STARFIST

FORCE RECON: RECOIL

BOOK III

STARFIST

FORCE RECON: BOOK III

RECOIL

DAVID SHERMAN & DAN CRAGG

BALLANTINE BOOKS • NEW YORK

A Del Rey Books Mass Market Original

Copyright © 2008 by David Sherman and Dan Cragg

All rights reserved.

Published in the United States by Del Rey Books, an imprint of The Random House Publishing Group, a division of Random House, Inc., New York.

DEL REY is a registered trademark and the Del Rey colophon is a trademark of Random House, Inc.

ISBN 978-0-345-46060-8

Printed in the United States of America

www.delreybooks.com

OPM   9   8   7   6   5   4   3   2   1

To Second Lieutenant Jose Lugo, Jr., USA
RVN 1967–1971

PROLOGUE

Montgomery Homestead, Haulover

Chad Montgomery stepped onto the porch of his house just as the sun rose over the eastern horizon. His face contorted and his jaw twisted side to side in a great yawn; his back arched and he flung his arms out to the sides to force more air into his lungs. The last dregs of sleep gone, breathing easily, he turned to face the red orb and watched its wavering disk, only its upper half yet visible. In moments the sun rose completely above the horizon, and the disk wavered less, became brighter, too bright to continue looking at. He rested his eyes on the green and red fields that spread halfway to the horizon to his east and south, to where they butted up against the native trees, and smiled. The grapelopes, beetpeas, and spinmaize were native to Haulover, but their proteins and amino acids were fully digestible by the human system and provided nutrition as good as any of the vegetables imported from older worlds in Human Space; imported seeds were so expensive to grow locally that the native foodstuffs quickly became standard fare. And they were mighty good tasting. Those fields were the Montgomerys' third crop, and Chad was certain the harvest would bring in enough to allow him to pay off the loan he'd taken out to start the farm.

He smiled again, hearing the homey sounds and tinkling voices of his wife, Connie, and elder daughter, Margery, as they fixed a hearty farm breakfast. A moment later the light voice of his younger son, Mitchell, joined with the voices of the women, and it was obvious from the "shoo"s and "careful there"s that the youngster was trying to help but was getting in the way more than helping.

Chad sucked in another deep breath then blew it out. He turned his head at a footfall next to him and smiled at his firstborn, Clement.

"Claire's still abed?" Chad asked.

"Sure is," Clement said with a shake of his head. "That girl'll never make a proper farmwife."

Chad chuckled. "We'll fix that. Your mother has another one in the oven. We'll give its care to Claire. Then she won't be able to be a slug-a-bed."

"Gonna be a 'C' name?"

"Of course. Clif for a boy, Corine for a girl."

Clement eyed his father. "You don't know yet?"

Chad shook his head. "We decided we'd like to be surprised this time."

"So how long do I have to wait before I know whether my youngest sibling is a brother or a sister? Mama's not showing yet."

"Seven months."

Clement looked out over the fields and nodded. "Smart timing, there. The crop'll be in, and Mama will have time to recover before the next sowing."

"Right. We might want to be surprised by the new one's sex, but that didn't mean we wanted an accident."

Clement nodded again. He remembered his father telling him the deciding reason for the family's emigrating was that their home world had adopted strict population-control measures, capping family sizes at three children. But Chad and Connie wanted a large family. Connie had been pregnant with Mitchell when they left to make a new home here. The first three had come at three-year intervals, but Mitchell was five years behind Claire. Thanks to the demands of settling in a new world and starting the farm, child five, whether Clif or Corine, would be four years behind Mitchell.

From inside, they heard Connie tell Mitchell to run upstairs and drag his sister out of bed before she missed breakfast. Mitchell laughed delightedly at the prospect and tromped away to do his mother's bidding.

"Life is good," Chad murmured.

"It is," Clement agreed.

"Let's—"

Whatever Chad was going to say was cut off by Mitchell's scream.

Strictly speaking, Spilk Mullilee had no business being there. The constabulary was treating it as a crime scene, and the police believed that the planetary administrator would only get in the way. Haulover's attorney general was also concerned that, if there was a political aspect to the alleged crime, the presence of the planetary administrator might jeopardize the findings of the crime scene investigation. And Haulover's minister of war chimed in with a protest that if the incidents were the work of an unknown enemy force, the planetary administrator could be putting himself in unnecessary danger.

Spilk Mullilee ignored them all. It was the thirteenth such incident in less than four months and, as planetary administrator, he believed it was his duty to see the site for himself. He couldn't continue to wait idly for Robier Altman, a Confederation of Human Worlds under minister of state who also happened to be an old friend, to reply to the message he'd sent almost a month ago.

So even though, strictly speaking, Spilk Mullilee had no business being there, he *had* to be present at the investigation. After all, the planetary administrator was responsible to the Confederation for everything that happened on his world.

Looking to the east and south, Mullilee saw fields of native vegetables, stretching halfway to the horizon, rich fields that would provide nourishment for thousands once they were harvested. If they were harvested. Looking north and west, where the farmhouse and outbuildings with the machinery needed to work the farm should have been, all Mullilee saw was devastation. He'd already looked at images of the farm when the buildings had been there. Now the view was biblical—not one stone left standing on another.

Literally.

Everything burnable had been turned to ash. The bricks and stone pulverized to sand and dust. Even the plasteel and the metals in the farm equipment had melted to slag.

Despite the concerns of the constabulary, Mullilee was careful to keep out of the way of the technicians who sifted through the wreckage. Mullilee flashed on a trid he'd once seen of twenty-first-century archaeologists excavating a Neolithic site, how they'd sifted dirt through a large sieve, winnowing out small bits that might be something other than dirt. Some of the techs on the site of the Montgomery homestead looked just like what he'd seen in that trid. Others, bearing objects that *pinged* or *bonged* or flashed colored lights, stepped carefully about the site, keeping off ground that hadn't yet been sifted. Whatever they were doing was, to Mullilee, indistinguishable from magic; he knew neither the tools they manipulated nor what they did.

What did Mullilee expect to see here, anything that the techs couldn't find more easily and quickly than he could? Nothing, which was why he kept off ground they hadn't covered, and otherwise stayed out of their way, carefully not doing anything to interfere.

He hoped the techs would find something that would tell them—and him—more than they'd gotten from the first three homesteads, and from the more recent ones that had been destroyed the way this one was. Something like what happened to the people. Eight people were missing here: the Montgomerys, their four children, and two hired hands. That brought the total missing in the thirteen incidents to sixty-seven people, people who seemed to have simply vanished, except for a few tiny bits of white stuff that may or may not have been human bone.

A new world such as Haulover expected to lose people in the

beginning. But not to have them simply vanish. With their homesteads so thoroughly destroyed.

Office of the Planetary Administrator, Haulover
We need help, I need help, Mullilee wrote in another message to Robier Altman. *The Haulover Constabulary and the Ministry of War have concluded that the homestead destructions and missing people are the work of enemy military operations. But they have no idea who, or why. Do you have contacts who can get us help, or can you direct me to the appropriate office in the Heptagon?*
I'm desperate.

CHAPTER
ONE

Home of Jimmy Jasper, Tabernacle, Kingdom

It was sunup on the sixth day of the seventh month when Jimmy Jasper and his wife, Zamada, sat down to a meager breakfast as they did every morning at that same time. As one of the Men of the Spirit, Jimmy had no time to dawdle over his meal that morning. He had a full schedule to meet that day: visits to the sick, a funeral in the afternoon, two prayer meetings, one with the swing shift going on duty at the mines, and a planning session with other elders for the Holiness Camp scheduled to commence later that month. So, preoccupied with his pastoral duties, he dug in with hardly a word to his wife.

The bowls of oatmeal steamed in the cool morning air and the chicory root coffee, sweetened with brown sugar and laced with goat's milk, filled their tiny kitchen with its rich aroma. Zamada, left to her own, would have preferred real coffee, but it was expensive and Jimmy insisted on chicory root because he believed it helped with digestion. And what Jimmy Jasper wanted in his home was law; Zamada obeyed her husband as any devoted consort would, to the letter of that law.

Jimmy had only lifted the first spoonful of oatmeal to his lips when the house shook violently and the air was split by a great explosion.

"Accident at the mine!" Zamada said, half rising out of her chair.

Jimmy paused, head canted toward the mines, as if anticipating another blast. A long, loud, screeching roar filled the air all about them and through the window the pair saw a brilliant flash of light. "No, I don't think so," Jimmy said calmly, reflectively. He stood as if in slow motion. The spoon in his hand clattered on the table unnoticed. An eerie calm seemed to have come over him. "Is it—?" he whispered. Then, "Stay here," he ordered Zamada, and in two long strides was out the door.

Jimmy caught his breath at what he saw outside. The sky was filled with tongues of fire almost too bright to bear looking at directly. Waves of tremendous concussive sound washed over Jimmy Jasper like a stiff breeze, ruffling his clothing, raising the dust in the street. His neighbors stood outside their houses, faces turned toward the heavens, eyes transfixed on the mighty display overhead. Someone began to wail in terror and immediately others began moaning and screaming and calling upon God to protect them. But not Jimmy Jasper. He, of all the assembled, knew positively and without question what was happening. That knowledge surged through him and suffused his spirit with the joy of heavenly rapture. He fell to his knees, his face filled with happiness, tears of glory streaming down his cheeks and arms uplifted to the sky, and he shouted in his powerful, commanding voice, "*Hallelujah!* Dear Father, it is the Sign! *It is the Sign!* Lord God Almighty, thank You! Thou hast given us *the Sign!*"

The Tabernacle Rock of Ages True Light Christian Church, established two centuries before in a remote mountainous region on Kingdom, had never boasted a very large congregation, but the faithful had been true to their Pentecostal roots through all those long years. Tabernacle itself began as a rip-roaring, everything-goes mining camp called Hard Times. It had grown to a town of about ten thousand inhabitants by the time Jimmy Jasper was born some forty years before the Sign. The name of the town had been changed to Tabernacle by Jimmy's great-grandfather when the members of the Rock of Ages sect came to outnumber the miners. In time, those workers who did not convert moved elsewhere.

The miners moved not because the Rock of Ages congregation persecuted them. No, they moved on because the hand-clapping, singing, shouting, weeping congregants, speaking in tongues and rolling in the dust in an ecstasy of religious fervor, were really hard to take, especially on Saturday nights when a hardworking guy only wanted to go out and tie one on. First the whores moved on, those that didn't convert; then the publicans; then the shops stopped selling thule and tobacco, and before you knew it, a working stiff couldn't even pee in the street after dark without a bunch of the Jesus freaks confronting him, singing, praying, begging him to convert, the Holy Spirit virtually oozing from every pore. No, those old boys moved because the Rock of Ages people were, for the ordinary, fun-loving workingman, one colossal pain in the ass.

So Jimmy grew up (Praise the Lord! as he often put it) surrounded by the loving, caring, righteous fold of his ancestors' church. Long before his time the mines had come into the possession of the Rock of Ages Church, which ran them with the same rigorous enthusiasm with which its adherents read their Bibles. Jimmy worked in the mines as a young man. The labor was hard and the work made him hard, physically and mentally, and it was good because it was dangerous and made him fear his God. He joyfully joined his companions far beneath the earth, singing an old miner's song (lyrics suitably sanitized!) as they worked:

An angel with his glimmering light
Guides us down into the night.
Some dig for silver, some dig for gold
As we lift our praise to the God of old!

By the time Jimmy reached his twenties he discovered that he had a voice for preaching—and could he preach! His voice was so powerful with the spirit of the Lord that it rang through the chapel during services and tickled the innards of the worshippers. His preaching particularly affected the women. Jimmy

Jasper was tall and handsome, broad-shouldered with an unruly mop of auburn hair and piercing blue eyes that transfixed
his listeners as he preached. Sometimes women fainted, especially when he preached on a text from the Old Testament, and
at such times he appeared to them as Moses himself come out
of the desert or Abraham about to sacrifice Isaac or even Noah,
herding them into the Ark of Paradise!

So by the time he was forty, Jimmy Jasper was a prominent
member of the Rock of Ages True Light Christian Church. "In
my name is Prophecy!" he often thundered to rapt congregations, quoting from the Book of Revelation, 21:11, " 'Having
the glory of God: and her light was like unto a stone most precious, even like a jasper stone, clear as crystal.' My message to
you, dearly beloved, is clear as crystal: Repent or be damned!"

The Rock of Ages sect consisted of four-and-twenty separate
congregations meeting individually in homes and common
buildings around Tabernacle. The sect did not approve of formal
church buildings but, like the Christians of old, preferred to
meet wherever the faithful gathered. Huge cathedrals were a
worldly abomination and a perversion of the Word to them. So
the members were free to worship wherever they wanted. They
propagated their faith among themselves with prayer chains,
worship services, family prayer, and mass gatherings. Formally
the sect had no ministers; it was led by laymen obsessed with
teaching the Gospel rather than enforcing rules or seeking power
through church offices. Church hierarchies were another corruption of the Spirit that the Rock of Ages condemned as blasphe-
mous. It avoided the power struggles so common among the
larger and older denominations.

Anyone among the brethren could preach; all that was required was the ability to read the King James version of the
Holy Bible and to demonstrate the presence of the Holy Spirit
in their hearts, which, when manifested during a meeting, was
seen as special authority from God to preach. Some were better at that than others, of course, and the best preachers were
often demanded by their congregations to preach before them.

Jimmy Jasper became one of the most popular of that breed, so popular, so forceful, so dynamic, that he began to take on the mantle of a leader and soon found himself, not by design, replacing many of the far older men of his church in that role. It was then that he quit the mines and devoted himself full-time to the business of the church.

But there was one slight area of disagreement among the Rock of Ages congregations: evangelism. Propagating the Word through missionary work was a basic tenet of the sect, but in the years immediately preceding Jimmy's birth, the evangelistic fervor had slackened. This was due, in part, to the remoteness of Tabernacle from the large population centers on Kingdom and, in part, to the lack of resources to support missionary work. Money from mining operations was needed for capital improvements and could not be diverted to other purposes because it was the only source of income for the people of Tabernacle.

But it was the bitter opposition to their preaching by the long-established and powerful churches and sects dominating religious life on Kingdom that had stymied the sect's evangelistic fervor. Their missionaries had been persecuted and laws had been passed to prevent their preaching in the cities and larger towns dominated by the other sects. Many members were uncomfortable with the sect's giving in to this opposition, but in time the majority, influenced by the practical-minded visionary preachers among them, was content to wait patiently for the Revival that prophecy said would begin with a Sign from heaven. Then and only then would the Word spread among humankind, followed by the Millennium. And until that Sign was given, the Rock of Ages people would keep the flame of faith burning at Tabernacle.

That Sign came with the arrival of the Skinks.

Tabernacle Village, Kingdom

The alien invaders did not bother the people of Tabernacle again after that first fateful day; with the arrival of the

Confederation Marines they had more pressing matters to attend to. When the creatures departed Tabernacle that day on tongues of flame, as they had arrived, the remaining inhabitants took stock. Sixty of their number had been taken. Some believed the visitors had been angels and that those taken had been translated directly to Heaven because some of the most righteous souls in their community had been among that number. Others, especially those who had *seen* the visitors, swore they were devils sent to punish them for their sins. One of those taken had been Jimmy Jasper, snatched from the street right in front of his own house as his wife stood in the doorway looking on. Blinded by the flashing light, she did not see the angels.

In the weeks that followed, the ones abducted came to be referred to as "the Taken." Of them all, only Jimmy Jasper was ever seen again.

The day of Jimmy's return was one of great rejoicing, although it started inauspiciously enough. Elmer Swaggart was tending his crops that morning, a brilliant, sunshine-filled day, when he noticed a figure staggering toward him across the rows of tomato plants. The plants were only knee-high and Elmer was busy staking them out so the vegetables would be kept off the ground when he heard someone stumbling toward him.

"I did not recognize him at first," Elmer said later. "He was thin and ragged and exhausted, but I did recognize him as a poor, wandering soul seeking succor, and so I rose from my knees and took him in my arms."

Even Zamada, when she first saw Jimmy that morning, found it difficult to recognize him as her husband. But as Jimmy regained his strength and his voice his true identity became known at last to everyone in Tabernacle. The first words he spoke as he began to recover were, "I have seen the Lord God Almighty and He has sent me to save humankind." A Day of Thanksgiving was declared and as soon as Jimmy had regained his strength, he preached to the multitude, small as it was, of the Rock of Ages True Light Christian Church.

"I was lifted unto Heaven," he began, "on the snow-white wings of Angels, and it was given unto me that the Lord has a mission He wants me to perform. I was given this mission by none other than the Archangel Gabriel. He told me that the devastation visited upon other parts of our world was the vengeance of the Lord upon the apostate sects that have for too long dominated life and suppressed the Truth in this land. We were spared because we are among the Elect, and I was selected by the Lord God Almighty, as He chose Moses, to go down and set His people free! Friends, I am to preach the Holy Spirit among humankind!

"We have failed in our evangelistic mission, but the Lord God has given me the responsibility of correcting that fault! I am to go forth and start a revival of Faith. Some of you say the spirits who came here and took us were Devils. I say you were blinded by Satan! Those who came here to fight them were blinded by Satan! All of humankind is blinded by Satan! But I was given to see them as they truly are, Angels of the Lord. All of humankind will see them in the True Light too, once they have regained their Faith! We are not to *fight* these spirits, we are to welcome them! We are to love them as *they* love us. They are truly the emissaries of the One True All-Loving, All-Powerful, All-Knowing Creator.

"And I warn you now," he thundered, transfixing each listener with a stare delivered across a rigid forefinger, "if any among you persist in opposing the Angels of the Lord, you shall be destroyed! Those who do not listen to me shall be destroyed. Eternal hellfire shall descend upon those who oppose me. Worlds will burn if the Word is not accepted!"

And so on.

When asked outright what had become of the other people taken by the angels, Jimmy would only say, "They are with Jesus. All those taken were the most righteous of the righteous and they now have received their reward in Heaven." Of course some people in the congregation knew that maybe, just maybe, some of those taken had not been all that "righteous," but no one was going to contradict Jimmy Jasper on the point, and besides, sometimes the Lord moved in mysterious ways.

"I must go," Jimmy announced to Zamada at breakfast one morning, "today."

"Of course, husband. Must I accompany you?" Zamada stood in their tiny kitchen, a ladle in her hand.

"No." Jimmy did not pause while shoveling oatmeal into his mouth. "I cannot be encumbered in my work, wife. I love only the Lord now and the work He has given me. You shall remain here and keep our home in order until you are called." In truth, he would never think of Zamada again after that morning.

Zamada knew that "until you are called" meant until she was safe in the arms of the Lord, that her husband would never return in this life. In a way she was relieved. Jimmy was not the same man who was taken that dreadful morning. Something about him now frightened her. She thought at first it was the spark of the fire of the Lord that burned within him, but he had always been zealous in his faith. No, his spirit had *changed* somehow and made him *different* from the man he once was. When she was alone with him now it was as if he were far away somewhere, in some place beyond human comprehension. If that was what happened to a man who'd been called to the Lord, Zamada would rather he lived somewhere else. There were others in Tabernacle who felt the same way, although none would admit it openly: Jimmy Jasper had become a scary man.

"Where shall you go, husband?"

"Earth. Earth is now the focus of the Devil's plan to destroy mankind's soul. The government there is a tool of evil. I shall go to Earth and I shall preach the Word and I shall defeat Satan. With the Lord's help, of course."

The church elders had raised a large sum of money to finance Jimmy's mission to Earth, and that very same day, amid prayers, tears, and hosannas, he departed Tabernacle for Interstellar City, where he booked a flight on a starship bound for Earth. While waiting for departure the Lord sent him his disciple. "I am Sally Consolador. I am from the Twelfth Station of Jerusalem and was also taken when the Angels of the Lord came unto us there," she announced, sitting next to him in the spaceport terminal, "and the Lord has directed me to accompany you and attend to the rod and staff He has given you in your Faith." Jimmy had been informed he would have help, but he neither asked about it nor questioned the fact. It was not his to question the Lord. The thought did not even occur to him that there might be many other evangels working for revival, only that he had been chosen to lead the movement on Earth. There were many other worlds in need of Salvation, but Earth was the center of the Confederation of Human Worlds, and it was from Earth that Satan was directing his war against the Angels, so Jimmy was very proud that the Lord had picked him to work against Satan in his very lair.

"I know, it was given to me that someone would join me on my mission." He put his arm around her. "To that end I have purchased one-way tickets for two, but I did not know who that other disciple would be until now." He smiled; Sally was a buxom woman. "We shall be a great comfort to each other in my work," he continued. "We shall preach unto the multitudes, you and I, Sally, and we shall create great joy in the land, and we shall turn the hearts of the people away from Satan and unto God."

And in time they did, and in time they became a great pain in the derriere of President Cynthia Suelee Chang-Sturdevant in the war against the Skinks.

CHAPTER TWO

Bill Clabber's Bar, Flambeaux, Lannoy

"Ahhhhh, it sure is gonna get drunk out tonight!" Puella Queege shouted to the barflies. She grinned lopsidedly at herself in the huge mirror behind Bill Clabber's bar. She thought she'd never looked better, although her dark hair, tied in a bun on her neck, military fashion, had started giving off loose strands. But her face was flushed with the glow imparted by a healthy dose of alcohol, and, just then, she perched on her stool, queen of all she surveyed.

Before she had enlisted in Lannoy's army, Puella had been a rather pretty young woman, if a bit on the heavy side. But for a long time she had striven to achieve a masculine look to blend in with the men of the battalion, had let herself go physically, and had hit the booze so hard it was starting to ruin her complexion. Still, when Puella was sober she possessed a very sharp intelligence, knew army regulations well, and was a master of the intricacies of orderly room procedures and functions. Without a doubt, she was the best company clerk in the battalion. When she was sober.

The barflies, the usual crowd at Bill's on payday night, were hanging on her every word, their sweaty mugs thirsting for the beer she had been treating them to since she'd staggered in around sunset. That was a bit of a disappointment, though, because she'd always imagined that, when she was the center of attraction in a bar, the barflies would be buying *her* beers, not the other way around. But what the heck, she reflected, the attention she got was worth the price of treating the old codgers.

"Queege," an old-timer sitting at a table up against the wall shouted, "tell us agin how yew done kilt them guys in the bank!" He knew the longer he kept Queege talking the more free beer he could count on.

"Naw, girl," another regular hollered, "tell us how it was to be a prisoner o' war at that Confederation camp. Did they, you know, make you do interestin' things?" He cackled so hard he started choking on his own spit. His partner pounded him hard on the back, forcing up a huge yellow-green mass of phlegm into his clawlike hand, which he wiped on his trousers.

"Thass ol' Queege, there, Hank," another barfly admonished the choker. "Don't *nobody* screw with our Queege! Ain't that right, girl?"

"Yar, girl, tell us 'bout th' bank agin," the first barfly insisted.

"Well," Queege said, and stretched and set her mug on the bar, shrugged her shoulders and shifted her weight on the stool, "it warn't nuttin' much. See, these guys, including the fuckin' *mayor*"—at this point in the story, which they'd all heard dozens of times before, everyone nodded their heads and roared with laughter, which they did now, on cue—"was robbin' the vaults. I come along 'n shot th' shit outta 'em." She tapped the ribbon representing the medal she'd been awarded for the act that now sat slightly askew above the left breast pocket of her tunic.

Surreptitiously she adjusted the tiny piece of cloth, hoping the barflies wouldn't notice its unmilitary positioning. Before the night was over it would, inevitably, fall off, and in the morning she'd go back to the post exchange and buy a replacement. But when Corporal Puella Queege, Seventh Independent Military Police Battalion, had shot it out with the three bank robbers at Phelps during the recently concluded war on Ravenette, she had performed a truly heroic deed, earned the Bronze Star Medal on her chest, and become the *only* soldier in the battalion to have such an award. Never mind that she'd been drunk at the time and was only on patrol in the streets of Phelps that morning because she'd lied about being a military policeman. But the medal was real and she had killed all three of the bank robbers despite the fact that they had shot back at her, at very close range.

"Ya see, I was on patrol that mornin'," Puella continued—

"Corporal Queege!" a voice cut through the barroom like howitzer blast. All heads snapped toward the door. A huge figure stood there silhouetted against the dim light from the street outside. *"Front and goddamned center, Corporal!"* the figure shouted. The barflies cringed and stared into their mugs. They might have been useless drunks sponging off a deluded corporal's generosity, but they knew the Voice of God when they heard it, and they realized with a sharp twinge in their guts that the free beer was about to dry up on them.

Puella's mouth dropped open. Then she straightened her tunic and slipped unsteadily to the floor, where fortunately she was able to steady herself against the bar before she fell flat on her face. Well, she'd had a *lot* of beer that evening . . .

"Y-Yes, First Sergeant," she mumbled. That was the only way anyone addressed "Skinny" Skinnherd, first sergeant of the Fourth Company, Seventh Independent Military Police Battalion. And nobody ever called him "Skinny" to his face either, because he wasn't. He loomed in the doorway, a massive mountain of a man, gesturing that Puella should follow him out into the street. "Jeez," he wrinkled his nose at the smell of stale beer and vomit that always pervaded Billy's place, "you keep hangin' out with these pigs, Queege, and you'll be needin' a liver transplant as well as a friggin' *bath.* Come on, we're shippin' out in the mornin'." He turned and stepped outside.

Fumbling to adjust her tunic, Puella staggered after her first sergeant. It was raining lightly outside and the cool air had a sobering effect on her—not that the sudden appearance of First Sergeant Skinnherd hadn't already begun the job. All up and down the street first sergeants and company charge-of-quarters NCOs were rousting men who until then had been enjoying payday binges.

"Queege old Squeege," a drunken sergeant from the Third Company shouted as he staggered by, "why don'tcha gimme some of yer—*oooops.*" He recognized First Sergeant Skinnherd and hurried on quickly. Everyone in the Seventh MPs believed Puella was putting out for her first sergeant, so, knowing Skinnherd, no one ever seriously tried to put the make on her. Not when he was sober, that is. But drunks can be very self-destructive.

"Wh-Wha—?" Puella stuttered.

"We're movin' out in the mornin'," Skinnherd said over his shoulder as he stomped down the street, staring bullets at the retreating back of the sergeant, whom he thought he knew. "We got a change-of-station mornin' report to do and we gotta close out the orderly room, and I need you, girl, drunk or sober."

"Wh-Where, First Sergeant?" Puella rushed to catch up with Skinnherd's long, determined strides.

"Asshole!" he shouted, not bothering to look back.

Puella blinked. He'd never called her *that* before! "Who? *Me,* First Sergeant? All I done was have a few beers with the guys 'n it's payday night, 'n I worked hard this—"

"Not *you*!" Skinnherd barked. "How long you bin in the army, anyway, Queege? *Arsenault,* the Confederation training world . . ."

"Never bin there," she muttered.

". . . We've been ordered there to form up with some kinda task force." He stopped and looked down at his company clerk. Then he smiled and put his arm around her shoulders. "You old beer barrel," he said, laughing. "If you could ever sober up . . . Army HQ has mobilized us, Queege. We're shipping out to Arsenault to be part of this task force that's gonna take on the Whatchamacallits, the aliens the Old Girl tol' us about. Now, come on," he said and squeezed her shoulder gently, "we got work to do."

Why us? she wondered.

Office of the Chief, Armed Forces Headquarters, Lannoy

"Now why in the name of Beelzebub are they bothering us with this shit?" General Reggie Fitzhugh, chief of the Lannoy armed forces asked his army chief of staff, General Rick Moreville. "Gawdam, Ricky, we ain't even reconstituted the units that come back from Ravenette, fer all anybody knows they're still full of hothead secessionists, 'n now they want us to furnish this Task Force Aguinaldo with a whole freakin' *battalion* of infantry? Do we even got one that's ready to ship out?"

General Moreville ran a hand under his huge nose, wiping away the constant dribble, then rubbing his hand surreptitiously on his tunic sleeve. Throughout the army he was known as "Slick Sleeve Moreville" because of this habit. "Hell no, Reggie, 'n besides, what if them *things* make Lannoy their first stop? Who's to protect us? That Marine and his 'task force' is light-years away; we'd all be baked potatoes by the time anybody got here. Naw, we gotta keep our forces intact. Screw this . . . this . . . gawdam order of his!" He snapped the flimsiplast sheet that read:

"IN ACCORDANCE WITH THE AUTHORITY INVESTED IN ME BY THE PRESIDENT OF THE CONFEDERATION OF HUMAN WORLDS, I HEREBY DIRECT THE CHIEFS OF THE ARMED FORCES OF THE FOLLOWING MEMBER WORLDS TO TRANSFER *IMMEDIATELY* TO THIS TASK FORCE ON PERMANENT REASSIGNMENT ORDERS THE FOLLOWING UNITS . . ." The list was very long but opposite Lannoy it read: "2ND BATTALION, 35TH INFANTRY REGIMENT . . . ADDRESSEES WILL ENSURE THAT DESIGNATED UNITS ARE UP TO FULL TO&E STRENGTH WITH AUTHORIZED LEVELS OF PERSONNEL, WEAPONS, AND EQUIPMENT."

"Sheesh, Reggie, the old boy did his homework. The 35th is the only combat-ready unit we got right now. They did good on Ravenette and this old boy"—he snapped the flimsiplast sheet again—"knows it."

"Then we'll send him someone else. You know the old army rule, when asked to furnish troops for any detached duty you send your ash and trash. Who we got we don't need and don't want around?"

"Seventh MP Battalion," General Moreville answered immediately. "They're the boys ol' General Lyons put up on the coast on Ravenette 'cause they wasn't good for nutthin' else, 'n the Confederation Marines steamrollered 'em. So they was taken prisoner intact—personnel, equipment, everything—'n when the peace treaty was signed, the Confederation give 'em back to us, like yer bad penny." He laughed.

"Yeah! We can beg off, saying we ain't got no other combat-ready units. Hell, MPs can carry blasters as good as anybody. We can tell 'em we ain't rooted out all the secessionists yet. That'll frost their nuts."

"This old Anders Aguinaldo is gonna be highly pissed, Reggie." General Moreville grinned as he said it.

"Fuck him. What's he going to do, send us to Ravenette?" They both laughed. Neither had been in the war.

Office of the Commanding General, Task Force Aguinaldo, Arsenault

"Don't these people realize the threat we're all up against?" General Anders Aguinaldo shook his head. "I asked for infantry and these fools send me this military police battalion!"

"I'm sure they don't, sir. But they know there's a threat and it's only natural nobody'll send their first-line units to our task force. It's the old army game, sir."

Aguinaldo regarded his chief of staff, Major General Pradesh Cumberland. At least, Aguinaldo reflected, he'd been able to get the best people for his command staff, and Cumberland was one of those. His frustration was with the member worlds who, in response to President Chang-Sturdevant's urgent directive requesting they furnish his task force with good troops, had been reneging, finding dozens of excuses not to send the troops or, like Lannoy, sending fifth-rate units. How could he possibly take on the Skinks with troops like the Seventh Independent Military Police Battalion?

"Well, Pradesh," he sighed, "we can probably use a good group of MPs when we deploy. We'll need them to attend to such things as population control in urban areas and so on. If the Skinks attack at more than one location, we can break the battalion into companies and send them with the combat forces. But I don't think we'll have much of a POW mission for them; even during the campaign on Kingdom, we never captured one of the Skinks. As usual, goddammit, the Marines will have to lead the way. How're the training teams progressing?"

"Just fine, sir. They've spread out to the selected member worlds and are doing an excellent job apprising their governments of the nature of the Skink threat. That may be one reason some of these people are less than enthusiastic about parting with their best troops. That might have been a mistake, sir."

"We had to do it. But dammit, we've only asked for selected units, and sparing them wouldn't have diminished anyone's combat power, and it'd have added to ours so when the time comes we can respond with a powerful, highly motivated, well-trained force." He was silent for a moment. "Well, we still can and we *will*. Okay, here's what we're going to do. Once the units arrive we'll do a top-to-bottom inspection—arms, equipment, personnel, training, combat experience, everything. I've drawn up a list of very capable officers to conduct those inspections and, if necessary, take command of the units. I've put out a call for those personnel and they're on the way here right now. For those units that measure up on their own, we'll put them into training immediately. For those that don't, we'll reorganize them, give them new commanders if that's necessary, or break them up and farm them out to capable units if it isn't. And if all else fails, send them home. Meanwhile, I'll keep the president informed and maybe she can put pressure on the politicos."

"Sir, what it's going to take will probably be a full-scale Skink invasion somewhere. That should get everyone's attention mighty fast."

Aguinaldo scratched his chin. "You're probably right, Pradesh, let's just hope their first port of call isn't Earth."

"Well, sir, wherever they hit us, let's hope that when they do, we're ready for them."

CHAPTER
THREE

The House of Pain, Undisclosed Location

He screamed and screamed, "Mumeeeee! *Mumeeeeeee!*" but the pain and terror only intensified.

The Brattle Home, New Salem, Kingdom

" 'And it came to pass in those days, that there went out a decree from Caesar Augustus, that all the world should be taxed. And all went to be taxed, every one into his own city. And Joseph also went up from Galilee, out of the city of Nazareth, into Judea, unto the city of David, which is called Bethlehem.' " Hannah Brattle smiled, put a marker between the pages of her Bible, and closed it. "And on that note, it's about time for lunch," she informed the three boys.

"More? More, Mumee?" Moses begged.

Hannah smiled at the boy, for she had come to think of him as human, and laid a hand on his head, stroking it gently. Moses loved it when she did that. He turned his strangely convex face up at her and smiled. It was the smile of an idiot, full of vacant pleasure. Moses loved to be stroked and he loved the sound of Hannah's voice, but she doubted he understood much of what she read to him. Hannah sighed. Joab and Samuel, her two sons, no doubt they would soon be soldiers in the Army of Christ, but poor little Moses—she shook her head sadly—he would never live up to the name she had given him.

"I've read the entire Gospel according to Mark this morning, Moses. I'm an old lady, my voice needs a rest. And my stomach tells me it's time to eat! Afterward you boys can go on down to the river if you want and see if you can find another Moses." Joab and Samuel had found Moses as a baby at the water's edge and brought him home with them. They wanted to call him "Jedo," because that was what they thought he had told them when asked if he had a name, but Hannah had quickly dubbed him "Moses" because he had been found abandoned among the bulrushes, and the name had stuck.

"Awrrrright!" Samuel chortled. "Down to the river, Moses!"

"Oh, good! Good!" Moses began to pirouette on his stubby legs. Any suggestion of play, especially play involving water, excited Moses because once in the water he was totally in his element. Then the webbing between his fingers and the toes on his large feet extended, helping to propel him through the water like a fish.

Zechariah Brattle, the nominal leader of the New Salem community, Hannah's second husband and stepfather to her boys, had returned to New Salem a few days after Hannah had agreed to let the boys keep Moses. "We have a *big* problem," he told his family as they sat in their living room one evening. He gestured at Moses who crouched on a blanket spread out on the floor, uttering contented noises, munching cookies Hannah had baked that morning.

"Why, father?" Samuel asked, apprehension in his voice. He glanced at his older brother for reassurance.

"Father, Jedo's harmless," Joab protested. "He can't possibly be one of *them*!"

"No doubt about it, son, he is one of them," Zechariah answered. "I've seen them up close, and believe me, he's a devil, or a Skink, that's what the Marines call them. Oh, he's not full grown yet, boys, but make no mistake about it, he *is* one of those creatures."

"Father," Hannah interjected, "he's been with us for days

now. He is no different in his manner than these boys of mine were at his age. I think he's just another of God's creatures. You aren't suggesting we turn him over to the government, are you? That we abandon him? I think he was given to us for a purpose, Zechariah, and if we reject him before we know what that purpose is, we're defying God's will."

Zechariah snorted. "Funny, how whenever someone wants to do something really foolish they claim they're only obeying God's will."

"Zechariah!" Hannah stamped a foot on the floor, a habit she had when angry.

"All right! All right! I'm sorry I said that." Zechariah sighed and wearily passed a hand across his face. "All this government business up in Haven has, well, secularized me a bit, I guess. But you should hear the excuses some of these sects up there give for not cooperating with perfectly reasonable government reforms! Let me ask you this: What do the others here think of this Moses?"

At first nobody answered. "Well, they haven't been around much," Hannah finally admitted, "except for the black woman and her family." She meant Judith Maynard, her husband, Spencer, and their boy, Chisi.

"The rest are wary of him, aren't they?"

"Yes, I guess so, Zechariah. Nobody's said anything because this is your house and nobody's going to go directly against you or your family; everyone respects you too much for that."

"Father?" It was Samuel. "Jedo already can speak a few words."

"I doubt that, son. You just think those grunts and mumbles mean something. It's like people who believe in ghosts; they see them everywhere." He smiled and playfully swatted the boy's head. "Okay, here's what we'll have to do. I don't have to return to Haven for a few days, but before I go we're going to settle the issue of this creature. Tomorrow I'm calling the entire congregation together and we're going to let everyone speak his piece about this thing here. If the majority votes to keep him among us then so be it. Otherwise I take him back to Haven with me and we turn him over to the government. You know perfectly well we've never been able to capture one of these things alive or dead. What he can tell us in captivity about his species will be invaluable when and if the big ones ever come back. We can't in all justice withhold that information from humanity."

"His name is *Jedo,*" Joab said sullenly. He did not like the way his stepfather kept referring to Jedo as a "thing."

"Well, we ought to call him 'Moses,' because you found him down by the river," Hannah said, and from that moment on the name had stuck.

Meeting House, New Salem, Kingdom

As was the custom with the City of God sect, each member of the community had a voice in deciding what to do with Moses. Samuel Sewall, the eldest member of the sect and, next to Zechariah Brattle himself, the most highly respected, moderated the debate.

Samuel and Joab Brattle were the first to speak, telling how they'd found Moses abandoned by the stream and how they had come to think of him as their little companion—not quite a brother, not quite a pet. They testified to his gentle, harmless, playful nature and urged the congregation to let him stay with their family. But because of their impressionable ages, their testimony was largely ignored by the assembled adults. Many felt giving him the name of Moses amounted to blasphemy.

Thereafter the arguments ranged widely as speakers referred to biblical texts to support their points while the rest of the congregation furiously turned the pages of their own books to follow along or to find other scriptural evidence to support new arguments. Most of the congregation was against keeping Moses in New Salem. The people had not forgotten that the Skinks had ruthlessly killed their friends and neighbors, almost destroyed the City of God, and, as one of them pointed out, to forgive them for that would be like forgiving Satan himself. That Moses had had no part in that massacre was considered moot; he was clearly one of *them*.

But it was Zechariah himself who pointed out that at the time of the massacre the survivors had agreed it was the just punishment of God because radical members of the sect had attempted an act of war against the Confederation of Human Worlds. To escape the anticipated retribution for that act, the sect had fled to the wilderness where it suffered the anger of the Lord. He reminded them of their belief that they had been spared for a reason, and of the long trek through the wilderness that had brought them to New Salem, and a new beginning. "We believed that was God's Plan for us. Now that you are living in prosperity and peace," he reminded them sternly, "do not forget where you came from and do not project your own sins or those of his fathers upon this creature."

Moses sat quietly at Hannah Brattle's side, sometimes a bewildered expression flitting across his strange face as he tried to follow the speakers. It was clear he understood that the discussions concerned him, but otherwise he had no idea his fate hinged on the outcome.

Finally Emwanna Haramu, baptized Judith after she married Spencer Maynard, spoke. "I come to you with my son, Chisi, as refugees. Kingdomite soldiers, they kill my people, the Pilipili Magna," she reminded them. "You taken us in and you showing us de Way and with God's grace I marry good Christian man and find new life and new hoping is to us among you given. We too, Chisi, me, we wander in the desert many days, like Children of Israel long, long ago, and de Lord, he show us de way here." Tears ran down her cheeks as she spoke but her voice did not waver, and although her Standard English was not yet perfect, what she said was clear to everyone. "Now I listen to all the talkings and you making me sad, 'cause the peoples of the City of God youselfs has lost the Way."

Several people protested these words loudly. "Silence!" old

Samuel Sewall demanded. "It is her turn to speak and you shall all listen." He nodded at Judith to continue.

"Devils not kill my people, mens do, mens, mens like we, mens with souls, mens who turn from de Way, dem mens, I forgive dem fo' dere sin and I pray that God forgive dem! I ignorant woman, I no can hardly read the Book yet, but I ask you why cannot our Father give souls to creatures He wishes? This little one? He no devil now! Mebbe like mens, like us, he get in de wrong way, he grow up devil! Sure. Can happen. But now? No, no! Now he with *us* and now we mus' save his little soul."

Judith sat down. No one spoke for a long time. Then old Samuel Sewall cleared his throat. "We have had great argument here today," he began, "and I am now, by this little woman, reminded of some lines by an old poet, not of our faith but exceedingly wise:

" 'Myself when young did eagerly frequent
Doctor and Saint, and heard great argument
About it and about: but evermore
Came out by the same door where in I went.'

"Friends, there is one here who has not yet said her piece." Samuel turned to Hannah Brattle and nodded that she should speak.

Hannah stood and, holding Moses by his little hand, said, "I vote we keep him among us."

Moses looked up at Hannah, smiled, and in a tiny but clearly audible voice that was heard by all said, "Mumee, I love you!"

Zechariah Brattle's Office, Interstellar City, Kingdom

And it came to pass that in the days immediately following the precipitous flight of the Skinks after their defeat by the Confederation forces on the world known as Kingdom, that Madam President Chang-Sturdevant decreed teams of specialists should be sent to that place to find out as much from survivors of the war as they could about the enemy aliens. This began even before Task Force Aguinaldo was formed. And so there came to Haven Dr. Joseph Gobels, who went down to New Salem, where Moses dwelt.

Dr. Gobels and his assistant, Dr. Pensy Fogel, whom Gobels kept calling "Fogy," sat impatiently in Zechariah Brattle's office, regarding the old puritan with evident distaste. To the offworld scientists he was a bureaucrat, worse, an old zealot, and was standing in their way. As an ambitious exobiologist, Dr. Gobels sensed a terrific scientific breakthrough if the rumors he'd heard about New Salem's newest resident were true.

"Do you, or do you not"—Gobels emphasized each word carefully, as if talking to a child—"have one of those things in captivity? Mr. Braggle."

"Brattle, Doctor, my name is *Brattle*." For his part, Zechariah regarded the two scientists with deep suspicion. The few hairs on Gobels's head stood erect with tension and he drummed fat little fingers nervously on the arms of his chair, leaning forward aggressively as he spoke. A thin sheen of perspiration covered his upper lip and saliva flecked his lips. His teeth were small and pointy, like Moses's. His assistant, who had said very little, sat quietly, his fingers steepled beneath his chin, his gaze fixed balefully on Zechariah as if trying telepathically to be more cooperative.

"Well?"

Zechariah knew he should lie to these men, deny Moses's existence, but the president had decreed full cooperation with their researches, which she and everyone else believed were in the best interests of humanity. He knew better than these men the threat the Skinks represented. He could not in conscience tell that lie.

"He is not in captivity. He is living peacefully among us as one of our own and he has taken to our ways."

Dr. Joseph Gobels's heart raced at the admission. Here it

was! A live Skink! *Oh, glory,* he thought, *a Nobel in my hands!* "Then"—he glanced triumphantly at his assistant—"we shall proceed to New Salaam, Mr. Braggle! At once." And he half rose out of his chair.

"New Salem, it's New *Salem,* Doctor. What will you do with him if we give him to you?"

"Ah, ah, well." Gobels had not expected this question. He gestured vaguely with a hand. "Nothing much, nothing much, I assure you, my dear fellow! Uh, we'll perform some tests and studies, of course. Isn't that right, Fogy?" He turned to his assistant, who nodded vigorously. "But nothing too intrusive, I assure you." He shrugged. "Fluids will have to be analyzed, you know, just like when you have a physical, Mr. Braggle, nothing more serious than that." He grinned nervously.

Zechariah did not trust the man. But duty was duty and he felt duty bound to render Moses unto Caesar. "You aren't going to keep him caged up, like some animal, are you, Doctor?"

"Oh, no, no, Mr. Braggle, certainly not!" He laughed, a nervous, high-pitched giggle, like a small child denying he'd been in the cookie jar.

"Where will you take him to perform these experiments?"

"Oh, not 'experiments,' I assure you! Tests, examinations, studies. Ah, but to answer your question, we'll take him to our headquarters at Universal Labs in Fargo, back on Earth."

"And will you return him to us when you're done, Dr. Gobels?"

"Well, it may be a while," Gobels answered cautiously, "but yes, indubitably, indubitably." The way he pronounced that word sounded to Zechariah like a fart in a bathtub.

"And so, we shall be on our way now, and thank you for your cooperation." Gobels rose as if to go.

"Not so fast. I'm going with you."

"Well"—Gobels grinned nervously—"that won't be necessary! Not at all! Why . . . why . . . you have"—he gestured about Zechariah's Spartan office—"your duties here, my good man. You cannot possibly spare the time," he added, hopefully, desperately.

"I'll be the judge of that, Doctor. I'm going with you because New Salem—not 'Salaam,' goddammit, and don't you freaking forget it—is my home, and the boy lives with my family."

A lot of Charlie Bass had rubbed off on Zechariah Brattle.

CHAPTER
FOUR

**The Snoop 'n Poop, Havelock, Near Camp Howard,
Marine Corps Base Camp Basilone, Halfway**

Thirdday evening was normally a quiet time on the streets of
Havelock, one of the liberty towns outside Camp Basilone, because the Marines who were the main patrons of its bars,
restaurants, and other establishments had duty early the next
morning. It was more so at the Snoop 'n Poop, which catered
more to the Marines of Fourth Force Recon Company than to
other Marines, and the Force Recon Marines who weren't deployed were often on training missions somewhere on Camp
Basilone during the week. But this night, the Snoop 'n Poop
was busier than usual for a weeknight. One hundred and
twenty members of Fourth Force Recon Company had recently
returned from the war on Ravenette, and Lieutenant General Indrus, the commanding general of Fourth Fleet Marines, had
given them two weeks' leave following their mandated debriefings and psych evaluations.

Having been drained of all the lessons learned and intelligence the Marines could provide, and been declared sane and
mentally sound—or at least as sane and mentally sound as men
whose business it was to roam in very small groups behind enemy lines to gather intelligence and raise havoc without being
caught could be expected to be—nearly all of them headed for
distant locations on Halfway. During the second week of their
leave, the Marines drifted back toward Camp Basilone. Not

that they were headed back to their home at Camp Howard, not yet. They gravitated to Havelock, and most of them gradually assembled—sort of assembled—at the Snoop 'n Poop. The members of the sniper squad preferred the Peepsight.

On that Thirdday forty-odd members of the company were in the Snoop 'n Poop for dinner and drink. Mostly drink. They didn't talk about the war in which they'd just fought; they'd talked about it enough in the debriefings and psych evaluations. That didn't mean they didn't have memories that needed to be drowned. Or maybe they hadn't had enough to drink during the week and a half that most of them spent at removes from Camp Howard—a hard-fought war can raise a powerful thirst in a man. It could simply be that they felt more comfortable in the Snoop 'n Poop than just about anywhere else on the friendly side of enemy lines. If nothing else, the staff of the Snoop 'n Poop was friendly, efficient, and easy on the eyes.

"What'll you have, Mikel?" a waitress asked Corporal Nomonon; she'd already served their first round of drinks. "I mean from the menu," she said when she saw the sudden glint in Nomonon's eyes.

Corporal Mikel Nomonon immediately changed what he was about to say to, "How are the mussels tonight, Gail?"

"Really good. There's enough garlic in the sauce to put hair on your chest."

"Then how do you know they're good?" he asked, looking at the large oval of bare skin between the high stock collar and the upper portion of her breasts left exposed by the mock dress reds of her waitress uniform. "You obviously didn't have any."

"You know what I mean," Gail said with a playful swat at the back of his head.

There was enough force behind the swat to sting, but Nomonon didn't even blink. His gaze slowly moved up to Gail's eyes and he gave her a crooked smile. "And you know what *I* mean. I'll have a double ration of the mussels."

"You got it." Businesslike, she turned her attention to Corporal Ryn Jaschke. "How 'bout you, Ryn? Your usual?"

"You've got me pegged, Gail," Jaschke said. He pointedly didn't look at the oval of bare skin on her chest.

"And—I'm sorry, I don't remember your name," she said to the third Marine sitting at the table.

"Hans Ellis," he said, courteously rising to his feet and giving Gail a bow. "I'm surprised you even remember my face; we didn't have much of a chance to meet before our last deployment."

Gail tapped the top of Nomonon's head with her knuckles. "You, sir, could learn a few things from Corporal Ellis—"

"*Lance* Corporal Ellis," Nomonon corrected her.

"—Lance Corporal Ellis about how to treat a lady. He's a gentleman. Now, Hans, what would you like for your dinner?"

"I dearly love stuffed flounder."

"An excellent choice; I can vouch for it because it's what I had for dinner myself. I'll be back to check on your drinks." She gracefully spun about and walked away to place their dinner orders. As she walked away, Jaschke admired her legs, most of which were visible below the hem of her skirt, the exact color and cut of the skirt of a female Marine's dress reds—except that Mother Corps would never condone a uniform skirt anywhere near that short. Ellis drank in the whole woman.

"Down, boy," Jaschke said when he saw Ellis's look. "I think she actually does like Nomonon—though I can't imagine why."

"Liking Nomonon's a dirty job, but I guess somebody's got to do it," said Sergeant Him Kindy from the next table. Normally, Kindy would be with his men, but that evening the squad leaders had segregated themselves from their men.

"You're absolutely right, Kindy," Sergeant Wil Bingh agreed. "But why's it got to be a nice girl like Gail? There's got to be five or ten—well, maybe not ten, four or five, I guess—scuts around who're low enough to like Nomonon."

"You know, Bingh," Sergeant D'Wayne Williams said, "I do believe you're right. I'll bet if we went out and prowled around it wouldn't take us much more than a couple of hours to find some scut so down on herself she'd go for Nomonon."

Kindy lit up with excitement. "You're on! I think it'd take two days, at least."

"I'll hold the money," Bingh said and held out his hands.

"Who said we're betting money?" Williams said. "And what makes you think we're dumb enough to let you hold it if we were?"

Nomonon growled at the three squad leaders and made to get out of his chair, but stayed seated when Jaschke put a hand on his arm.

"Ignore them," Jaschke said. "Remember, when a Marine makes sergeant, he gets docked twenty IQ points. They don't know what they're talking about."

At another table, Corporal Harv Belinski and Lance Corporals Santiago Rudd and Elin Skripska were already well into their third pitcher of ale when Mom Kass came to check on them.

"Come on, boys," she said, "get some food inside you. I don't want to have to throw you out for being skunkly drunk."

"Ah, you wouldn't do that to your favorite Misguided Children, would you, Mom Kass?" Belinski said, giving her his most innocent wide-eyed smile.

She gave him *that* look, the one that said she was giving him a chance to retract his question.

Kass wasn't called "Mom" because she was old enough to be the mother to any of the other waitresses, though she *was* the oldest of them. Neither was it because she was older than the Snoop 'n Poop's customers; perhaps half of them were older than she was. Nor was it because her build was stout and motherly; she was one of the more svelte and shapely women on the staff of the Snoop 'n Poop. It wasn't even because she dressed in a more matronly manner than the rest of the young women who worked there. Indeed, her skirts were the shortest, the bare back of her mock tunic extended around her sides, and the oval between the stock collar and the slopes of her breasts displayed more decolletage than the norm.

No, Kass was called "Mom" because of her motherly approach to the eating and drinking habits of the Snoop 'n Poop's customers. Well, not *completely* motherly—few mothers would allow their sons to drink as much as these Marines did.

"We're just warming up, Mom Kass," Rudd said, laughing.

"Right, we're whetting our appetites," Skripska agreed. He emptied the pitcher, pouring it more or less equally among their three mugs, and held it out to Mom Kass for a refill.

She gave Skripska *that* look, and said, "I'll be back with some food. *Then* I'll get you a refill."

The three Marines looked at one another with surprised amusement, then burst out laughing.

Mom Kass was back well before they'd emptied their mugs, bearing a tray with a Boradu-style nacho platter and three plates. As soon as she finished placing the platter and plates on the table, Rudd hoisted the empty pitcher and said, "Mother, may I?"

Mom Kass gave him *that* look, pointed at the platter, and said, "Eat."

"Yes, ma'am," Rudd said, and used a handful of the grain chips to scoop cheese, ground meat and sauce blend, peppers, and greens onto the plate she'd put in front of him. Throughout, he kept the pitcher aloft for her to take.

Mom Kass gave the other two *that* look until they also filled their plates from the platter and started eating. Only then did she take the pitcher from Rudd's hand and go off to refill it at the bar.

Raucous laughter sounded from the next table, and a voice crowed, "Mom Kass sure has you three under control!"

Belinski looked over and glowered. "That's enough out of you, Musica," he snarled.

Corporal Gin Musica barked out another laugh. Corporal Dana Pricer and Lance Corporal Stanis Wehrli joined in. They cut off and switched their attention to their own food and drink when Mom Kass came back and bestowed *that* look on *them.*

Before Belinski could laugh, or say anything to Musica, a hush fell over the Snoop 'n Poop, and all movement ceased—even the waitresses stopped in their tracks—and all heads swiveled toward the entrance. Where a most strange sight presented itself. A group of women was coming through the door. None of them wore anything that could be identified as part of a uniform, but the cut of their hair and their bearing declared them to be Marines. A whole platoon's worth of female Marines—a reinforced platoon. Entering the Snoop 'n Poop. An establishment that catered to male Marines, where the most commonly seen women were waitresses in mock female-Marine-uniform costumes.

For a long moment, the only sounds in the room were the light treads of the women Marines' feet as they moved about finding tables for themselves, the scraping of chairs on the floor as they took seats, and the light titters of their voices as they talked back and forth.

Sergeant Kindy was the first to speak. He was afraid of how the platoon of female Marines would react to the waitresses' uniforms, and his murmured "Oh shit" carried quite clearly through the room. Kindy had been coming to the Snoop 'n Poop frequently during his three and a half years with Fourth Force Recon, and this was the first time he'd ever seen a female Marine in the place—unless the rumors that some of the waitresses were off-duty Marines were true. His murmur spoke for everyone.

Kindy's two syllables were enough to break the few men in the place who weren't Force Recon out of their paralysis. They began frantically signaling the waitresses for their checks. They were the only ones who showed intent to leave, though. Even when the door opened again to admit two more women. The two newcomers, even bereft of uniform and insignia, were instantly identifiable as Marine gunnery sergeants, most probably acting as sheepdogs, there to protect their flock from the wolves who inhabited the Snoop 'n Poop.

The non–Force Recon Marines couldn't exit fast enough, but the Force Recon Marines weren't budging from their place, nossir! It was *their* place after all, and *nobody* was chasing them out of it. And if the women didn't like it, well, they could just pick their cute little derrieres up and prance right out!

The women didn't seem to object to the waitress uniforms— except maybe for the two gunnery sergeants. Then again, those two looked like they disapproved of *everything* in the Snoop 'n Poop, quite possibly even the very existence of the establishment. Not only didn't the women Marines seem to object, but one said to the nearest waitress, "Nice outfit! Who's your tailor?" Her voice carried clearly throughout the room.

A hush washed over the men, who turned their heads to the women anew. The quiet was broken by the women Marines, who burst out in delighted laughter. Realizing the laughter wasn't directed at them, the waitresses joined in.

All the women were laughing except for the two gunnery sergeants. One of whom not only looked like she used ten penny nails for toothpicks, she looked like she was chomping on one *right now*!

Gradually, the noise level in the room returned to the way it had been before the "Who's your tailor?" remark. The tables weren't big; round and designed to seat four comfortably, six if they were very friendly and didn't order too much to eat or drink at one time. The men sat three or four to a table, eating and drinking—mostly drinking—while the women grouped five or six to a table, huddled close together, talking in low voices over their food and drink—mostly food.

After a time, Lance Corporal Ellis got up and went to the MusiKola, slotted some credits, and made several selections. When the melodious strains of the HekKats "I Sit and Watch" filled the room, Ellis began solo dancing with his back to the room. He slowly turned around and, feet, shoulders, and arms moving to the music, wended his way to a table where five women sat watching him.

At the table, feet, shoulders, and arms still moving to the music, where the women still watched him, some expectantly, some nervously, one with glowing eyes and parted lips, he nodded at them, looked each of them in the eye, and said, "Excuse me, ladies, but would one of you care to dance?"

"I would!" said the one with parted lips and glowing eyes. She was on her feet and leading Ellis to the small dance floor before any of the others had found their voices. The Snoop 'n Poop didn't have a real dance floor; it wasn't that kind of place. But the small space in front of the MusiKola would do.

Back at Ellis's table, Corporals Nomonon and Jaschke gaped at Ellis and the woman dancing with him. Sergeant Kindy leaned over from the adjacent table at which he sat—he had to stretch to reach—and rapped both of them on the back of their heads with his knuckles.

"What are you doing, letting him get away with that?" Kindy demanded. The two corporals, rubbing the backs of their heads, glared at their squad leader.

"He didn't ask permission!" Jaschke snapped.

"He didn't even say what he was doing; he just got up without so much as a by-your-leave and did it!" Nomonon declared.

"You can't let the junior man get away with that, you know," Kindy told them.

Nomonon and Jaschke looked at each other.

"He's right," Jaschke said.

"Watch me," Nomonon said back. He got up and swaggered over to another table of women.

"Hey, babes, who wants to dance?" he boldly said.

They laughed at him, and a couple said, "No thanks," while the rest simply shook their heads.

Red-faced, Nomonon marched back to his table. Gail got there with a fresh pitcher of beer just as he resumed his seat.

"What did I tell you, Mikel? You should take lessons from Hans on how to treat a lady."

"What?" Nomonon squawked, looking offended.

"Hans asked politely, in the manner of a man who just wanted to dance. *You* strutted over there like you expected them to rip their blouses off and spread their legs for you. Not the way to win a woman's heart." She spun about and flounced away.

"Don't say it," Nomonon snarled at Jaschke. "Don't say *anything*." He made sure the squad leaders at the next table knew he was talking to them too.

In another part of the room, Corporal Harv Belinski wasn't about to be outdone by a mere lance corporal. He got up and walked, not strutted, to a nearby table, bowed to the six women seated there, and asked, "May I have the pleasure of this dance with one of you?"

Four of the women gave him skeptical looks, but the fifth, bopping along to WizzinWacks' "All Day Short," looked in his eyes and said, "Thank you, I'd love to dance." But when he reached for her hand to lead her to the impromptu dance floor, she said, "No touching."

Ellis and his partner were still dancing when Belinski and his reached the front of the MusiKola. There was room enough for two couples, but when a third, Sergeant Williams and a woman who looked like she might also have three stripes on the sleeves of her dress reds, tried to join in, the space was entirely too crowded. But Marines are resourceful, and in moments enough tables and chairs were pushed out of the way to make a reasonable dance floor. It wasn't much longer before the available space was filled with dancing couples.

In another half hour, the only table that held only men or only women was the one with the two sheepdogs, who did everything but stand up and howl to make sure the wolves knew they were there to protect their flock, and woe be to the wolf who dared trespass.

That was the scene into which Gunnery Sergeant Alf Lytle and Staff Sergeant Kazan Fryman, respectively the platoon sergeant and first section leader of second platoon, Fourth Force Recon Company, walked. The two Force Recon leaders almost instantly assessed the situation and, without needing to exchange any words, acted. They headed directly for the sheepdogs, sat at their table, introduced themselves, and engaged the women in conversation.

The sheepdogs may have been intent on protecting their flock, but Lytle and Fryman were just as intent on running interference for their wolves.

And who knows, maybe the sheepdogs actually wanted some wolvish company.

CHAPTER
FIVE

Fourth Force Recon Barracks, Camp Howard, Marine Corps
Base Camp Basilone, Halfway

"There's never a corpsman around when you need one,"
Sergeant Wil Bingh moaned late the next morning.

"Arrgh," Sergeant Brigo Kare said in agreement.

They occupied overstuffed chairs in the squad leaders' lounge
of the Force Recon barracks. Bingh sprawled, Kare curled fe-
tuslike.

It was the morning after the Snoop 'n Poop had been invaded
by the reinforced platoon of off-duty female Marines. The two
were in the company's squad leaders' lounge because when
they got to the barracks the night before, second platoon's first
section squad leaders' room was locked and the door barri-
caded from the inside. When they banged on the door and demanded entry, Sergeant Kindy, from inside, told them firmly to
go away. When they persisted, Kindy unbarricaded the door,
slipped out, grabbed them by their scruffs to march them to the
lounge, where he deposited them on the overstuffed chairs and
told them he'd let them know when they could return to their
room.

Kindy wasn't bigger than Bingh and Kare, but he wasn't
shit-faced drunk like they were, which was why he'd been able
to handle them so easily.

Bingh and Kare were among the last to leave the Snoop 'n
Poop in the wee hours of the morning. By then, more than half

of the Force Recon Marines who had been in the place had left, as had all of the women Marines; unlike the men, who were still on leave, the women had to report for duty in the morning. Some of the stragglers, as had some of the earlier Marines to leave, went in search of rooms in Havelock to spend the night. The rest, as had some of the earlier departers, caught a liberty bus back to Camp Howard and the barracks. But not all those who left earlier left alone. Alone in this case meaning with only other men.

So there they were, Sergeants Wil Bingh and Brigo Kare, muscles and joints kinked and cramped from sleeping in the chairs, heads aching and mouths dry, suffering from monumental hangovers.

"Corpsman up," Kare moaned.

"Water," Bingh groaned. He pulled his sprawled limbs inward as the first step in rising, thought better of it, and went limp. "You try," he rasped.

"Try what?" Kare opened a bloodshot eye and rolled it toward Bingh.

"Getting up."

"Why?"

"Find a corpsman. Get water."

"Uhn." Kare slowly began straightening from his curled position, stopped when his upper hip encountered the arm of the chair, preventing him from rolling onto his back. "Can't."

"*Can't* isn't in the Force Recon lexicon, Sergeant!" a jovial voice boomed at them, making both sergeants flinch and groan in agony. "My, my, I spy—two sergeants who did *far* too much partying last night."

Bingh's eyes painfully fluttered open and oriented themselves on the source of the entirely too cheerful and loud voice: Hospitalman Second Gruff, one of the company's five corpsmen. Like the two Marines, Gruff was in civilian clothes. Unlike theirs, his were clean and neat and had not been slept in.

"Did you get any?" Gruff asked jovially.

Bingh's valiant attempt to glower at the corpsman died a painful death; even his lips hurt.

Kare didn't even try; he would have had to turn his head to see Gruff, and turning his head was simply too difficult.

"I didn't think so," Gruff said. "If you had, you wouldn't need these." He held up a large bottle of water and a smaller bottle of what Bingh immediately recognized as hangover pills.

"Gimme," Bingh groaned as he thrust an arm in Gruff's direction and partly rose from the chair. He moaned and fell back.

"Wha . . . ?" Kare struggled into a position from where he could see Gruff.

Gruff smiled cheerfully as he twisted his wrists, shaking the bottles that dangled from his fingers. "The cure," he murmured.

"You're a sadist, Doc," Bingh mumbled.

"Torturing sick men you could cure so easily," Kare added.

"Say pretty please."

"Kill you if you . . ." It took more effort than Bingh could manage to complete the sentence.

"P-Pretty p-please," Kare croaked.

"Yes, Sergeant Kare, Doc Gruff has the cure for you." He circled Bingh, making sure he was out of easy reach, to Kare's side and decanted a pill from the smaller bottle. "Drink this down with a liter of water," he instructed, dropping the pill into Kare's open mouth and handing him the water bottle. He turned back to Bingh and pulled another bottle of water from out of nowhere. "Wil?"

"Oooh . . ." Bingh worked his mouth to dredge up some saliva. "P-Please."

"Pretty please. With a cherry on top."

"Kill you." Bingh struggled without much success to climb out of the chair.

"You know, Doc, he probably will if you make him get better on his own," said Sergeant Kindy from the entrance to the squad leaders' lounge. Unlike the other two squad leaders, Kindy was freshly shatshoweredshaved and wore fresh civvies. He was also grinning like a legendary cat.

"Hmmm," Gruff mused. "You may be right, Him." He turned to Bingh. "Open wide, like a fish going after a worm on a hook." Back to Kindy. "You look nice and fresh. Did you stay in last night, instead of going out carousing like these two?"

Kindy's grin widened. "Only part of the night, Doc. Only part of the night."

By then, the hangover pill and water were taking effect on Kare so he was able to turn himself around and sit up. "Him," he asked softly so as to not upset his still unstable equilibrium, "are you saying you had, ahh, contraband in our room last night, and that's why you wouldn't let us in?"

Kindy's grin grew more broadly yet. "What I don't tell you can't be used against me in a court-martial."

"Lemme at 'im," Bingh croaked. The pill and water hadn't had time to do much for him so it took massive effort for him to lever himself out of the chair. He stood tottering for a moment, then leaned forward until he had to step to avoid falling on his face. He moved forward by alternately leaning, nearly falling, and stepping. Kare got to his feet and followed him past Kindy into the corridor, toward the squad leaders' room, along with Gruff. Kindy hung back but went along as well.

The pill and water worked on Bingh, and by the time he reached the squad leaders' quarters, he was almost walking normally. Inside, he wasn't able to look and see everything from one place; each of the squad leaders had his own small room, cubicle really, separated from the common area by low partitions. Bingh made a circuit of the main room, looking into each cubicle. His and Kare's racks were unslept in, as was Sergeant Williams's. So was Kindy's—but his had fresh bedding.

Bingh sniffed loudly. Sniffed again. "Fee fi fo fum, I smell the musk of a woman," he snarled. He turned around, looking for Kindy, saw him. "You brought a *woman* into the barracks last night? Are you out of your ever loving *mind*? Do you realize what could happen to you if the officers found out?"

"Find out what?" Kindy asked, all innocence, looking all around. "You're saying a woman's in here? Where? I don't see a woman."

Fists clenched tightly at his sides, Bingh advanced on Kindy. "You brought a *woman* into the barracks last night?" he snarled. "And made me and Brigo sleep in the *lounge,* and you want to act like nothing *happened*?"

"What happened?" Kindy demanded indignantly. "Nothing, that's what!"

Doc Gruff stepped in front of Bingh, blocking his advance. "Calm down, Marine. Nothing happened."

When Bingh went to step around Gruff, Kare grabbed his upper arm to hold him back. "Let it go, Wil," he said. He immediately regretted the sharpness of his tone—he wasn't recovered enough yet from his hangover to not feel a painful physical reaction to his own voice.

"But—"

"No 'buts,' " Gruff said. "Nothing happened. And if Kindy got lucky and you didn't, so what? It's the breaks of the game."

"I had to sleep on a chair in the lounge!"

"Beats sleeping in the mud on Ravenette."

Bingh turned his still bloodshot eyes on the corpsman. "This isn't the bush. This is different."

"You could have gotten a room in town; you didn't have to come back to the barracks," Gruff insisted.

"Wanted to save m' money for more liberty," Bingh mumbled.

"We've slept in the lounge before, Wil," Kare said. "Come on, let's grab a shower. We'll both feel better. Then we can take Him back into town and see who gets lucky tonight."

Bingh looked at Kare for a moment, then said, "A shower. You're right, I feel like shit." He twisted his arm out of the other's grasp and aimed himself at his own cubicle, shedding his clothes as he went. A moment later, a towel wrapped around his hips, he was headed for the squad leaders' showers.

When he heard the water running, Kare stepped up to Kindy and said, "You son of a bitch," and punched his shoulder. It was a friendly punch, but still hard enough to sting.

Havelock

Not much more than an hour later, the three squad leaders were sitting at a table in a Havelock diner, having a steak-and-egg breakfast even though it was late in the lunch hour. They were far from being the only Marines in the diner but, thanks to the hangover pills Doc Gruff had given Bingh and Kare, they were in much better shape than many of their fellow diners, who were still showing the effects of the previous night's drinking. Others of their number looked quite chipper and self-satisfied—Bingh and Kare had a very good idea of why they looked so pleased with themselves and glowered at them. Then:

"Either of you know where D'Wayne is?" Kindy asked between bites. The others shook their heads.

Kare thought for a moment, swallowed a mouthful of steak and eggs, and said, "The last time I remember seeing him, he was hanging out by a side door at the Snoop 'n Poop."

Bingh thought back, then nodded. "Right, I saw him there too." He looked at the other two and mused, "I seem to remember, the woman he'd been dancing with slipped out that same door right before I noticed him. Good-looking woman." He glanced at Kindy. "When we find him, I'll bet he looks just like this guy."

Kindy gave him an eyebrow-raised, "Who, me?" look, but opted for taking another bite of steak instead of saying anything.

"Him," Kare said, chewing slowly and swallowing, "I don't remember you dancing with any one woman in particular. So who'd you nail?"

"Brigo, please!" Kindy said with exaggerated indignance. "A gentleman never discloses such things."

"I know. That's why I'm asking *you*."

"Yeah, who?" Bingh demanded. He hefted his mug and took a sip of hot kaff.

"No, no, no," Kindy said, waving his fork. "You believe I had a woman in our quarters last night, and that's why I didn't let you in when you came knocking. If I say, then you'll know. If I *did* bring a woman into the barracks—and I'm not saying I did, because we all know that's a violation of regulations—I'd be admitting I did something wrong. You can't expect me to convict myself now, can you?"

"You already admitted it when you said a gentleman doesn't talk about it," Kare told him.

"Ah ha! But not telling can also mean maybe I *didn't*."

"You're jerking on us, Him," Bingh snorted. "Confess! We both know you did."

"Are you going to see her again?" Kare asked, and took a bite of toast.

"My lips are sealed on the matter." Kindy put a hand to his face and pressed his lips together with his fingertips.

"Now, listen here," Bingh leaned onto his elbows and poked his fork at Kindy. "I'm the senior squad leader in the section, and—"

"Speaking of senior," Kindy cut him off, "did either of you see Gunny Lytle or Staff Sergeant Fryman leave?"

Bingh and Kare looked at each other.

"You know, I think you're right," Kare said. "They must have left earlier than we did."

"And the sheepdogs were gone early too," Bingh added.

"Well, what do you know," Kindy breathed as he mopped up the last of his egg yokes and steak juices with the end of his toast.

Kare thought about the implications of their own leaders and the two sheepdogs leaving the Snoop 'n Poop while some of the women were still there. He shuddered. "That's going above and beyond. Can you imagine doing a female gunny?"

Bingh and Kindy also shuddered.

"That'd be almost as bad as doing a male gunny," Bingh admitted.

"Maybe worse," Kindy said, then gave the others a "What now?" look in response to their shocked expressions.

"What might be worse?" a familiar voice asked. The trio looked up and saw Sergeant Williams, who had come to their table unnoticed while they were contemplating the above-and-beyond heroism of Lytle and Fryman pairing off with the sheepdogs.

"Where the hell have you been, D'Wayne?" Kare demanded.

"Sit down," Bingh ordered.

"Have you had breakfast yet?" Kindy realized that Williams's expression must be much like his own had been an hour or so earlier.

"I had an early breakfast."

"So where have you been since then?" Bingh asked.

Williams gave the others a smug smile. "She had duty this morning and had to go back to Basilone. So I went back to sleep."

"And you just now got up?" Kindy asked, trying to deflect questions about who she was from Bingh and Kare.

"A little while ago. I had breakfast earlier, but I could use a bit of lunch now." He pulled the menu to himself, but his angelic look told the others he was giving more thought to the woman he'd spent the night with than he was to the menu.

"So who is she?" Bingh asked.

"And does she have friends for us?" Kare wanted to know.

Kindy leaned back with an almost inaudible sigh; it looked like Bingh and Kare would soon be off his back about who he'd spent the night with. At least for the time being.

When Williams placed his lunch order, the other three decided to join him. So what if they'd just finished breakfast; it was lunchtime!

CHAPTER
SIX

Brattle Household, New Salem, Kingdom

Moses was engaged in his favorite pastime—playing in the mud outside the Brattles's home—when Dr. Joseph Gobels stepped out of his hopper. Moses took one look at the doctor and ran screaming into the house. "Mumee! Mumee! Devil! Devil!"

"Good God!" Gobels gasped. "It can speak English! You didn't tell me that, Braggle!" he said, turning to Zechariah accusingly.

"You didn't ask," Zechariah answered. He'd given up correcting Gobels's mispronunciation of his name and wanted now only to get the unpleasant business over with and see the scientists' departing backs. He was not looking forward to what he knew was going to happen. Zechariah had not informed his family they were coming; otherwise, he was afraid, they would have tried to hide Moses somewhere. He felt badly about that but his sense of duty to the Confederation overrode his guilt.

Gobels turned to Fogel. "It can speak English! My, my," he chortled, rubbing his stubby hands together enthusiastically. He began laughing that annoying, high-pitched giggle of his that cut through Zechariah Brattle like a knife blade.

The flight down to New Salem from Haven with the two scientists had been very unpleasant in the cramped passenger compartment because Fogel farted and Gobels's breath stank.

Zechariah endured most of the flight with a hand over his nose. About halfway into it he could stand the pair no longer. "Next time you go on a flight somewhere, Bogel, kindly move your bowels before you leave, and as for you, Bobels"—he derived great pleasure from mispronouncing *their* names—"try brushing your teeth once in a while, would you?" For the rest of the flight they sat in frigid silence staring out the ports at the landscape passing beneath them.

Hannah Brattle, wiping her hands on her apron, stood looming in the doorway as the three walked up to the front door. Moses, clutching her skirts, peeked out from behind her. She knew instinctively what was about to happen. *"No, you don't,"* she said menacingly as the three approached. Hannah had always been a formidable woman.

"These men have come for Moses, Hannah. We must give him up to them. It is the law."

"To hell with the law! Moses belongs to us and not to Caesar!" Hannah bellowed.

"Hannah—"

"Madam," Gobels said, wiping the perspiration from his forehead as he stepped forward, "we shall not harm him and he shall be returned to you when we are done with him." His insincere smile revealed dirty teeth, and Hannah visibly recoiled at the sight as much as from his foul breath.

"No! Joab, Samuel!" The two boys emerged from the back of the house where they'd been studying their Bibles. They realized immediately what was happening and took up protective positions on either side of their mother.

"Hannah, you will give him up *now.* These men are scientists on an important government mission. Moses will be returned to us when they are done with him. Now stand aside and give him to me. I will tolerate no more of this foolishness." Hannah and her boys began to cry now. Zechariah made a sudden grab for Moses but the boy was too quick and scuttled away into the house grunting in terror. "You stay here!" Zechariah told the scientists and brushed Hannah aside.

What happened next was heartbreaking. Moses, motivated by mortal fear of the scientists, scooted away from Zechariah. He was aided by his small size, which permitted him to crawl into narrow spaces and under pieces of furniture, and he was very quick on his stubby little legs; he was even faster on his belly, zipping across the floor as though he were in water. Zechariah stumbled after him, barking his shins against furniture and knocking things over. "Moses, come here! Moses, come here!" he shouted, to no avail.

Outside, Gobels and Fogel stood by apprehensively, listening to the crashing and yelling, keeping a wary eye on Hannah and her boys. But the Brattle family's attention was focused on Zechariah inside the house, not on the scientists who didn't dare take part in the chase. Gobels turned to Fogel and whispered, "This is fucking hilarious!" He glanced slyly at Hannah but she had not heard him, thank God. "Reminds me of a goddamned cartoon show," Fogel whispered back, and the two giggled surreptitiously behind their hands. "Nobel, Nobel, Noble Nobel," Gobels chortled happily. It was hard for him to resist dancing on the spot. *A live Skink! All mine, all mine!* He felt like singing.

At last Zechariah, flushed with anger and exertion and breathing heavily, emerged from the house grasping Moses firmly about the waist. "Dada! Dada! No! Nooooo!" Moses shrieked.

"Now, you two," Zechariah gritted, "you take him and get the hell out of here!" He handed Moses, still struggling, to Fogel, who carried a harnesslike device that he strapped onto Moses; as he did that Hannah screamed and might have collapsed if Joab and Samuel had not supported her.

"It is all right, it is all right," Gobels cautioned. "We won't hurt him!"

By now a curious crowd had gathered. It was obvious and disheartening to Hannah and the boys that most of the people in the crowd were pleased at what was happening. Although they had voted to keep Moses among them, few had been happy with that decision. For the first time, Hannah Brattle began to doubt that the spirit of Christ still dwelt with the City of God.

"Now leave!" Zechariah commanded the scientists. Gobels and Fogel scuttled off with their precious burden. Zechariah was certain Gobels was laughing hysterically as he climbed back into the hopper. He turned to the crowd. "We all have our duty," he said bitterly, "and I have just done mine. Go home now and leave us in peace." He stomped back into the house without saying another word to anyone. It was fully a month before either Hannah or the boys would even speak to him.

Dr. Gobels's Laboratory, Wellfordsville, Earth

"Mumeeeee! Mumeeee!" Moses screamed, but the pain and terror only got worse.

"Uh, don't you think we ought to lighten up on him?" Fogel asked. "If it dies"—he shrugged—"we're in the shit."

"A moment, a moment! This thing tolerates pain very well, Fogel. One more jolt," Gobels said, and twisted a dial on the control panel. Moses shrieked. "Look! The heart rate has not increased appreciably, Fogel! That much current would knock out a human being. Truly amazing." He turned off the machine and Moses, sobbing and gasping, went silent. "These things were bioengineered, Fogel. Bioengineered to endure pain and hardship. That is why it hasn't succumbed to what we've done to it! I believe aside from deliberately killing it there's nothing we can do with our tests that will permanently harm the thing."

Lying in his cage, Moses quietly murmured what sounded like a name to Fogel. "Well, it certainly feels pain, Doctor. You know, I think it's calling for its mother."

"Ridiculous, Fogel! Ridiculous. The thing has no mother. It was designed, I tell you, bioengineered."

"Well, that Brattle woman—?"

"Oh, come now! What's gotten in to you, Fogel? They were

attached to the thing the way many people are attached to their pets. Obviously it was birthed while the Skinks were fighting us on Kingdom and somehow got separated from its litter when they took off in such a hurry. I've never been able to understand that, how people can become so attached to dumb animals."

"But it's not a dumb animal, sir. It's educable. It has learned Standard English; it has a vocabulary, emotions, that's obvious. It thinks the Brattle woman is its mother."

"Oh, humbug! Well, of course we know the adults are highly intelligent, Fogel. They have a highly developed technology, FTL capability, are highly organized. Yes, a formidable species, no doubt. But don't forget how poorly this one did on the intelligence tests."

"Well, it has been under considerable stress, sir. I didn't do well on exams either after a night out on the town."

"No, no, no, Fogel! This one was bred to have a low order of intellect. But our goal here is not to make friends or pets of the damned things, it's to find out what makes them tick and then use that against them. Look, prepare it for another gastrointestinal probe, will you. Feed it first and set the monitors to work their way through its system in twenty-four hours."

"Again? The damned thing will start that screaming all over, boss!"

"Yes, again! If your ears are too sensitive, go outside. I don't care if they hurt the thing or not; they won't kill it."

"There was considerable blood in its stool last time, Doctor."

"Set it up, Fogel! Now, dammit. I want to do another analysis of its stomach acids and its fecal material. Its digestive system is almost like our own, truly amazing, and I want to pin that down, Fogel, pin it right down. Analysis, analysis, analysis, Fogel! Facts and figures, man. We are on the verge of a tremendous breakthrough here. Well, get to it, man, get to it!"

Gobels had not taken Moses to Fargo and Universal Labs. He did not even report that he had found Moses. He returned to Earth on his own, to a small town known as Wellfordsville in the hills of what had been the state of Virginia during the age of the United States. There he had his own laboratory. It was where he planned to conduct his examination in his own time and in his own way.

The first thing Gobels did was to view a series of trids taken by combat reporters embedded with the Confederation forces during the war on Kingdom. He compared the physical features of adult Skinks with those displayed by Moses. "Compare the teeth." He pointed them out to Fogel. "See how sharp they are on the adults but those on our specimen are closer in form to our own. Pointed, yes, but still very much like our own. They've been *dentified* on the adults, not bred that way but fixed some time after birth. Extraordinary! It has a four-chambered heart and pituitarylike glands in the brain that regulate its body temperature, like the mammals of Earth. We've compared voice patterns from the sound on the vids to the voice of our own Skink. His is not as harsh and guttural as those of the adults, but that's probably because it's not fully mature yet."

"Yes, and language analysis has identified fricatives very much like those of human speech," Fogel pointed out. "We need to subject them to analysis by an expert."

Gobels shrugged. "Not of interest to me, Fogel. We aren't trying to communicate with the bastards, only finding out how best to kill them."

"I think the Marines know how to do that already," Fogel said drily.

"Not just shoot them up, Fogel, but wipe them out as a species before they wipe us out! Damn, you've got to think big! Now, look at this"—he produced a printout of Moses's blood analysis—"these fatty oils in the blood. Something very strange, very unnatural about these oils, Fogel. Perhaps they aid in maintaining body temperature, but they're highly volatile. When the creatures are struck with any kind of flame—and *poof*! That's why we haven't been able to recover a dead one from the battlefield! Brilliant! Amazing! The thought that has gone into engineering these creatures." Gobels shook his head. "We're dealing with scientific geniuses here, Fogel, no doubt about it! And look at the gill slits along the lateral sides of the thorax. They're vestigial, but with a minor surgical operation they can be altered so the things can breathe underwater! Truly amazing! Fogel, we've only scratched the surface here. In a couple of days I'll have the results of some *definitive* tests I've been running and then we'll have a complete picture of what this thing is made of!"

"Do you think we'll find out it has a soul after all?" Fogel asked archly.

"Your sense of humor, Fogel, is wearing mighty thin on me. But you can laugh all the way into the history books when we publish our findings."

Zechariah Brattle's Office, Interstellar City, Kingdom

Zechariah Brattle rubbed a hand wearily across his brow. He'd been had, hoodwinked, fooled and he was sick to the depths of his soul that he could have let the scientists get away with it. His routine inquiry to Universal Labs in Fargo on Earth had just been returned. According to the lab, Dr. Joseph Gobels was still on Kingdom and had reported nothing about finding a living Skink. "If you have any further information on this matter, please communicate it to us at once as it may be of the greatest importance to the Confederation," the message concluded. There was no denying the imperious tone of the message or that it was perfectly justified.

"So what am I to do?" Zechariah asked himself aloud. "Admit how serious a mistake I made?" He smashed a fist onto his desk in frustration. Well, admitting to that publicly wouldn't be half as bad as when he told Hannah and the boys that Moses had been kidnapped by a pair of rogue scientists. He thought about taking it to the Lord in prayer. "No, Lord," he said quietly, "You have given me this cup for a reason and I've got to drink from it."

So what does a man do when God has given him a job and then stands back to see how well he handles it? Zechariah knew. "Lord, I'll try this first," he said aloud, and then he sat down and wrote a long letter, which he sent by FTL drone to the one person he knew who could help him. He sent it to Charlie Bass.

CHAPTER
SEVEN

Office of the Commanding General, Task Force Aguinaldo, Camp Swampy, Arsenault

The rain fell in sheets outside the headquarters building. General Aguinaldo had set up his training base in the tropical region of Arsenault because he was certain the Skinks came from a watery world and he believed that when the place was finally discovered his Marines and soldiers would have to be prepared to fight them there under the worst conditions. His mission was twofold: to find their home world and destroy them once and for all, and to be prepared at a moment's notice to fight them if and when they appeared again anywhere in Human Space. But just then he was not quite ready to do either, at least not with the forces currently available.

Colonel Rene Raggel, late aide to General Davis Lyons, who had commanded the secessionist army on Ravenette, sat quietly in General Aguinaldo's office, waiting for him to return from a staff conference. The Marine corporal who was Aguinaldo's enlisted aide had given him a delicious cup of coffee and told him to make himself comfortable. Raggel was tired. He had only just arrived from Ravenette, but his orders had been to report immediately and directly to the task force commander. So there he sat, still dripping from the downpour outside. When he'd first arrived at Camp Alpha, Arsenault's main spaceport, he'd been impressed by the beauty of the world in that northern hemisphere. But deep in the tropics in the middle of the monsoon season, he wasn't so sure anymore about the "beauty" of the place. And, of course, everyone was still talking about the tsunami that had killed so many in that region only recently.

The room was not climate-controlled and one of the windows was open. The roar of the rain was muted but it was a constant background noise. A damp breeze wafted in through the window. It actually felt good. Suddenly several tiny blue flashes winked at the window. Obviously the building was equipped with some form of the commercial Silent Guard system that fricasseed insects trying to fly through it. Raggel was getting comfortable. That breeze, laden with moisture as it was, felt delicious. He wondered what it'd be like in the room without the Silent Guard system. If he sat there much longer, Colonel Raggel realized, he'd doze off.

He yawned and looked around the room. It was absolutely bare of the usual memorabilia with which flag officers decorated their office suites. A stand directly behind the general's desk held three flags: Confederation of Human Worlds, Confederation Marine Corps, and one with two gold novas—the insignia of the Marine Corps Commandant, which Aguinaldo had been before being given command of this task force. As the rank of commandant was also the position—the Marine Corps only had one person of that rank at a time—he wondered what insignia Aguinaldo was wearing as a full general—a rank the Confederation Marines hadn't had before Aguinaldo received this assignment. It was a Spartan office. Raggel smiled. This General Aguinaldo and Raggel's erstwhile commander, General Davis Lyons, had in common a disdain for military pomp. He liked that.

"Keep your seat!" Aguinaldo said as he burst suddenly through the door. "Johnny!" he called to his enlisted aide, "another cup of joe in here! Refill, Colonel?" He extended his hand to Raggel and shook it hard, then plopped into the chair next to him at the small coffee table. He stretched his legs out and sighed. "Damn staff conferences, endless conferences, Colonel, you know what I'm talking about."

Colonel Raggel regarded Aguinaldo carefully. He was dressed in a combat field uniform, as was everyone he'd seen at the headquarters. He was short, sinewy, his dark complexion bespeaking more of his Filipino father than his Dutch mother. He was not an awesome person—he did not try to overpower people with a "commanding" presence—but he was a man who radiated *confidence* and energy. And Raggel's insignia question was answered; Aguinaldo wore four silver novas on each collar, one more than any other Confederation Marine Corps general officer.

The corporal served Aguinaldo's coffee and poured some more into Raggel's cup. "May I call you Rene, Colonel? Thanks, Johnny," he told the corporal, "please shut the door and tell Dottie we're not to be disturbed, will you?" Dottie was the Marine commander who ran Aguinaldo's personal staff and his office, which included keeping his daily agenda.

Aguinaldo regarded Colonel Raggel over the rim of his coffee cup. "Think we'll have rain, Colonel?"

"Intermittent showers, sir. Quite normal for this time of the year," Raggel replied, and they laughed. Even though he had no idea why he had been called there, by name, from Ravenette, the Marine's personality was having its effect. Raggel was beginning to relax in Aguinaldo's presence.

"Rene," Aguinaldo began, "I know you just got down here, haven't had a chance to check in, get quarters even, but we've a lot to do and I want you to start right now. To make a long story short, Rene, when I went out looking for reliable officers to work with me getting my task force combat-ready, your name came up. You worked with General Cazombi, didn't you?"

"Yes, sir. I worked with him on the surrender terms and POW repatriation process after General Lyons surrendered our army."

"I know. I know we were on opposite sides in that war. But that was then, this is now. The president has ordered that we forget all that. The Coalition worlds are back in the Confederation and we are facing a mutual danger far, far more potent than the late, short-lived secessionist ambitions. I need good men to face that threat, and you, Rene, have been recommended to me as someone I can rely on."

Raggel wiped a drop of perspiration running down the side of his cheek.

"Wondering why it's not climate-controlled in here, Colonel?" Aguinaldo asked with a grin.

"Um, it is rather warm in here, sir."

"We believe the Skink home world is very much like it is here right now: hot and wet. We're training to invade that place when we find out where it is. So I am acclimating the task force for those conditions—and that includes my staff and me. Get used to life in the tropics, Colonel."

"Very good, sir. May I ask to whom the honor goes for recommending me?"

"Volunteered you is more like it." Aguinaldo grinned. "Alistair Cazombi. You've had police experience, Rene?"

Raggel had come to like General Cazombi very much but the question surprised him. "Yes, sir, but that was a long time ago."

Aguinaldo leaned forward and placed his coffee cup carefully on the table. "Okay, Rene, here it is. I have a military police battalion that's been assigned to my task force. It's full of misfits and virtually useless as a military unit. I want you to take command of this battalion, knock it into shape. You have unlimited authority to do that. Promote, demote, transfer anyone who doesn't cut the mustard. Whatever equipment or training they need, you ask and you shall receive. You have thirty days from today to get those duds ready for training. For all I know, we may not even have that much time. This could be a come-as-you-are war, Rene; the Skinks could show up anywhere at any time and we'll be off to the races. That is why you'll see no dress uniforms of any kind in this task force, combatticals only, because we have to be ready to go at a moment's notice. Can you handle this assignment? I'm not asking if you will—you have no choice—but I'm asking if you *can*."

"Uh, sir, that sergeant major sitting in the outer office—?" On the way in Raggel had nodded casually at the senior non-com sitting stiffly in a corner, a massive man with bumps on his clean-shaven head. He'd noticed the crossed pistols on his uniform, the traditional insignia of the Military Police Corps, and wondered what the man was doing sitting outside the task force commander's office.

"That is Command Sergeant Major Krampus Steiner, formerly the senior NCO of the Seventh Independent Military Police Battalion. Dottie will give you the personnel records for every man—and the one woman—in the battalion. Go over them with Steiner. Dottie'll give you an office to work in. See if you want to keep Steiner. If you do, fine; if not, get rid of him. But I think you'll want to keep him. Oh, I'll formally introduce you to the rest of my staff after you've vetted the Seventh's personnel files and selected whom you want to work with down there.

"So I ask you again, Rene, can you work with these guys and make something out of them?"

"Yes, sir, I can."

"Good! Dottie!" he shouted, "send the sergeant major in here right now!"

Headquarters, Seventh Independent Military Police Battalion, Fort Keystone, Arsenault

Colonel Raggel and Sergeant Major Steiner sat in a small office cubicle just down the hall from General Aguinaldo's office, methodically going through a manning roster and personnel summary sheets on the men and one woman currently assigned to the Seventh Independent Military Police Battalion. With Steiner's help—mainly his candid appraisal of each man—Raggel formed two piles of summaries: on the left, those who would be sent home; on the right, the ones who'd remain assigned to the battalion. The left-hand stack was very small, by comparison, and consisted mostly of officers and noncoms and a few other ranks whose records revealed total inexperience or monumental incompetence or men about whom Steiner had nothing good to say. That stack consisted only of the *worst* incompetents and drunkards. Colonel Raggel soon came to realize that if drinking to excess were the only criterion for sending a man home, the Seventh Independent Military Police would soon cease to exist.

Conspicuously missing was the sheet of Lieutenant Colonel Delbert Cogswell, the officer who commanded the battalion on Ravenette. He had retired as soon as the battalion had been repatriated. "A decent enough officer, Colonel," Steiner had remarked, "but too fond of the booze." Steiner did not drink, at least not to excess, a rarity in the Seventh MPs, and he despised those who did, although under Colonel Cogswell he had been powerless to do anything about it. Things had changed. Raggel had gone over Steiner's sheet first. A professional police officer in civilian life, he had earned several citations for bravery and two or three complaints for excessive use of force. When Raggel asked him about those incidents he had replied, "I only beat the bastards that deserved beating. Ya gotta understand, Colonel, when ya deal with scum sometimes they gits to ya." Raggel had decided on that basis, and his sobriety, to keep Steiner as his sergeant major.

When they began their review, Steiner had leafed through the printouts and handed Raggel the one for the CO of the First Company, a Lieutenant Keesey. "Git rid of this bastard, Colonel."

Raggel glanced at the man's sheet. He could see nothing amiss with his record. "Why, Top?"

"He's a fuckin' pervert, sir. He gits his rocks off hurtin' people." Keesey's sheet went into the left-hand pile.

Steiner pawed through the stack of sheets again and withdrew two more. "This here's the sheets on First Sergeant 'Skinny' Skinnherd of Fourth Company 'n his company clerk, Corporal Queege. I'd git rid of both of 'em."

Raggel reviewed the sheets silently. "Well, Top," he said,

scratching his head, "this Skinnherd appears to be a good first sergeant, and this corporal, hell's bells, she's got the Bronze Star for valor! 'N lookit the schools she's been to and her efficiency ratings! Looks like to me she's eminently qualified in all phases of company administration, Top. Why the heck would I get rid of a good clerk?"

"Skinnherd *is* a good top soldier, sir, most of the time. But two strikes against 'im: He's a big boozer 'n he's been porkin' that corporal, at least that's what every man in the battalion believes, and what they believes is what's real to 'em. That ain't good for anybody's morale, sir, troop leaders formin' love-bird relationships with the junior enlisted." And then he told Raggel about the bet Skinnherd had made with Queege, one hundred credits if she could eat baby slimies and drink a liter of ale within a specified time.

"Ohmigawd," Raggel groaned. He felt sick even thinking about such a thing. He'd grown up on Ravenette and knew very well how disgusting the slimies were. "That's, uh, *inhuman!*" he gasped. Furthermore, and he did not have to say this, Skinnherd's conduct was unbecoming of a senior noncommissioned officer, abusing a lower-ranking soldier like that. "Uh, did she win the bet?"

"Yes, sir, 'n then puked all over Skinnherd. Colonel Cogswell was there 'n he presided over the whole affair."

"Jesus God, Top, no wonder the Marines rolled you guys up like a rug." And without another word Skinnherd's sheet flew into the left-hand pile, but Raggel held on to Queege's. "I don't know about this corporal though. Good clerks are hard to come by."

Steiner shrugged. "Well, ever'body likes the girl; she's sort of the battalion's mascot, if you know what I mean, sir. But she is a good clerk. When Skinnherd was recovering from too much booze, she ran the company. The lieutenants who was appointed to command Fourth Company, they ran through there like a dose of salts, one after th' other, 'n left the orderly room exclusively to them two. Queege held the place together more than once, when she was sober. But she's a boozer, sir, a big one, 'n she's got the reputation that she put out for Skinnherd. I'd send her home."

"Um . . . no, Top, I'm gonna keep her here. In fact I'll bring her into battalion HQ, make her our chief clerk. Anyone who can choke down, what was it, five or six slimies, has got to be a *determined* individual. Think you can sober her up?"

Steiner shrugged. "I kin try, Colonel." He did not look very enthusiastic about the prospect.

"We'll both try. If she doesn't work out, okay, I'll send her home. But I'll tell you what, Top, there's more to this girl than meets the eye. I think if we can wean her off the booze, we'll find us a mighty fine soldier under all those suds. I think her problem might be that nobody's ever given her a chance to show what she can really do when she puts her mind to it. All right"—he set Queege's sheet aside—"let's winnow out the rest of the deadwood."

They spent the rest of that day going through the records. Once they'd decided on who was going to be relieved, they went back through the keepers and decided who would fill the positions of the men being sent home. It was already dark by the time they finished.

"Top, take the files on these rejects down to battalion personnel. If they've gone back to the barracks for the day, roust 'em out. I want reassignment orders on these men in my hands by zero-six hours tomorrow morning. First thing tomorrow I want this Queege standing tall in my office at HQ. I'm going to talk to her. Next, I want the men we're sending home assembled so I can talk to them. I'm telling them precisely why they're being relieved and then you will see that they're on their way. Once that's done, call the battalion into formation. I want to talk to everyone who's left over. I apologize for keeping you up like this, Sergeant Major, but we're both going to lose a *lot* of sleep before this battalion is ready to go into its deployment training phase."

"Well, sir, I had an old first sergeant a long time ago who

used to say, 'You git yer best work done between retreat and reveille.'" Steiner chuckled and stood, extended his hand. "Thanks for keepin' me on, sir. We'll surer'n shit shape this outfit up, 'n it's about gawdam time someone did!"

Office of the Commander, Seventh Independent Military Police Battalion

"Funny, isn't it, how our paths have crossed, Corporal," Colonel Raggel said. "Did you know we heard about what you did in that bank at Phelps all the way up to General Lyons's headquarters?"

"N-No, sir," Puella answered. It was "oh-dark-thirty" in the morning, she'd had no booze since leaving her home world, Lannoy, and she was very apprehensive that her new battalion commander had called her into his headquarters office at that ungodly hour for an "interview." Everyone in the battalion knew vast changes were coming and they all expected this new broom of a colonel to sweep the unit clean. She shifted her weight in her chair and licked her lips nervously. Colonel Rene Raggel was of medium height and weight, broad at the shoulders, eyes a bright blue, close-cropped hair light yellow. Everyone knew he'd been close to General Davis Lyons during the Ravenette War. It was mystifying to Puella how such a man had gotten appointed CO of the battalion, but here he was, fresh as a daisy and full of energy even at such an ungodly hour.

"Well, we did know about you, Corporal. That"—he gestured at the ribbon on her tunic—"is partly the reason I'm not sending you home with your first sergeant."

Puella gasped, "Yer sendin' Top *home,* sir?" She knew better than to ask why although she really did not know why. She felt a sinking sensation in her stomach. Who would run the company now?

"And I'm bringing you up here to be my chief clerk, Corporal Queege."

"S-Sir?" Surely she hadn't heard him right. Colonel Raggel smiled at the mixed expression of horror and astonishment that crossed Puella's face.

"And, as of right now, you are *Sergeant* Queege."

"Sir?"

"You heard me. The TO&E calls for a sergeant major, but that's Steiner and I'm keeping him on up here, and a senior sergeant as chief clerk in my office. I am also authorized two junior clerks but they won't be available for a while yet, so you're it, three-in-one, my one and only administrative honcho. You do well for me in this job and before this is all over you'll have a senior sergeant's stripes to go along with that Bronze Star there."

"Ah, ah—" Puella could not get the words out.

"Some other things you need to know, *Sergeant*." He smiled briefly. "I'm going to work you harder than you've ever been worked before. We'll be up before dawn each day and we won't hit the sack until long after dark. We're going to get most of our important work done between retreat and reveille. That's a promise. You ever come in here with the smell of alcohol on you, you're finished, and believe me, I won't just send you home. You probably won't have time for much off-duty shenanigans, Sergeant, but you will not engage in same. You're a full noncommissioned officer now and you will conduct yourself accordingly, is that understood? If anybody in this battalion gives you a hard time about anything that you can't handle yourself, you let me or Top know about it. No hesitation. You work for me now and I won't tolerate *anyone's* giving my chief clerk a ration of shit. Is that clear?"

"Yes, sir!" But she wondered just what he meant by that remark. Who in the battalion would ever give "Queege old Squeege" a "ration of shit"?

"Very good, then. Your first day on the job begins right now. Sergeant Major Steiner's got a heap of work for you to get started on. He also has your promotion orders and a new set of chevrons; pin 'em on. So go on out there and get busy. Two final things: If you ever need to see me about anything, don't hesitate to come in here or grab my attention wherever I may be. As my chief clerk, you're the next closest person to me after my sergeant major. Don't abuse that position, but take advantage of it whenever you feel it's necessary. And last, everything you hear and see up here stays up here. Guys will constantly pump you for information. Don't utter a word to anybody, clear? Okay, big day dawning, we gotta get cracking."

Puella jumped to attention and raised her arm in a salute. "No, no, none of that!" Colonel Raggel smiled. "Henceforth and for as long as you are in Task Force Aguinaldo, you are in a combat zone, Sergeant. That's the reason the uniform of the day is always field combat, no Class As, no mess dress. We're in the field, no saluting required. Now"—he stood and extended his hand—"get to work, *Sergeant*!"

As she left the colonel's office, Puella was walking on air. She'd already forgotten what he'd said about anyone giving her a hard time.

CHAPTER EIGHT

Office of the C5 Military Assistance to Newer Worlds, the Heptagon, Earth

Robier Altman did have a contact at the Heptagon, the headquarters of the combined military of the Confederation of Human Worlds. Altman prepared a report for his contact, an army colonel by the name of Akhen Farbstein. Farbstein was an assistant director in C5, the civil affairs division of the Combined Chiefs of Staff. His specific job was to liaison between State and the military, and he was responsible for making recommendations for military assistance to recently colonized worlds. Farbstein was very conscientious about his work, and very good at it. But he was on leave when Altman's report on Haulover reached the top of the queue on his console. His desk was being covered by a colonel named Archibald Ross.

Every bureaucracy has someone in it who doesn't read memos or daydreams through meetings or doesn't pay attention to the news. If a bureaucracy is big enough, it will have someone who embodies all three of those failings. And face it, the Heptagon constitutes one of the largest bureaucracies ever devised by humanity.

Colonel Ross didn't read all the memos that came to him, daydreamed through many meetings, and didn't always follow the news. His superiors knew that, though their realization hadn't come until he'd reached his current rank. By way of making amends for their negligence, Ross's superiors had resolved not to promote him again. They didn't give him a negative, or even a marginal, officer efficiency report. They just neglected to put the simple word *outstanding* anywhere in their reports. Nobody had *asked* him to submit a letter of resignation, but that lack of an "outstanding" rating anywhere gave him to understand that he had reached his terminal rank and might as well begin his retirement proceedings—without expecting even a graveyard promotion to commemorate his forty-five years of service.

Knowing his days in the army were numbered in small numerals, Ross had been paying even less attention to memos, meetings, and the news. If that wasn't enough, the previous night he and his wife had a fight that lasted into the wee hours, and resumed that morning before he was fully awake. So he merely skimmed Altman's report, getting just enough out of it to know that attacks by persons unknown were taking place on a recently colonized world called Haulover, and that the local planetary administrator was requesting military assistance in dealing with whoever was making the raids. Up to the time of his latest—it might as well be negative—officer efficiency report, he'd paid enough attention to be aware that pirates and other freebooting miscreants had taken advantage of so many army divisions' being involved in the war on Ravenette, and had increased their nefarious activities in those areas from which army and Marine forces had been withdrawn or drawn down for deployment to the war. Similarly, there had been a number of skirmishes between neighboring worlds that bore ill feelings toward one another after they were free to do so because of the absence or low staffing of Confederation military forces.

So Colonel Ross made the obvious—to him—assumption that whatever was happening on Haulover, pirates, other freebooters, or hostile neighbors were behind it.

Disgruntled, and angry at the army—not to mention furious at his wife for what he saw as a totally unjustified attack on his abilities as an officer, which were forcing him into retirement before reaching flag grade—he decided to endorse and forward the request to the Marine Force Reconnaissance Company of the—he had to check which Fleet Marine Force was responsible for that sector of Human Space—Fourth Fleet Marines. If any glory, or any commendations, was to come out of the deployments, let them go to someone the army hated and let the army stew in its own juices for underappreciating the abilities of Colonel Archibald Ross!

Had Colonel Ross been in a better frame of mind, he might have remembered that President Cynthia Chang-Sturdevant had just made a startling revelation to the Confederation Congress, and had a press conference scheduled to make public news of strange developments on the fringes of Human Space. Such a memory might have had him hold off in forwarding Haulover's request until he learned what the president's announcement was. But he didn't remember, so he sent off his recommendation without any consideration of the fact that there might be more to the incidents on Haulover than a rebellion, bandits, pirates, or a hostile government.

Office of the Company Commander, Fourth Force Reconnaissance Company, Camp Howard, MCB Camp Basilone, Halfway

Commander Walt Obannion, company commander of Fourth Force Recon Company, ignored the sudden rush of upraised voices in the outer office in favor of continuing his review of the planned training schedule for the next month. Not that the schedule would be rigidly followed; deployment orders could come down at any time that would take away part of his unit, or even every available Force Recon Marine. Besides, he had a good idea what the hubbub was about. He was proved right when he looked up at a sharp rapping on his doorframe.

"Sir, Ensign Jak Daly reporting for duty!" said the newly commissioned, recruiting-poster-handsome officer standing in the doorway.

Obannion blanked his monitor and rose to step around his desk, hand extended.

"Welcome aboard, Ensign," he said, shaking Daly's hand. He let go and stepped back to look the ensign up and down. "Well, Jak, it doesn't look like your second trip through Arsenault did you any harm. None visible, anyway. I heard you had quite a fight with the elements. You fully recovered from that?" He waved Daly to one of the two visitor chairs and returned to his own seat behind his desk.

"I've recovered, sir," Daly said; he'd waited for Obannion to resume his seat before sitting himself. "But a lot of other people never will." His gaze briefly went to a different place and time while he flashed back on the tsunami that had hit the town of Oceanside on Arsenault while he was on liberty there. He shook himself and returned to the here and now to look Obannion in the eye. "It was like being in a war where we couldn't shoot back. All anybody could do was try to save himself and as many other people as possible. I did what I could."

Obannion nodded. Daly's words were modest but the way he said them implied that he'd acted heroically. It looked to Obannion to be the same kind of arrogance Daly had exhibited when he'd been a squad leader—just a little more than the other squad leaders. But it was an earned arrogance, proved when he'd taken command of his platoon when everybody above him was killed or wounded on a platoon raid during an ultra-secret mission.

"You did good on Arsenault, Jak," was all Obannion said. He'd been thoroughly briefed. "Now, you're probably wondering how it happened that you got reassigned to Fourth Force Recon as soon as you got commissioned."

"Yes, sir, that question did cross my mind. I'd expected, per policy, to be assigned to a FIST to get experience as a platoon commander before I returned to Force Recon."

"Then I guess you haven't heard much about our part of the war on Ravenette."

"Not much, sir. Fourth FR raised hell behind enemy lines, but I haven't heard any details."

Obannion nodded; he wasn't surprised that word of individual actions and casualties hadn't made it to Arsenault before Daly graduated from Officer Training College. He'd just returned to Camp Basilone a couple of hours ago, so he hadn't had time to talk to anybody in the company yet.

Obannion raised his voice. "Sergeant Major, would you get Captain Qindall and Warrant Officer Jaqua, please. I'd like to see the three of you."

"Captain Qindall and Gunner Jaqua, aye aye, sir."

There was the sound of the sergeant major's chair pushing away from his desk, followed by footsteps. Captain Stu Qindall, the company executive officer, appeared in the doorway of Obannion's office and entered, followed by Warrant Officer Krispin Jaqua.

"Detail reporting as ordered, sir," Sergeant Major Maurice Periz said as he entered the office behind Jaqua.

Obannion shot him a look then shook his head slightly. He should have known that everybody he wanted to see would be right outside, waiting for his summons. "At least I don't have to worry about having to repeat anything," he said drily, then stopped while Qindall and Jaqua greeted Daly and congratulated him on his commissioning.

When they were through, he said to Daly, "You heard right about the company raising hell on Ravenette. General Cazombi said we were worth three divisions." He paused while Periz muttered, "Showed that damn Billie a thing or six," then continued. "One of the company's actions was a two-platoon raid. Captain Wainwright was in command." He hesitated before continuing; the memory was painful. "He was severely wounded and won't be fit to return to duty for several months so we need an officer to fill in for him in the Three Shop. Lieutenant General Indrus didn't want to disrupt the company by having me shift one of the platoon commanders into operations, and he didn't want to take the time necessary to get an officer transferred from one of the other Force Recon companies so he contacted Corps G1 and told them he wanted you back." He shrugged. "What a lieutenant general wants, a lieutenant general usually gets, no matter what policy says. So you're here." He held up a hand to forestall whatever remark Daly was about to make.

"No, you're not going to be running my S3, and I'm not putting you in command of one of the platoons. Krispin"—he nodded toward the warrant officer—"is acting S3 until Pter returns. Even though, technically, you outrank him, you'll be the assistant S3 and training officer—that latter under his direction."

Daly looked at Jaqua. "Sir, I'm sure Gunner Jaqua will teach me everything I need to know about the Three Shop."

Periz snorted. "What Krispin doesn't know, no ensign who ever lived needs to know."

Jaqua grunted, and looked stern.

"There's no time like the present to get started," Obannion said, standing. "Maurie, see to quarters for Jak and have someone put his bags in his room. Krispin, take your new assistant in hand and put him to work. Stu, stick around for a couple of minutes."

When the others had gone, Obannion gestured for Qindall to close the door and sit down.

"I'm not totally happy with having Daly back," he said when the XO was seated.

"Jak's a good Force Recon Marine," Qindall said. "And he proved he can run a platoon on the Atlas mission."

"And too many of the Marines who were his peers, or superiors, when he was a squad leader are still with the company. That can make integrating him awkward."

"I know. That's why you put him in the Three Shop."

"I wonder if it might not be better to get him offworld for a while."

"How so, Walt?"

In way of reply, Obannion pushed a button on his console and turned the monitor to Qindall. "This came in right after I got the word that Daly was on his way."

Qindall read what was on the screen: a deployment order. When he finished he looked his commander in the eye and said, "I imagine you're thinking of sending Jak. It's kind of hard to justify sending an officer on a two-squad mission."

"The two squads will have to deal directly with the planetary administrator and the Planetary Board of Directors. Those local dignitaries might resent having mere sergeants running the show, might even think they're being slighted. Our Marines will need their cooperation if they're going to do their job. Right after I got this, I contacted Colonel Szilk. He agreed that the locals might have thin skins, and approved sending Jak out with the two squads." Colonel Lar Szilk was the operations chief for Fourth Fleet Marines.

"On the theory that an officer is more impressive to the yokels." Qindall grimaced and shook his head. "If they only knew," he murmured. Nobody became a squad leader in Force Recon without being intelligent, educated, highly experienced, and extraordinarily competent. Force Recon Marines believed that dealing with one of their sergeants in their field of expertise was the equivalent of dealing with at least a colonel, if not a brigadier in the regular forces. Most people who had dealings with Force Recon Marines thought they were arrogant—until the Force Recon Marines proved their worth by saving those with whom they dealt. Force Recon Marines believed they were the best of the best, and weren't shy about letting others know. The Corps allowed Force Recon Marines to be arrogant—because they lived up to their arrogance.

When Obannion nodded, Qindall asked, "So why the charade about assigning Jak to the Three Shop?"

"To give him something to do and keep him out of the way for the few days before he and the squads deploy. The main mission he and Krispin will be planning is the one he's going on." He grinned. "So when I spring the assignment on him, he'll already know everything we've got about it."

Qindall returned the grin.

"I want a mix of Marines on this mission, some who served with or under Daly when he was a squad leader, and Marines who joined the company since he left for Arsenault."

"That means second platoon."

"That's right."

"I'll review the platoon roster."

"Do it."

"Aye aye." Qindall rose and left his commander's office.

Office of the Company Commander, Fourth Force Reconnaissance Company, Camp Howard, MCB Camp Basilone, Halfway

Commander Walt Obannion gave WO Krispin Jaqua time to overburden Ensign Daly with his new duties before summoning his staff to the initial planning session for the mission to Haulover. Sergeant Major Maurice Periz stood easily inside the door to Obannion's office. Periz didn't say anything; he knew that Obannion would say what he had to say when his staff arrived, and anything else he, Periz, needed to know, he'd get from the commander after the staff meeting. Captain Stu Qindall, the executive officer, was in his office, on the comm alerting the platoon commanders that something was coming down, while Ensign Arvey Barnum, the S1 personnel officer, remained at his desk in the outer office waiting for the other staff officers to arrive. Lieutenant Jimy Phipps, S2 intelligence, and Captain Alphonse Gonzalez, S4 logistics and support, entered the outer office together just moments after Obannion put out the call for them. Jaqua was next to last to enter the outer office; he was trailed by his new assistant. Qindall and Barnum joined him in entering Obannion's office. Barnum, the last man in, closed the door behind him.

"Are you settled in your quarters yet, Jak?" Obannion asked Daly.

"No, sir." Daly suppressed an ironic laugh. "Gunner Jaqua's had me so busy I haven't even had time for a head call."

"Now you know why the company staff always seems harried." Obannion quickly turned to the reason he called for his staff. "We have a deployment. Two squads, one officer. Isolated homesteads on a new world called Haulover have been attacked by parties unknown, for reasons unknown. There has been total destruction of all buildings, and the people resident in the homesteads have simply vanished. The Haulover planetary administrator states he has no idea who is behind the hostile activities.

"All that and further details are in the briefing packets the sergeant major will give you on your way out.

"The first thing we need to decide is which squads are going. Suggestions?"

Qindall recognized his cue. "Sir, how about third and fourth squads from second platoon?" he asked.

Obannion seemed to consider the suggestion. Fourth squad's Sergeant D'Wayne Williams was new, and Sergeant Him Kindy had been promoted to succeed Daly when Daly had left for Arsenault. Lance Corporal Santiago Rudd had been in the platoon when Daly was still there, and Corporal Mikel Nomonon had been one of Daly's men. The others didn't know him. Obannion gave a sharp nod and said, "Inform Kady and Alf," Lieutenant Kady Rollings and Gunnery Sergeant Alf Lytle, the platoon commander and platoon sergeant of second platoon. "Arvey, see to it that the records of everyone in those two squads are up-to-date. Jimy, find whatever you can about Haulover's history and interactions with its neighbors, and past pirate activities in its sector. Then add the information to the briefing packets and give it to Krispin for his planning. Alphonse, triple-check everybody's weapons and equipment, make sure they'll stand up to a possibly prolonged deployment without support—including the, ah, 'special' equipment. Krispin, stay in close touch with Jimy and integrate whatever he finds into your op plan. You're also responsible for establishing the routines for the special equipment.

"Are there any questions?"

Daly hesitated; he didn't want to sound stupid, but he knew that asking dumb questions was part of the learning process. "Sir," he said.

"Jak."

"Sir, this is a two-squad mission. Why does it require an officer?"

Obannion studied his newest officer for a brief moment, then said, "Politics. We're dealing with a newly colonized world here. They don't have a lot of self-confidence yet, and their egos are liable to get bruised if they think the Confederation believes they don't rate anyone higher than a sergeant. An officer will be along to hold the hands of the planetary administrator and the board of directors.

"Now, if that's all, you've got work to do."

Ensign Barnum opened the door and stepped aside to let the others precede him.

CHAPTER
NINE

The day for the Seventh Independent Military Police Battalion began at five-thirty hours, even though reveille didn't sound until six hours. That was followed by calisthenics, which consisted of a warm-up followed by an eight kilometer run. No exceptions. The run was led by Colonel Raggel and Sergeant Major Steiner. Sergeant Queege was not excused. At first she, and more than half of the others in the battalion, did not make it all the way. By the end of the second week, though, she was completing the run, toward the end of the column to be sure, but she was making the entire eight kilometers. She'd also lost six kilos. By the beginning of the third week Colonel Raggel had extended the run to twelve kilometers. And so it went.

If the training schedule did not call for an all-night or early-morning exercise, chow—field rations, not prepared meals; they were only provided one day a week—followed the morning run. Then first call, when the respective company commanders took charge of their units for the day's scheduled activities, which might include classroom instruction, practical exercises—to include firearms training on the ranges—or a variety of other courses from driving instruction to handcuffing, the laws of land warfare, battalion general orders, and so on. The MPs should have known all subjects by heart, but few did because before coming to Arsenault the battalion had not been commanded properly and what training the men had received had grown very cold.

In two other areas that had become "traditional" with the Seventh Independent MPs, Colonel Raggel broke with that tradition. He personally developed the battalion training schedule, which, under its previous commander, had been a joke. Normally, maintaining a training program is the job of the battalion S3, the operations officer. But under Raggel's command the S3 merely assisted in the program's development and oversaw its execution; the battalion commander actually wrote the schedule himself. Raggel also rewrote the battalion's general orders book, which before he came to the Seventh MPs had been an even bigger joke than the virtually nonexistent training schedule. The general orders was a set of instructions governing every activity performed by military police officers in their law-and-order operations. The book contained precise instructions governing everything an MP could or could not do when dealing with civilians under the laws of Lannoy, and each man in the battalion was required to memorize them. Raggel rewrote them to make them consistent with Confederation laws, which were stricter than those enacted on Lannoy. The Seventh Independent Military Police under Colonel Raggel's command were losing their reputation as renegades.

But the bible for the Seventh Independent Military Police Battalion from Lannoy became Confederation Army Field Manual 3-19.1, "Military Police Operations." Raggel used it to define the battalion's mission in area security, internment and resettlement of local nationals, law-and-order operations, police intelligence operations, and MP support to echelons up to army level. It also told him his responsibilities in the areas of offensive and defensive combat and force protection operations. He paid particular attention to battlefield workload analysis. For instance, he determined that the battalion, if assigned main supply-route security, could protect 360 kilometers of road during a twenty-four-hour period without degrading its other assigned missions. Likewise, the battalion could control an estimated 150,000 refugees a day along a specified control route, and so on.

Since no one had ever captured a Skink, instructions governing the treatment and handling of prisoners of war were left as written as for the treatment of humans with the provision that if more became known about the Skinks, the instructions would be modified accordingly.

The battalion was organized under "Lannoy Army Heavy Division Military Police Battalion Table of Organization and Equipment No. 8-0-161-169, as changed through 24 December 2453," which authorized four companies, each company consisting of two platoons divided into two squads of three teams each, for a total of 33 men; the battalion at full TO&E strength numbered 528 men plus authorized equipment and arms to include vehicles, radios, night-vision equipment, and personal weapons as well as crew-served weapons. After Colonel Raggel finished cleaning out the so-called deadwood personnel, the battalion mustered somewhat fewer men than authorized under its TO&E, but General Aguinaldo had promised to fill those vacancies with good men drawn from other units. Until that time, Raggel worked with the men he had.

A normal training day for the Seventh MPs ended around twenty-three hours. Raggel, his battalion command sergeant major, and his battalion clerk kept the same hours as the rest of the personnel. During the day, CSM Steiner and Sergeant Queege often kept their commander company as he roamed the battalion area and the training facilities monitoring activities. They did their office work between retreat and reveille. This made for some very long nights. When Colonel Raggel was absent, which was often because he was required frequently to attend meetings involving General Aguinaldo's staff and the commanders of the task force components, Steiner and Queege virtually ran the battalion because an executive officer had not yet been nominated. But the two NCOs did such a good job that Raggel was not sure he even needed an exec.

The effect of all the training was that gradually the men and one woman of the Seventh Independent MPs began to see themselves in a different light. They were becoming physically fit, which gave them pride of appearance; they were mastering the long-lost or never acquired skills of soldiers; and they had a leader who shared their ordeals and really seemed to care about their welfare.

Office of the Commander, Seventh Independent Military Police Battalion

Puella's feet hit the floor at four hours that particular morning. She'd only gotten to bed at midnight, but the sleep she'd had was good, deep, refreshing and she was ready to begin her day, even though reveille wasn't for another two hours. Since she was an NCO and the only woman in the battalion, she had been given a small room in the battalion headquarters shack. But that meant she was responsible for getting things ready for Colonel Raggel when he came into the headquarters, always around five hours. That meant coffee.

In the time she'd been under Raggel's command, Puella had come to realize what a wonderful drink coffee was. It had been two months since she'd had a taste of alcohol; she'd lost twelve kilos, and was finishing the twelve-kilometer run each morning without even being winded. She was remembering what it was like to wake up in the morning without the stomach-churning nausea and head-throbbing ache of too much booze the night before. The pasty whiteness of her complexion had disappeared along with the extra fat in her jowls, and when she looked in the mirror in the mornings her eyes were clear. Her hips, stomach, and buttocks had shrunk and the muscles there had hardened, and, miracle of miracles, her breasts had regained their firmness. Even her hair had taken on a healthy sheen. The only thing about her appearance that still made her feel a bit conspicuous, now that she was looking at life sober, was that she had no left ear. That had been shot off during the shoot-out in the bank at

Phelps on Ravenette. But for some reason even she couldn't fathom, she kept putting off getting a simple graft to replace the missing ear.

Beer was available to the men of the Seventh MPs but only at Mainside, about eight kilometers from their training area. Colonel Raggel had a hard rule that none could be brought back to the battalion unless it came back in someone's stomach, and that man had better be able to handle it. The last time Puella had been at Mainside some men from the Fourth Company, her old company, had begged her to join them in the beer garden, to relive "old times." But she just shook her head, smiled, and walked on. She knew very well what would happen if she took that first beer. As she walked away she heard someone mutter mournfully behind her, "Ole Queege ain't our squeegee no more," and, someone else added bitterly, "She's sucking up to the CO. That's how she got them stripes."

She went to Mainside only to buy items she needed to maintain her uniform and personal appearance, which, since she had stopped boozing, seemed to be improving every day. And she had discovered she really liked sobriety.

The civilian employees and permanent party military personnel who occupied Mainside enjoyed all the luxury of climate-controlled facilities, but the Seventh Independent MPs did not, neither in their barracks nor at battalion HQ. The rainy season was ending but the nights could be uncomfortably damp. Puella slept in her underwear with her windows open, a ceiling fan circulating, and the insect-repellant fields turned on. Before she put her feet on the floor in the morning, she was careful to check that nothing had gotten through during the night. Each morning she emerged from her room in her skivvies, got the coffee ready, and straightened up the CO's and the sergeant major's offices before testing the coffee and performing her ablutions.

"Hi, Queege old Squeege," someone said from behind Puella as she bent over the coffeemaker that morning.

She whirled, startled. "Oh, Nix, what the hell you doin' up this early?" She smiled, her face turning red with embarrassment to have been caught in her undies. It was Sergeant Nix Maricle from the Fourth Company. She and Nix had "lifted" a few together and one particularly drunken night they'd gone all the way. Puella's memory of the occasion was vague now except she thought she had enjoyed it. But that was then, this was now.

"Oh, thought I'd bring up the charge of quarters report from last night," Sergeant Maricle said, never taking his eyes off Puella, whose nipples were clearly visible through her T-top. Her face turned even redder.

"Hey, you know it goes to the company commander first, Nix. He up this early? He sign it off? You know the colonel doesn't want 'em closed out until after first formation."

"Oh, yeah," Maricle answered, "musta got ahead of myself." He grinned evilly. "Hey, Queege, we don't see much of you down in the comp'ny no more."

"Yeah. Well, the old man keeps me too busy up here for socializin', Nix. You don't mind, I gotta get dressed." She turned back toward her room. *Damn that lyin' sonofabitch, what's he want at this hour?* she wondered, but she knew what he wanted.

"Hey! Puella! Not so fast." Maricle came toward her. Her shorts clung tightly to her buttocks and her breasts were clearly visible to him through her T-shirt. A thin sheen of perspiration glistened on her neck and face and her dark hair hung tantalizingly down the left side of her head, hiding the scar where her ear had been. "Hold up. Let's have us a cup of coffee, huh?"

Puella turned to face the man and said, "Don't mess with me, Nix. That coffee's for the CO and the sergeant major—"

"Oh, yeah, not for us peons, huh?"

"—'n I got a lot to do to get this place ready for the colonel, who'll be here in a few minutes, if Steiner doesn't beat him to it. And you kin explain to 'im what the heck yer doin' up here so early. So clear off, old buddy."

"Aw, Queege old Squeegee"—Maricle imitated a falsetto moan, stepping closer, a leer on his face—"come on, gimme a little smooch, jist fer old times' sake?"

"Sergeant, get the heck out of here! I don't have time for this crap."

"Okay, okay, Queege old Squeegee, you jist ain't no fun no more, you know that? Yer mighty high hat now you been screwing the battalion commander, or is Steiner doin' yer ass?"

Puella exploded. "Don't you call me 'old Squeege' anymore, you sonofabitch! You do and I'll bust your fuckin' chops for ya! 'N I hear any more bullshit about me screwin' the CO or the sergeant major, motherfucker, I'll put yer stupid ass so deep in the shit that not even fuckin' Hercules'll be able to dig it out!"

"Then fuck you, bitch!" Sergeant Maricle shouted, his face turning brick red. He spun around and stomped angrily out of the orderly room. Puella stood there, fists clenched, breathing heavily, fighting to get control of herself. It felt good that she'd told Maricle what she thought of him—and all the others who'd been insinuating things about her relationship with the battalion's leaders, because he would surely tell everyone he knew what she had said—but she also felt intensely embarrassed because the way she had just talked to Maricle was the way she used to talk to everyone—when she'd been on the booze.

Colonel Raggel arrived at a minute past five hours. "Good morning, Sergeant," he said cheerily as he came through the door. "We should have some sunlight this morning." He stopped beside Puella's workstation and looked down at her, an expression of concern on his face. "Everything all right this morning, Sergeant?"

"Fine, sir," she answered, but she was still smoldering from Maricle's visit.

It was obvious to Raggel that something was wrong. "Coffee smells good," he said, and turned away and poured himself a cup. "Refill?" he asked Puella, who nodded. "I ran into Sergeant Maricle on the way in," he commented as he poured. "Looked like he was coming back from here."

"Yes, sir, he was. He said he brought the CQ report for Fourth Company early. It hadn't been signed by the company commander and I told him it wasn't due until after reveille," she lied, looking away, "which he should've known," she added, looking back at Colonel Raggel sharply.

"I see." The battalion commander sipped his coffee slowly and sat on the edge of Puella's desk. "Well, the sergeant major will be out on the range all day today with Second Company and I have a meeting with General Aguinaldo's G1 at 0830, so can you run the battalion by yourself for a while?" He grinned at his clerk as he said this.

"Oh, yes, sir." Puella brightened at the chance to change the subject. "Are they gonna fill the vacancies we asked for, sir?"

"Mebbe, mebbe," Raggel said, taking another sip of his coffee. "You make a good cuppa, Sergeant. How's it goin' otherwise?"

Yes, Puella thought, *he is probing. Do I look* that *upset?* she asked herself. "Oh, just fine, sir, just fine."

"Um, huh," he set his cup down. "You know, Sergeant, when I first took over this battalion the sergeant major told me I should send you home. He thought you'd been too tight with your first sergeant—Skinhead, Skinnard, whatever—and the men in your company. I disagreed and now both he and I are very happy we kept you here. You are doing a superb job. You keep it up and I'll see to it that you're rewarded. I have the authority to promote every enlisted person in this battalion to whatever grade the TO&E calls for."

Puella almost started to cry at this point, not because she hadn't known that the colonel liked her work and was going to promote her eventually, but because coming so soon after the run-in she'd had with Maricle, it was wonderful to know how much the man supported her. "I-I—" she croaked.

"Hey, let me change the subject, okay?" He knew perfectly well what some of the men said about Sergeant Queege. Sergeant Major Steiner had already busted the lips on one man who had been rash enough to make a snide remark to the old soldier's face. The man had been smart enough to know he'd been out of place so he never lodged a complaint. Besides, every man in the battalion feared Steiner because before Raggel's advent as battalion commander he'd settled many disciplinary problems with his fists. But the battalion really did not have many of those problems under Raggel's leadership. "I'd like to ask you a personal question, Sergeant."

"Okay, sir, fire away."

"Well, I've been wondering why you haven't seen the medics and gotten that left ear of yours fixed." He laughed. "You got that at the bank back on Ravenette, didn't you?"

"Um, yes, sir, that's right. Well, I just haven't had the time—" She knew immediately that was not the right answer. "I mean, I just don't, well . . ." She shrugged.

"When you put your hair back it shows up mighty ugly, Sergeant. Hell, it'd be an outpatient operation, over in fifteen minutes, and nobody'd ever know it wasn't the ear you were born with. Go over to see the medics when I get back."

"Well, sir, it just is"—her face turned red—"it just is, it's the only damned reminder I got about what happened that morning. See, when I got this Bronze Star, sir, I got it for running away from a fight when we got overrun by th' Marines on th' coast! I was still hungover that morning and when these Marines started coming out of nowhere, I nearly shit myself, sir! So I beat it back to Phelps and warned the general. 'N that's how I got this medal." She flicked the ribbon on her tunic with a finger. "I *deserved* a medal for what I did in the bank, sir, but then everything collapsed, we were all taken prisoner, and"—she shrugged—"I never got nothin' so I really don't feel I deserved this valor medal. That's why I've kept this scar ever since."

"Um, I figured it was something like that. Who were you with at Phelps that day?"

"Third Company, 78th MPs. We was part of the 222nd Brigade of the Fourth Independent Infantry Division under Major General Barksdale Sneed, sir. My company commander was Captain Maxwell Smart. My platoon sergeant said I'd get a medal for shooting it up in the bank, but we was all captured and nobody had time to put in any recommendation. Story of my life, sir." She grinned at her battalion commander.

"I know General Sneed very well. Gallant soldier. Well, you probably wouldn't have gotten another Bronze Star for the bank shoot-out, that wasn't combat-related," he said speculatively, "but they'd have given you the Soldier's Medal for Heroism, that's for sure. Too bad, Sergeant." He picked up his cup and drained it. "Well, get to work," he said, sighing. "Give me all the data on the vacancies we have, personnel, equipment, armaments. I want to take that with me to my meeting." He stood. "You make a damned good cup of coffee, Sergeant! I might just give you a medal for that alone." He winked at Puella before going into his office.

CHAPTER
TEN

Main Conference Center, Office of the President,
Confederation of Human Worlds, Fargo, Earth

Accompanied by some of her closest advisers, the president watched the man on the vid screen closely. His words swept out over the tens of thousands of faithful gathered in the stadium. Even watching him on a vid, it was difficult to resist the hypnotic cadences, the almost irresistible force of his compelling gaze, his wonderfully pitched and mellifluous voice, speaking extemporaneously and without mannerisms, illustrating his points by using examples from the common lives of his audience, images that everyone could understand.

"Yield, sinners!" The command rang through the small studio where Chang-Sturdevant, Marcus Berentus, General Alistair Cazombi, and Huygens Long sat, transfixed. "I bring you the Final Awakening! Through me you shall find a New Birth, a Regeneration, and your very nature shall be changed as was mine when, Lord Be Praised! I was lifted unto the Kingdom of Heaven and Born Anew!" He varied his tone from whispers to shouts, swaying left and right to the rhythm of his words. He spoke in colloquial English, never referring to his listeners in the third person but as "you," all of whom, he told them, were sinners and damned—*unless* they came forward *now* to the "Anxious Bench," a large area reserved before the podium where the sinners knelt and wept and confessed sins while the audience prayed for them. Several hundred people were kneeling there, arms raised, hands clasped, professing and beseeching absolution. "I cannot give you absolution!" Jimmy Jasper thundered down at them. "Only God can do that! Open your hearts now, you sinners! Let the Holy Spirit enter your hearts and save your souls from damnation and the eternal fires of Hell! Come to the Anxious Bench and cleanse your souls of evil!"

Behind Jimmy, slightly raised, as if on a pedestal, where all could see her, stood Sally Consolador, Jimmy's "Consort in Christ," arms raised to Heaven, cheeks stained with tears, shouting "Amen!" and "Hallelujah!" her exclamations carefully synchronized with Jimmy's preaching—a professionally choreographed performance. She swayed left as he swayed right, as though the two were the pendulums on heavenly metronomes. As she lifted up her voice, so did the tens of thousands gathered in the stadium until the joyous roar from the host of voices thundered through the air in an almost palpable wave of sound, but never overwhelming the powerfully amplified flow of words that issued wonderfully from Jimmy's mouth.

The cameras swept over the huge gathering in Hector Stadium on the outskirts of Fargo, near its spaceport. The stadium could seat one hundred thousand people, and that day, as every day so far that week, it was filled to capacity. Hundreds of people massed at the Anxious Bench as scores of others leaped into the aisles, blinded with tears of ecstasy, and staggered down to join them.

Jimmy was silent for a long moment, arms raised heavenward, eyes tightly closed, perspiration and tears streaming down his cheeks. Perfectly tuned now to his every mannerism, the crowd too fell immediately silent. It was as though he were the conductor and they the orchestra, so totally in control of this mass of humanity was Jimmy Jasper at that moment. When at last he spoke it was in a normal tone of voice: intimate, friendly, as if he were talking in private to every single person listening to his words. "My friends! Truly beloved! Satan is here, among us now, but he is powerless. He is thwarted, he is discomfited. By God, we have got him by the tail and we're giving him the old heave-ho!" At this the thousands of listeners roared, "Praise the Lord! Victory to the Holy Spirit!" Jimmy held up his hands for silence, which fell instantly upon the multitude. "I have been blessed. I have stood before our God as Moses stood before the Burning Bush, and my Lord God has told me to come down here and free His people from the grip of the Devil! I am God's optician; I have come among you to grind you a new prescription! I am God's surgeon; I have come among you to remove the cataracts from your eyes! With me, you shall read God's eye chart with the twenty-twenty vision of the Holy Spirit!"

"Jesus!" Huygens Long whispered. "This guy's as full of shit as—"

"Shhhh," Chang-Sturdevant hissed.

"My friends!" Jimmy continued, "your president, your government, your military, they want you to believe that this Confederation is under attack from monsters, alien beings they call 'Skinks.'" He pronounced the word as if it were wormwood on his tongue. "Where your government officials see these beings as only one-eyed jacks, I have seen the other side of those beautiful faces and I recognize them as Messengers of the Divine sent by our Creator to warn us away from the path of Satan and the eternal damnation to which it leads the unwary! We must convince our president and her ministers to abandon this unholy campaign against the angels of God and accept them as harbingers of the Millennium!"

"Okay, that's *it*!" Attorney General Huygens Long exclaimed, half rising out of his chair. "He's into politics now; revoke his goddamned tax-exempt status—"

"Hugh!" Chang-Sturdevant said sharply. "Sit down!"

"Dearly beloved!" Jimmy shouted, "before the fires of Hell descend upon mankind we must turn this world into a 'burned-over district,' a world burned over by the Holy Spirit! We must burn Satan out of our hearts and the hearts of those who govern us! I leave you with the words of the Apostles. First Peter, who in his Second Epistle General warned, 'But there were false prophets also among the people, even as there shall be false teachers among you, who privily shall bring in damnable heresies, even denying the Lord that brought them and bring upon themselves swift destruction.' He is writing here of your government. And finally, John 6:37, 'All that the Father giveth me shall come to me; and him that cometh to me I will in no wise cast out.' Remember these words, my friends, and may the good Lord keep you and bless you until we meet again. Let us all join hands and pray."

"Whew!" Chang-Sturdevant sighed as she winked out the vid screen. "If that's how this guy comes across on a vid, what's he like in person? I need a drink and a smoke. Come on, gentlemen, help yourselves."

"Well, if you don't mind me saying so, ma'am, what *he* needs is a great big enema!"

"You're a hard case, AG." The president laughed, pouring herself a generous dollop of Lagavulin. "But what do you know about this extraordinary man?"

Huygens Long, attorney general in Chang-Sturdevant's government, glanced briefly at Marcus Berentus and General Cazombi before he answered. The adjective Chang-Sturdevant had used to describe a man he clearly believed was a charlatan made him nervous, not certain what words he should use. He had been observing the president closely, and the way she had reacted to Jasper's preaching made him wonder. "Well, he's from the world now calling itself Kingdom. He was formerly a prominent member of a Pentecostal sect known as the Rock of Ages True Light Primitive Christian Church based in a remote village known as Tabernacle. Sometime after the Skink invasion of Kingdom was defeated, he emerged in his present role as the founder of the Burning Flame Mission to Humanity. His 'Consort in Christ'"—here the attorney general could not suppress an outright sneer—"Sally Consolador, is also from Kingdom, from a small town known as the Twelfth Station of Jerusalem. Before she joined up with Jasper she was a thoroughly respectable but harmless religious fanatic, just like Jasper himself."

He shrugged. "The one thing they have in common is they were both abducted by Skinks."

"Many of the Kingdomites were," General Cazombi, Chairman of the Combined Chiefs, Confederation Armed Forces, interjected, "including one of our Marines even."

"Oh, yes, one of Ted Sturgeon's NCOs, if memory serves," Marcus Berentus, the minister of war volunteered. "But he wasn't brainwashed like this Jasper fellow, was he?"

Chang-Sturdevant glanced up sharply at Berentus's choice of words.

"No," General Cazombi said, chuckling, "you can't brainwash a Marine!"

"Hugh"—Chang-Sturdevant turned back to her AG—"what's this Sally woman to Mr. Jasper?"

"Well, I don't know. Jasper's married, no children. His wife, Zamada, is back on Kingdom, presumably dusting off his Bible collection or whatever. I can find out how intimate Consolador and Jasper are, if you want me to."

"No!" Chang-Sturdevant replied quickly, a bit *too* quickly, Huygens Long thought. "No. It's one thing to research background on a religious figure but another to spy on him."

"I wouldn't call it 'spying,' ma'am," Long replied. "After all, what this man is telling people to do amounts to treason. And I'm sure if I looked hard enough I'd find the dirt on this guy—"

"No, Hugh, that's going too far. The public wouldn't stand for such government probing. We guarantee freedom of speech and freedom of religion in this Confederation and I will not authorize any interference with those rights. Do you have any idea where he gets the money to hold these rallies, Hugh?"

Long shrugged. "Personal donations, ma'am. At today's rally—he calls them Holiness Camps—he'll take in maybe as many as a million credits. He'll take in who knows how much after this broadcast is seen worldwide and the contributions flow in. We won't know how much he makes off these camps until he files his personal income tax return, *if* he files one. But in the short time he's been working on Earth he's raised a *lot,* I can tell you that." As he spoke, Long speculated how he could put a spy into Jasper's entourage, someone close enough to the preacher that he could find out just how much money he was taking in and from whom.

"This man has managed to tap into ordinary people's lives, ma'am," Berentus volunteered. "He's giving them something they want. I don't know how long the effect lasts when they get home or after the vid screen goes dead, but you saw how powerful his preaching is! And one more thing, he's not alone. Others like him are preaching the same doctrine on several of our member worlds. They may not be quite as effective as he is but they are reading off the same sheet of music. Now, how could that be? Well, I'll tell you. They all have one thing in common." Berentus paused. "They were all abducted by the Skinks. I have to agree with Hugh on this. Look at what he's preaching. These people have been indoctrinated!"

"Ma'am, this has not yet spread to our military forces, but if it does"—General Cazombi shrugged—"our whole campaign against the Skinks could collapse. I can't stop it if the troops pick this up. I don't have the authority to dictate their religious convictions or to prevent them from practicing them. If this man's preaching gets in the way of our mission, though, I'll have to take action and it'll get very messy. It'll become a constitutional matter and wind up in the courts, and you all know what that'll do to our readiness, to General Aguinaldo's options as the anti-Skink task force commander. And we know what these things are. They're not angels, they're hostile aliens bent on the destruction of humanity. We've *fought* them, we *know* what they are." Cazombi did not raise his voice but the way he spoke made it a major emotional outburst. Huygens Long nodded his head energetically at every word.

"Hmm," Chang-Sturdevant replied. They were all silent for a moment, sipping their Scotch. "Well, gentlemen," the president said at last, "I've done my homework too." She nodded at her attorney general. "This Jasper is right out of the nineteenth century. Have any of you ever heard of the Reverend Charles

Grandison Finney and the Great Revival? He was a charismatic Pentecostal preacher of the 1820s and 1830s in the old United States. Perhaps he was the greatest of the Pentecostals. The language Jasper uses, even the Bible quotations, are right out of Finney's sermons. He even uses what he calls Cottage Prayer Meetings, where he meets with small groups in private and preaches to them, probably well-heeled individuals who give generously to his crusade. It's uncanny if you know your history."

"I've never heard of this Reverend Finney," Marcus Berentus said quietly, "but I don't need to hit the history books to remind you all that whatever this Finney was back in those days, he was no traitor."

"It's a bit early, isn't it, Marcus, to be throwing that term about?" Chang-Sturdevant replied sharply.

Huygens Long's mouth dropped open. He cast a desperate glance at the other two men as if asking them to say something, but he knew Chang-Sturdevant well enough to know when not to argue with her. So did Berentus and Cazombi.

"Gentlemen, I'll tell you what I'm going to do." Chang-Sturdevant leaned forward and clasped her hands together. "I'm going to meet this Jimmy Jasper," she said, nodding her head with conviction, "have a personal interview with the man; not"—she grimaced slightly—"a 'Cottage Prayer Meeting,' but a tête-à-tête, to size him up myself."

"What?" Huygens Long almost shouted, nearly dislocating his jaw.

"You heard me, Hugh. I'm going to invite him up here for lunch. I'll have my minister of public affairs arrange it. Now, you gentlemen maintain low profiles but keep me informed. All right"—she glanced at her watch—"that's it for now. Please excuse me." Chang-Sturdevant got up abruptly and left the room, followed closely by her minister of war, who exchanged significant glances with the other two as he went out the door.

Cazombi and Long sat rooted to their chairs, staring helplessly at the closed door. "Well," Long said at last, "it could well mean my ass as far as this government is concerned, but I *am* going to look into this guy and I *am* going to dig up the dirt on the bastard."

"I wouldn't do that," Cazombi cautioned, "but if you've made up your mind, Hugh, well, keep me informed, would you?" He leaned over and tapped Long on his knee. "Keep her informed too, whatever the cost to your career. She's not some ditzy broad, we both know that, and she'll listen to facts and reason. We have *got* to do something about this character and the others, but we've got to go about it the right way. Do you agree?"

"Very well, Alistair. I won't do anything until I've got all the facts together, and then I'll present them to the president. Meanwhile, will you keep me informed on how this is impacting on our military forces?"

"I will."

"And when the time comes to, er, put my neck in the noose, will you at least hold my hand?"

"You bet I will," Cazombi replied, and they shook on it.

Marcus Berentus had to hurry to catch up to Chang-Sturdevant as she walked rapidly down the corridor toward her office.

"Suelee," he whispered, placing a hand gently on her shoulder. She shrugged it off angrily. "Suelee, don't. Listen to me, will you?" This time she did not shake his hand off, but she whirled and faced him, her face flushed with anger. "For the love of God," Berentus said, "*do not* meet with this man! I'm begging you. Don't do it!"

"Marcus," she answered in burning words, "if you persist in opposing me this way, then everything between us is over, do you understand me?"

Berentus stepped back as if shocked by an electric current. "What?"

"You heard me. Now get *out* of my way."

"Suelee—"

"I mean it, Marcus! Just why are you trying to tell me what's good for me with this . . . this holy man?"

Berentus could not believe the conversation was really taking place. He swallowed hard and then his own face turned red with anger and he shouted so loudly that heads in adjoining offices turned toward the hallway.

"Because, love, this son of a bitch thinks he's Jesus H. Fucking Christ!"

CHAPTER
ELEVEN

She floated in a vast, warm bath. Someone was talking to her but she could not make out the words. The voice sounded like it was inside her head, she was sure of that. Maybe it wasn't a voice, after all; maybe it was her own mind reciting a mantra, a low, monotonous chant over and over again. What difference did it make; it was soporific, comforting. She was vaguely aware of *things* attached all over her body—wires, cables, things like that—but no pain. No, far from it, she felt wonderful in the torpid liquid that surrounded her. She wasn't breathing, she was sure of that. How, she wondered vaguely, could that be? Why worry? It was good not to breathe. But she did have a body, she could feel her fingers and toes, and, out of the corner of her eye, she sensed more than saw vague shapes moving somewhere outside the murky liquid bath, just shadows on her retinas, actually, not definable shapes, not shapes she recognized.

Suddenly Sally Consolador was sitting beneath the spreading pawpaw tree in Senator Maxim's garden, where she'd come to read her Bible. Dreams of sitting in that bath had been occurring more frequently since she had come to Earth but this was the first time one had come during the day, while she was still awake and fully conscious. She shook her head and closed her Bible. She could prepare for tomorrow's Holiness Camp later. She arose and began threading her way down the garden trail in the direction of the villa. An idea was beginning to form in her mind about what the visions really meant.

Sally gently fingered the engraved invitation. "Looks like I ain't invited," she pouted. "Fancy invite," she mused. The invitation was engraved on heavy, cream-colored paper and read: "The President of the Confederation of Human Worlds cordially invites the Reverend Jimmy Jasper to a private reception . . ."

"Mighty fine, mighty fine," Sally muttered, turning the card over.

Jimmy stood before the mirror, carefully examining his appearance. "It is an affair of state," he said solemnly, "and it means that the Word has at last reached the highest levels of Satan's regime. My preaching has finally had the desired effect, and you, Sally, have played your part." He turned and smiled at his consort. "How do I look?"

"Like John the Baptist come out of the desert into Herod's palace. Beware Phasaelis's treachery."

Jimmy was wearing a plain, high-collar tunic, intentionally frayed at the elbows and sleeves as if it had long ago seen its better days. His hair, streaked with gray like his scraggly beard, hung down the back of his neck and over the collar of his tunic.

"I am Moses, come to warn Pharaoh of dire consequences if he does not comply with God's commandments," he reminded Sally sternly.

Jimmy did not like the comparison to John the Baptist, betrayed by Herod's wife, Phasaelis, and beheaded. He was beginning to wonder if Satan at last had reached his consort and driven out the Holy Spirit. Had she turned into a weak vessel, he wondered. Her jealousy at not being invited to visit the president was disturbing, not in keeping with his holy mission. It smacked of cynicism, defeatism, in fact. Instead, she should be delighted that his evangelism had so impressed the president of the Confederation that she had requested a private meeting. No, Sally's potential backsliding could mean serious trouble for his crusade. Often before, he reflected, those who had received the Word had not kept it. Satan was a wily devil who delighted in the corruption of saints and sinners alike. He would have to keep an eye on Sally.

"Sally, are you having those dreams again?" he asked suddenly.

"Yup, just had one out back, in the garden."

"Satan's wiles are powerful, Sally. He often comes to us in our dreams—"

"Wasn't dreamin' this time, Jimmy."

"—in our dreams, Sally, when we are most susceptible to his temptations."

"Well," she said, "I 'spect I will just have to amuse myself in the garden until you get back from"—she tossed the invitation on the bed—"this invite."

Jimmy stepped forward quickly and retrieved the invitation. "You can amuse yourself by getting ready for the Holiness Camp scheduled to begin tomorrow," he replied sharply.

"But Senator Maxim's gardens are so wonderful." Sally smiled archly, glancing sideways at Jimmy. Senator Luke Maxim of the Kingdom delegation to the Congress of Human Worlds, an early convert to Jimmy's preaching, had given the pair the full run of his country estate, including its formal gardens, which were then in full bloom, and Jimmy had made the villa his headquarters for the duration of his stay on Earth.

Is she teasing me? Jimmy wondered. A prophet, he reflected, can tolerate anything—torture, persecution (the more of that the better!), disputatious disbelief—but a prophet cannot tolerate *laughter*. "Well, Sally, gardens can be a dangerous place. Ask Adam."

Sally stretched luxuriously and opened her robe wide. "Don't I look like Eve?" she said with a wicked grin.

Jimmy punched the egress button on the door console and as it hissed open turned back toward Sally. "I'll be back as soon as I've finished. Meanwhile, get ready for the—"

"The apple trees hang heavy with their fruit," Sally said, laughing and letting the robe fall to the floor.

"Stay out of the goddamned garden!" he shouted as he stomped angrily out of the room.

Office of the President, Confederation of Human Worlds, Fargo, Earth

"Madam President." Jimmy Jasper took Chang-Sturdevant's hand and brushed his lips softly over it. His hand in hers was hard, firm, warm. "I am so very pleased you invited me here today," he murmured.

"Very nice of you to come, Reverend Jasper."

"Call me Jimmy, Madam President, please do. I never went to divinity school, none of that scholarly stuff for me; just like Jesus Himself and His Disciples, I received my license to preach directly from God," he said, smiling. "All that education," he said, shaking his head, "it only confuses. A great poet once wrote:

'Myself when young did eagerly frequent
Doctor and Saint, and heard great argument
About it and about: but evermore
Came out by the same door where in I went.' "

Chang-Sturdevant recognized the quatrain immediately and was surprised that Jasper knew it too. There was a sharp wit behind the man's folksy puritanical facade. "Well, Jimmy, please." Chang-Sturdevant gestured toward some easy chairs and they seated themselves. It was not lost on Jimmy that she did not offer to let him call her Cynthia.

She noticed Jimmy's trousers were wearing thin at the knees. "Refreshments?"

"Springwater, please, Madam President, if you have it. I take neither spiritous liquors"—he nodded disdainfully at the wet bar in a corner—"nor tobacco products. Our bodies, Madam

President, are temples of the Lord who has created the souls that inhabit them and we shall not corrupt them by consuming harmful substances. 'Garbage in, garbage out,' as they say." He smiled briefly.

"Well, I happen to like my 'garbage,' Mr. Jasper. Will I go to hell because of that?"

"Yes, but not because of anything you drink or smoke."

"I'm going to hell?"

"Yes, Madam President, you are. You shall sink straight down, like a stone in a lake of brimstone. You shall burn and suffer there forever, writhing and screaming horribly. You shall roast like an overstuffed sausage on a barbie, your flesh splitting and oozing for all eternity. White-hot iron rods will be inserted into your anus and sear their way into your innards with a horrible intensity and burning. You shall turn slowly on a spit as devils puncture your flesh with red-hot pitchforks and horrid monsters constantly gnaw and rip at your palpitating flesh, consuming your tortured body, which will never be consumed, never diminish through the feasting but always be the same and always feed their insatiable appetites. You shall scream terribly and beg forgiveness but it shall never be granted, never." He sipped primly at his water and smiled. "But that does not have to be, Madam President."

Chang-Sturdevant regarded her guest with revulsion and fascination. His rugged face was strikingly handsome; his huge hands, scarred and veined from heavy manual labor, held the large glass of water as if it were a thimble. His voice, although he was not now speaking with the same volume and power he used when preaching, was deep, laden with conviction, and its timbre penetrated straight through her body. But it was Jimmy Jasper's eyes that held her attention. They were the brightest blue she had ever seen and they virtually shimmered with conviction. She could hardly avoid staring into them. "You . . . you are as impressive in the flesh as on a vid screen, Mr. Jasper. How—"

Jasper held up his hand. "It is not me that impresses people, Madam President; it is the Holy Sprit that resides within me."

"How do you know all this about hell and its tortures?" She winced visibly at the thought of white-hot spits and all that. How could the man in one breath quote Omar Khayyam and in the next talk so lovingly of the tortures of hell?

Jasper smiled gently. "I have been told, Madam President, by God Almighty Himself. But you can find out by reading the Scriptures. Read Psalms, Isaiah, but particularly, Madam President, beware of what Our Lord saith in Mark 9:47, 'And if thine eye offend thee, pluck it out: it is better for thee to enter the kingdom of God with one eye, than having two eyes to be cast into hellfire.'" He leaned forward and placed his hand gently on Chang-Sturdevant's knee. "You must pluck out an eye, Madam President, and it is my mission to help you do that."

Jasper smiled. He fixed Chang-Sturdevant's eyes with his own. Staring into those brilliant blue orbs, she felt she could not break away from this man. His hand resting on her knee seemed to be throbbing with power. With great effort, she closed her eyes and then looked away. The spell broken, he removed his hand, sat back in his chair, and sipped at his water. Chang-Sturdevant almost sighed with relief. "That is a mighty big sacrifice, Mr. Jasper, to pluck out your own eye," she said, smiling weakly.

"Oh, call me Jimmy, please." He chuckled. "Our Lord did not mean that literally, Madam President. He meant only that to enter the kingdom of God one has to make huge sacrifices."

"What's my sacrifice, then, Mr. Jasper?"

Jimmy smiled before he answered. Then: "Get rid of those around who refuse to shake off the clutches of Satan. I mean your minister of war in particular, who is known to be close to you." He nodded his head. Chang-Sturdevant thought, *How in hell does he know that?* Jasper saw the expression that crossed her face at that statement and smiled knowingly. "Call off this war against the Angels of the Lord, Madam President!" he continued. "Let them come among you and purge your souls of the Devil and expel from this land Satan and his demons! Let the Millennium begin! Welcome the messengers of Christ and accept His blessings and salvation!"

Afraid to look directly into those eyes, Chang-Sturdevant stared at the wet bar for a long moment before answering. Yes, she badly needed a drink! "You are talking about the Skinks, Mr. Jasper."

"As you call them, Madam President; as you call them, as Satan has made you call them. But I have been to the kingdom of God and I know the true nature of these entities, and they are here to bring you peace and salvation."

"There are people in my government, Mr. Jasper, who are saying words to that effect. Senator Maxim, for one, who I understand is your host. But we have seen those creatures, Mr. Jasper. They have murdered hundreds of thousands of innocent people! My soldiers and Marines have fought them and beaten them back. All these victims, these fighters, they cannot all have been deceived. How could God have chosen this way to save us? We aren't Sodom! We aren't Gomorrah! I am not Lot's wife, Mr. Jasper, you can be damned sure of that," she said, looking directly into Jimmy Jasper's eyes. She blinked. Nothing happened.

"Have you yourself ever seen one of these entities, Madam President?" Jasper asked quietly.

"Well, no."

"I have. I have seen them closer up than any of your soldiers. I know what they are, Madam President; you don't. None of your people do either. I am offering you and your people salvation. I know *I* won't, but all of you may perish despite my best efforts to save you. If that happens it's the will of God." He shrugged. "I can only try, using my puny intellect and insubstantial powers to make you see the Truth. But only you, Madam President, can make that glorious covenant with God; only you can accept the Holy Spirit. It was in fact the Holy Spirit that inspired you to ask me here today, I know it. I know it is not too late! There is hope! But"—he set his glass on the table—"I must leave now." He got to his feet. "Thank you for inviting me here, Madam President, and may God bless you and keep you and show you the Way." He bowed and walked to the door.

Chang-Sturdevant stood, her hand halfway extended, an expression of bewilderment on her face as Jimmy left the room. The officer in charge of Jasper's escort stuck his head in the door and looked questioningly at the president. She nodded weakly; the interview was over. "Whew!" she muttered and walked on shaky legs to the bar. She poured herself a generous shot of Scotch, which she drank neat in one swift gulp. She poured another immediately but sipped at it slowly as she made her way back to her chair. She looked at her hand. It was still shaking.

Jasper's visit had brought back to Chang-Sturdevant with sharp poignancy memories of her own childhood. The Changs had converted to Christianity generations before Cynthia had been born, converted to a fundamentalist Protestant sect in fact. At every meal in the Chang household, grace was pronounced by Cynthia's father, and he led the family in Bible readings before bedtime every night; attendance at Bible school and church every Sunday was required. The Bible was the King James Version. In their religious beliefs, the Changs were throwbacks to an earlier time. Cynthia's mother swore that the Catholic Church was engaged in a clandestine plot to destroy Protestantism and take over the world. When the local Catholic church, St. Boniface, rang its bells for vespers, Cynthia asked her mother, "Momma, it's only seven o'clock, so why are the bells striking *thirteen* times?" "Hush, daughter," her mother always answered in a whisper, a faint twinkle in her eye, "their clocks are set on Vatican time!"

But the denomination the Changs belonged to did not practice infant baptism. According to their beliefs, a person had to be old enough to understand what baptism meant before a minister could perform the rite. By the time Cynthia was old enough to understand, she knew that she did not believe in it, and her parents never pressed her about taking the plunge (they believed in full immersion). Her husband, Jakob Sturdevant, was a rationalist, and before their marriage was ended by his early death, Cynthia Chang-Sturdevant had come to realize that she too was an avowed rationalist.

But hellfire, the wiles of Satan, the Holy Ghost, salvation, and Jimmy Jasper had brought all that back to her, so President Cynthia Chang-Sturdevant sat for a long time, thinking about what Jimmy Jasper had told her.

The Home of Attorney General Huygens Long, Fargo

"What we have here is another goddamned Rasputin!" Huygens Long muttered over his cooling coffee.

"Oh, come on, Hugh! She's no doddering czarina, consumed by religious fanaticism! You're talking about our president! I know her too well to put any stock in this Rasputin crap. You both know her too; you've seen her in a crisis. She'd never give in to this foolishness, not in a million years." Marcus Berentus poured more coffee into Long's cup.

"I don't know," Alistair Cazombi said, leaning forward over the coffee table. "Stranger things have happened. You saw that guy on the trid. He almost had me convinced! And Jasper already has a following in the Congress. Senator Maxim is introducing a bill to reduce the Task Force Aguinaldo funding in the next defense appropriation. It won't pass, but the germ is there."

"He's right, Marcus. Look," Long whispered conspiratorially, leaning across the table, "I've been doing some snooping. I think his Sally is about to rally." He grinned. "She's the weak link! She was taken by the Skinks too. If we can get *her* to tell us what really happened . . ." He shrugged.

"I say we let the president do her job," Berentus protested.

"Are you going to help her, Marcus? We hear you're on the outs with her right now," Long ventured. Marcus Berentus did not respond. He did not have to: Word gets around quickly in any government, especially when its cabinet officers are heard yelling at their president in the hallway just outside her office.

"I agree with Marcus," Cazombi said quickly, glancing reassuringly at the minister of war. "But let's discuss a 'just suppose' scenario. Suppose Hugh's right and our president has gone the way of Senator Maxim and those others. Just suppose!" Cazombi held up a hand to stave off the protest he could see forming on Berentus's lips. "Just suppose. What would we do then, we three"—he looked hard at the other two men—"knowing what we do? Knowing that the fate of humanity lies in the hands of this one person? Gentlemen, we do not have much time. What would we do?"

"What they did to Rasputin," Huygens Long said softly.

CHAPTER
TWELVE

Fourth Force Recon Barracks, Camp Howard,
MCB Camp Basilone, Halfway

The Confederation Navy had only one frigate and a single supply ship on station in the sector that contained the newly colonized world of Haulover, and no plans to add starships to the mission. Neither of the starships on station was due for relief for several months, nor was the navy willing to redirect another starship from Halfway to Haulover. Consequently, Fourth Force Recon Company was authorized to send its detachment via commercial shipping. There was no direct commercial transport between Halfway and Haulover, so the Marines caught the next scheduled flight of the SS *Accotink* to Cecil Roads, a major transshipment point for the commercial craft that serviced a huge part of Human Space. There the Marines would change to another carrier to get them closer to their destination.

Ensign Jak Daly flinched when he learned which starship he was taking his Marines on; he'd shipped out of Halfway on the *Accotink* on the first leg of his voyage to Officer Training College on Arsenault the year before. On that voyage, he'd thought the starship would have been better named the SS *Neanderthal*.

The day before heading to orbit to board the *Accotink,* Daly inspected the two squads assigned to the mission. As he fully expected, all eight of the Marines had everything the mission order called for, and everything was in proper shape.

"At ease, gather close," Daly said when he returned to his place in front of the squads at the end of the inspection. "I want to give you a mild heads-up about the starship we'll be on during the first leg of our march to Haulover."

The Marines exchanged glances as they broke ranks and grouped closely in front of Daly; a "heads-up" about their transport vessel wasn't a normal part of the premission briefing.

"I sailed on the *Accotink* on the first leg of my voyage to Arsenault last year. If she was a navy starship, she would have been sold for scrap years ago. I haven't been able to find out if her crew is the same as it was then, but her captain is. The navy probably would have retired Captain Smithers when his starship was scrapped—if not earlier. As near as I can tell, all he does to run his starship is the minimum he must do to assure that she reaches her next port of call within a more or less reasonable period of time after her scheduled arrival. There's almost no discipline; and the crew does just enough to get the *Accotink* to the next port without its falling apart along the way and killing them. They seem to spend most of their time playing cribbage for money, and they fight among themselves a lot. They're the most surly bunch of sailors I've ever encountered. Internal maintenance is . . . well, I heard about the bunkers the Marines took over from the army in the Bataan Peninsula on Ravenette. The common spaces and passenger accommodations are close to what I heard about the Bataan bunkers. The cook . . . I don't think she *deliberately* tries to poison the crew or passengers, but we might have to take over the galley ourselves to make sure she doesn't *accidentally* poison us.

"Fortunately, we should reach Cecil Roads in no more than two weeks." In response to a quizzical look from Sergeant Kindy, Daly added, "I know, I know, the itinerary calls for ten days. But I wouldn't want to sail on the *Accotink* if I had to make a tight connection. That leg could be nine days, it could be double that. I'm splitting the difference.

"On Cecil Roads we'll be able to get another starship to our second transit point quickly; it's a major transshipment point.

We might even be able to get a ride on a navy starship for our second leg.

"Any other questions?" When there weren't, he said, "All right, then, I'll see you at four-thirty hours. Transportation for us to Glenn Field at that time has already been arranged."

The SS <u>Accotink,</u> En Route to Cecil Roads

Captain Smithers was still the master of the *Accotink,* and greeted the boarding Marines with such total disinterest they may as well have been sealed cargo that he didn't care whether or not got delivered to its destination. The crew, at first sight, was just as surly and unwelcoming as the previous time Daly was on the *Accotink.* He couldn't tell much about the cook yet. When he'd been a squad leader with Fourth Force Recon, Daly had made friends with people who might prove useful in the future. This was one of those future times, and one of the friends he'd made was a mess sergeant. Daly prevailed on their friendship to get sufficient prepared mess hall meals to feed himself and his Marines during their first full day aboard the *Accotink.*

The next morning, en route to the jump point, Daly discovered that, yes, the *Accotink*'s chow was just as bad as before—if not worse. So he *did* have his Marines take over the galley. They spent the morning cleaning it, then drew straws to see who would get stuck fixing the midday mess. To the Marines, the result wasn't very satisfactory, but it was sufficiently better than what they'd forced down for morning mess that the crew stopped grumbling and Captain Smithers stopped threatening to clap them in irons or heave them out of the air lock into Beam Space. He even went so far as to say he'd expunge the mutiny charges from the ship's records if their cooking improved enough by the time the *Accotink* reached Cecil Roads.

The only person aboard who *wasn't* pleased with the improved meal quality was the cook. She was so loudly and volubly *dis*pleased that Daly briefly considered mounting an overnight security watch on the passenger deck. But the cook hovered in the galley and gradually began helping out, and by the time the *Accotink* jumped into Beam Space she had retaken her assigned duties as ship's cook—with much better results than before.

Still, Daly and his Marines were quite happy to disembark at Cecil Roads, where they shipped out again a few hours later on the CNSS *Trumbull County,* bound for Aardheim, where they found another commercial freighter, the SS *Briny Stars,* about to depart for Haulover. During the entire trip, Daly had his men studying everything they had on Haulover and the incidents they were to investigate. There wasn't much; the colony was still in its first generation, and there was little information on the destroyed homesteads and missing people other than who and what had been there before the incidents. They got to the point where each of them, including Daly, could recite the history of Haulover and the biographies of its founding fathers and current leaders, as well as the bios of each of the missing people. This was more than a squad usually memorized on its way to a mission, but Daly had his reasons for the intensity of the study. Sergeant Kindy, Corporal Nomonon, and Corporal Jaschke had been in his squad before he'd left for Officer Training College. He had to get them, and himself, to the point where they would never look to him as the squad leader. Fourth squad's Sergeant Williams wasn't a problem that way, as he joined the company after Daly had left for Arsenault, but Corporal Belinski and Lance Corporals Rudd and Skripska all had known Daly as a squad leader.

The SS Briny Stars, out of Aardheim, En Route to Haulover

Captain Jonas Belzaontzi, master of the SS *Briny Stars,* read the orders Ensign Jak Daly tight-beamed to his comp and grimaced. He didn't like having to spend the extra time and effort unloading into orbit the cumbersome package the Marines were lugging with them. Then he looked again at the payment voucher attached to the request—order, really—and nodded curtly. The payment voucher was for enough to make launching a cumbersome satellite worth his while.

"All right, Marine, you've got it," Belzaontzi said. "I'll put that sucker in so secure an orbit it won't begin to decay for a couple of standard centuries. Don't sweat anything. Before I retired from the Confederation Navy and got my master's ticket, I was the launch officer on the CNSS *Grandar Bay,* in which capacity I stung a lot of pearls. You may have heard of the *Grandar Bay;* she was a *Mandalay* Class Amphibious Landing Ship, Force, carried a lot of Marines during her life." His eyes drifted to the side, and he added softly, "She was lost in Beam Space a few years ago."

The SS Briny Stars, in Orbit Around Haulover

Captain Belzaontzi personally directed the placing in orbit of the cumbersome satellite the Marines had brought aboard his ship. He allowed Daly to observe the placement and gave him full access to the launch and orbital data. Orbital mechanics weren't Daly's specialty, but the Marine knew enough to see that the orbit was good.

"So what is that sucker?" Belzaontzi asked before the Marines boarded the shuttle to make planetfall.

"It's a multiple-drone launcher, so we can communicate with higher headquarters if we have need for quick comm," Daly said.

"I thought so," Belzaontzi said with a curt nod. "A Mark IX Echo?"

"Yes, sir," Daly answered, not surprised that a retired navy launch officer would recognize the satellite.

"We didn't have them when I was in but I've read about them in the satellite supplement to *Jane's War Starships of Human Space.*" Belzaontzi smiled at Daly's expression. "There are some nasty people roaming the spaceways. The wise starship captain keeps current on what's out there."

Beach Spaceport, Haulover

Beach Spaceport wasn't situated at the shore of an ocean or large lake, it was on a broad plateau three hundred kilometers from the nearest sizable body of water. It wasn't named for its proximity to water but rather after Dr. Martin Beach. Dr. Beach had been a xenobiologist with the initial exploratory team sent by the Bureau of Human Habitability Exploration and Investigation—BHHEI, pronounced "Behind"—to the exploratory world that was then called Society 689. He had brought the attention of the expedition to the existence of a carnivorous and dangerous life-form on Society 689 in rather dramatic form.

In full view of several other members of the expedition, Dr. Beach, on foot, slowly approached an animal that bore a vague resemblance to an Earth moose. The animal stood calmly watching Beach's approach, working its jaw in what the observers swore exactly resembled the cud chewing of Earth ruminants. When Dr. Beach approached to about three meters from the beast, it suddenly sprang at him with its mouth spread wide and chomped down on his shoulder as it bore him to the ground.

There was little agreement among the witnesses as to the exact sequence of events after that; they couldn't even agree on whether Dr. Beach's cries cut off almost immediately or if his blood-curdling screams continued for a relatively lengthy period of time. They did, however, all agree that the animal didn't appear to bunch its muscles before it sprang, that they were surprised at how much wider its mouth opened than they'd thought possible, and that said mouth was filled with huge, very long fangs.

Having taken Dr. Beach to the ground, the beast commenced devouring him, a repast at which it continued until it was driven off by the terrified, but brave, witnesses to the attack. By then, of course, it was too late for Dr. Beach. His entire left shoulder and arm, a substantial part of his upper left thorax, and most of his gut were gone before the other scientists, screaming and throwing things, drove the animal off.

A few days later, a hunting party found the animal, by then unofficially dubbed a "beachivore," a couple of kilometers from the scene of the killing. It was dead. A necropsy determined that it had been poisoned by human tissue, or possibly by something in the scraps of clothing it had swallowed along with large chunks of Dr. Beach. It was further speculated that there was some form of communication among the "beachivores," as ever since that one attack, the beasts had kept their distance from humans.

Ensign Jak Daly was the first person who departed the orbit-to-ground shuttle, followed in quick order by the eight Marines of the two squads. He immediately recognized Planetary Administrator Spilk Mullilee standing at the head of a line of greeting dignitaries. Even if he hadn't known what the planetary administrator looked like, his appearance would have given him away—he was a Confederation bureaucrat; no matter what he was wearing, he looked gray despite the brilliance of his chartreuse suit and magenta shirt. And no matter how resplendent the Marines looked in their dress reds, Mullilee seemed very disappointed when Daly saluted and introduced himself.

"Wh-Where are the rest of the soldiers?" Mullilee said when Daly halted in front of him and saluted.

"Soldiers?" Daly said. "There are no soldiers here, sir. We are Marines, and we can deal with whatever your situation is." Behind him, Sergeant Kindy got the squads into a two-rank formation.

"B-But . . . there are only"—Mullilee paused to count—"only nine of you. Unless"—he gave Daly a hopeful look—"your commanding officer is still on the shuttle. Or in orbit?"

"Sir, I am the commanding officer."

"Damned by all the gods!" exclaimed the next man in line. He was stout and dressed in the style of a moderately prosperous businessman on one of the more settled worlds. "*This* is all the Confederation thinks of us, that all we rate is a tiny gaggle of fancy-dress soldiers?"

"Mr. Miner, sir," Daly said, dipping his head politely to the stout man, "I say again, we are not soldiers, we are Confederation Marines—Force Recon Marines." He had to stifle a grin at Smelt Miner's occupational name—the man controlled most of the ore mining and smelting on Haulover. Daly thought Miner could have been more clever in picking his name, as had the other directors, such as Manuel Factor, the manufacturing kingpin, or Rayl Rhodes, whose long-haul rail system already connected all of Haulover's cities and was expanding to the secondary settlements. Even Agro Herder, whose industrial-scale farming and ranching operations were aimed at ultimately providing exotic foodstuffs for export, had given himself a more imaginative name.

Miner blinked at being addressed by name, but almost immediately realized that the Marines must have made at least some cursory study of the dossiers of the principal leaders of Haulover, and the dossiers surely included their pictures. He went on at a shout. "We need an army division, or at least a battalion, and those spy satellites of the navy's, to find and destroy the pirates that are terrorizing our countryside. And all the Confederation sends us is an understrength squad under the command of a very junior officer! And a not very good officer, given your evident advanced age."

The squads stood easy in their ranks: feet at shoulder width, hands clasped behind their backs. While their bodies were still, their eyes were in constant motion, seeking eye contact with the other members of the greeting party—all of whom except for Mullilee were members of the Haulover Board of Directors. The directors quickly looked away when one of them happened to make eye contact with one of the Marines.

Daly briefly let a smile crease his face. "Sir, you evidently aren't very familiar with military capabilities. In a situation such as yours, a normal deployment would be *one* four-man Force Recon squad under the command of a sergeant. The fact that the Confederation sent *two* squads under the command of an officer demonstrates the very high esteem in which the Confederation holds Haulover. As for my age, yes, I am older than the typical navy ensign or army second lieutenant. That is because the Marine Corps commissions all of its officers from the ranks. I have fifteen years experience as an enlisted man and noncommissioned officer behind me. Before I went to the Marine Officer Training College and was commissioned, my last assignment was as a squad leader in Force Recon. I know a great deal more than a junior officer who received a direct commission.

"Now, if we are through with the reception, my Marines and I have a job to do, and we need to get ready to do it."

"One question before we break up." Daly looked at the speaker; it was Finn Bankley, Haulover's finance and banking kingpin. "I know you Marines have a high opinion of your capabilities—I'm familiar with your reputation, and it seems your high self-opinion is at least somewhat deserved. But what happens if you find something out there that you *can't* deal with on your own?"

Daly nodded at him. "Thank you, Mr. Bankley, that's a good question. If we find something bigger than we can handle ourselves, we'll be able to determine exactly what it is and what it will take to defeat it. Then we can make a recommendation to the appropriate authorities on what they need to send here to resolve matters."

"And just how long would that take?" Bankley asked.

"There is a FIST two days Beam Space travel away at Thorsfinni's World, and Fourth Fleet Marines headquarters on Halfway isn't much farther. The Confederation Army also has garrisons in this region. And the navy can get warships here in a short period of time."

"But how long will it take to get a request for assistance

from any of those units to Earth and then for authorization for action to get to any of those units?"

Daly gave Bankley a chilling grin. "Sir, when Force Recon finds a need for immediate action from a larger unit, we don't have to send a request to Earth; we can contact the units we need directly. Such units rarely decline to grant our requests. And we have already emplaced an orbital station with interstellar communications drones in orbit so that we can send necessary requests in a timely manner."

CHAPTER
THIRTEEN

Marine House (Temporary Quarters), Sky City, Haulover

The Marines were given quarters in a large, newly built house in Sky City that the town had originally constructed to house the offices of the Confederation of Human Worlds administration on Haulover, and to service Beach Spaceport, but had since been designated for use by visiting dignitaries. The Marines promptly renamed it "Marine House." The house was in an area of large homes on larger lots. A big living room took up most of the front, with a fully equipped kitchen to the left. A hallway led to the rear of the house from near the living room's junction with the kitchen. Two rooms and two baths led off each side of the hallway. Another shorter hall led from the middle of the living room to a bath and two bedrooms, the rear of which was windowless and must at one time have functioned as a walk-in closet or classified documents library. Another room, which could be either another bedroom or a meeting room, was on the right just behind the living room.

Ensign Daly took the windowless bedroom so he could have the equipment to communicate with the Mark IX Echo satellite at hand and out of sight of the locals. Sergeants Kindy and Williams took the adjacent bedroom, and the other Marines occupied the two bedrooms closer to the living room on the long hallway.

They went through the motions and chatter of unpacking and stowing their gear but mostly paid surreptitious attention to the bug-detection devices they put about—the "special" equipment Commander Obannion had so casually mentioned when he'd first told Ensign Daly that he was going on the mission. Every room in the house had multiple audio and vid bugs except for one bathroom, which only had audio. The Marines gravitated to the house's living room once they'd located all the bugging devices, leaving all doors open behind them.

The living room was well, if modestly, appointed, with sufficient chairs, sofas, and occasional tables to accommodate the nine Marines. It was bereft of decoration, but there was a reasonably well-stocked bar in one corner. For the moment, none of the Marines did more with the bar than look to see what it held. They'd also noted a goodly supply of a local beer in the kitchen.

"I'm going to shower," Daly announced. He held up a small overnight bag in his hand, a bit larger than needed to hold a change of clothes.

"Good idea," Sergeant Kindy quipped. "Can't have our commander going around smelling like he just spent the past month confined to the cargo hold of a civilian freighter."

"He was in ossifer country," Sergeant Williams shot back. "So if that's what *he* smells like, what do *we* smell like?"

Daly flashed a rude gesture at them and headed to the bathroom off the bedroom he'd picked for himself, the only bathroom that didn't have a vid pickup, where he'd already put his toiletries. He left the door ajar.

Corporal Nomonon sniffed his own armpit. "Whew! I know a certain corporal who stands in serious need of a serious cleaning."

Corporal Jaschke snorted. "Gonna take more than a shower to clean *you* up!"

"Why you—!" Nomonon mock-swung at Jaschke, and the two grappled in mock wrestling while the others stood back and cheered them on.

In the bathroom, Daly hummed off-key as he emptied his overnight bag. Not much seemed to come out of it—it sometimes looked like his hand went in and came out empty. The apparent empty hands held, of course, his chameleons. The visible items he withdrew from the bag were innocuous in appearance, resembling ordinary containers of household products. Closer examination would reveal a tail on each of the items, tails of varying lengths and thicknesses. He put all but one of them into a chameleon bag.

After emptying his overnight bag, Daly turned on the water in the shower, attached one of the items from his bag to the single audio pickup in the room, then stripped naked and pulled on his chameleons, including gloves and helmet with its chameleon screen lowered. Now invisible, he took the chameleon bag and slipped out of the bathroom. He padded through the living room to the first bedroom, where he attached devices from his bag to each vid and audio pickup in the room. Then into the adjacent bathroom where he attached more. Onto the second bedroom and its bath, then the third and the fourth and fifth, with their respective bathrooms, and finally the kitchen.

When Daly was done with all the other rooms, he returned to the living room. Nomonon and Jaschke were no longer wrestling, but were collapsed on sofas, breathing heavily from their exertions. The others were scattered about the room, commenting on the wrestling they'd just watched or chatting about other neutral topics. Still invisible, Daly slipped behind Kindy and tapped him on the shoulder that faced away from the vid pickups.

Kindy didn't visibly react to the touch but stood up and announced, "All right, you scuzz-buckets, it's time for everybody to hit the head and police your bodies."

Williams led the way, standing and heading for the room he was sharing with Kindy. Kindy stood, arms akimbo, looking in turn at each of the junior Marines until they were all on their feet and moving to their rooms.

As soon as Kindy closed the door to his room behind himself, Daly went to work putting the spoofers on the living room's pickups. When he finished, he returned to the bathroom off his bedroom, and stripped and stepped into the still-running water; let the listener think he took a long shower.

Fully clean for the first time since transshipping from the CNSS *Trumbull County* to the SS *Briny Stars* at Aardheim, and changed into fresh garrison utilities, the Marines reassembled in the living room. The first one back, Ensign Daly, came by way of the kitchen, where he had filled a cooler with bottles of beer, which he deposited on a low table in the middle of the living room. Each of the Marines grabbed one before picking a place to sit.

Sergeant Williams wasted no time getting things started. With only a quick glance at one of the spoofs, he said while opening a beer, "I've had an uncomfortable feeling about this board of directors from the first time they were mentioned in our mission briefings. And now that we've encountered them—"

"I really don't like them," Sergeant Kindy cut in. He opened a beer and took a swig.

"They give off bad vibes," Corporal Belinski said.

"Especially that Smelt Miner," Corporal Nomonon added. "I'd like to take him behind a mine head and teach him a thing or three."

"I'll help," Lance Corporal Rudd said, wiping imagined foam from his upper lip.

"What's the deal with those names?" Lance Corporal Ellis asked. "I can understand people wanting to create new identities for themselves when they go to settle a new world, but *those* names . . ."

"I think it's a case of the big frog, small pond syndrome," Williams said. When Ellis looked blank, he explained. "In a large pond, only the very biggest frogs are powerful. But take a medium-size frog from the big pond and put him in a small pond, he has a chance to be the big frog without actually being big. When I read the dossiers of the members of the board, I saw that none of them were important people on their home worlds—they were medium-size frogs. Here, with a small population and no resident big frogs, they get to be the big ones. So they adopted names that they think reflect their imagined size."

Rudd chuckled. "So they picked names that make them sound like a bunch of small-time con men, out to fleece the rubes."

Ensign Daly sat back in an armchair outside the circle of NCOs and junior men and smiled to himself. Kindy and Williams were both on just their second missions as Force Recon squad leaders, and their first as squad leaders on an (almost) independent mission, but they were doing exactly what he would have done when he was a squad leader—get everybody's first impressions out in the open. He took a deep draft of his beer, then settled back to nurse the rest of it.

"The planetary administrator doesn't seem to be in charge," was Lance Corporal Skripska's first contribution. He'd barely touched his beer.

Lance Corporal Ellis nodded. "He backed off in a hurry when Miner opened his mouth."

Jaschke looked introspective. "Not one of them was willing to look us in the eye," he said softly, and took a thoughtful sip.

"Except Miner and Bankley when they challenged Mr. Daly," Kindy said.

"How much you want to bet nobody at Diplomatic Services has any idea that their on-site man isn't running things?" Williams asked. He got no takers.

Daly listened with half an ear; he gave most of his attention to the spoofs he'd mounted on the pickups. They were clever devices that noted who was in a room and whether or not they were talking, then altered the transmissions of their movements and words to something that would seem innocent to the observers. The technology was new and hadn't been fully tested, but Fourth Fleet Marines G2, intelligence, and

G4, logistics, believed it was solid enough to spoof spy devices a generation or two beyond anything Haulover was known to have—and beyond the abilities of Haulover techs and equipment to override even if they managed to detect something amiss in what they were receiving from their pickups.

Daly certainly hoped G2 was right; he and his Marines needed to be able to discuss all aspects of the mission without fear of being overheard. His men were right; there was something amiss in the governing of Haulover. He wondered just who was behind the bugging of Marine House.

His ears perked up when he heard Rudd say, "The board of directors. Every member of the board is the richest, most powerful person in an industry or trade. Reading between the lines of the reports we have on Haulover, it seems pretty evident that each of them is intent on controlling *all* of his industry. Independent mines get bought up. Regional intercity transit systems get bypassed and forced out of business by lower rates offered by Rayl Rhodes. Small energy companies are eaten up by Alec Powers's continental operation. Et cetera."

Kindy's eyes grew wide. "The destroyed homesteads we know of were all farms or ranches. Could Agro Herder be behind it, forcibly putting small farmers out of business so he can take over their holdings?"

"Possibly," Williams said. "He *has* bought up their holdings."

"Damn," Nomonon said, "are we dealing with an inside job instead of off-worlders?"

"Wouldn't that be a bitch," Jaschke said; his beer bottle dangled from his hand, half-forgotten.

Office of the Planetary Administrator, Sky City, Haulover

Ensign Daly and the two squad leaders went to meet with Planetary Administrator Spilk Mullilee to get the details of the most recent raids on the homesteads. Chairman of the Board Smelt Miner was there, and so was another member of the board to whom the Marines hadn't been introduced: Goode Sales, who owned all of the major goods distribution and sales operations on Haulover.

"Our most recent information is a couple of months old," Daly said. "What's happened during that time?"

Miner glared at Daly. "What's the matter with you people that you can't keep up?"

Daly looked at him with the kind of blank expression that can be more threatening than a glare, then said calmly, "Sir, we were in transit for nearly four weeks; it wasn't possible for us to receive updates during that time. Prior to that, our headquarters hadn't received anything directly from Haulover, but only data that had been relayed from Earth. It took a month for the data to be transmitted from Haulover to Earth, be analyzed there, and forwarded to Halfway. Ergo, we're two months behind on what's happening here."

Miner glowered. "So, when a member world sends to Earth for assistance, it's likely to be destroyed before the cavalry arrives."

"Yes, sir, that's possible. It's also possible that the situation will have resolved itself before the arrival of any military assistance. But usually help arrives before things have gotten too far out of hand." He turned to Mullilee and ignored the anger radiating from Miner. "Now, sir, about incidents in the past two months."

Mullilee spoke hesitantly, with frequent glances at Miner and Sales, as though asking permission to continue. "There have been eleven more since the Montgomery homestead."

"All of them farms?" Kindy asked, leaning forward.

Mullilee nodded. "Eight farms and three ranches. Seventy-five more people are missing." He seemed shaken by the missing people. Neither Miner nor Sales seemed so much disturbed by the missing people as by the destruction of the properties. Except:

"Dammit," Sales grumbled, "those ranchers were good customers. Herding animals is hard on clothes."

Daly didn't acknowledge Sales's comment, but Sergeant Williams fixed him with a hard look. Uncowed, Sales returned the look.

"Where were these homesteads located?" Daly asked. "The first dozen plus that we know about were scattered pretty widely."

Mullilee looked at Miner, who nodded curtly. "So were these," Mullilee said. "They're all over the continent." He looked to Miner again, got another curt nod, and tapped the console on his desk. A map was projected onto the wall behind him, with the attacked homesteads marked on it.

"Can you show them in the order they were attacked?" Daly asked.

Mullilee again looked for Miner's permission before touching his console again. Numbers appeared next to the markings for the homesteads.

"Show which ones Mr. Herder has acquired." Williams didn't *ask,* he *told* Mullilee to put the data up.

"Ah," the planetary administrator said when Miner made a slight sideways movement of his head, "I d-don't think I have that information in my database yet."

Kindy snorted. "Sure you don't."

Mullilee put his fingertips to his throat, swallowed.

"Now see here!" Sales snapped.

Daly gave no sign he was aware of the byplay. He got out his comp and set it on Mullilee's desk. "I'll need all of the data you have on the homesteads. Then we will examine a few of the sites—particularly the most recent ones. There are two more things I'll need: one is secure satellite communications; the other is two all-terrain vehicles."

"Ah," Mullilee said, looking plaintively at the Marine, "we don't have secure satellite communications."

"But you do have commsat, don't you?"

"Y-Yes. We have a Lodestar in geosync."

"Surely it's got an unused secure channel that we can use."

"I-It doesn't have s-secure channels installed."

Daly looked at Mullilee with disbelief.

"We're an open society, Mr. Daly," Miner interjected. "On the rare occasions we have for secure communications, we use a scrambler at each end. And before you ask"—he held up a hand—"no, we don't have any unused scramblers we can lend you."

"All right," Daly said slowly, not believing Miner. He turned to Mullilee. "We still need the vehicles."

Before Mullilee could respond, Miner said, "Give it to him." Mullilee began transmitting data from his comp to Daly's. Miner turned to Daly. "I'm sure if I ask him, Mr. Rhodes will supply you with vehicles and drivers."

Daly addressed the metals boss for the first time since he'd begun talking directly to Mullilee. "The drivers won't be necessary, sir. The vehicles are all we need."

"Of course you need the drivers," Miner insisted. "How else will you find your way around without getting lost?"

Kindy barked out a laugh. Williams looked amused. Daly maintained his calm demeanor.

"Sir, we're Force Recon. Every time we go on a mission, we find our way around without getting lost, and without local guides. We wouldn't be Force Recon if we couldn't do that."

"I still think you need the drivers, and you'll have them." Miner looked as though he thought the matter was settled. Daly didn't press it.

Mullilee indicated that the data on the vanished homesteads had been downloaded to Daly's comp. Daly looked at him. Mullilee almost choked saying, "It's all there. Everything I have."

Daly stood; so did the squad leaders. "Thank you, sir. We'll study this then go out first thing after we have the vehicles. If there are any further developments before then—or at any time at all—kindly notify me immediately." He nodded to Miner and Sales. "Gentlemen."

The three Marines left and walked side by side back to their quarters. They talked about all things Haulover except for their mission—and the thing uppermost in Daly's mind.

Marine House

"I didn't see," Ensign Daly said as soon as they were inside the house. "Where'd you plant it?"

"Did you see me lean forward when I asked if all the home-steads were farms?" Sergeant Kindy asked. Daly nodded, and the squad leader continued. "I'd already dropped it on the floor by my toe. I slipped my foot forward and fed it to the leg of the desk. It crawled up to the bottom of the console base."

Daly clapped him on the back. "Very good. With luck, we'll find out what Mullilee's putting into his comp or getting out of it, as well as hearing everything that's said in that office." The office of the planetary administrator was more effectively bugged than Marine House had been.

By the time the three leaders returned from their meeting with Planetary Administrator Mullilee, all of the Marines were feeling hungry. Haulover was new enough that it didn't have many of the labor-saving conveniences of more settled worlds, such as automatic kitchens—the Marines would have to prepare their own meals. Fortunately, the kitchen was as well stocked with food as with beer. Corporal Belinski claimed he knew how to cook, so the others let him do the honors. It wasn't the worst meal any of them had ever had on a deployment but it was far from the best. Except for Corporal Nomonon and Lance Corporal Ellis, who admitted they couldn't do as well, the other Marines all swore they'd do the cooking themselves before they'd let Belinski try to poison them again.

They'd barely had time to clear the table—Belinski was assigned kitchen police duty as punishment for not being as good a cook as he claimed—and begin studying the data Mullilee had downloaded to Ensign Daly's comp when Daly got a call.

Another homestead had been attacked. Seventeen people were missing this time.

The homestead wasn't a farm or ranch, it was a small mining operation.

The Marines were ready to move out in minutes. They each carried food and water for two days; one man in each squad carried a blaster—the others only had knives and sidearms. They were going on a reconnaissance—if they found a trail they could follow—not a combat raid.

CHAPTER
FOURTEEN

Marine House, Sky City, Haulover

"Where are our vehicles?" Ensign Daly snapped into the comm. "They aren't here yet."

"I-I don't know." Planetary Administrator Spilk Mullilee's voice was almost a whine. "B-But you can travel with my convoy, we'll make r-room for you in our v-vehicles."

Daly swore under his breath, but said out loud, "How soon will you be here to pick us up?"

"F-Fifteen minutes? M-Maybe twenty."

"Make it ten." Daly cut the connection and turned to his Marines. "Showtime. Let's get ready to find the bear."

In less than ten minutes, the Marines were ready and assembled in front of Marine House.

Sergeant Williams grinned. "They're going to shit a brick when they see us." They were in chameleons with their helmets and gloves off and sleeves rolled up so Mullilee and his people would be able to see them.

Corporal Nomonon hooted. "They've probably heard of chameleons but don't believe what they've heard."

"Got that right," Sergeant Kindy said, poking Nomonon's shoulder.

Daly faced his men. Despite the many years he'd been a Marine, he still sometimes found the sight of disembodied heads and hovering hands disconcerting.

"Just don't go out of your way to frighten the natives," he told them.

"Aye aye, sir," Corporal Belinski said and made to put his helmet on. He lowered his helmet and grinned when Daly gave him a stern look.

It took more than thirty minutes from Mullilee's call for the small convoy to reach Marine House.

"What is this?" Chairman Smelt Miner yelped from the front seat of the lead vehicle when he saw the Marines' heads and hands. Mullilee sat staring slack-jawed in the vehicle's back-seat.

Daly ambled over to the landcar, not showing the annoyance he felt at the delay—or the presence of the overbearing Miner. He pointedly looked at the three vehicles of the convoy—two of which bore the markings of the Haulover Constabulary, and were already full—before leaning to look into the backseat at Mullilee. "Sir," he said, "I still don't see the vehicles for my Marines."

"You c-can sit with m-me," Mullilee said. He tried to look at Daly's eyes so he wouldn't have to look at the way the Marine's head hovered in midair.

Miner twisted around in the front seat to watch, but didn't say anything.

"My Marines, sir. I was promised two vehicles."

"I-I'm sure they'll be here by the time we g-get back from the Johnson h-homestead."

"If we find something we can follow, my Marines and I aren't coming back. If we have to come back, we may lose valuable time and the perpetrators have a greater chance of getting away and raiding more homesteads. I need those vehicles *now*."

Mullilee lowered his eyes, blinked when he realized he couldn't actually see *through* Daly, and looked past him toward the other Marines. "Ah, do . . . do you ha-have weapons and . . . and . . ."

"We have everything we need, sir. Except vehicles."

"You'll get 'em," Miner snarled. He yanked his comm out of a pocket and spoke sharply into it, listened for a few seconds, then snapped it off. "They'll be here in ten minutes. And if they aren't, we'll leave without you."

"They better be here in ten minutes," Daly said, far more calmly than he felt.

True to Miner's word, when the extra vehicles didn't show up in ten minutes, the three-vehicle convoy pulled out, leaving Daly and the other Marines behind when Daly refused to leave without his men. Less than two minutes later, two Land Runners, the civilian version of the Confederation Army's Battle Car, pulled up in front of Marine House. The Land Runner had thinner armor, no firing slits in the window armor it didn't have anyway, and a less powerful engine.

"Nomonon, Belinski," Daly said, and gestured sharply at the two vehicles.

The two corporals moved sharply to the Land Runners, pulled the drivers' doors open, and ordered the drivers to get out.

"No, these are ours!" the driver of the lead vehicle objected. "We're driving—we have our orders."

Daly used his parade-ground voice to say, "I told Mr. Miner we didn't need drivers, that we'd do our own driving."

That voice, and the sight of hovering heads and bodiless hands, rattled the drivers enough that they dismounted.

"B-But, Mr. Miner," the first driver said, "he told us we have to drive. He'll be awful pissed when he finds out that you took the Land Runners from us."

"What's the matter," Kindy said, sneering, "do you think he'll fire you?"

The first driver's head bobbed rapidly.

"He'll do more than just fire us," the second driver said.

Daly considered that for a second, then ordered the drivers, "All right, get in the back. *I'll* take care of Mr. Miner."

The drivers did as Daly said, and in a moment the Marines were mounted and chasing after the convoy.

Johnson Homestead, One Hundred Kilometers
Northwest of Sky City

Although Ensign Daly was annoyed by the delay in the convoy's arrival, and the further delay caused by the wait for the Land Runners, he'd put the time to good use by studying the data Planetary Administrator Mullilee had downloaded to his comp. His Marines also studied during that time. The data, contrary to what Mullilee had said during the meeting in his office, *did* have the timing of the attacks on the homesteads. But he had to work at getting the data in such shape that he could clearly see the sequence of disappearances. He didn't have enough time to study the sequence before they arrived at the Johnson homestead, as all the vehicles heading there pushed at two hundred kilometers per hour and arrived half an hour after leaving Sky City.

The Johnson homestead was—or had been—a dozen buildings situated along the bank of an ancient, dry riverbed. The three vehicles that carried Planetary Administrator Mullilee and the police arrived scant minutes before the Marines and parked just outside a disturbed area. The Marines parked their Land Runners next to them. Mullilee and Chairman Miner stood on the edge of the disturbance, along with a uniformed man the Marines hadn't seen before, watching the constabulary forensic people, who were setting up to examine what they were treating as a crime scene. A platoon of local soldiers were in a defensive perimeter around the site.

"This is General Pokoj Vojak," Mullilee introduced Daly to the stranger, "Haulover's minister of war."

"Ensign Daly, I'm pleased to meet you," Vojak said and extended his hand. Even if his civilian masters weren't, Vojak was respectful of the Marines. He'd been a major in the Confederation Army, and had experience with Force Recon, so he had an idea of their capabilities.

"General," Daly said, saluting, then shook the offered hand.

"My army isn't much, but I'll offer you every bit of help we can give," Vojak said.

"Thank you, sir. Once we locate the base of these raiders, we'll provide you with assistance in dealing with them."

Before they could say anything more about cooperating, Miner stepped forward, shouldering Vojak aside. "That's all good and well," he snarled. "But in the meantime, what are you going to do about this?" He waved a hand at the devastation.

Vojak didn't protest Miner's treatment and moved away.

Daly looked around but didn't see anything that looked like the entrance to a mine, so he asked, "What were they mining here?"

"Platinum and ru-ruthenium," Mullilee said. Miner shot him a harsh look.

Daly's eyebrows went up. "Ruthenium?" He looked around again and saw gouges in the riverbed where the alluvial deposits had been dug out to be shoveled into sluice boxes. "What did they do, pay for their initial operation with the platinum and use the profits to go after the ruthenium?" Ruthenium was commonly found with platinum. As a necessary metal in the manufacture of Beam interstellar drives, it was an extremely valuable export commodity. Platinum, while a precious metal, wasn't as valuable on the interstellar export market. It was probably worth more on the domestic market; no matter how far they were removed from the bright lights of high society, women always liked to adorn themselves with sparkly and shiny things.

"Ah, I . . . I th-think so."

Miner spat onto the alluvial deposit that contained the rare metals. "Johnson had some romantic idea about striking it rich like an old-time gold prospector," he growled. "He spent all the time he could over four years prowling around, looking for the big strike. Every now and then he found a few nuggets of gold, but never enough to justify a commercial mining operation. Then he found this." He shook his head. "The son of a bitch knew the value of the ruthenium. He wouldn't sell out to me when he had the chance. Now look at where it got him." He looked away. "People know I wanted this mine. Now some of them are going to blame me for what happened here."

Daly looked at him levelly. "Are you?"

"Allah's pointed teeth, no!" Miner yelled. "If I was, why would I have taken out two dozen farms and ranches? *They* don't do me a damn bit of good. So don't you think I'm in any way responsible for this, mister!"

They would if you were trying to deflect attention from yourself, Daly thought. He abruptly turned from Miner and Mullilee to direct the two squads in examining the ground surrounding the destroyed mining operation, leaving the locals to stand staring after him. Miner's chest heaved with deep breaths as he tried to calm himself and bring his fury at this junior officer under control.

The Marines didn't need to be directed by their officer; the squad leaders knew exactly what they needed to do and already had their Marines doing it. Daly remembered the "dumb question" he'd asked at the preplanning briefing: "This is a two-squad mission. Why does it require an officer?" He now felt every bit like the excess baggage he had feared he'd be.

A few minutes later, a raised voice caused Daly to look toward the parked vehicles. He saw Miner angrily talking to the two men who'd been the assigned drivers of the Land Runners loaned to the Marines. He lowered his sleeves and put on his helmet and gloves before briskly walking toward the trio.

". . . to scrounge whatever odd jobs you can find, because nobody on the board will give you any assistance," Miner was saying to the two terrified-looking drivers when Daly stepped unseen between the director and the two men. The drivers didn't say anything, didn't look like they *could* say anything.

Daly whipped his helmet off in a move that created the impression that he had simply appeared out of nowhere. The helmet removal was a move practiced by Force Recon squad leaders to startle people who needed to be put off balance; the sudden appearance of a disembodied head usually distracted whoever for long enough that the Marine could peel his gloves off, leaving the impression that he'd suddenly appeared exactly as seen.

"Mr. Miner," Daly said in the voice noncommissioned officers have used to put fear into the hearts of recalcitrant soldiers for as long as there have been armies, "I believe you are threatening these men because they obeyed my orders!"

"I tol—"

"I don't give a hair off Muhammad's ass *what* you told them! They are *civilians.* I told you I *don't* want or need drivers. Maybe I didn't make myself *clear.* Let me do that *now.* I am *not* going to put the lives of my Marines in the hands of *civilians.* I am *not* going to take *civilians* into situations where their mere *presence* might endanger the lives of my *Marines.* And I am *not* going to take them into situations where they might get *killed!"* As he spoke, Daly edged closer to Miner, until his nose was mere centimeters from the other's face. Now he moved those final centimeters, forcing Miner to lean back off balance. "Or do you *want* these men to get *killed?* Do you want my *Marines* to get killed? *Do you?"*

Those last shouted words sent Miner staggering back a step or two.

"You can't talk to—"

"I can talk to *anyone* anyway I please when the success of my mission is at issue!" Daly lowered his voice to a tone that implied he had the weight of the entire Confederation of Human Worlds behind it and said, "I will not tolerate anyone placing their own lives or those of my Marines in jeopardy. If you punish these men because I won't allow you to use them to interfere with my mission, you will have occasion to regret it. Do you understand me, Mr. Miner?"

A step away from Daly, barely within arm's reach, Miner felt more confident. He drew himself up to his greatest height and shouted, "You're insubordinate, mister! I'm going to lodge a complaint and have you removed from command here. I have connections, and by the time I'm through with you, you'll not only lose your commission, you'll be lucky if you don't wind up in Darkside!" He began to turn to stalk away, staggered again when Daly stretched to grab his shoulder and yank him back.

"By the time your complaint reaches my superiors and their reply comes back here, my mission will have been completed and my Marines and I will no longer be here. And you will look like a fool, because my superiors will back me." It looked like Daly merely flicked his fingers, but he did it with enough force to stagger Miner. He turned his back on the furious chairman and said to the drivers, "Let me know if he does anything to you."

Miner wrapped himself in as much dignity as he could and stalked away, snarling over his shoulder, "You're done here, mister. You'll be sorry that you ever crossed me, *Ensign!*"

The two drivers waited until their boss was no longer looking back, then grinned.

"The son of a bitch deserved a chewing out," one said.

"But you bought yourself some trouble," the other added.

Daly shook his head. "He doesn't know what trouble is until he goes up against a few good Marines."

Before either driver could respond, Daly heard a voice on his helmet comm and raised the helmet to his head to hear.

"Boss, we found something," Sergeant Williams said. "Look to your eight o'clock. Use your magnifier."

Daly put on his helmet and looked slightly to the rear of his left through the magnifier screen. He saw Williams waving an arm at him from a couple of hundred meters beyond the razed area. "On my way," he said. He circled the destroyed area so as not to disturb anything for the constabulary's forensics people.

Two Hundred Meters West of the Johnson Homestead

"What do you have, Sergeant?"

"They traveled by aircraft," Sergeant Williams said. He pointed at marks on the ground.

Daly squatted to get an up close look at one of the faint marks on the hard ground, sighted along them to see how far they went. They were about sixty meters long, traces left by skids rather than by wheels. Toward one end there was blown debris in the kind of pattern thrown out by breaking engines;

scorch marks in the other direction were those of thrusters launching an aircraft. The twin skid marks were roughly six meters apart.

"How long is the aircraft?" Daly asked.

"Hard to say," Williams answered, "but look here." He led the way to the central area of the skid marks. "The marks are very slightly deeper from here to there, like something sat there for a while." He used a laser pointer to pick out "here" and "there"; they were almost distinct, about fifteen meters apart.

Daly considered the marks for a moment, then asked, "What kind of aircraft is six meters by fifteen?"

Williams shook his head; he'd been wondering the same thing.

"Or it could be wider or narrower, depending on where the skids are under it. And the skids probably aren't the full length of the aircraft, so it could be twenty meters long or even longer." He checked his comp. It didn't have data on an aircraft with skids six meters apart and fifteen long. "What about footprints?" he asked.

Williams showed him what his squad had found, which wasn't much. The alluvial plain was hard enough that it didn't take footprints very easily. What traces there were seemed to be of smallish feet. "Women, or adolescents?" the squad leader wondered aloud. His squad hadn't found any prints farther from the homestead than the midpoint of the deeper skid traces, or any beyond a path that indicated whoever made them went directly to the homestead and back again. Nor had they found any that had a high probability of having been made by the missing homesteaders. There weren't enough prints, or any distinct enough, to make an educated guess as to how many individuals there might have been in the raiding party. For that matter, it was only an assumption that the marks had been made by whoever had destroyed the Johnson homestead, and made seventeen people disappear—but that was a reasonable assumption.

Daly got on his comm and called Sergeant Kindy. His squad hadn't yet found anything to the east of the razed area.

"Keep looking," Daly ordered.

The Marines kept searching, but didn't find anything else by the time the forensics team finished its work and was ready to return to Sky City.

"We'll head back now too," Daly decided. "I want to examine satellite, radar, and any other surveillance data available for this location over the past several days. Then we'll come back with better equipment to see what more we can learn about these tracks."

CHAPTER
FIFTEEN

Government Center, Confederation of Human Worlds,
Fargo, Earth

Every visitor to any government office in Fargo was required first to pass through an ultra-sophisticated biomedical scanning system. The individual was identified by fingerprints and retinal and voice scans which were compared to readings already on file in the vast database maintained on all citizens over the age of twelve. If for some reason that information was not already in the system, as sometimes happened with people born and raised on distant worlds, it joined the billions of others already on file there and the Ministry of Health and Human Services was duly notified and in time the planetary administrator on the unrecorded person's home world was goosed to do a better job imprinting citizens' personal data.

But the main purpose of the system was for security. Each individual was subjected to several kinds of scans and minute quantities of moisture were collected from the person's hands when palm prints were taken. This was subjected to instant blood chemistry analysis. Bone and tissue scans determined if a person might be carrying an implant of any kind. Spies with miniaturized transmitting and recording devices had been detected in that way, as well as would-be assassins. In one notorious case, a well-endowed woman carried a powerful bomb embedded in her breasts. It detonated in the screening station, killing her and everyone else within a radius of ten meters.

The woman had been on her way to testify before a congressional committee investigating a well-known criminal organization. After that incident guards did the screening from behind bombproof barriers.

Blood chemistry analysis was done to determine if visitors had any mind-altering drugs in their system that could make them a danger to other persons, or otherwise affect their conduct or embarrass politicians. Wags often joked that none of the members of Congress would ever notice any difference.

One of the recent visitors to pass through the system was Jimmy Jasper. He had been admitted with a clean bill of health to visit President Cynthia Chang-Sturdevant.

The results of his scans were provided routinely to several government ministries, among them the Ministry of Justice.

Office of the Attorney General, Confederation of Human Worlds, Fargo

Attorney General Huygens Long sat at his desk, scanning the lab analysis on Jimmy Jasper. "Gobbledegook. What's it all mean, J.B.?" he asked, waving the report at his chief of forensics, Dr. Hans Jeroboam.

J.B. leaned forward and gestured at the report with a long index finger. "He's on something, AG."

"Well, *what*? There's a question mark in the column where all the other stuff, natural, harmless stuff, is identified. What's he on?"

"That question mark is there because we don't know what it is or what it does." J.B. shrugged and pulled at his short beard. "It does not match any known substance, natural or manufactured. There is nothing in our formulary like it."

"Hmmm. Anything else?"

"Look at the MRI. It's the right-hand column on the sheet."

Long frowned. "Okay. So what?"

"Enlarged thyroid lobes, AG, that's what."

"So? Plenty of people have them. Nothing unusual there. *Is* there? J.B., stop playing these games with me. Come right out and tell me what you are driving at."

"We're getting there, AG," J.B. said, grinning, "and no, enlarged thyroids are not that unusual. But upon closer examination we determined Jasper's lobes had been surgically altered. Something was grafted to the gland, AG. Surgically implanted." J.B. grinned again, as if that explained everything.

"But our agent on Kingdom, I've read his report. Jasper's never been in the hospital, never been sick a day in his life, J.B.!"

"Right. Now, attached to the lab analysis are two printouts we took off a trid of Mr. Jasper preaching the Gospel to the faithful. Take a look at them."

Long flipped over the lab report. Attached were several full-color printouts, the first two of Jimmy Jasper's neck and throat. Someone had circled two tiny scars over the trachea. "Holy jumpin' Jehosephat," Long whispered. "Never been in the hospital, never been sick a day in his life. J.B., the Skinks, *they* did this." He tapped the printout with a finger.

"Yep. I'll bet that substance in his blood is being released by those implants. We don't know what it does, but I'll also bet it blocks his memory of whatever it was the aliens did to him while he was in captivity, and it also may be helping him 'see Jesus,' if you get my drift." J.B. sat back triumphantly.

Long glanced at the other printouts. "Who's this? Looks like a woman."

"Sally Consolador. She has the same marks."

"So she *does*! They've *both* been fixed." Long rubbed his hands. "We're on to something here, J.B. Now, I've had people reviewing the reports coming back from the survey teams sent to Kingdom to interview the people taken by the Skinks and later released. They haven't been subjected to any biomedical scanning, but none has much memory of what happened while he was a prisoner, and they all are acting normal, or as normal as anyone on that world ever acts. Except for the other preachers, like Jasper, who've shown up on some of the other member worlds, and we haven't been able to get to all of them yet."

"Call them in and have them scanned."

"No, no, J.B., we start doing that and Senator Maxim'll be standing up in the Congress and accusing us of religious persecution. I have to tread lightly here."

J.B. nodded. "I understand. Can't have you playing Pontius Pilate to his Messiah, can we?"

Long laughed and patted his stomach. "Some already are calling me 'Paunchy Pilot.' But fuck anyone who can't take a joke. We get the goods on this guy, we'll go to the president and arrest him. Can't crucify him though. That's gone out of style."

"Seriously, AG, you know some people are already comparing Jasper to the Messiah, some of them believe he *is* the Messiah and that the Second Coming is upon us."

"*That* would sure solve all our problems," Long answered archly.

"Seriously, AG, we've got a real problem on our hands with this guy. If this is the doing of the Skinks, they've really figured out a way to fuck us over but good. He's *got* to be stopped before too many more people buy into this Messiah stuff."

Long nodded. He was silent for a moment, drumming his fingers thoughtfully on his desk. "But the president ordered everyone taken by the Skinks to be interviewed. We don't have anything on this Sally Whatshername, Consolador, Jasper's assistant. She's not in our database either. Those Kingdomites never cooperated with us in getting their people's vital statistics into the system. But that has turned out to be a good thing, J.B." He grinned. "I'm going to get her in here for that interview; good excuse to run her through the scanner, see what's floating around in her bloodstream. I want you to sit in on the interview with me. If she has the same alterations as her mentor, all these preachers will probably have them too." He looked at the printouts of Sally's throat. "Nice neck on this girl. But why have some of the abductees been treated like this and not the others, J.B.?"

"I don't know. Maybe it didn't take on some, maybe the candidates weren't susceptible to the drug, maybe they felt they didn't need to convert everyone they took. Only the Skinks know the reason for that. I suspect all they wanted from most of those prisoners was information about the human species, and they selected a few likely specimens out of all those people for infiltration. And you know, plenty of the people on Kingdom who were taken have never come back. Maybe the Skinks think they're doctors and bury their mistakes," he said, chuckling. "However you cut it, AG, our Jimmy Jasper is a damned traitor; they all are."

"Well, J.B., maybe not. Maybe the poor bastard doesn't even know what he's doing."

Senator Maxim's Villa, Outskirts of Fargo

"What shall I do, master?" Sally asked Jasper. She was referring to the summons issued for her appearance at the Ministry of Justice to undergo an interview. Jimmy had recently begun to insist that his assistants and acolytes refer to him as "master."

"Child, thou must render unto Caesar that which is Caesar's." Jimmy smiled, laying a hand on her shoulder. He fixed her with his hypnotic, compelling eyes, something he had only recently started doing, as if an inner light had begun to burn inside him that had not been there before. She had to blink to get away from that gaze. "Go now, woman, and prepare thyself. Upon your return, thou shalt accompany me into the city this holy night, where I shall preach to twelve learned men whom my disciple, Luke, will have gathered to hear me." Luke was the Confederation's powerful Senator Maxim.

Sally had begun to have her doubts about Jimmy's ministry of late, and she was beginning to fear him. He had not yet come out and said to anyone, even her, that he thought he *was* the Messiah, but he had started acting like it, and many of his followers had started talking as if the Second Coming was already upon them. Worst of all, the daymares, the frightening visions, had started occurring with much more frequency and vividness. The faces of her tormentors in those visions were becoming clearer, and she was horrified that they were the visages of the devils whom men called "Skinks," the creatures that had ravaged her home world. In her visions, they were not angels, and they were hurting her, putting things into her, doing terrible things to her. She was terrified that one day the visions would not go away and she would find herself sucked down into the bowels of hell.

"Then I shall prepare, master." She bowed in resignation. Jimmy said nothing, just stood, regarding her with a beatific, all-knowing smile. She turned and rapidly left the room, leaving Jimmy staring after her. Her heart skipped a beat. She realized that he *knew* what was happening to her, knew what the visions meant, knew everything about her. He *knew* that her faith in him was slipping as if it had been foreordained.

Getting into the landcar the Ministry of Justice had sent to convey Sally to her interview was like breathing fresh air. She sat back and closed her eyes as she was driven away from the villa. The farther she got from Jimmy Jasper the better she felt. She looked about her as they entered Fargo, at the soaring buildings, the crowds teeming in the streets, all the brightly lit shops and stores, the happy crowds vibrant with life. Clearly, it was not the Sodom Jimmy kept calling it; Fargo was a great metropolis, a thriving, dynamic city full of normal human beings going about their normal human business, enjoying the fruits of their honest labor.

Sally covered her face with a hand. *What is happening to me?* she asked herself. *What has happened to me? Why am I being punished like this?* Back on Kingdom, in the small town where she'd been raised, where she'd spent her whole life until she had been taken, Sally Consolador had been a happy, carefree girl, a believer, yes, but not a zealot. She wept silently behind her hand.

Ministry of Justice

Passing through the biomedical scanner proved to be a simple, noninvasive process. Sally was asked to place her hand on a pad, look into a camera, and state her name. She then stepped into a very ordinary-looking doorway, was asked to stand still for a moment, and then a smiling female guard walked around the barrier, gave her a visitor's pass, and escorted her through the corridors of the Ministry of Justice to Huygens Long's office.

Two men rose to greet her as she was ushered in. "Good morning, Miss Consolador," a man with a heavy paunch greeted her, coming forward to take her hand. "I am Huygens Long, the attorney general. Call me Hugh. Please have a seat. This gentleman here is Dr. Jeroboam; we all call him J.B. because nobody can pronounce his name correctly." The fat man chuckled. He had pleasant laugh lines around his eyes and his hand was warm and dry and held hers firmly, reassuringly.

"I am very pleased to meet you, miss," J.B. said. He gently brushed his lips across the back of Sally's hand. He had long, tapering fingers with big knuckles, the hands of a man who used them in his work. He held her hand gently, like a precious porcelain. His lips brushed its back ever so lightly. To her he seemed an elegant, old-fashioned gentleman, and she found herself enormously flattered.

"Are you any relation to the king who caused Israel to sin?" Sally blurted the question out inadvertently and then grinned as her face turned red with embarrassment at her forwardness. She surprised herself with the remark because it was the first attempt at humor she had made since returning from—*them*.

Jeroboam started and looked intently at Sally for a moment, then he too smiled. "In First Kings, somewhere, isn't it?"

"Yes, sir, 1 Kings 14:16. 'And he shall give Israel up because of the sins of Jeroboam, who did sin, and who made Israel to sin.' "

"You do know your Bible." J.B. smiled. "Please have a seat."

"Refreshments, Miss Consolador?" Long asked, rhetorically because he'd already ordered coffee. "You do drink coffee, miss?"

"No! Oh, yes! Yes, I would like some, sir."

They sat around a low coffee table in comfortable chairs, almost like friends having a chat. They talked for over an hour.

The longer she sat there the more comfortable Sally Consolador grew in their presence. It was the first time since leaving Kingdom that she had felt such ease and pleasure in talking, even though they kept asking her questions about her abduction. She tried, unsuccessfully, to skirt around the visions she'd been having, but both Long and Dr. Jeroboam sensed her resistance.

At one point they were interrupted by an aide who laid a computer printout on Mr. Long's desk. He glanced at it and smiled at Sally. "Are you ready for a refill?" Long gestured at Sally's coffee cup.

"Oh, yes, sir!" She had almost forgotten how wonderful a good cup of coffee could be. Jimmy Jasper hated drugs of all kinds. "Your body is the Lord's temple," he would thunder during a sermon, "and it is a sin to defile it with man's evil concoctions!" She realized suddenly how silly that prohibition was.

They engaged in small talk for a while after the supposed object of the meeting, the Skink abduction, had been covered. Sally noticed, idly, that neither man had bothered to take any notes of the conversation. But she liked talking about her family and friends back on Kingdom. She hadn't thought of them in a long time. At last Dr. Jeroboam stood up. "Well, Miss Consolador, we want to thank you for coming to see us and being so cooperative."

"You have been a great help to us, miss," Long said, coming around the coffee table to give her his hand. He helped her to her feet. A guard appeared silently at the door to escort her out of the building. "Please have a safe trip back to Senator Maxim's villa, and feel free to visit us here again anytime."

Sally felt like yelling, *No! Keep me here! Help me! I do not want to go back there!* but she could not. "Thank you, sirs," she said instead, and let herself be led out of the room.

"Whew!" J.B. said. "That girl is desperate, AG. We should have kept her here for her own good. I shudder to think of that poor girl returning to Jasper's clutches."

"Not ready to do that yet, J.B. Here are the lab analyses.

Compare Consolador's with Jasper's. Oh, she has the thyroid grafts, just like he does, but look at this blood serum analysis."

Jeroboam glanced at the printouts briefly and whistled. "The level of that stuff in his blood is 240 milligrams per milliliter. Hers is—holy jumpin' Jehosephat—*40* milligrams! The stuff is wearing off on her!"

"Right. Come on, J.B. We're getting all this stuff together and we're going to see the president. I'm going to get her to agree to get one of the justices to issue us a warrant for the arrest of Mr. Reverend Jimmy Jasper."

Sally Consolador wept quietly all the way back to Senator Maxim's villa.

CHAPTER
SIXTEEN

Marine House, Sky City, Haulover

Since the dawn of professional standing armies, seasoned non-commissioned officers have found it necessary to take newly commissioned officers aside and teach them how to be good officers. That's because, no matter how well educated or trained a new officer is, he lacks the experience to put his education or training to its best use. High among such "best uses" is the art of dealing with people, commonly called "people skills." The Confederation Marine Corps didn't have that problem because all of its officers were commissioned from the ranks, most new ensigns being elevated from the ranks of sergeants and staff sergeants, and already had the requisite "people skills."

Usually.

But there was the occasional exception. And Sergeant Kindy and Sergeant Williams were of the opinion that Ensign Daly had become such an exception. So when they returned to their quarters in the capital to plan their next steps, the two squad leaders took Ensign Daly aside.

"Don't you think you're overdoing it a bit, boss?" Kindy asked.

"What do you mean?" Daly asked.

"You virtually accused Miner of being responsible for the raids," Kindy said. "That's pretty damn harsh. Especially when we don't have a bit of evidence."

"I think the son of a bitch is behind them, and that's why

he's stonewalling us. So I'm on his case. What?" The last word was directed at Williams when the latter smiled and shook his head.

"You do have a reputation, sir," Williams said.

"Reputation?" Daly demanded. "What are you talking about?"

Kindy leaned close and stuck his face in Daly's. "What he means is, you've got a rep as one arrogant SOB, that's what."

"Arrogant! I'm not—"

Kindy stepped in even closer. "I was with you for a long time when you were my squad leader, *sir*. Take my word for it, you *are* arrogant." He pulled back slightly. "Hell's bells, we're all—all of us Force Recon Marines—we're all arrogant. We damn well *earn* the right to our arrogance just by being what we are! But *you,* Mr. Daly, *you* have always been a little more arrogant than the rest of us. And you've gotten worse since you became a damn ossifer!"

"Now, you see here," Daly roared, red-faced, leaning into Kindy so his nose nearly touched the sergeant's, "I am *not* arrogant!" He poked a stiff finger into Kindy's chest. "You seem to forget that when I was your squad leader, I taught you everything you know about being Force Recon!"

"That's right," Kindy roared back, nearly as red-faced as Daly, slapping Daly's finger away from his chest. "And you seem to have forgotten some of the things you taught me! One of them that you forgot"—he edged closer to Daly—"is don't lean too hard on civilians. Civilians don't cooperate when you lean on them."

"Well, Miner's *not* going to cooperate with us, not if he's behind the raids—and I believe he is!"

"Well, I think he is too. And your arrogance is putting him on guard. So he's going to be more careful to see that nothing slips that'll prove he is!"

"Kindy's right, sir," Williams interjected while trying to insinuate himself between them. "I think you've alerted Miner to watch himself."

Daly stepped back and turned away. After a moment, Daly turned back, his color almost back to normal.

"You know, you're right. I *have* been pretty insufferable." Daly gave his head a sharp shake. "It's one thing to act superior to a field grade doggie, but it's a mistake to act that way to one of the leading citizens of a world."

"Even if he *is* guilty," Kindy said, nodding vigorously.

"Until we have the proof," Williams said with a relieved grin.

"But," Daly said thoughtfully, "I can't take back the way I've already acted. What I can do, though"—a grin spread across his face—"is push the arrogance all the way to buffoonery. Make him believe I'm an incompetent fool."

"And then maybe he'll let his guard slip."

"And then we'll get the proof we need to nail him."

Daly put a call in to the office of the planetary administrator, requesting an appointment for first thing the next morning.

Kindy listened to the bug he'd planted in Spilk Mullilee's office, and laughed when the planetary administrator placed a panicky call to Smelt Miner, telling the chairman of the board about the early meeting.

Office of the Planetary Administrator, Sky City

"You want what?" Planetary Administrator Mullilee croaked. He leaned back in his chair and looked up at the Marine officer standing on the other side of his desk.

"I want satellite, radar, and any other surveillance data you have for the area of the Johnson homestead," Ensign Daly repeated his request. His expression was blank, impassive. He was in garrison utilities.

Smelt Miner, sitting on a settee along the side wall of the office, where he thought Daly couldn't see him, shook his head when Mullilee darted a glance in his direction. But Daly had better peripheral vision than Miner realized.

"W-We don't have mu . . ." Mullilee started to say, but let his voice trail off when Daly turned away from him.

"Mr. Miner," Daly said, facing Haulover's chairman of the board, "is there a particular reason you don't want the Confederation military to have access to intelligence that could lead us to whoever it is that is conducting raids on remote homesteads? I'd think you'd be eager to give us all the help you can to stop the abductions or murders of the people on your world."

Miner replied calmly. "Mr. Daly, if you had let Spilk finish speaking, you would have heard him say that we don't have the kind of data you are asking for. What we have in orbit are weather satellites, and a communications satellite in geosync. And we don't have radar installations anywhere near the Johnson homestead.

Daly momentarily showed confusion on his face before he resumed his impassive mask. "But radar doesn't have to be in the vicinity of the Johnson homestead to show the tracks of aircraft heading in its direction. And, if you only have weather and communications satellites in orbit . . . I could have sworn the Confederation Aviation Orbital Administration gave Haulover five Global Trekker satellites some years ago," he added, uncertainty in his voice.

A glint of superiority and victory flashed in Miner's eyes. He said, "That's right, the Aviation Orbital Administration *did* give us the Global Trekker satellites. *But,* several members of the board were concerned that using the Global Trekkers would be a violation of the Intra-Confederation Arms Control Act of 2368. So after careful consideration, we decided not to launch them." He shook his head. "You see, *Ensign,* we don't have the satellite data you are asking for."

"B-But, Mr. Miner, surely the board isn't that naïve. The Act of 2368 prohibits the sale of military *weapons* to civilians. The Global Trekker is a *civilian* satellite designed to conduct land use surveys."

"Be that as it may," Miner said through gritted teeth, "we never launched the Global Trekkers—and we *don't* have any satellite data to show you."

Daly stood off kilter, projecting confusion and uncertainty.

"All right," he finally said, "I'll settle for radar and what other surveillance data you might have."

Miner smiled condescendingly, and nodded at Mullilee. Then he turned back to Daly and said, "You'll have what you need."

"I-I'll have the radar data for you tomorrow," the administrator said. "W-We don't have o-other surveillance data."

"We're going back to the Johnson homestead today, Mr. Mullilee. I really need that data before we leave."

Mullilee swallowed. "I-I'll do what I can."

"Thank you," Daly said, sounding positively contrite.

Miner dismissed Daly with a flick of his fingers.

As Daly closed the door of Mullilee's office, he heard Miner say, "I took *that* pup down a peg or two." Daly thought that the board chairman meant for him to hear it. He smiled inwardly as he left the building and headed back to Marine House.

Office of the Director, Resources and Survey Department, Ministry of the Interior, Sky City

While Ensign Daly was wearing garrison utilities for his visit to Planetary Administrator Mullilee, Sergeants Kindy and Williams paid a visit to the forensics department of the Haulover Ministry of the Interior. Unlike their commander, the two squad leaders wore their chameleons—the better to throw their hostess off balance.

"Ms. Silverthorp, I'm—"

"Mrs.," the blond woman behind an impressive desk centered in a surprisingly opulent office said, wagging the fingers of her left hand at the two sergeants to display the rather impressive diamond-encrusted ring on its third finger. She looked at her wagging fingers, as they were far less disconcerting than having to look at the disembodied heads and hands that hovered before her.

"Mrs. Silverthorp," Sergeant Kindy said, correcting himself, "I am Sergeant Him Kindy, Force Recon, Confederation Marine

Corps. We—that is, Sergeant Williams and I"—he gestured with the hand that wasn't holding his helmet—"are in the team tracking down whoever is conducting the raids on remote homesteads."

"Yes, I've heard that the Confederation sent military assistance." She clasped her hands on the desktop behind the silver-plated name plaque that announced her as Phyllis Silverthorp, and kept looking at them rather than face the upsetting sight in front of her.

"And we would like some assistance from your department," Sergeant Williams continued.

"Oh, but we don't have any expertise in fighting or . . ." Her hands fluttered at the mention of assistance, and she looked up in frightened surprise, only to clutch her hands back on the desktop and fix her eyes on them again. She continued talking but in so low a voice the two Marines couldn't make out her words.

"No, no, Mrs. Silverthorp," Kindy said in a soothing tone. "We don't want *people* from your department. We want *equipment.*"

"Oh! That's different. Why didn't you say so?"

"We just did," Williams said, but Silverthorp continued talking and she didn't hear him.

"I have no idea what kind of equipment my department might have that fighting men could possibly need, I mean, after all, we survey land and locate natural resources of all kinds that can be utilized to build our society here on Haulover, and we assist homesteads all around the continent in getting established, and assist homesteaders in deciding what kinds of homesteads they want to establish and surveying their holdings so correct information can be given when they apply for their land grants and determine the resources, both surface and sub-surface, not to mention water and minerals, that are available to them on their homesteads, and we also survey and map un-settled and unpopulated areas of the continent so that the information is already on hand when our population increases to the

point where we need to expand, *lebensraum,* if you are familiar with the term—"

Kindy leaned forward and placed a hand on Silverthorp's
clasped hands. "Yes, Mrs. Silverthorp, we know what *lebensraum* means."

At Kindy's touch, she abruptly stopped talking and stared at
the disembodied hand on top of hers for a moment before
yanking her hands out from under it and spinning her chair
around so she was facing away from the two Marines.

"What do you need?" she asked, her voice squeaking. "No"—
she lifted a hand—"don't tell me, I don't need to know, m-my
secretary can take care of you; I'll instruct her to give you all the
assistance you require and you can sign out any equipment my
department has that you can use and I won't even ask what
you're going to do with it. I'll even instruct my staff to let you
have whatever you want without question, and if anybody
doesn't cooperate report it to me for—no, you don't need to report it to me, tell Miss Domiter and she can tell me so I can take
the necessary disciplinary action against the miscreants, so I'll
call Miss Domiter right now and instruct her to give you all the
assistance you need." She began to grope blindly behind herself
for her comm. "After all, the Department of Resources and
Survey is all about assisting people, even the Confederation military, and what the Confederation military wants my department's equipment for is none of my business nor is it the
business of any of my staff—" She jumped and gave out a small
shriek when Williams placed the comm in her hand. Her back
still turned, she pulled herself together and babbled into the
comm for a moment. When she'd finished giving her secretary
instructions, she went on. "Miss Domiter is ready to assist you,
gentlemen, it's been a true pleasure meeting you but now I have
important work to get to so if you'll excuse me . . ."

Sergeants Kindy and Williams didn't hear the rest of what
Director Phyllis Silverthorp had to say; they were on their way
out of her office as soon as she said her secretary was ready to
assist them.

Barbora Domiter wasn't as put off by the hovering heads and hands as was her boss; she seemed amused by the way her superior had reacted to the Marines.

"She's a political appointee," Miss Domiter whispered to the Marines. "Almost everybody knows to see me or one of the deputy directors if they need anything done." Then, in a normal speaking voice, she said, "What can I help you gentlemen with?"

Kindy and Williams grinned at each other and smiled at her. Her blond hair was obviously the result of outside intervention, but her charming smile implied that she'd altered the color for fun rather than vanity. Her eyes were so dark they were almost black. Even seated behind her desk, they could tell she had a shape that would turn men's heads when she walked past.

They told her what they wanted. She placed the order for everything but the comm scramblers. "We don't have scramblers in the inventory," she explained. "Only members of the board of directors have scramblers." She gave them a printout, along with another slip of paper.

"Go to this address." She marked a box on the printout. "They'll have everything ready for you. That's my personal number," she said, tapping the other piece of paper. "If you find yourselves at loose ends some evening and would like to see the sights of Sky City with a local guide, give me a call. I'll bring a friend."

"Thank you, Miss Domiter, we just might do that."

"Please, it's Barbora."

Kindy and Williams smiled broadly at her.

"My name's Him. He's D'Wayne."

"Pleased to meet you." She held her hand out.

Kindy shook it, then silently cursed himself for being so restrained when Williams kissed her hand and said, "The pleasure is ours."

They were back at Marine House with everything Ensign Daly had asked them to locate shortly after Daly returned from the meeting with Planetary Administrator Mullilee. The Marines all had a fine laugh when they listened to the recording of Daly's encounter with Mullilee and Miner.

"You may have turned him, boss," Kindy said.

Daly nodded. "I think I managed to convince him I'm highly fallible.

En Route to the Johnson Homestead

Ensign Daly was disgruntled when Planetary Administrator Mullilee failed to have the requested radar data ready by the time the Marines left for the Johnson homestead, but he didn't show it. Instead of discussing the lack of cooperation they were getting from the local government authorities, Daly encouraged his men to discuss the overall situation.

"They're hiding something," Sergeant Kindy said. His squad was in the lead Land Runner with Ensign Daly. The equipment he and Sergeant Williams had collected from the Department of Resources and Survey was in the second vehicle with Williams's squad.

"I know that, we all know that, and you keep saying it," Daly said.

"Johnson had a small mining operation," Kindy said, ignoring Daly's comment. "Miner controls most mining on Haulover. That put Johnson in direct competition with Miner."

"And Johnson was mining ruthenium," Corporal Nomonon added from the driver's seat, "a valuable element that Miner just had to want for himself."

Corporal Jaschke pitched in, saying, "So it sounds like a damn good motive for Miner to wipe Johnson out—so he could take over the ruthenium mine for himself."

"Then why were the couple of dozen earlier attacks against agricultural homesteads?" Daly asked. "Agro Herder is the agriculture baron." He looked at Lance Corporal Ellis.

Ellis took the hint. "Those raids may have been to throw off suspicion. Unless Herder's in on it with him."

"Or unless Herder was wiping out independent farms and Miner decided to sneak in and grab the ruthenium the same way Herder's been grabbing up independent farms," Nomonon said.

"That doesn't wash," Jaschke said. "The board wouldn't have let Mullilee call for help if they were behind the raids."

"Mullilee used a back channel instead of submitting a formal request," Daly told him. "The board might not have known about his message to Fargo."

Kindy snorted. "If Mullilee sent that back channel on his own, it's probably the only time he ever did something without getting Miner's permission first." He shook his head. "I don't think that man takes a shit without asking the board 'mother may I' first. How the hell does he keep his job? He's not doing anything for the Confederation; he just does the board's bidding."

"Planetary administrators are assigned to newly colonized worlds," Daly explained. "Maybe for a generation or so. Their job function is intermediary between the new world and the Confederation, making sure that the colony gets whatever assistance it needs to succeed, and to let the proper authorities know if anything is seriously out of line. So if things are going well, just about all a planetary administrator has to do is file progress reports."

Jaschke picked up the thought. "And things were going well on Haulover until the raids on homesteads started."

"Except for the board of directors running everything," Nomonon said.

"Some other worlds have boards of directors," Ellis objected.

"Yeah, but they don't run their worlds like a band of robber barons," Kindy snorted. "I still think Miner's involved."

Johnson Homestead, One Hundred Kilometers Northwest of Sky City

Only a few hours of daylight remained when the Marines reached the site of the former Johnson homestead, so they got to work immediately. Sergeant Kindy and his squad used ultra-violet lights and goggles, along with laser range finders and chemical sniffers, to examine the route the raiding party had followed between their aircraft and the homestead. Sergeant Williams and his squad plotted the destroyed area and used the same equipment, along with DNA sniffers, attempting to work out the sequence of events during the raid. They had no idea what they might find that the constabulary's forensics people hadn't found the day before. Nor had they any idea to what use they might put such information—or the findings of the police. But intelligence gathering is like police detective work and scientific research; you don't often know what you're going to find or what it means until you find it. Even when found, you don't always know what it means until sometime later—if then.

What that means, especially on a mission like this, is that you gather every bit of information you can find and hope it leads to some understanding. Unlike science, and more so than in police work, in military reconnaissance and intelligence, the information you don't have can kill you.

But they found nothing in the remains of the Johnson homestead to tell them who the raiders were, where they'd come from, or where they'd gone.

After two frustrating days at the Johnson homestead, Ensign Daly used one of the Mark IX Echo drones to send his first report back to Fourth Force Recon on Halfway. In it, he gave an update on the number and increasing frequency of the raids. He detailed the lack of cooperation from the local authorities and briefly noted his suspicions of what might be behind the raids. He also included trids of the site they'd examined, in the hope that someone in Fourth Fleet Marine G2 might be able to find something he and his Marines had missed.

During the following several days, the Marines visited the sites of the Claymont and Vijae homesteads. Each of them came up as empty as had the Johnson homestead.

They hadn't gone over even half of the Humblot homestead

when Daly got a call that caused him to shut down the operation there. The call was from the Sky City Police Department. Another homestead had just been wiped out—and this time, they had everything they needed to gather the intelligence.

"Saddle up," Daly ordered into his comm. "The raiders just hit somewhere else. We're going there while everything's still fresh."

In fifteen minutes they had everything loaded into their Land Runners and were driving away from the Humblot homestead, headed toward the Shazincho homestead.

CHAPTER SEVENTEEN

In the Air, En Route to the Shazincho Homestead, Haulover

The Pilot Master skillfully flew his aircraft nape-of-the-earth, keeping ridges and high trees between his craft and any radar stations whose reach might extend to this stretch of the world the Earthmen called Haulover. Usually the Pilot Master enjoyed his job; he loved flying for the greater honor and glory of the Emperor. But this was the eighteenth raiding mission he'd flown on this operation, and the mere display of his skill for the edification of the Master, Leaders, and Fighters carried in the cabin of his flyer had lost much of its luster—he had naught to do between touchdown and takeoff save wait. The Pilot Master did not take easily to waiting on the ground. He didn't even need to display his flying skills on these transport missions; the transport craft were stealthed, invisible to all the detection systems known to be on the Earthman world.

Oh, how the Pilot Master yearned for the honor of going along with the ground fighters, and reaping a share of the glory when they slaughtered the Earthmen in the outpost that was the target of the raid, and razed the outpost to the ground so that no stick stood together with another. *That* was where the glory was on this operation, not in flying, no matter how skillful that flying.

Until the Earthman Marines arrived. *Then* the Pilot Master would have his chance for glory, flying a killer craft to slaughter the Earthman Marines as they scattered on the ground like ants fleeing a stomping foot. Or flying against the so-called Raptors of the Earthman Marines, and swatting them out of the sky like so many mosquitoes.

That would be glory greater than these tiny raids against the small Earthman outposts.

But just then all the Pilot Master could do was demonstrate his flying skills in ferrying the ground fighters on their raids. And that ferrying was becoming a tedious chore.

The Pilot Master set his aircraft down in the exact center of his assigned landing zone and the thirteen-man raiding party disembarked and set off at a trot to the outpost they were to utterly destroy. The Pilot Master settled back in his seat to await their return.

Approaching the Shazincho Homestead, Three Hundred Kilometers North-Northwest of Sky City

The Master commanding the raiding party snarled orders at the two Leaders. The Leaders in turn growled the orders to the Fighters. The snarling and growling of the orders was hardly necessary; this particular raiding team had already conducted nine raids on the Earthman world called Haulover and rehearsed their raids so often they could nearly conduct them while estivating. The Master didn't bother inspecting the members of his raiding party, he'd inspected them before they boarded the transport craft. The Leaders gave the Fighters a cursory inspection, just enough to assure themselves that the Fighters hadn't left anything behind on the aircraft, and that the tanks on their backs were properly balanced and hoses connected.

The orders given, the ten Fighters assembled in two parallel lines behind the Leaders, who spaced themselves twenty meters apart, with the Master between them. At the Master's barked order, the two squads trotted rapidly toward the Earthman outpost. Nearing it, they heard the sounds of saws cutting through wood and the shouts of the Earthmen felling trees here and there as they thinned the forest and hauled trunks to the sawmill. About two hundred meters from where the trees were being cut, the squad on the left peeled away from the squad on the right, and the Master closed on the right-side squad. The Master stopped the remaining squad just out of sight of the Earthmen, and had the Leader of the squad with him emplace his Fighters. Then he waited for the signal from the Leader who was taking the other squad around to the opposite side of the outpost, near the sawmill, from which the Master heard a mechanical whining.

The Master concealed his impatience; he knew the wait was necessary if they were to let none get away. The Leader was less impatient, so he didn't attempt to conceal his mild eagerness for action. The Fighters were not at all impatient; the desire to do anything except what they were told had been bred out of them, and they waited docilely.

At the Shazincho Homestead

On the far side of the outpost, the Leader positioned his Fighters. Once he was satisfied that they were in the best positions to take their initial actions, he hefted the incendiaries and approached the sawmill in a crouch, staying out of sight of anyone who might happen to look into the forest behind the sawmill. There was no need for him to go quietly, the *zzzzz-zzzRRR-WHOMPF!* of the saws cutting tree trunks into planks covered any sounds he might have made; even the nearby gurgling of the stream that moved the mill's waterwheel, providing power for the saws, was drowned out by the saws. But the Leader could not shrug off his many years of training; he moved so silently he could not have been heard approaching even if saws weren't buzzing, planks thudding, and the stream gurgling.

Forty meters from the sawmill, a small movement in a window halfway up the wall facing him caught his eye and he froze. He looked, not moving his head, merely angling his eyes upward. An Earthman was there, just inside the window, leaning against the frame. His head was down, as though he was asleep.

Except the Leader knew that Earthmen didn't sleep standing up any more than true People did. A closer look at the details showed the Leader that the Earthman was armed—he was an armed guard! The first the Leader had seen on any of the raids he'd gone on. The Earthmen must be worried about the raids, and hoped to defend themselves against them. As if they could.

The Earthman's body began to slump, and he jerked, his head flipping up. Blinking, he looked around, even into the interior of the sawmill. Evidently satisfied that no one had seen him falling asleep on guard, he shifted the weapon in his arms and peered at the forest.

The Leader wasn't particularly worried about the Earthman's seeing him; his mud-colored uniform with its black and brown splotches blended in with the damp ground below the forest canopy, and he was still deep in the shadows of the trees. He waited patiently, and in a few more minutes the guard's head began to dip again.

The Leader rose from his crouch, made sure of his grip on his incendiaries, and sprinted on soft feet to the base of the sawmill's wall. Working quickly, he placed the incendiaries and daisy-chained them together.

That done, he had a decision to make: He could stay where he was and die in glory when he set off the incendiaries, and trust that his Fighters were well enough trained to perform their assignments without further leadership from him; or he could chance making it back into the trees unseen, and set off the charges from there. He slipped silently along the wall until he was directly under the window. He listened there, trying to discern any sounds below the din of the cutting inside. After a few moments he heard, as though from a remote distance, a cry, answered immediately by a shout from directly above, followed by faintly heard taps that might have been running feet.

Cautiously, the Leader leaned away from the wall and looked upward. He could see no part of the Earthman in the window. He took a step backward, still looking at the window, still saw nothing of the Earthman on watch. He spun about and dashed away from the wall, toward the safety of the forest shadows, his thumb on the ignition button of the controller clutched in his hand, half expecting the impact of fire or projectile in his back, resolved to press the button before he died.

Panting, he reached the trees without hearing a weapon fired anywhere in the outpost. He dove for the cover of a tree trunk and carefully looked around its base. The window was empty, the sentry was gone.

The Leader pressed the button. He had planted and daisy-chained his incendiaries properly; all along the length of the wall there were small explosions, and flames erupted at the base of the wall. Accelerants spewed upward by the shaped charges inside the incendiaries splashed on the wall and drew the flames higher and higher. In seconds, the fire reached the level of the window from which the sleepy guard had watched the forest.

Inside, the saws continued to whine, but the *thump* of falling boards ceased and the whine rose sharply in pitch. Cries of panicked Earthmen sounded from within, and men started racing out of the sides of the sawmill.

The Fighters were well positioned for what they had to do— they began firing at the Earthmen fleeing the burning sawmill. Greenish fluid streamed from the Fighters' weapons, arching at the Earthmen. The panicked cries of the Earthmen turned to shrill screams of agony when the green fluid struck them, and their flesh began to dissolve where the fluid stuck to them.

The Master watched as the Earthmen fled the sawmill before the flames became visible above the top of the building. It was the sign he'd been waiting for, and he barked out an order. The Leader began directing the fire of his Fighters, and green arcs struck out at the Earthmen felling trees at the edge of the clearing. In less than a minute, all of the lumberjacks were down, writhing in the throes of death. Then the Leader had the Fighters stand and advance, shooting as they went at the Earthmen visible in the open between the edge of the trees and the sawmill.

Sword in hand, the Master trailed behind the squad, checking the Earthmen who fell at the edge of the trees. Where one still gasped, the blade slashed across the Earthman's throat. The Master continued into the clearing, ignoring the sporadic gunfire that came from the clearing's remaining buildings, and dispatched any Earthmen he found still alive.

The Leader saw that his Fighters were fully engaged in killing Earthmen, and the Earthmen's attempt at defense was too feeble to cause much concern, so he ran zigzag to the nearest building and tossed an incendiary through a window. The Leader didn't wait to see the flames, but ran to the next building, from which someone was firing a projectile weapon. He ignored the flaming Earthman who ran out of the building he'd just ignited. When the Earthman collapsed and began twisting into a fetal position directly in front of him, he sidestepped the body without more than a glance to note its position.

Alongside the next building, the Leader readied another incendiary, and sidled to the window through which the projectile weapon was firing. He got a good grip on the incendiary, thumbed off the safety, and shot his hand inside the window to whip the device down, to go off when it struck the floor. He yanked his hand back out before the Earthman inside could react to it—but not before the incendiary went off, splashing the Leader's hand and wrist with flame and accelerant. He didn't have time to scream before flame completely engulfed him and vaporized him.

The Master saw the incident, and his nostrils flared above gritted teeth. That Leader had been with him on all of his raids, and knew how to lead his Fighters. But evidently he didn't know all ways of best using the incendiaries, or he wouldn't have immolated himself. The Master curled his lip and snarled. Now he would have to waste time integrating a new Leader into his section. That meant he would be held back from raids until he and the Senior Master commanding him were satisfied with the performance of the new Leader. It would be weeks before he was allowed again to gather glory slaughtering Earthmen.

He cursed the dead Leader.

The Leader beyond the sawmill had been busy making certain his Fighters killed all the Earthmen who fled the burning building. When the sawmill was totally aflame, and all of the Earthmen who had gotten out of it lay still on the ground, he ordered his Fighters forward, three to the upstream side, where they swam across the millpond, the other two with him on the downstream side, where they splashed across the mill run. The squad reassembled beyond the flames. No living Earthmen were in sight. But buildings still stood untouched. The Leader ordered his Fighters to be alert and to shoot immediately any Earthmen they saw—especially any Earthmen who might threaten him—and ran to the nearest building to set it afire.

When all the buildings in the Earthman outpost were aflame, the Master ordered the remaining Leader to consolidate all the Fighters into one squad and put them to work gathering the Earthman bodies and undamaged weapons. The corpses were then doused with accelerants and tossed into whatever buildings were still burning.

At length, satisfied that no board would be left standing against another, and that the bodies of the Earthmen would be fully consumed by the conflagration, the Master ordered his section to pick up the captured projectile throwers, formed the Fighters into one column, and led them at a trot back to the transport craft.

The Pilot Master noticed that the returning raiding party was short one Leader but he made no comment.

CHAPTER
EIGHTEEN

En Route to the Shazincho Homestead, Haulover

Planetary Administrator Mullilee's office had not been very informative about what had happened at the Shazincho homestead when they radioed Ensign Daly. Mullilee had already left and the clerical person he had call the Marines had only the most basic information, only the name and coordinates of the homestead, and that it had been destroyed and there was no sign of the homesteaders.

Haulover might not have had surveillance satellites, but it did have the geosync comm satellite. Daly had Corporal Belinski use the comm net to get into the planetary database and ferret out everything it had on the Shazincho homestead. Which was enough to give the Marines what they needed to know going in. The database even had information on the results of the attack.

The Shazincho homestead had been established only a couple of months earlier as a logging and woodcutting operation specializing in the hardwoods most desired for the finishing details of new housing in the colony. The Shazinchos had laid claim to a twelve hundred square kilometer stretch of forest at the foot of a spur of the Northern Range Mountains. In addition to the six members of the Shazincho family, the homestead employed nine lumberjacks and sawmill workers. They intended to practice sustainable forestry, cutting down selected mature trees rather than clear-cutting the forest. Thanks to the cost of equipment, and construction of the living quarters, sawmill, and other buildings, the Shazinchos didn't expect to break even, much less show a profit, for at least three years. Now it looked as though they would never break even—everything was destroyed, and it seemed likely that all fifteen people at the homestead were dead.

From the Marines' point of view, the worst part of what the data showed was that the raid had taken place right after dawn that morning. Yet the planetary administrator hadn't seen fit to notify them until *after* he and the forensics people reached the site.

The Marines might have been able to track the raiders immediately had they been notified right away. They were worried that the delay could cost more homesteads.

Ensign Daly had had to calm himself down during the three-hour drive to the Shazincho homestead; his anger at the notification delay kept threatening to overwhelm him. Fortunately, he hadn't tried to keep it bottled in, but talked it over with Sergeant Kindy and his squad during the trip.

The thing that eventually tipped the balance in favor of calm was Kindy's reminding him, "Remember what Sergeant Williams and I had to say to you."

Daly took a deep breath and held it for a long moment before letting it out again. "You were right then," he admitted, "and you're right now. Thanks." He turned to the other three Marines in the landcar and said, "No, I'm not going to tell you what that was about."

The Shazincho Homestead

The road through the forest didn't cut straight through the trees, but wound its way, so that the smallest possible number of young trees was sacrificed to make it. So the Marines were nearly on the site before they could see it. The data they'd downloaded from the planetary net had them prepared for what they saw, including the small number of trees still standing in

the cleared area. Corporal Nomonon parked the landcar near a
severely burned tree. Lance Corporal Skripska, driving the
other landcar, parked with its nose almost touching the tail of
the lead vehicle.

The Marines saw Planetary Administrator Mullilee and
Chairman Miner, along with eight or ten people in constabulary jackets, some of which identified them as from the forensics division. But General Pokoj Vojak was notably absent, and
no soldiers were in evidence.

"Helmets on," Daly ordered on his all-hands circuit. "Two
men from each squad, keep your infras in place, and watch for
hot spots that don't belong to the fires. Squad leaders, with
me." He opened the landcar's door and dismounted.

Spilk Mullilee was already approaching him at a brisk walk,
almost a trot. The planetary administrator glanced nervously
over his shoulder right before he stopped in front of Daly.

"I-I'm sorry, Mr. D-Daly," Mullilee stammered. "I wanted to
n-notify you as soon as I h-heard about th-this, but Mr.
M-Miner insi-insisted that our people investigate before you
c-came and . . . and m-messed things up." He swallowed. "Th-
That's what h-he said."

"Don't worry about it," Daly told him, though that certainly
wasn't what he was thinking. Miner's deliberate delay in noti-
fying the Marines just made him more determined to learn if
the chairman of the board had any connection to the raids.
"Where are General Vojak and his soldiers?"

Mullilee shook his head. "W-We didn't th-think we needed
them here. N-Not with the M-Marines."

The corner of Daly's mouth twitched. He was going to have
to review the recordings from Mullilee's office and see if the
absence of the minister of war and his soldiers was Miner's
doing.

He asked, "What have your people found so far?"

Before Mullilee could answer, Miner came up. "All they've
found is exactly what was found at the other destroyed homesteads," the chairman said. "Exactly nothing that we can use to

find out who's responsible." He looked sour, as though the lack of evidence was a personal affront.

"Did your people find where the raiders came from?" Daly asked; his voice was almost meek, causing Mullilee to look at him with something approaching despair.

Miner shook his head and waved a hand. "Out there someplace. That's all I can tell you." He looked Daly in the eye. "You're supposed to be the trackers. So start tracking." With that, he turned on his heel and stalked away.

Daly watched Miner's back for a moment, then gave his orders. "Sergeant Kindy, take your squad and find out where they came from. Sergeant Williams, track their movements in the compound." Then to Mullilee: "I need to speak to your people, learn what they've found out. Don't worry, we'll get to the bottom of this. And when we do, whoever is responsible is going to be very, *very* sorry."

"Y-Yes, right away," Mullilee said. He looked at Daly with confusion; unlike when the Marine had spoken to Miner, there was nothing whatsoever meek in his voice now.

"One more thing, Mr. Mullilee. It took us three hours to get here by landcar. We need an aircraft."

Mullilee swallowed and looked to the sides before saying, "I can probably get an aircraft and p-pilot for you."

Daly shook his head. "Thank you, sir, but all I need is a light aircraft. Three of us have licenses to pilot light aircraft."

Mullilee's surprise was visible. There was more to these Force Recon Marines than he'd realized—and, he thought, more than Smelt Miner suspected.

Overlooking the Shazincho Homestead

The Master lay hidden by bushes that grew along the side of the watercourse that led to the destroyed sawmill and observed the homestead through powerful optics. His location was on the side of the mountain down which flowed the stream that powered the mill. He grinned around pointed teeth as the

Earthmen sifted futilely through the ash and rubble of the outpost, knowing that they would find little or nothing to tell them
what had happened—or who had done it. *Watching* the Earthmen conduct their pathetic forensic examinations was almost
as amusing as actually *leading* a raid. He wished the Over Master commanding the People's operation on this world would
send Masters to observe the aftermath of every raid, instead of
only half of them. Moreover, he wished that he himself was
assigned to observe more aftermaths. That and be assigned to
lead more raids. But there were many Masters who deserved
to lead raids and observe aftermaths, though not enough to observe all and still be able to properly supervise the Leaders who
kept the Fighters in proper discipline. He could not expect to be
given as many assignments as he would like.

Movement at the far side of the raid site caught the Master's
eye, and he shifted the optics. Two more landcars entered the
site but from a different direction from which the Earthmen already present had come.

At the approach of the two vehicles, an Earthman supervising
the sifting looked up and raised a hand. The landcars closed on
him and stopped a few meters away. The doors of the landcar
nearer the supervising Earthman opened and closed—but the
Master saw no one get out. Then the other landcar's doors
opened and closed, but the Master couldn't see whether anybody
got out since his view was occluded by a tree trunk. He wondered what was going on, then wondered even more when two
of the supervising Earthmen began talking to the air before
them, and gesturing. The Master shifted his view to the space
just in front of the Earthmen and his heart leaped in his chest.

Heads hovered in the air!

Earthman Marines had finally arrived!

The Master slithered from under the concealing bushes, and
scooted along the bank below its top, to where three Leaders and
six Fighters awaited his pleasure. Speaking curtly in a low growl
he gave instructions to one of the Leaders.

After the designated Leader repeated the message he was to

deliver, he ran, crouched, accompanied by a Fighter, along the stream's edge until he reached a tributary that runneled out of the forest and changed direction to follow the smaller streamlet.

When his runner had gone, the Master returned to his observation post. The two remaining Leaders and five Fighters were more alert than they had been before. None of them had experience fighting the Earthman Marines but they all knew the reputation of their foes. They mentally prepared themselves to die in the service of the Emperor.

The Other Side of the Mountain

"Earthman Marines," the Leader barked when he reached the aircraft that waited in a defile on the far side of the mountain down which the millstream flowed.

The Pilot Master's eyes widened with anticipation. Finally, he would have his chance to kill the Earthman Marines! But he knew his duty; first he had to transport the Leader to the base of the People's Army so the Leader could report what the observing Master had learned. The Pilot Master lifted his aircraft high enough to clear the low-lying brush and trees, then headed at the greatest speed he dared, keeping at all times below the level of the ridgetops so his transport craft wouldn't be spied by Earthman radar.

Headquarters, Emperor's Third Composite Corps

The Grand Master listened intently to the Over Master who knelt before him, forehead to the reed floor mat. Four Large Ones were arrayed behind the Grand Master, long swords in their hands, ready to protect their lord from interlopers who might enter the cavern used as the Grand Master's Hall. Lamps with mirrored backs stood around the perimeter of the cavern and hangings behind the lamps disguised the walls, making the cavern look more like a constructed room than a natural cave. Unseen Leaders and Fighters lurked behind the hangings, providing far more security against interlopers than the Large Ones possibly could. A Great Master, the Grand Master's chief of staff, stood next to the kneeling Over Master, sword in hand, ready to decapitate the kneeling Over Master should he sufficiently displease the Grand Master.

The Over Master was the Grand Master's chief of intelligence, and the intelligence he was delivering was most interesting. So much so that when the report was finished the Grand Master commanded the Over Master to sit back on his heels and deliver it again. The Grand Master's voice was rugged, raspy; as with nearly all Masters of the Emperor's army who attained such high rank, the Grand Master had not exercised his gills in so long that they had atrophied; the atrophied gill slits were warped, as were some of the underlying gills, allowing air from under his arms, as well as from his lungs, to exit through his larynx, affecting his voice. The change in the voices of high-ranking Masters did not bother them; when they growled or barked with their rugged, raspy voices, they sounded so much more threatening than the growls and barks of lesser-level Masters who routinely—or at least occasionally—did breathe underwater.

The Over Master rocked back onto his heels and raised his face to his Grand Master, but respectfully kept his eyes on the mat before his knees. He repeated the report of Earthman Marines being seen at the site of the latest raid.

Pleased not only with the report but with the high degree of respect with which it was delivered, the Grand Master clapped his hands imperiously. A diminutive female glided into the hall, half-bent at the waist, eyes on the floor before her, and awaited instructions. The Grand Master growled and the female glided out of the hall. A moment later she and two other diminutive females glided into the hall.

The first female bore a tray on which stood a slender vase with a single flower from Home and a delicate cup. She gracefully knelt and placed the tray on a stand next to the Grand Master. The second female carried a tray with short legs, also adorned with a flowered vase and cup. She knelt gracefully next to the Over Master and placed the tray next to his knee. The third female brought a tray with two steaming pots. She approached the Grand Master, bowed low at the waist, and extended the tray to the kneeling female, who took one of the pots and poured a small amount of hot beverage from the pot into the delicate cup. After lowering the pot to her tray, she picked up the cup and drank it dry.

The Grand Master watched with seemingly minor interest and, after a couple of moments during which the kneeling female showed no signs of distress, gestured for her to pour the cup full, and for the female with the tray now bearing one pot to deliver it to the Over Master's servant. The Grand Master's servant poured beverage into the cup and raised it in the fingertips of both hands, lifting it to where he could easily reach it. She kept her eyes averted downward.

Instead of taking the offered cup, the Grand Master growled at the Great Master, instructing him to assemble the staff; now that the Earthman Marines had finally arrived, it was time to begin planning to annihilate them.

While the Grand Master was instructing the Great Master, the Over Master drank deeply and accepted a second cupful of the steaming beverage, which he sipped more sedately. He listened intently while the Grand Master instructed him to gather more intelligence on the numbers and disposition of the Earthman Marines.

Some minutes had passed since the Grand Master's servant had sipped from his cup, and neither she nor the Over Master were displaying any signs of distress. The Grand Master finally accepted the cup and drank from it.

CHAPTER
NINETEEN

The commanders and staff officers of Task Force Aguinaldo perspired quietly as the huge overhead fans languidly stirred the stultifying air. Nobody noticed the sticky heat. All eyes and ears were on General Anders Aguinaldo. He was not a big man and, in his sweat-stained utilities, he looked no different than the dozens of other officers crammed into the big hall. But when the short brown man opened his mouth he seemed to grow in size. He spoke with a powerful voice using a soldier's vocabulary, and he had the uncanny ability to appear to be looking each officer straight in the eye as if he were speaking to each man and woman personally, saying to them as individuals, "You are good enough to be on my team so I know you're good enough to make this work."

"People, I have called you here to announce the next phase in the preparation of this task force for battle. You have all done a fine job training and reorganizing your respective commands and I hereby commend all concerned." The Marine four-star smiled. "And I expect official commendations to be showing up for signature in my office for those of your personnel who were most outstanding in this long and sometimes painful process. Now we are ready to put this task force through its paces.

"We are all going into the field, people, every last one of us. I have scheduled the first of several field training exercises designed to test the ability of your commands to work together under simulated combat conditions. I don't want to hear anybody refer to these exercises as 'war games.' War is no game, as those of us who've been there know. So-called war games are plotted by eggheads far removed from battle, men who *think* they know their asses from their elbows—but they don't know jack shit about war, off in their 'war rooms' playing with their sand tables and virtual battlefield arrays. We won't have any of that here."

Colonel Raggel, sitting in the back of the room with Sergeant Major Steiner, whispered, "This is going to be good, Top!"

"I have arranged for permanent-party units stationed here on Arsenault to be the aggressors. They have been fully trained on all known aspects of Skink tactics. They'll be out there somewhere," he said, gesturing at the surrounding jungle, "waiting for you to come and get them. I worked personally with those people to set up their mission. Nobody on my staff has a clue about who they are or how many of them there are or where they are. I've also arranged with Arsenault Training Command to flood the operational area with an 'indigenous' population that has the express mission of getting in your way. . . ."

"We'll straighten that out," Raggel whispered.

". . . When this operation kicks off, General Cumberland, my chief of staff, will assume overall command of the task force. I will remain loose and go out with the umpires. Your job will be to work together, use your reconnaissance and intelligence assets, find the enemy, fix him, and fight him. You will learn to work together.

"We still have a few units that haven't yet been briefed on the enemy's capabilities and operational tactics."

"That's us," Raggel whispered.

"Most of you have. When every command is up to speed on that this exercise will commence. We're going to call it Operation Slogger because that's what you'll all be doing out there. I expect it to last ten days. Every swinging Richard and every pendulous Jane will deploy to the field, including my head-quarters staff.

"I am going to leave you now with General Cumberland. He will give you the order of battle for this exercise. Get to know your sister units. Liaise, people, liaise. Next time we meet it'll be for the postoperation debriefing. It's going to be a rough two weeks but hardly as rough as actual combat will be, and when we come to that you will be ready and you will kick some Skink ass."

Lecture Hall, Seventh Independent Military
Police Battalion, Fort Keystone

"Tennnns-*hut*!" Command Sergeant Major Steiner bellowed as General Aguinaldo, followed immediately by Colonel Raggel and a Marine corporal marched onto the stage.

"Take your seats, men, take your seats," Aguinaldo said, standing at the podium. Large circles of perspiration stained the armpits of his utilities but nobody noticed; everyone perspired in this region of Arsenault. Fans slowly stirred the hot, humid air in the lecture hall. The men of the Seventh Independent MPs were used to it.

"Men, I apologize that it's taken me this long to get around to visiting you, but I have been unavoidably detained elsewhere." He smiled and a murmur of laughter circulated through the hall. He liked what he saw there, five hundred men under arms, fit, alert, ready for action. He nodded appreciatively at Colonel Raggel. At that the men broke into a thunderous cheer.

"I also apologize, gentlemen, that we couldn't have given you today's lecture a lot earlier." He nodded at the Marine corporal sitting just behind him on the stage. "Everyone in this task force is receiving the same course of instruction but, since we don't have that many men with the experience Corporal Wade here has, we just had to work our way to you. The maneuver elements had to come first because they're going to have first contact with the enemy. That's not to denigrate you or anybody else in this task force, but you all know the infantry leads the way. Corporal Wade will be with you for several days. During that time he will impart to you everything we know about our enemy. He has seen that enemy up close and personal. Pay very close attention to what he's going to tell you.

"Now, you all know we're going to have a big field training exercise soon, a major maneuver operation. I am going to put this task force through its paces, see how we operate as an army in a combat zone. The Seventh MPs will have a role in these maneuvers." Aguinaldo smiled again. "I've arranged to have several thousand recruits from the training depots on Arsenault participate as refugee role players and it will be your job to process them and keep order among them and"—here he paused, grinning—"do anything else that might pop up. This is to prepare you to deal with our own people if and when the Skinks show up in force somewhere in Human Space. If—make that when—we find their home world, your role there will be to keep our men from killing them all." At this the crowd burst into a long roar of cheering and whistling. Aguinaldo, grinning, held up his arms for quiet. "Well, I like your spirit." He laughed and the cheering broke out all over again.

When the men were silent at last, Aguinaldo said, "All right, men, I'm going to withdraw and leave the stage to Corporal Wade. He has seen the Skinks.

"Men, you've done a good job and I'm proud to have the Seventh Independent Military Police Battalion as a part of my task force." To the men assembled in the hall that was the finest compliment anyone had ever paid them. All the embarrassment and disgrace that had followed them from Ravenette, the years of neglect and lack of discipline that had marked them as the "renegade battalion" at home, all that vanished at Aguinaldo's words and every man present knew that when the task force finally went up against the enemy, he would have the chance to squash some Skink ass.

"Tennnnns-*hut!*" Sergeant Major Steiner roared. The men jumped to attention. General Aguinaldo and Colonel Raggel left the hall. "Awrrrright, ladies," Steiner said, "at ease. This here is Corporal Wade and he is in charge here until he's finished with you. I catch anybody goofing off or dozing during these lectures—you officers excepted, of course—I am gonna kick his ass for him.

"Now here's how this is gonna work: First and Second Companies remain seated. Today's your day, you lucky bastards. I guarantee ya, when Corporal Wade gets through today you'll *never* go near swampy ground again." He grinned evilly at Corporal Wade who nodded grimly. "Third and Fourth Companies will report here at zero-eight hours tomorrow. Staff and support, you get it the third day. Awrrrright, move, move, move!"

After the excused personnel had left the hall, Steiner turned to the Marine. "Corporal Wade?"

The Marine stepped to the podium. "My name is Corporal Manning Wade of the Twenty-sixth Fleet Initial Strike Team. I was on Kingdom." With that he removed his tunic and exposed his left side to the audience. This drew a collective gasp. "These scars are mementos of a Skink acid gun I ran into on Kingdom." He grinned as he put his tunic back on. "Another graft and I'll be as good as new. Before we deploy, you will all be issued acid-resistant field uniforms. But, gentlemen, I show you this so you will have some idea of what we were up against. Rest assured, however, the enemy knows our weapons too. They learned about them the hard way. Those Skinks don't fool around and they don't worry about getting themselves wasted. They are experts at sneaking up on you and pulling a kamikaze attack. Next time we meet up with them you can expect they've compensated for our superior firepower. Meanwhile, I'm going to teach you everything we know about them, so settle back, smoke 'em if you got 'em, and enjoy the show."

Nobody in the Seventh MP Battalion talked about anything for the next three days but the Skinks. Corporal Manning Wade, Confederation Marine Corps, was the most popular man in the battalion during that time.

Puella Queege and Sergeant Oakley sat together during the lecture on the third day. By then it was clear to her and everyone else in the battalion how deadly serious the threat from the aliens was and how important their mission was in support of Task Force Aguinaldo. Each man in the battalion knew perfectly well that he'd been sent to Arsenault by his army command to get rid of him, how much work had gone into shaping up the battalion, and how abysmally shortsighted army command back on Lannoy really was about the threat the Skinks posed to all of humanity. Each man in the battalion was very proud that he had qualified to remain part of the task force. Those Colonel Raggel had sent home had bragged before they left that they were getting the better part of the deal, but the men remaining behind came to understand that they'd been given a great honor.

"Goddamn," someone was heard saying after the first day's lecture, "glad we got them Marines on our side!"

Headquarters, Task Force Aguinaldo, Camp Swampy

General Aguinaldo's field training exercise, or FTX, involving two hundred thousand men operating over ten thousand square kilometers of jungle, was not entirely successful, at least not by his standards. The major problem he encountered was the lack of communication between maneuver elements, which led to poor coordination of battle operations. That was complicated by the rugged terrain over which the troops had to operate. Units moving through triple-canopy jungle on foot, subject to ambushes at any time, found it very difficult to link with other units moving against the enemy, which upset the ambitious time schedules devised by staff officers operating just behind the battle front. But by the end of the first week, everyone in the task force was beginning to get a clear idea of what it would be like to encounter the Skinks in terrain favorable to the enemy's weapons and tactics.

If time was on his side, General Aguinaldo planned to move

his training activities into the temperate zone of Arsenault and even to one of its moons so that if the Skinks were encountered in those environments his troops would be able to deal with them properly. Considering the apparent cold-blooded nature of the Skinks that had been encountered thus far, he did not think it worth his time and effort to train the task force under polar conditions.

General Aguinaldo's mandate gave him control over every aspect of operations on Arsenault. All normal training operations ceased during the FTX because all military personnel, cadre and trainees, and every civilian employee working in support of Training Command were detailed to support the exercise. Marine and army reconnaissance personnel, together with infantrymen in their final weeks of advanced training, were designated as aggressor forces and given instruction in the use of Skink tactics; basic training and boot camp personnel, along with designated civilians, made up the "indigenous population" encountered in the maneuver areas that had to be protected and evacuated. That is where the Seventh MPs came into their own.

"Rene," Aguinaldo told Colonel Raggel after a staff conference critiquing the recently concluded FTX, "your battalion outdid itself. I am amazed at what you've done with those men—oh, and that one woman." He smiled because, during the course of the exercise, he'd several times met Sergeant Queege in Raggel's retinue.

"Thank you, sir, and I'll pass that on to my men."

"You do. Give them a training holiday; they deserve a break."

"Sir, one question?" Aguinaldo nodded. "Do you think we'll ever get a chance to capture one of those Skinks?"

Aguinaldo hesitated briefly. "No, Rene, I doubt it. If any are captured, the scientific boys will grab them and haul them off to a lab somewhere. And you know how careful the Skinks are about letting their dead fall into our hands." He shook his head. "Even so, Rene, your men will have their hands full when the time comes, no doubt about that. They performed magnificently during this FTX. The umpire reports just glowed with praise for your people. Every man and woman in this task force is dedicated to beating these things, and together that is just what we are going to do. We are going to win."

But far, far behind General Aguinaldo's back, forces were hard at work to ensure that did not happen.

CHAPTER
TWENTY

Rooftop Landing Pad, Ministry of Justice, Fargo, Earth

Dr. Hans Jeroboam's face turned white as he looked at the huge storm coming in from the northwest. "Maybe we should take the underground, AG?" he asked Huygens Long nervously, casting a fearful sidelong glance at the approaching blackness. A sudden, powerful gust of wind tore at the pair as they got into the hopper.

"Nonsense, J.B.! We've got a meeting with the president in ten minutes and we're not going to be late." He patted the pocket where he was carrying all the evidence he thought they'd need to get Chang-Sturdevant to agree to Jasper's arrest. He was secretly amused at the scientist's nervous reaction to flying in a storm.

"Sir?" The crew chief leaned over and yelled at the two officials as they boarded the flier. "That storm is moving slowly but there's a lot of turbulence, so please strap in during the flight. The pilot says you may have to take ground transport coming back. We'll let you know, sir."

"Oh, hell," Jeroboam muttered, but his words were snatched away on the wind.

"Hell of a night to be up high!" Long chortled as he strapped himself in. Jeroboam groaned.

Office of the President, Confederation of Human Worlds

"I don't know, I don't know," President Cynthia Chang-Sturdevant said as she shook her head.

"Ma'am, the evidence is all there. It's quite clear. We have to act and we have to do it right now." Huygens Long's face was red with frustration. He'd never seen Chang-Sturdevant so indecisive. He wondered if Jasper had somehow cast a spell over the president when he met with her. He shook his head. Ridiculous. But why was she dithering?

"Madam President, the AG is right. These tests, these analyses, everything points to the fact that Mr. Jasper is an agent of the Skinks. If not a conscious agent, he's working under their influence. If he is not stopped he could destroy this Confederation." Dr. Jeroboam was also frustrated, although he did not show it as plainly as the attorney general. "Everything fits," he added.

Chang-Sturdevant sighed. "Marcus?" She turned to Marcus Berentus, who had had his doubts about the relationship between Jasper and the president, especially after the way she had talked to him in the hallway after his visit.

"Ma'am, Hugh is right. The man must be arrested."

"You gentlemen know that if we go forward with Hugh's recommendation, we're liable to have serious riots on our hands? Jasper has created an enormous following in only the short time he's been preaching. We'll have to deal with that. We are going to become very unpopular over this."

"Madam, we are going to become very *dead* if this man succeeds in weakening our preparations against the Skinks. The fate of all humanity hangs on the decision you are about to make," Long said.

"Senator Maxim has already introduced a rider on the upcoming appropriations bill that would reduce funding for Task Force Aguinaldo," Marcus added grimly.

"I know, I know. And he's gathered forty cosigners to the measure." Chang-Sturdevant pursed her lips pensively and scratched the side of her face, considering. She looked at the three men. She was not that familiar with Dr. Jeroboam, but she knew Long and Berentus intimately and had always relied on their advice—she trusted them. She sighed. "During my administration we've done some mighty extralegal things out of expediency. But this time we're doing it right. We're going to have to lay all this out to the public, and we'd damned well better have all our ducks lined up. Dan," she spoke into her intercom, "get Chief Justice Borden on the screen."

Chief Justice G. F. Borden of the Confederation Supreme Court was still in his chambers when Chang-Sturdevant appeared on his vid screen. He was not happy to be disturbed at that late hour and said so. The president had interrupted the weekly poker game with his colleagues and he was losing. The call came through just as he looked at his cards. Aces over on the jacks or better deal. The best hand he'd had all evening.

"We're coming over, G.F.," Chang-Sturdevant said. "On a matter of the utmost importance. I'll explain when we get there."

"Well, it damned well better be, Madam President," Borden growled. "I got a matter of importance myself. How long till you get here?"

"Five minutes." The screen went dead.

"Goddamn, goddamn, goddamn," Borden muttered. "I open for five hundred." He lost the hand to another justice who had three deuces. So he was not in the best of humor when he excused himself to talk to the president.

Office of the Chief Justice, Supreme Court of the Confederation of Human Worlds

"G.F., you know Marcus and Hugh. This is Dr. Jeroboam, chief forensic scientist at the Ministry of Justice," President Chang-Sturdevant began without preamble.

"Who do you want to arrest now?" Justice Borden said.

"You know," Chang-Sturdevant said in a conversational

tone, "I *never* would have appointed you chief justice, never in a million years."

Borden snorted. "I'm aware of that, Madam President, but you have to deal with me, and I plan to head this court for at least another million years, long after you are no longer the president of this Confederation. Now who in the hell do you want arrested?

"I want you to issue a warrant to the AG for the arrest of Jimmy Jasper."

Chief Justice Borden started violently and looked askance at his visitors. "What's the matter, you don't like his preaching?" Borden growled. "You'd better have a mighty damned good reason."

"We do," she replied, and laid it all out for him.

Eight Hundred Meters, Descending, over Senator Maxim's Villa, on the Outskirts of Fargo

The two officers from the Presidential Security Detachment, their faces white with fear, sat across from Huygens Long and Dr. Jeroboam as the hopper lurched and plummeted up and down in the turbulence; large hailstones pelted the machine. "Hold on!" the crew chief said over the headsets. "Only a couple of minutes and we'll set 'er down!" The floor in the passenger compartment was slick with vomit, but the four men strapped into their seats hardly even noticed.

The flight out of the city in the storm had been terrifying, each of the four men certain the next moment would be his last as the machine flew between and around the high government buildings of the inner city. No one on board was more upset than the pilot, who had argued with Long that they shouldn't try flying out to Senator Maxim's villa until the storm abated. They'd had a shouting match on the presidential hopper pad.

"I'm the pilot and I say if we can fly or not. It is not safe to fly in this weather! This is a supercell storm and we've been warned that a tornado has been spotted to our west. It's crazy to fly in this weather!" the young woman had shouted into Long's ear.

"Goddammit, we're on business of the *utmost* importance to this Confederation! If you don't get us out there in this thing you'll be lucky to fly a kite after today. I mean it. Now get this thing airborne and let's get on out there!" Long had screamed at her above the wind. She had given in but she was regretting it.

Miraculously, just as the villa came into sight, the storm abated. The hopper landed smoothly in the senator's garden. "You'll all get medals for this!" Long shouted into the cockpit as he unsnapped his harness. "Let's get in there and nab this guy!" he told the security officers. He jumped out into a flower bed. It was eerily quiet all around them. "Wait for us here!" he told the pilot as he slogged ankle deep through the senator's pansies. "If the storm starts up again, we'll hold out here until it's over. Come on!" he yelled at the two officers, and, trailed by them and Dr. Jeroboam, he headed for the villa.

"I don't like these weather conditions," the young aviator said to her copilot. "Keep an eye out. This is too weird."

"It's a hell of a relief, after that storm," the crew chief said.

The three sat silently for a few minutes and then the pilot suddenly said, "Holy shit! Shut 'er down, guys. We're going inside. Now!"

The four men stormed into the house and began searching the rooms. It was empty. "Jesus H. Christ!" Long swore. He stood in the living room. "Nobody?" he asked the two officers, who recovered their professional faces and were all business as soon as the chopper landed. They shook their heads.

"Now what?" Jeroboam asked. "Don't tell me we're flying back into the city in that thing, AG! No thanks, I'll walk!" He laughed. He had just learned what it was to cheat death and he enjoyed the rush it had given him, and his lunch.

"You can't get out of this, J.B. I've deputized you." Long scratched his head.

At that moment the hopper pilot, her copilot, and the crew chief came crashing screaming into the living room. "Take cover!" she shrieked. A tremendous roar quickly grew louder outside the house. Long looked at her in disbelief and was about to say something when she yelled, *"Tornado!"*

"Where's the basement?" the crew chief asked.

"Doesn't have one!" a security officer shouted. "Find the johns! Take cover in the bathrooms!" He ran to the back of the house and everyone else followed him. They all piled into a rather small bathroom. The next few seconds were pure terror as the twister roared over the house, ripping it to pieces and passing on as quickly as it had struck.

Huygens Long couldn't believe he was still alive. "Is everybody all right?" he asked, brushing plaster fragments out of his hair. He could see someone's legs under the sink; someone beneath what looked like a door groaned. Jeroboam was sitting up in the bathtub, looking around in amazement at the wreckage.

The hopper pilot, about thirty with pretty blond hair that hung in bedraggled strands about her face, sat up painfully. She looked back the way they had come and groaned. The entire house was gone. She could look straight into the garden. She gasped. "My hopper! It's *gone*!" She turned to Long. *"You owe me a new hopper!"* Something had hit her just above her right eye and a long stream of blood dripped down her face and jaw. Her right eye was closed. She glared at Long fiercely with a big, bright, blue left eye.

"Madam," Long sighed, "I'll get you a new hopper. You can have all the bells and whistles on it you want. But after what you've been through for us today, anytime you like you call Huygens Long, give him five minutes to gather a crowd, and he'll gladly kiss your beautiful little derriere."

She seemed to consider that proposal for a moment and then said, "That's okay, sir; after what you've put me through today, I'll settle for that fucking kite instead."

Long nodded and said, "Well, people, I guess we'll just have to go after our man tomorrow."

Senator Maxim's Penthouse Apartment, Fargo

Jimmy's meeting with the twelve disciples—twelve believers, twelve powerful and influential men that Senator Maxim had arranged—was to take place in his penthouse apartment in downtown Fargo. Aside from the villa on the outskirts of town, which he'd given over to Jimmy, the senator owned several other properties in and around the capital. But the fashionable penthouse atop the Dirlik Building, named in honor of the famous Wiccan priestess and philanthropist, was where he lived when Congress was in session. It had all the modern conveniences. From its position atop the ninety-story complex, one had a spectacular view that on a clear day stretched over a hundred kilometers in every direction.

To beat the incoming storm, Jimmy and Sally had arrived early at the apartment. Senator Maxim's long white mane glistened in the bright lighting and contrasted brilliantly with the darkness that had fallen outside. Tremendous flashes of lightning lanced the horizon and the wind outside had risen to gale force. But inside the penthouse, the storm outside was hardly noticeable.

"I'm going down to the lobby, Reverend," the senator said after making his guests comfortable, "to escort our visitors up here. We'll meet in the party room. Can my servants get you refreshments?"

"Thank you, my son. Natural springwater, if you've got it." Jimmy smiled. Sally, sitting by his side, grimaced inwardly. She could still taste the excellent coffee the attorney general had given her that morning.

"Then, Reverend, Miss Consolador, I shall leave you now, but for just a few moments. I expect the storm will have delayed some of our guests. I hope that will not inconvenience you?"

"Why should it when eternity lies before us, Senator? Besides, the heavens are God's handiwork, a testimony to mankind, Senator, that He is all-powerful. We shall enjoy the display with reverence until thy return."

Sally and Jimmy sat together silently after the senator departed, sipping springwater. "What," Sally ventured at last, "is this meeting all about tonight, master?"

"Tonight, my child, I shall reveal to these men, these believers, my true mission to humankind, that I bring unto humanity the Truth and the Way to eternal salvation through faith in Me. The Lord has sent me once again to—"

Sally screamed and jumped to her feet. Her water glass flew from her hands and bounced off the carpet. "I can see them!" she screamed. In her mind she did see them, the Skinks, their sharp little teeth gleaming, strange instruments in their stubby fingers. They were gathered around her. She was prostrate, restrained somehow, unable to move. Pain flashed through every fiber of her body. She tried to scream but no sound would come from her throat. The vision passed as quickly as it had come upon her. She stood in the center of the room, panting, her face covered in perspiration.

"Child, come unto Me," Jimmy said gently, holding out a hand. "I will ask My Father to make this terror pass from you and cast the demons into hell. Come, come." He stood and held out his arms to her.

"Nooo!" Sally screamed. "No! No! You are a blasphemer, a *man,* a bad man! Get away from me! *They* did this to you!" She clenched her fists so tightly that her nails bit into her palms and blood oozed between her fingers.

Jimmy noticed the blood. "Stigmata, my child," he said and smiled. "The spirit of the Lord is upon thee! Come unto Me. Come. Come." He advanced toward her.

"Goddamn you!" Sally shouted, stepping backward, away from him. "I swear, I'll scratch your eyes out if you come near me, Jimmy!"

Jimmy smiled and held out the palms of his own hands toward Sally. "Thou canst do no more unto Me, child, than mankind has already done. See my wounds and kiss them."

Sally gasped. Jimmy's palms were perfectly normal. "You are crazy!" she shouted. Her screams had brought the servants, who stood cringing on the edges of the room.

At a gesture from Jimmy the servants fled into nearby rooms, fearfully closing the doors behind them. *"I am the Messiah,"* Jimmy whispered almost reluctantly, as if the role were being forced on him against his will. "Come to Me, child, and I will prove it."

"Show me a miracle!" Sally croaked. "If you are the Messiah, show me!"

Jimmy smiled again and nodded. He stepped closer and fixed Sally with those eyes of his. They stood like this for several moments. Sally was unable to tear away her gaze. Looking into his eyes, Sally thought, *Yes, maybe there is something there.* She took his hand as if in a dream and he led her across the room. The doors to the patio hissed open. They stood under the Lexan covering. Now the roar of the storm was clearly audible and gusts of rain pelted the roof. It was black outside, the darkness illuminated only by the frequent flashes of lightning.

"Open!" Jimmy commanded. A window panel slowly hissed open. In fine weather this portal gave one a magnificent, exhilarating view out over the rooftops of Fargo to the northwest. But now, in the raging storm, a powerful gust of wind surged through the opening, drenching and chilling them, splashing rainwater on the flagstone floor and knocking over a light table that stood between them and the storm. Jimmy moved toward the window. He climbed the low parapet that formed the sill and turned to Sally. Wind tore at his clothes and buffeted him, but somehow he kept his balance. "Come up here with me, child, and behold a miracle!"

One part of Sally's mind screamed *Don't do it!* but she took Jimmy's hand and stepped up beside him. Jimmy put his arm around her waist and turned them both to face into the storm. Her heart jumped into her mouth. Lightning flashed and crashed all over the city in such an awesome display that despite herself Sally was fascinated by it. Wind ripped at her clothing, and she would have pitched forward but Jimmy, somehow rooted safely to the parapet, kept her from falling. Far, far below through the swirling torrents of rain, the light of Fargo blinked and winked beckoningly. Sally smiled. She could be down there right now, in a boutique or in a coffee shop or standing under a marquee, watching the traffic pass through the rain.

Far to the northwest, on the outskirts of the city, they watched as the cloud base began to lower and a funnel formed that quickly extended to the ground. Around the base of the funnel tiny objects, debris, swirled around. "It is the Finger of God!" Jimmy yelled, pointing his own finger at the tornado. "Behold the glory of our Father!"

From behind them, back inside the apartment, someone yelled at them, but they could not distinguish the words above the roar of the storm. The senator and his guests had arrived at last and stood in the living room, eyes bugging out, staring at the pair standing in the open window. At that moment the tornado surged directly at them, "hopping" over the ground, rising and lowering as it came on, growing larger and larger. "Our Father is coming for us, child! Fear not! If thou believest in Me, thou wilt come to no harm! For I *am* the Messiah and I have returned and whoso-ever believeth in Me shall have eternal life!"

Sally's father had been a lumberjack. His specialty was topping tall trees. She once asked him, "Father, isn't it dangerous up there? What if you fall?"

Jack Consolador had put his arm around his daughter, drawing her close to him. "Sally, remember one thing about climbing trees. It's not the fall that kills you, it's the sudden stop when you hit the ground."

"Daddy!" Sally yelled as Jimmy was snatched away from her. "I am not afraid!"

The funnel came right down on the top of the Dirlik Building, sucking up Senator Maxim, his servants, and the twelve disciples. Their bodies, like overripe apples, thudded to the ground all over Fargo that night.

Jimmy Jasper and Sally Consolador were never seen again.

CHAPTER
TWENTY-ONE

Senator Luke Maxim's Villa, Fargo, Earth

Jimmy Jasper sat opposite Senator Maxim in the living room of the senator's villa, sipping a hot cup of unsweetened barley tea.

"I don't see Sally." The senator smiled. He had spent the night in the city and had only just returned to the villa for his meeting with Jimmy.

"She hath been called unto Fargo by the Ministry of Justice," Jimmy replied. "They will try to turn her against me, Senator." He shrugged. "There is always a Judas among us."

"Reverend, I can hardly believe—"

Jimmy smiled. "The Lord hath given me the gift of prescience; I have seen the future, Senator. You have the list?"

"Yes." He handed Jimmy a handwritten list of names. "I hope you can read my handwriting. I'm so used to using voice dictation, I've almost forgotten how to write in longhand."

"That is fine, Senator, I already know who they are," he said, unfolding the paper, "but I shall glance at it anyway. They are all in town now, you say? Ah"—he smiled broadly—"von Styles!" He referred to Henrietta von Styles, lead vocalist and founder of the gospel group known as the Doxology Chicks. "Her music hath done more to promote my ministry than anything else aside from my preaching." He began to hum the tune to one of their most successful songs composed expressly in honor of Jimmy Jasper's ministry:

There are good times coming
Good times coming.
Everyone shall heed
Jimmy's godly creed
In the good times coming.
In the good times coming,
Mankind shall be shorn of pride,
And flourish all the stronger.
In the good times coming,
In the good times coming,
Angels shall light their lamps,
Wait no longer!

Senator Maxim grinned. "It went to the top of the charts."

"And they hath donated the proceeds to my ministry. These girls hath done more to finance my work than any others, and their music, it toucheth the hearts of billions, Senator, billions! Music is one of the most effective means of reaching into the human heart. It appealeth directly to the emotions, bypasseth the reason, or what the majority of mankind calleth 'reason,' which is actually prejudice and selfishness—some of the devil's most effective tools, aside from pride."

"There are those in very high places who speak out against you, Reverend."

"I know, I know. They believe only what their eyes can see and what others tell them, all those who hath been blinded by Satan into believing the Confederation is under attack. These poor souls are deluded. They see reality only darkly, as flickering, distorted shadows on the walls in the caverns of their souls. They live in the darkness of fear and unbelief, but I shall free them. I shall cast light into the shadows that shall reveal the true face of God's love and cast out the demons who besiege humankind. Satan fears and hates me because of that. He would have me martyred, Senator, but that shall not come to pass, not this time. I shall not go that route again." He studied the list.

Senator Maxim looked up sharply. Had he heard Jimmy

correctly? *"I shall not go that route again"?* He began to sense that something very strange and exciting was dawning upon him but he remained silent, awestruck at the thought creeping up his backbone. Quickly, his hand shaking, he downed half a glass of barley tea and coughed into his hand.

"All these people"—Jimmy held out the list—"they shall be at the meeting?"

"Yes, Reverend. My penthouse, tonight. They are eager to meet with you again."

"I shall tell them something tonight, Senator. I shall tell you all something, that shalt open a new door unto salvation, and begin the Millennium." He leaned back in his chair and crossed his legs comfortably. "This list thou hath prepared is exceeding fine. I knew when first I spoke with these people that they would come unto me. The Lord is very pleased at what thou hast done, Senator."

"More tea, Reverened?"

The list consisted of the following names:

Carla Morales, owner of Universal Multimedia Systems, the greatest news and entertainment enterprise in Human Space.

John Drago, religion editor for *The Galaxy Times,* an acknowledged and respected authority on comparative religions.

Henrietta von Styles, beautiful lead vocalist and founder of the gospel band known as the Doxology Chicks; their recordings had sold billions.

Fenelon McGuire, a very popular science fiction novelist and poet whose books had sold in the billions. Her six-volume heroic saga, *Fungible Fungi,* had won the Nobel Prize for Literature and was rumored to be short listed for the Nebula.

Professor Quincy C. Orchard, renowned holder of the Chair of Charismatic Religious Studies at Miskatonic Seminary.

Wang Ng, director of Universal Labs, a Nobel Prize–winning exobiologist.

Hillary Snead, gossip columnist for Universal Multimedia Systems. Her columns were eagerly read by billions.

General Wilkie Warner (Confederation Army, Retired), president of the Veterans of Interplanetary Wars, highly decorated combat veteran of six wars and numerous campaigns.

Senator Dixie Rhapsody, from Kingdom, member of the Senate Armed Services Committee and an outspoken critic of Chang-Sturdevant's government.

Senator D. Barkus O'Lear, from Carhart's World, also a member of the Senate Armed Services Committee and a virulent opponent of the military.

Senator Clayton P. Fogg, from Earth, senior member of the Senate Finance Committee, currently under indictment for felonious misuse of senatorial privileges, but never more popular with his constituents.

Those eleven people, along with Senator Luke Maxim himself, formed a very respected and influential group, movers and shakers all, whose influence reached to the far regions of Human Space. All had committed themselves to support Jimmy Jasper's missionary work. Together they could have a profound impact on public opinion.

"I must return to the city now," Senator Maxim announced. "I have to vote on a very important bill this morning. Then we shall all gather at my penthouse apartment, at the Dirlik Building, tonight at six?"

"Yes, my son. Now let us pray."

As Senator Maxim's car drove off from his meeting with Jimmy Jasper, it passed in the driveway the Ministry of Justice vehicle returning Sally from the city. Maxim thought he could make out Sally in the back, but the figure slouched there in the semidarkness of the car's interior did not acknowledge his wave as the cars passed.

Drying her eyes, Sally darted from the car directly into the garden. She found a seat under the spreading branches of a chestnut tree and plopped down on it. She dreaded facing Jimmy and needed time to compose herself.

"My child, why are you out here?" Jimmy asked.

Sally started violently. She had not heard his approach. "I-I wanted to enjoy the day, master."

Jimmy smiled and sat down beside her. "Actually, it's not a very nice day today, is it? Humid, overcast. Storms are predicted for the late afternoon." He put his arm around her and drew her close. "We shall never have to worry about the weather again when we are in my Father's House, Sally, and that time is nigh. Rejoice, for thou shalt sit there with me on my right hand. Tell me what happened at the ministry."

Sally cleared her throat nervously. "Nothing much, master."

"How much 'nothing much,' child? Come, thou canst tell me." Jimmy knew that Sally was the weak link in his ministry, that she'd been called into Fargo by the minister of justice because the minister was trying to use her to get at him. The visions she'd been having of late were proof to Jimmy that her faith was weakening. The visit to Fargo had upset her so much that she had fled into the garden and been crying. He knew he would have to deal with her.

"Well, they asked me questions about myself, master, and about the time when I was in the presence of the Angels of the Lord."

"Did you tell them about the visions?"

"No!" she answered too quickly.

"Did they ask about me, child?"

"No, master."

Jimmy raised an eyebrow. "They did not? Were you scanned?"

At first Sally did not understand what he meant, then said, "Oh, I passed through a machine on the way in. It was nothing, master."

"Did they say anything about what they found on that machine?"

"No, master."

"Did they ask you to do anything after you returned here, do anything for them in the future?"

"They only invited me back again, if I were to wish so."

"And who were they, child? Their names?"

"One was Mr. Long, the attorney general, and the other was a doctor, his name was Jeroboam. Mr. Long kept calling him 'J.B.'"

Jasper pronounced the names to himself and smiled. "The attorney general himself? That is quite extraordinary. 'Jeroboam.'" He smiled. "A very appropriate name! These men and their president, they are leading the people to sin, child. I had thought Chang-Sturdevant a believer, but I could see not long into our meeting that she was of two minds and the lesser of the two defied me," he mused. "Satan was strong in her that day." A breeze stirred the leaves in the branches above them, but otherwise it was utterly still in the garden. Jimmy lifted his head to the breeze. "Yes, a storm is coming, I can smell it on the air. It shall come in from the northwest, I think. And that was all, child? Did anything else happen that you should tell me about?"

"No, master, that was all." Sally looked at the ground. "I *had* to go, master, you know that."

"Why are you so nervous, my child? Ah, fret not. We must, for now, render unto Caesar. I am sure they will be calling me soon also. But they should make it very soon because things are about to change." He sighed. "Thou art a comely woman and mature, and thou hast upon thee the veil of chastity. Thou hast never been with a man, hast thou?" He put his hand under her chin and turned her face up toward his own. His brilliant blue eyes looked into hers.

"No, master," she answered in a small voice. She knew what was coming and she wanted it, and she didn't want it; she was terrified by the thought that she was about to be taken by God. In the back of her mind a tiny voice seemed to ask, *"What took Him so long?"*

When they were done Jimmy stood. "We shall go into the house now, child. I must prepare for a very important meeting tonight with people at Senator Maxim's apartment in Fargo. I want you to come with me, Sally. What I am going to say tonight will change you and the world. I want you with me, at my side when the trumpet shall sound and the dead shall be raised, incorruptible. Now, let us go down on our knees right here; let us give thanks to the Lord for having chosen us as his vessels. Let us pray."

President's Private Office, Fargo, Earth

Marcus Berentus shook his head sadly and said to Cynthia Chang-Sturdevant, "How can people be fooled by this guy?" They had just left Huygens Long and his party as they departed for Senator Maxim's villa and were now back in the president's private office.

"People must have something to believe in, Marcus. Jasper gives it to them."

"But all the evidence, all the eyewitnesses, all the devastation on Kingdom, how can anyone deny that was caused by the Skinks, enemy aliens bound and determined to destroy us? It flies in the face of reality, Suelee."

"People deny all kinds of things, Marcus. I was about ready to tear your head off the other day after my meeting with Jasper, and I'm one of the most rational people in Human Space— except around election time. I grew up in the evangelical-Pentecostal environment. They take their name from the biblical feast of the Pentecost, when early followers of Christ gathered and were filled with the Holy Spirit. It's this emphasis on the Holy Spirit that sets them off from all the other Christian sects. These guys have waxed and waned since biblical times. I guess Jimmy Jasper is waxing."

"Yes, and this could be the last time, not because of the Millennium but because the Skinks are going to screw us permanently."

Chang-Sturdevant nodded and they were silent for a moment. "Ever hear of the Reverend Willie Gahan?" she asked. "He was a much beloved and respected evangelist when I was still a kid. He got his message across through his preaching and crusades, which were revival meetings but much more sedate and intellectual than Jimmy Jasper's. Gahan had a divinity degree and was a noted biblical scholar; he knew his Greek and

his Hebrew and his sermons were respected as legitimate inter-
pretations of biblical prophecy. Oh, he preached the same Bible
as Jimmy—salvation through faith, eternal life for believers
and all that. He believed in a literal interpretation of the Scriptures, but none of this shouting and screaming or 'witnessing'
that we saw on that trid of Jasper's preaching."

"I confess I don't know much about that sort of thing."

"Most people don't. I bet you never heard of Moral Bob-
berts or Matt Roberson either. Now, they were Pentecostals,
like Jasper. Pentecostalism has its own internal dynamic that
sets it apart from the established churches. It has no church hi-
erarchy, no doctrine; it's all based on direct experience of the
Holy Spirit; everyone in the congregation is a preacher and
everyone participates directly in the worship. You saw it, people
screaming, singing, weeping, dancing, and that awful music by
the Doxology Chicks." She shook her head. "All thundering
and blasting away."

"Papa Haydn would've been outraged." Berentus laughed.

"Pentecostal preaching is like religious karaoke, Marcus.
Everyone gets a chance to perform. Oh, Jimmy preaches, but
he's more like a band leader than a shepherd. Old Willie Gahan, he was a shepherd, a teacher, you sat there listening to his
preaching and admiring it. He appealed to both your heart and
your brain. You could argue theology with a man like him. But
Jimmy Jasper goes straight to the lonely heart and there is no
argument, it's all emotion and testimony, where experience of
the Holy Spirit trumps theology every time. The Pentecostal
preachers are shrewd businessmen too. Look at the millions
Jasper has raised. And there's something else, and this should
really concern us, Marcus—Jimmy's Pentecostal preaching
appeals to everyone, not just the poor and downtrodden, the
people who normally turn to religion for hope and spiritual
sustenance, but to the rich and powerful, the movers and shakers of society. Senator Maxim is a good example."

Marcus shook his head in wonder. "You know what trou-
bles me, Suelee? That the Skinks, who set this guy up, who

engineered him into this ministry of his, evidently know much more about us than we know about them."

They fell silent as the storm raged outside. "This is a bad one, Marcus." Chang-Sturdevant moved to the window. "I hope Hugh makes it out there."

"They'll be all right and within an hour all this Jasper nonsense will be over and done with." He came and stood beside her at the window. Hailstones thudded against the reinforced Lexan material. "I've flown in far worse than this," he added. "But not in a hopper. That storm could rise as high as twelve thousand meters. A hopper can't fly over it. I hope the pilot returns after all, or lands somewhere to wait it out."

Chang-Sturdevant turned to him with an anxious expression on her face. "Marcus, you're scaring me!"

"Sorry, Sueelee, sorry. I was just thinking out loud. They'll be perfectly all right." They were silent for a moment, watching the approaching storm. "I've never been a very religious person, except right now, maybe, as nature shows me how helpless I really am." He chuckled.

"You don't believe in ghosts either, do you, except when you're all alone around midnight?" Chang-Sturdevant added.

"Suelee, I've always considered the Holy Trinity, for instance, an exercise in the ridiculous, but I know that hundreds of millions of people, decent, intelligent people, believe in it. And some pretty smart people believe in ghosts. When alone, around midnight." He grinned.

"Just as many believe that the angel Gabriel spoke directly to Muhammad," Chang-Sturdevant added. "I don't find it hard to believe, or an anomaly either, that Jasper has been able to convince a lot of people that we're being deceived about the Skinks. Evidently he believes it himself, although maybe not by his own choice. But Marcus, the whole point I tried to make just now is that religious faith like his doesn't come through a process of reason and analysis, and if you don't have it you'll never understand it."

Berentus put his arm around the president. "Good God!" he

shouted suddenly and pointed. "Look! Away out there! It looks like a goddamned tornado has touched down!"

"Well," she said drily, "I see God does enter into your life— your vocabulary at least. Hey, I believe that damned thing is heading straight for the city! Let's get away from this window and down to the Emergency Operations Center. If it hits the city there'll be damage and casualties and I need to see what help my office can render."

"Jesus, am I ever glad we aren't out in this storm," Marcus replied.

Senator Luke Maxim's Penthouse Apartment, Fargo

As they entered the palatial lobby of the Dirlik Building one by one, shaking the rainwater off their coats, Senator Luke Maxim greeted his guests effusively, "Greetings, brothers and sisters! Greetings!" he chorused, embracing each in turn. "The Master awaits us. But let us gather here until we are all present and then go up to my apartment." His face glowed with good-will and happiness.

The Dirlik Building was home to many notables and the staff was used to seeing the rich and famous come and go through the lobby, but that night they stood in awe of the luminaries gathered around Senator Maxim. That dignitary had had the foresight earlier to usher Jimmy Jasper into the building through a private entrance to avoid the attention that inevitably disrupted his arrival in public. But his guests were too many and time was growing too short, so Maxim held them in the lobby until all had arrived. He counted noses. "Ah," he announced at last, "we are all present. I do not want to keep the Master waiting, friends, so we'll take the high-speed elevator to the roof. You will get a very good view of the city as we go up." He led them to the elevator bank.

The high-speed elevator ascended the outside of the building, and the view from it was in fact splendid. It was glassed in on all six sides so that occupants had the impression that nothing separated them from the sheer drop of ninety stories to the streets of Fargo. On a clear day, riding in the device was an exhilarating experience. But that night it was *not*.

"Oh, lordy, lordy, lordy," Henrietta von Styles sighed as the elevator quickly rose into the storm. She turned around to face the building, vertigo so strong in her that she could not bear looking out over the city into the raging storm.

General Warner snorted. "Humpf, I've seen worse. The artillery fire during the assault on Bulon was worse than this." Nobody else in the group could even remember where or when that battle took place. The general's words were punctuated by a tremendous clap of thunder that vibrated the elevator. He was secretly pleased that Henrietta was showing her nerves. He had no ear for music of any kind and often said, to make a point of it, "I only know two tunes, one is 'Yankee Doodle' and the other isn't." Hailstones suddenly rattled fiercely against the glass panels. "Ah," the old general sighed, "reminds me of when I was pinned down on the beach at Sanford! How I love the sound of automatic weapons in the morning!"

At the seventy-fifth floor the elevator stopped abruptly and the lights went out. "Oh, God!" Hillary Snead cried in a high falsetto. Wind shook the carriage violently and someone screamed in terror. "Open the door! Open the door!" Professor Orchard yelled, his scholarly detachment abandoning him momentarily. Brilliant lightning flashes illuminated the riders' faces starkly, revealing them twisted grotesquely in fear.

"It is only a temporary power outage," Senator Maxim announced, his voice shaking. With effort he managed to control it. "Do not be distressed! The Master awaits us and no harm can come to us because we are here to do His calling! Be calm. Trust in the Lord." He reached out and clasped the sweaty hand of the person nearest to him, Dr. Ng, who was shaking violently, and announced, "Let us pray!" At that moment the power came back on and the elevator resumed its ascent to the joyous hosannas of the riders. When they disgorged on the rooftop Senator Maxim's face was as white as his hair.

CHAPTER
TWENTY-TWO

Marine House, Sky City, Haulover

Day after day, the two squads went out to examine destroyed homesteads. Day after day, they returned with nothing to show for their efforts. All the homesteads were the same: nothing was left standing, not one stone on another. Nor was there any sign of the people who used to live at the homesteads; no sign of who the raiders were, or where they went afterward, except that they came and went via air, in craft that never showed up on any of the radar scans the Marines had been able to wrest from Planetary Administrator Spilk Mullilee. And Spilk Mullilee always had Chairman of the Board Smelt Miner looking over his shoulder—or pulling his strings, as the Marines thought. It got tedious.

Painfully tedious.

When the two squad leaders had finished dressing after showering the dust and ash off themselves after another futile day, Sergeant Him Kindy turned to Sergeant D'Wayne Williams and said, "We've *got* to do something to break the routine. Let's do something different tonight before I go totally bugfuck."

"What, going out drinking isn't enough of a break from the day for you?" Williams asked.

Kindy held up a slip of paper with a comm number written on it.

Williams looked at the slip of paper, then grinned. "Why, you devil! I'd ask if you'd been holding out on me, but I was there when she gave us that number." He reached for it, but Kindy jerked it away.

"I've got it, *I* make the call."

"So how come you haven't begun calling yet?"

"But I am, I am!" Kindy replied as he punched the number into his comm. A moment later he said into the comm, "Miss Domiter? I don't know if you remember me, but I'm Sergeant Him Kindy. Sergeant D'Wayne Williams and I were in your office a few days ago, and I want to thank you for your assistance." He paused, listening. Williams could barely make out the sounds of a delighted female voice coming from the unit held to Kindy's ear. "Oh, yes, the equipment you procured for us has been very helpful. So helpful, in fact, that D'Wayne and I would like to express our gratitude by taking you out to dinner." Williams heard the tinkle of female laughter and words inflected in a question from Kindy's comm. "That's right, tonight, if that's not too short notice." Kindy nodded, listening. "Eight o'clock local? Let's see, that's twenty hours military; yes, that's fine. We're strangers here so you have to pick the place—price no object. Uh-huh, that sounds fine. Now"— Kindy signaled Williams for a stylus—"what's your address?" Kindy jotted it on the slip of paper on which Barbora Domiter had written her comm number. "No, it's not necessary to give me directions. We're Force Recon, we specialize in unerringly finding our way to places we've never been. Now, you said something about a friend?" Her excited voice came through almost clearly enough for Williams to make out what she was saying. Kindy's eyes widened at what she said next, and he broke in with, "That's no problem, bring them all! The more the merrier, yes indeed. Eight o'clock. We'll be there. I"—Kindy saw the anticipatory expression on Williams's face—"we look forward to seeing you then too. And meeting your friends." He cut the connection and grinned broadly at Williams.

"Well, tell me, dammit! How many is 'them all'?"

"She was meeting three of her friends for dinner. I told her to bring all of them!" Kindy beamed.

Williams looked reflective. "Two of us and only four women. Do you think there's enough of them to go around?"

Kindy roared in laughter. When he recovered, he asked, "How much cred do you have left in your chit? She said we should go to a place called The Upper Crust. Sounds expensive. And we'll be paying for six."

Williams put a hand on Kindy's shoulder and leaned in close. "Him, don't worry your ugly little head. Uncle D'Wayne is flush. *You,* on the other hand, might have to go to the boss and ask for an advance."

"No way, not never. We tell him, he's liable to want to go with us."

"You're right, it's better nobody else knows."

"Anyway, I've got plenty of available cred myself." Kindy's eyes twinkled when he said, "I'll just tell Dad we need the car keys tonight." The two of them burst out laughing.

518 North Hamilton Street, Sky City

Barbora Domiter lived in an attractive, white, wood-frame house on a quarter-acre lot in a quiet residential neighborhood within easy walking distance of the government center where she worked. The well-lit streets all had paved walkways. Not only was the exterior of the house well maintained, care had been taken in its modest landscaping. The lights glowing through the windows and on the porch made the house look very welcoming and cheery. Williams was driving one of the two Land Runners on loan to the Marines; he parked along the curb even though there was plenty of room on the drive leading to the attached garage.

"Shall we?" Sergeant Kindy said enthusiastically, opening his door.

"Yes, let's," Sergeant Williams agreed while getting out, though with not quite as much enthusiasm. They'd flipped a coin before leaving Marine House. One of them was to drive from Barbora Domiter's house *to* The Upper Crust; the other to drive *back* to her house at the end of the evening. Both of them believed whichever of them was in the backseat at the end of the evening would have more fun during the drive than the one in the backseat at the beginning.

The front door opened as soon as they reached the porch, side by side, almost marching.

"Him! D'Wayne! You're here, and right on time!" Barbora Domiter glowed as welcomingly as her house. The two Marines saw three other women peering expectantly from behind her.

"Barbora," Kindy said, beating Williams by half a beat, taking her hand, and kissing it. Then he felt chagrined when Williams, instead of taking her hand, put his hands lightly on her shoulders and leaned in to brush a kiss to her cheek.

"It's so nice to see you again," Barbora Domiter gushed. "I'd almost thought you weren't going to call!"

"We were always going to call," Kindy said.

"It's just that we've been in the field every day," Williams amplified, "and get in too late to bother you."

"You wouldn't have bothered me," she said in a low voice. She cocked a critical eye at them. "You know, I thought you'd show up in those invisible suits like you were wearing when we first met."

"Oh, no," Kindy objected. "Those are our *field* uniforms. We only wear them when we don't want the enemy to be able to see us."

"But think of how much fun we could have if we never knew where you were until you said something—or until we felt your touch!"

"Next time," Williams said decisively. "Definitely next time."

That made Barbora laugh. Then she said brightly, "What am I doing keeping you outside? Come in, come in." She took each of them by a hand and stepped back, drawing them through the entrance, then deftly spun about and back-stepped so that she stood between them, still holding their hands. "Sergeant Him Kindy and Sergeant D'Wayne Williams, I'd like you to meet my very dear friends, Jindra Bednar, Marketa Knochova, and Petra Zupan."

The three other women had been standing back, but now they came forward to meet the two Marines. It was the first time Kindy and Williams had seen Barbora standing. She was slightly taller than either had imagined, but every bit as shapely. Petra Zupan was the same height as Barbora. Her hair was red, her smile impish. Jindra was a bit shorter, honey blond hair and hazel eyes, prominent cheeks, a bit on the thin side, and if she wasn't careful her face would bear permanent smile creases one day. Marketa was the shortest. Her blue eyes contrasted with her long, dark brown hair. Like the others, she looked like she knew how to have fun. They wore dresses, silvery gray or burgundy or amber or scarlet, that floated and shimmered, clung and billowed with every movement. All four wore jewelry that shone and sparkled.

When they shook hands, Petra held her hand up so that the men could brush their lips across its back. Marketa shot her a look, then went back to smiling.

"I made reservations for nine o'clock," Barbora said. "So we've got time for a drink before we have to leave." She cocked her head questioningly.

"I brought a bottle of Wildcatter schnapps," Jindra said. "Is that all right with you?"

"Lovely lady," Williams said, "we are Confederation Marine sergeants. We have yet to meet any alcoholic beverage that *isn't* all right with us."

"With pleasure, Jindra," Kindy said. He suspected Williams had called her "lovely lady" because he didn't remember her name. *Score one for me,* he thought.

Barbora hustled away to get glasses—but not so fast that her hips didn't sway. Jindra went with her to open the schnapps.

"Now, don't you two go trying to steal them," Barbora called over her shoulder. "They asked *me* out to dinner. You two are just add-ons."

That made Marketa and Petra laugh, and Marketa reached out to take both Marines by the hand.

Petra, standing to Marketa's left, smacked her nearer hand away from Kindy's. "Now, now," she said, "don't be greedy." She took Kindy's hand in both of hers and gazed into his eyes.

The two men very carefully did not look at each other. Were the women *already* fighting over them?

"You must be *very* strong," Marketa said to Williams. She slipped her hand up his arm to his biceps.

"I'll bet you've been all over Human Space," Petra said to Kindy.

"We're strong enough," Williams said proudly.

Kindy cleared his throat before saying, "I've seen a lot of it, yeah."

"Oh, yes, *very* strong," Marketa husked, kneading his upper arm.

"I was born in Sky City," Petra pouted. "I've never been off-world."

"Come, come," Barbora said suddenly, insinuating herself between the other two, "I saw them first." She handed glasses of amber fluid to the two Marines. "Why are we standing here? Let's sit down and make ourselves comfortable." Her hips swayed with delightful grace as she led the way to a love seat, a sofa, and three comfortable chairs. She artfully put the men in chairs that had been placed so they were the twin foci of the room. The women took seats facing them, moving so their dresses settled cloudlike until they rested as dew upon their bodies.

And they chatted, chattered, until it was time to leave for the restaurant. Afterward, neither Kindy nor Williams could re-member what they talked about; they'd only been able to hear the tones and tinkles and trills of the women's voices, see the shimmy and shimmer of the dresses caressing their bodies. They were entranced. And preening.

Williams snickered to himself on the way to The Upper Crust. The women had piled into the rear of the Land Runner straightaway and closed the doors, leaving Kindy to sit in the front with Williams. Any chance of Kindy's having fun on the way to the restaurant, Williams thought, is cut off.

The Upper Crust, Sky City

Even though on most missions to strange worlds they spent nearly all of their time in the field, away from civilized amenities, Sergeants Him Kindy and D'Wayne Williams had been around enough to have dined in some of the finest establishments in all of Human Space. So even though The Upper Crust was one of the best restaurants on Haulover, to the two widely traveled Marines it had more pretension than class.

But that was fine with the Marines. The pretensions didn't extend to the prices, which weren't much higher than at the Snoop 'n Poop in Havelock, or to the dress code—a restaurant with more class than pretensions wouldn't have let them in dressed as they were. Besides, the four lovely women with them provided all the class Kindy and Williams could possibly desire.

The table at which they were seated was shaped like a half-moon. The maître d' sat the four women along the curved side and the men on the straight, once again at the focus, with neither sitting next to a woman. They examined the menus—Kindy and Williams accepted the women's suggestions—had an aperitif, ate when the food arrived, had a flaming concoction of something local for dessert, and talked.

Oh, did they talk. In Barbora's living room, they'd chatted and chattered about things of little interest to anybody, other than their value as icebreakers—and for the men to hear the voices of women. At dinner—before the entrée; during dining; before, during, and after dessert; and afterward until they had to leave—the women asked questions about the Marines' work. Between them, Kindy and Williams had enough stories, mostly true, to keep them all talking for more than a week. And enough of those stories were unclassified that they could take several days to tell them without risk of revealing secrets.

The women punctuated the men's stories with gasps, shivers, occasional laughs, and, once in a while, a hand stretched across the table to touch a hand or wrist, and exclamations of "You're so brave!" were heard.

Kindy and Williams ate it up.

They were in love. Not with any one of the women in particular; each of them would have been happy with any of the four.

By the time they noticed that they were nearly the only people left in The Upper Crust, and the maître d' and waiters were surreptitiously checking their watches, Kindy and Williams were actively wondering exactly how they were going to pair off for the night. Or trio off—they wouldn't want to hurt anybody's feelings by leaving her out. Or whether they'd all stay together in one big mash.

Kindy signaled for the bill, which he and Williams split, adding a tip generous enough to make the staff smile.

By the time they were all back in the Land Runner, the two Marines were suspecting that matters weren't going to work out the way they'd thought: The women once more piled into the back of the vehicle, leaving Kindy and Williams to ride together in the front, *sans* the anticipated contact with wonderful female flesh.

"Where to now, ladies?" Kindy asked from the driver's position.

"Back to my place," Barbora said in a voice dreamy enough to restore hope in the men's hearts.

518 North Hamilton Street

"I had a *wonderful* time!" Barbora gushed as they all stood at the foot of her porch steps. "Thank you, both of you, for an absolutely delightful evening."

"Oh, me too," Marketa chimed in.

"Thank you so much!" Jindra and Petra added.

"It was my pleasure," Sergeant Williams said, giving a shallow bow. "You're such wonderful company."

"My pleasure too," Sergeant Kindy said, reaching out to pull one or more of the women into an embrace. The women hardly seemed to move, but his hands and arms snared none of them.

"But it's late now, and we all have to be at work early," Barbora said, "so I'm afraid it's time to bid you a fond adieu."

"Yes," Jindra said, " 'adieu' rather than 'good night.' "

"We'll have to do this again," Petra said.

"And go someplace where we don't spend the entire night in a restaurant," Marketa said.

"Well, you're home," Williams said, looking at Barbora. "Can we give the rest of you a lift home?"

"Oh, no need for that," Marketa said. "I'm just a few doors down."

"Jindra and I came together in my landcar," Petra said, "so we don't need a ride."

"Call Barbora to set up another time for us all to get together," Jindra said. "Please. I'd really like to see you again." She looked at both of them.

Williams swallowed a sigh.

"We will," Kindy assured her, and looked at Barbora who smiled back at him and nodded.

"We'll still see you home," Williams said, "even if none of you need a ride."

There was a quick flurry of women stepping close, leaning forward with hands touching shoulders or chests, and the brushing of lips across cheeks. By the time each of the Marines had been lightly bussed four times, Marketa was more than halfway home, skipping all the way. Jindra and Petra jumped into Petra's landcar and headed off. Barbora danced up the steps to her front door, opened it, and blew a kiss over her shoulder before she disappeared.

And then Kindy and Williams were standing alone on the walkway. They looked at each other for a moment then, as though in response to a parade ground command, turned about and got in the Land Runner.

On the way back to Marine House, Williams asked, "Do you think we just got taken?"

"We're Force Recon, Marine. We find ways in where others don't even try."

They rode in silence the rest of the way. After he parked in back of Marine House but before opening the door and dismounting, Williams had another question.

"Remember that night in the Snoop 'n Poop? When all those women Marines came in? Remember the two gunnys who followed them in?"

"Yeah, the sheepdogs."

"I've got a funny feeling that all four of them were acting as sheepdogs for each other."

Kindy thought about it for a moment. "You know, you might be right. You just might be."

Williams nodded as though to a great truth. "There's nothing a Force Recon Marine likes better than a good challenge."

"Got that right, brother."

Marine House

When Sergeant Williams woke the next morning, he found Sergeant Kindy already awake, sitting half dressed on the side of his bed, staring at something in his hands, looking distressed.

"What?" Williams asked.

"I just found these in my shirt pocket," Kindy said, handing over two small slips of paper. "They must have put them there when we were saying good night."

Williams gave him a curious look, then looked at the slips. The first one had three words, "Call me, please!" and a comm number. Williams raised his eyebrows at Kindy while he shuffled the other slip of paper to the top. He read it; a comm number with the words, "I'd love to see you again. Soon."

Williams remembered his own chest being touched near the shirt pocket; he dropped the two slips of paper and dove for his own shirt, but the pocket was empty.

"You son of a bitch," he swore.

Kindy nodded as he scooped the numbers off the floor. "I probably will be," he agreed. He displayed the numbers, one in each hand, as though balancing them. "All I know is, neither of these numbers is Barbora's. Jindra? Petra? Marketa? Who is who here? I'm going to be in trouble when I call one and probably use the wrong name."

Williams stared at him for a moment then held out a hand. "Give me Barbora's number and I'll help with the recon to find out which number goes with which woman."

Kindy stared back, then scrabbled for Barbora's number and handed it over. "Force Recon!"

"We find out what others only guess."

CHAPTER
TWENTY-THREE

Flitterette Homestead, Haulover

During the week after the raid on the Shazincho homestead, the Force Recon Marines split into squads and doubled the number of raided homesteads they could visit. They continued to find nothing that could lead them to the raiders. None of the sites they visited was new; the raiders didn't strike that week. It was as though the raids had stopped.

"What do you think, boss," Sergeant Kindy asked Ensign Daly when the search came up empty on a sixth homestead, "did we scare them off?" The two squads met up and the Marines of both squads were gathered around.

Daly looked around the debris of the Flitterette homestead, another small timber operation, and shook his head. "No," he said slowly. "Whoever did this isn't likely to be scared off by a few Force Recon Marines. They're too well organized, and too able to conceal their tracks coming and going. They might be lying low to see what we'll do next, but we haven't scared them off."

"I was afraid you'd say something like that," Kindy said. "So what are we going to do about it?"

Daly gave him a quizzical look. "Him, that's the kind of question I used to answer when I was a squad leader. You're a squad leader now; why aren't *you* answering instead of asking?"

"Because you're here, and you're in command," Kindy answered.

"And once you see what kind of—" Daly began, but was cut off by Sergeant Williams.

"—mistakes the officer makes, the squad leaders will divulge a better plan."

Daly shot a withering look at Williams, but the sergeant just looked at Daly with a bland expression.

Corporal Nomonon nodded sagely. "That's the way it always works."

"But sergeants don't normally say it in front of the officers concerned," Daly said.

"Or in front of the peons," Lance Corporal Skripska murmured.

Williams elbowed Skripska in the ribs. "Ellis should have said that," he said sotto voce. "He's junior to you."

"Yeah," Skripska murmured back, "the *only* one on this mission who's junior to me." Ellis looked back at him; in his chameleons his shrug went unseen.

"Do what you think is best," Daly told the squad leaders. "But until somebody comes up with a better idea, we're going to continue with what we've been doing. Maybe we'll catch a break somewhere, find someplace where they didn't simply vanish, left some sign we can follow, or something else that will lead us to them. In the meanwhile, I'll send a drone back to Basilone, with a request for string-of-pearls assistance."

The squad leaders allowed as how that was a very good idea, one worthy of a former squad leader.

Before Daly's message drone had time to reach Halfway, a drone came in *from* Halfway, telling the Marines to expect a navy starship that would take up station around Haulover and lay a string of pearls. That was the problem with interstellar communication; it took time, seldom less than two weeks, and sometimes as long as a few months, for a message to reach its destination and a reply to return, and sometimes an answer came before the question was asked.

Office of the G3, Fourth Fleet Marines, Camp Basilone, Halfway

Lieutenant Miltiades Atticus was far more on the ball than Colonel Archibald Ross from the Heptagon's C5 had been. When he received the dispatch from headquarters Marine Corps that contained information on the announcement from President Chang-Sturdevant about the Skinks, he had just read the first report from Ensign Daly, commanding the two Force Recon squads on Haulover. Daly's report gave what few details the Marines had managed to glean from the homesteads they'd investigated, and mentioned the lack of cooperation from both the planetary administrator and the board of directors. Atticus immediately made a connection between the two messages. He raced to the office of his commander, Colonel Lar Szilk, the G3 operations officer of Fourth Fleet Marines, and rapped on the door.

"Come," Colonel Szilk said without looking up from his console.

"Sir, I believe we've got a problem," Atticus said, rushing into the office and handing the flimsy to Szilk.

Szilk's eyes popped when he read the brief message. He looked up at Atticus and murmured, "Hostile aliens? I'd say we *do* have a problem."

"Sir, Haulover. The incidents there. We sent two Force Recon squads to deal with the situation."

"By Buddha's blue balls! If these"—he glanced back at the flimsy for the word—"Skinks are there and all we have in place is two squads . . ." He jumped to his feet. "Thanks, Miltiades. Return to your post. I'm going to see the big guy." Szilk bustled out of his office.

Office of the Commanding General, Fourth Fleet Marines

As was his habit, Lieutenant General Indrus left his office door open, so Colonel Szilk marched right in without waiting to be announced by Commander Eddit Gyorg, Indrus's aide-de-camp.

"Sir," Szilk said without preamble, "have you seen the latest dispatch from HQMC?" He placed the flimsy on Indrus's desk.

"I'm reading it now," Indrus said, waving Szilk to a visitor's chair near his desk. He finished reading and looked up from his console. "So, she's finally decided to go public with it."

"Sir?" Szilk asked, confused.

Indrus tapped a command into his console and his office door silently closed. "This isn't to be repeated," he told his G3. "I wasn't on the need-to-know list, but I've known about the Skinks for a few years now. Someone who *is* on the list realized that, since one of my FISTs had made contact with the Skinks on two different occasions, I should know about them. I'm sorry I couldn't tell you, but I was sworn to absolute secrecy."

"One of our FISTs has had contact with hostile aliens?" Szilk said, shocked. "I had no idea."

Indrus nodded. "A platoon from Thirty-fourth FIST was the first—the first that we know of. That was on Society 437. That religious war on Kingdom a couple of years ago?" The general shook his head. "It wasn't about religion, it was against an alien invader—the Skinks the president just announced. Thirty-fourth FIST went in to deal with what was reported to be sectarian violence and found a strong alien force. They needed assistance, and Twenty-sixth FIST was sent to help them.

"Over the years, there have been unexplained disappearances of small military units and nongovernmental explorers. The thinking now is that at least some of them may have run into the Skinks. Anyway, the Skinks are why Society 437 hasn't been colonized, even though it seems an ideal choice." He cocked his head. "Do you know that those two FISTs are quarantined?" When Szilk shook his head, Indrus said, "That was to keep knowledge of the Skinks from getting out. They were threatened with Darkside if they told anybody about the aliens. As far as that goes, everybody who has knowledge of the Skinks faces a Darkside penalty for divulgence—as does everybody unauthorized who learns of them. Or did, I should say." He lifted the flimsy Szilk had placed on his desk. "But now it's public knowledge."

"Kali's bloody arms," Szilk whispered. "I had no idea."

"If my G3 didn't know, that tells me security was as tight as it should be." Indrus looked back to the reports he'd been reviewing. "And now it seems the Skinks are back," he said softly, "and we sent two lone Force Recon squads to face them."

"If that's the case," Szilk said, "those Marines have no idea what they're facing."

"They need intelligence and help," Indrus said, nodding.

"I believe the first thing they need is to launch those Global Trekker satellites Haulover has," Szilk said.

"Get a drone message off to Mullilee ordering the launch. And my compliments to Admiral Marsallas requesting he dispatch a warship to Haulover posthaste to install a string-of-pearls. And make an appointment for me to see him at his earliest convenience." Admiral Marsallas was commander in chief of the Confederation Navy's Fourth Fleet, also headquartered on Halfway.

"Aye aye." Szilk began to leave Indrus's office, but turned back at the door. "Should I notify Thirty-fourth FIST to stand up?"

"Thirty-fourth FIST, and the rest of Fourth Force Recon."

CNSS Broward County, at a Jump Point in Interstellar Space

Staying awake on the bridge of the destroyer escort CNSS *Broward County* at midwatch was not an easy thing to do. The lights were dimmer than during other watches and the only sounds were the *pings* and *blips* of the instruments, and occasional murmured voices. On other watches, the crowded bodies on the bridge could keep a sleepy sailor awake. On midwatch, Bosun's Mate First Tigure Sean saw to it that the duty officers and sailors remained awake and alert. The junior petty officers and sailors under him said that was because he was bucking for chief. Many of the starship's officers thought Sean would make a fine chief petty officer, and a couple had already written endorsements to go as attachments with the captain's recommendation for his promotion.

So nobody on the bridge was surprised when PO1 Sean was the first to notice the blip: "Jugo, that pip looks like a drone. Bring it up."

Radioman Third Class Eric Jugo blinked at the display in front of him and belatedly saw the blip Sean had noticed from across the bridge. His fingers almost tripped over themselves from his embarrassment as they danced over the controls to bring the blip into sharp focus and get data on it.

"You're right, First, it's a drone." He blinked again when he finished reading the data, and glanced over his shoulder at Ensign Hedly Tallulah, the watch officer, then looked at Sean. "It's addressed to 'any Confederation Navy starship.'"

Sean merely nodded, but he thought, *Very interesting.*

"Give me the azimuth, range, and vector," Tallulah ordered crisply. If he picked up on the significance of "any Confederation Navy starship," he gave no sign.

Jugo rattled off the numbers. Tallulah made a quick calculation for an intercept vector and gave the orders to engineering that put the starship on course to retrieve the drone.

Navy starships on cruise were allowed to go wherever in their sectors their captains chose. But they were out of communications with Fleet when they were out on their own, or even as part of a task force. So starships were assigned specific times to be at specific jump points in order to meet drones that might carry alterations in orders, and often also personal messages from family, friends, or other associates for the officers and crew of the starship. On arrival at the designated jump point, the drones broadcast identifying data that included the name of the starship they were for. A drone addressed to "any Confederation Navy starship" usually meant an emergency, and quite possibly combat was in the offing for the next warship to arrive at the jump point.

It took fourteen hours, standard, for the *Broward County* to intercept the drone and bring it aboard. Even though he wasn't on bridge duty when the drone's message reached the bridge, Bosun's Mate First Sean made sure he was present when it did; he was *very* curious about this "any Confederation Navy starship" message. He wondered if it had anything to do with that news report he'd seen just as the ship was undocking to begin this cruise. All he'd gotten was a glance at the headline, but he thought it had said something about hostile space aliens.

A smile creased the face of Lieutenant Commander Aladdin Bhimbetka, captain of the *Broward County,* as he read the message. He didn't show it to anyone while he spent a moment in thought. Then he picked up his microphone and keyed it to all compartments and pressed the bosun's key.

A whistle piped throughout the ship, followed by a carefully modulated female voice saying, "Now hear this, all hands, now hear this," followed by another whistle.

"This is the captain speaking," Bhimbetka said into the mike when the whistle had finished. "We have just received new orders. The *Broward County* is ordered to proceed at flank speed to a world called Haulover. There is an unidentified hostile force on Haulover. We are to lay our string-of-pearls to assist the Marines already planetside in locating the base of said hostile force. We will intercept and either capture or destroy any spaceships or starships we discover that belong to said hostile force. We will conduct other operations as required in support of the Confederation Marines planetside, and to the civilian authorities in conjunction with support of the Marines."

He finished drily, "I do not anticipate declaring a liberty call while we are in orbit. That is all."

"Flank speed" was an inaccurate term, as the only place a starship could go at full engine speed was in Space 3. Nevertheless, the Confederation Navy used it to designate the most direct and swiftest means of reaching a destination. So Captain Bhimbetka briskly gave the orders that would have his starship back in Beam Space in less than three hours, and once again in Space 3 in the vicinity of Haulover two days later.

"Sir," Sean asked when the captain finished giving orders and sat back in his chair, "does this have anything to do with the hostile aliens I saw something about right before we left port?"

"The message didn't say, Chief." Bhimbetka had taken to calling Sean "Chief" ever since he'd decided the first class deserved the promotion, and began the proceedings to get him his crow. "But it well could be."

"Sir, how many FISTs do the Marines have in combat at Haulunder?"

"Haulover."

"Right, Haulover." Sean shook his head. "Never heard of it."

Bhimbetka grinned. "They have an ensign and two Force Recon squads there. Nine Marines facing who knows what." Sean's eyes bugged, The captain's grin broadened. "You know the Marines, Chief. They believe that if they'd had a single blaster squad at Little Bighorn, they would have beaten those five thousand Sioux and Cheyenne warriors without any help from the Seventh Cavalry."

Sean looked at him blankly for a moment then returned the captain's grin. "Right, sir. And one squad could have replaced the Spartans and beaten the Persians at Thermopylae."

Bhimbetka nodded then shook his head. "Yep. That's the Marines for you."

Later, when the *Broward County*'s captain returned to his cabin, he opened his safe and installed the sealed orders that accompanied the orders to Haulover, orders that he had palmed without anyone's seeing.

Headquarters, Emperor's Third Composite Corps

The Grand Master had followed the reports from his scouts with great interest for an entire week. The more reports came in the more interesting he found them—and the more puzzling. He had expected a force of more than a thousand Earthman Marines to respond to the raids his troops had been making against the isolated Earthman outposts, or at least several hundred. But so far it appeared that the Earthmen were not responding with any great power. The faces of only nine individuals appeared in the recordings made by his scouts. And one or more of those nine faces appeared in every recording made of visual contacts with the Earthman Marines.

Where were the rest of the Earthman Marines? Or were those nine the only ones who ever exposed their faces and hands? The scouts had never gotten close enough to sense the presence of others but had kept outside the range of the motion detectors the Emperor's soldiers knew the enemy carried.

It was most strange.

What about aircraft and vehicles? The Earthman Marines had killer aircraft nearly as potent as the aircraft the Third Composite Corps had brought, but none had been seen since the arrival of the Marines. And there was no sign of their amphibious vehicles.

It was most curious.

Even more curious was the fact that the scouts sent to look for a base camp could find no sign of one for a unit of any size. Indeed, the scouts who had trailed the Earthman Marines from the destroyed outposts determined that they seemed to bivouac inside the city on the plateau, the capital of the isolated world. The scouts who entered the city disguised as adolescent Earthmen found much evidence of nervousness and concern among its inhabitants but they saw or heard nothing to indicate the presence of an offworld military force.

It was most peculiar.

Was it *possible* that the Earthmen had only sent nine of their Marines to this world in response to the raids conducted by the Emperor's Third Composite Corps? The Grand Master pondered that question for a time, and finally concluded that it *was* possible. After all, he had instructed his troops to leave no evidence of who had wrought such destruction on the outposts, who had killed the people. Perhaps the results were too subtle for the Earthmen to interpret correctly. Perhaps there was sufficient dissent among the inhabitants of this world that the local authorities mistakenly believed that the people who established the outposts destroyed them themselves then vanished into even more remote areas of the planet to escape the attention of the authorities and build new lives in anarchy. If that was indeed the situation, then the Earthmen might well have sent only nine Marines. But if the authorities believed that, then why had Earthman Marines come instead of police investigators?

It was most baffling.

The Grand Master made a decision; one of the Earthman Marines must be captured and made to answer the questions. Then, if necessary, the commander of the Emperor's Third Composite Corps would plan a new operation, one that would guarantee that the Earthmen would send a proper force of Marines—Marines that the Grand Master and his army would most joyfully destroy for the greater honor and glory of the Emperor!

CHAPTER
TWENTY-FOUR

Shortly after he began to pull his task force together, General Aguinaldo let it be known that every man and woman assigned to his command would go armed at all times with their individual weapon.

"I want them to learn to live with their weapons, Pradesh," he'd told newly promoted Lieutenant General Cumberland, his deputy. "We will all carry our weapons 24-7, 365, until they become an extension of our bodies. I want everyone in this task force to know that a weapon is all that stands between them and a Skink acid bath."

"There'll be accidents," Cumberland warned.

"We'll do our best to keep those to a minimum. Except when they're in the field, we'll make it an offense to be caught with a 'round up the spout' as they used to say. That'll cut down on accidental discharges in the barracks. I want all NCOs and junior officers to be especially alert in that regard. And I want all commanders to know that if they catch anyone *without* his or her weapon, even when they're in the latrine, it'll cost them. They'll sleep with their weapons, eat with them, shine, shit, shower, and shave with them, and if there are any romantic liaisons among our people, by God they'd better fuck with them too."

Cumberland chuckled as he tried to imagine what *that* would be like. "The two times when a soldier is most vulnerable to attack is when he's on the shitter or on his squeeze, that's right," he said. "We'll emphasize constant maintenance too, Andy. All that moisture and dirt will accumulate as they, er, you know . . ." He began to laugh.

Aguinaldo slapped his knee and joined in the laughter. "But I am serious, Pradesh. You know, I don't give a damn how these people *look*. There'll be no uniform inspections in this task force, none of this 'junk on the bunk' foolishness. This command is not a freaking marching band or some kind of ceremonial garrison outfit. We're going to turn it into a lean, mean fighting machine, one ready to deliver immediate fire on a wily and unpredictable enemy."

And he meant what he said. When General Aguinaldo made visits to subordinate commands and found officers requiring their troops to work on garrison beautification details or shine the floors in their barracks—the bane of life in a peacetime military garrison—he tore them a new aperture. "I don't want them living in filth, gentlemen," he emphasized at staff conferences, "but a little dirt under an infantryman's fingernails is perfectly natural, as is a little mud in the barracks, and that can be taken care of in two minutes with a robomaid. And if you don't have one of those, a good man behind a goddamned push broom."

Briefing Room, Headquarters, Task Force Aguinaldo, Camp Swampy

"Hold up there, old man," someone said as Colonel Raggel was leaving a staff conference at General Aguinaldo's headquarters. It was Lieutenant Colonel Pommie Myers, an infantry battalion commander whose unit was billeted not far from the Seventh Independent Military Police. While the two commanders were not precisely on friendly terms, they were cordial to each other whenever they met at headquarters conferences or held staff meetings to schedule the ranges that troops from both units used for firearms training. There had been some minor disciplinary incidents that the two commanders had had to resolve—usually fistfights at the local beer garden, but nothing very serious. Still, there was a subtle air of tension between the two commands, an unspoken rivalry where it was clear the infantrymen considered the MPs a very inferior breed of soldier.

Myers was a beefy, barrel-chested man who perspired constantly in the tropical heat. His face was always bright red and the tiny veins in his nose stood out like those of a boozer. He always talked in a very loud voice, leaving everyone with the impression that he considered himself the cock of the walk in all military matters. Although he never came out and said it, Raggel was quite certain Myers considered him, as an ex-rebel and commander of an MP unit, to be very much the lesser soldier. Myers himself had never been in combat. His battalion had never been called up during the recent war on Ravenette. Truth be told, he'd been passed over for promotion and was very close to the mandatory retirement age for combat arms officers in his own army. Task Force Aguinaldo was his last chance to see real action.

And although Rene never told Myers, he was an infantryman himself, not an MP, and he'd commanded a battalion before being assigned to General Davis Lyons's personal staff during the war on Ravenette.

"Raggel," Myers said, coming up and putting a sweaty hand on Rene's shoulder, "let's talk."

"Well, Myers, I am on my way back to the battalion." Another thing about the infantryman that irked Raggel was that Myers always used people's last names, never their first or their rank, and as a *full* colonel, Rene outranked Myers, and it was a violation of military courtesy that the lower-ranking officer presumed to call him only by his last name. Rene let it go though because he did not see any value in locking the other officer's heels for him. He just returned the insult whenever they met.

"Only take a minute." Myers guided Raggel over to an open window. "Let's organize a little competition, you and me." He grinned. "Like, say, a pistol competition on the range. You MPs are sidearms freaks, my men are experts with real weapons, so we'll take the handicap and challenge your guys to a shoot-out with sidearms. We can organize prizes for the high scorers. Be good for morale, fun for us all. What do you say?"

Raggel wondered about Myers's real motive but without hesitation he agreed.

"Understand you did well on the FTX," Myers said, changing the subject abruptly. "Of course you MPs were mostly in the rear, weren't you?"

"Tolerably well, yes. And your battalion?"

Myers made a face. "Ah, the goddamned umpires were enlisted men, *Marines,* can you imagine that?"

"Yes, they were from those FISTs that fought on Kingdom. They know the Skinks better than any of us do."

"Bullshit, Raggel! That goddamned Aguinaldo just loves his Marines! *Enlisted* umpires, never heard of such a thing."

Raggel regarded Myers carefully for a moment before saying, very calmly, "Myers, talk like that can get you sent home mighty quickly."

"Yeah, Raggel?" Myers shot back. "You've turned mighty loyal for having been a goddamned rebel."

"At least I saw real combat, old bean. If General Aguinaldo sends you home, why, then you'll never get a chance to be a real soldier." He grinned in a friendly manner. Evidently Myers's battalion had not done very well on the exercise.

"Well," Myers said, clearing his throat, "we all know infantry is held to higher standards than military police, and we all know the history of the Seventh MPs, don't we?"

"None better than me, Myers old man, but that was then, this is now. When do you want to have this shoot-out?"

"You know how I came up with this idea, Raggel?" Myers grinned craftily. "I was out by the range t'other day and I saw two of your people out there, poppin' away. One was that split-tail clerk of yours. I could see she was doing pretty good out there, and I figured if a *woman* could shoot that well, maybe your *men* could give mine some real competition."

"Well, as I just asked you, Myers, when do we do it?"

"Soon as we can put our teams together. Let's say we each pick three men, our top marksmen. You set up the range."

"All right. Standard police pistol team rules, fifty-meter range, solid-shot projectiles. We'll time the shooters, go through combat reloads, shoot at different distances out to fifty meters, shoot from behind barricades, in the open, offhand, keeling, prone, strong hand, weak hand, all that."

Myers grinned. "Fine. We'll accept the handicap. Let's say ten days from now? The rainy season's over for this year."

"Doesn't give you much time to practice."

"We won't need that much time."

"Prizes?"

Myers shrugged. "The losers host the winners to a steak cookout."

"No booze, just eats."

"You're on." They shook. Raggel was not about to agree to his MPs drinking with the infantrymen; too much opportunity for old habits to revive, and that would mean big trouble.

"I'll go back to my battalion, form up my team. You have your coaches get with mine and we'll see that the rules are understood in advance. We'll all meet on the range ten days from now."

"Very good, Raggel. Ta-ta for now. Don't arrest yourself by mistake, old man."

"Write if you get work."

Battalion Commander's Office, Seventh Independent Military Police Battalion, Fort Keystone

"Sarge," Colonel Raggel began, "let me tell you about a conversation I just had with the commander of our neighboring infantry battalion."

Senior Sergeant Oakley sat expectantly beside his CO's desk. This is why he'd been called up to battalion HQ? Because that infantry lieutenant colonel, a true garrison rat, had had a conversation with Colonel Raggel?

Quickly Raggel explained the challenge Myers had offered. "So what do you think, Sarge?"

"Well," Oakley said, grinning, "long guns and crew-served weapons? The ground pounders might offer some competition, but hand cannons? We'll shoot circles around them, sir!"

"I want you to form a team; you coach it and set up the range for me. Who will you pick to shoot for us?"

"Three marksmen? Well, first would have to be Sergeant Nix Maricle of the Fourth Company. Then"—he thought for a moment—"well, sir, Sergeant Queege over there. She's a natural."

"Me?" Puella squeaked, looking up from her work consolidating the company morning reports. "Me?" she asked again.

"Yep," Oakley nodded.

"Fine! I can spare you for this, Sergeant," Raggel said with a grin. "Whose your third choice?"

"Me. I'll coach and shoot, sir."

"Damned good choices!" Sergeant Major Steiner said, patting Puella on the shoulder. "Yer th' only soldier in this battalion that's ever fired an M26 in anger. You'll show 'em."

"Very well, then. Take Sergeant Queege here, police up Sergeant Maricle, and get started. Top, get us a clerk from one of the companies or one of the staff offices to replace Sergeant Queege here for a couple of weeks. I'll call the CO of Fourth Company and tell him to release Sergeant Maricle to Oakley until after the match. And I'll tell you something else, you two," he addressed Queege and Oakley. "Aside from the steak cookout the mudpushers are going to treat us to, you three will get a forty-eight-hour pass to enjoy yourselves anywhere you want on this shithole world. Dismissed." He stood and offered Sergeant Oakley his hand.

Puella's heart sank. She was delighted and excited to be chosen as a member of the pistol team but privately she dreaded being anywhere near Maricle, who, as a nasty reminder of her past, she considered worse than a virulent dose of VD. And the thought of spending a weekend anywhere with that man made her sick to her stomach. Now, a weekend with Oakley, that was a different matter! But it was with great trepidation she accompanied Senior Sergeant Oakley down to the Fourth Company.

Commanding General's Office, Task Force Aguinaldo, Camp Swampy

As soon as the arrangements had been made for the pistol match, Colonel Raggel requested a few moments of General Aguinaldo's time to inform him of the contest and to extend an invitation to him.

"Splendid!" Aguinaldo enthused. "It's high time you army guys began to realize the importance of marksmanship! I'll be there. Cumberland," he said, turning to his deputy, "why is this the first I've heard about this match?"

"First I've heard of it myself, Andy."

"Uh, well, I'm sure Lieutenant Colonel Myers was just about to—"

"Was he now?" General Cumberland said, exchanging glances with Aguinaldo, who just shook his head. "Myers is CO of the First Battalion of the Third Brigade in Major General Miles's division. They're off Hancock's World."

"Oh, shit," General Aguinaldo sighed. "I remember now. *Them.*" He turned back to Raggel. "Rene, these competitions are very important to morale, and I wish more of my commanders would take the initiative you have and organize them."

"Well, sir, it was Colonel Myers's idea. He challenged the Seventh MPs, actually."

"Was it now?" Aguinaldo leaned back. "That's interesting."

He exchanged another look with Pradesh. "Who'll judge the contest?"

"We haven't decided yet, sir."

"Don't give it another thought, Rene. Pradesh, you're an old shooter; get together a team of judges, you head it up. Rene, I'm putting the word out. Everyone's going to be there. As soon as you've worked out the rules, let General Cumberland know. Keep me informed. We have an old expression in the Marines, but it's still a good one for any commander to live by: 'Send me men who can shoot.'"

CHAPTER
TWENTY-FIVE

Pistol Range, Seventh Independent Military Police Battalion, Fort Keystone, Arsenault

Senior Sergeant Billy Oakley, S3 operations sergeant and firearms instructor for the Seventh Independent Military Police, put his hand lightly on Sergeant Queege's right shoulder. Colonel Raggel had asked him to give Queege some individual marksmanship training, so they were alone on the range. Oakley had never much liked Puella although they'd never had much contact; her foul-mouthed, boozy reputation had not set well with him. Oakley, along with Command Sergeant Major Steiner, was one of the few men in the battalion who hadn't been a professional drunk or ne'er-do-well. For his part, Oakley could not understand why Raggel had selected her to be his battalion clerk, but on the occasions when they had met and worked together preparing training schedules, the senior NCO had been surprised to find Puella in person a lot different than he'd expected.

The firearms ranges the Seventh Independent MPs were using were fully automated but not the usual virtual ranges they were used to on Lannoy. These were genuine outdoor facilities with pop-up targets at marked intervals. When it rained or the sun beat down on them the shooters felt it. Shooters, depending on the instructor's lesson plan, could blast away from stationary firing points or advance on their targets and shoot at them while moving. Different kinds of barriers and obstacles were available for use in shoot/don't shoot scenarios both out of doors and inside buildings constructed for that purpose. The facilities had been designed specifically for the training of military police and law enforcement personnel. The handgun range was only one of the ranges the Seventh Independent MPs were using. Others accommodated much heavier weapons and were designed to engage targets up to several kilometers distant.

The first day of Queege's instruction, Oakley would run her through a standard outdoor course; the shoot/don't shoot training would come later. Colonel Raggel had told both of them that he wanted her to become an expert marksman with the M26 hand weapon. "When we deploy," he'd said, "I'll be constantly on the move, so will the sergeant major, but Sergeant Queege here will be with me. I want someone by my side who can *shoot,* Sergeant Oakley, and it'll be your job to teach Queege how to do that."

That first day on the range had started with classroom instruction in the functioning and field stripping of the M26, sight picture and trigger squeeze and so forth. "When we leave the range later today," Sergeant Oakley had told Puella, "I'm going to give you a set of weights and some exercises to perform with them. It is important that you work on your upper body strength—hands, arms, shoulders—because the stronger you are the better you will be able to handle this weapon, any weapon." Then they moved outdoors to the firing points.

"Okay, Queege old Squeege, put your left foot a bit forward, that's right. Now bend a bit forward at the waist, like a boxer. Fine. The reason I want you to take that position when shooting the M26 10mm hand weapon is because it'll give you a steadier aiming platform. There's no recoil with this caseless ammo, you know that, but if you hold steady your aim will be steady. Shot placement is the only thing that matters, and if you get that standing on your head, okay. But I'll teach the standard marksmanship method now, so you wait until you get on your own before you develop any fancy techniques, all right?" He paused and regarded his student. "You're the only soldier in this battalion who's ever fired one of these in combat, did you know that? What range did you fire it at in that bank holdup?" Puella had not been with the Seventh Independent MPs when that incident happened, but in the battalion they all knew the story, more or less.

"Oh, I guess three meters, Sarge."

"Well, most hand weapon fights take place at less than three meters. You were prone when you fired, weren't you?"

"Yes, I was lying under one of the writing benches."

"The prone position is the safest and most accurate firing position. But today, with this weapon, I'm going to teach you how to fire offhand, standing up. We'll start at seven to ten meters, then move to twenty, twenty-five, and finally fifty."

"*Fifty meters,* Sarge? I can hardly see that far! You can hit something with this thing at that distance?"

"You sure can, with projectile ammunition. We're going to fire two different types of ammo though, one magazine of fléchette ammo, one with solid projectile ammo. We'll use the fléchettes on the closer targets, the projectiles on the farther ones. We use the fléchettes in the law-and-order mission, so you don't get overpenetration if you have to fire when there are innocent people around, and projectile ammo in actual combat, when you don't give a shit if the rounds overpenetrate or hit more than one target.

"Let me see your magazine pouch." He moved to Puella's left side and examined the four magazines she was carrying there, with the rounds pointing backward. That was so when the magazines were withdrawn they were ready, rounds now pointing forward, to be inserted into the weapon's magazine well. He withdrew them one by one to make sure they were all loaded with fléchette rounds. He handed them back to Puella the wrong way, to be sure she checked them before putting them back. She did. He smiled broadly. A big problem with their magazines was that they could also carry projectile ammunition, so a shooter had to be doubly sure what he was carrying.

"Okay, Sergeant, lock and load one magazine of fléchette ammo and holster your weapon! Remember what I told you about sight picture and trigger squeeze. Remember, finger off the trigger until you're ready to engage your target. When you do, I want to see Queege squeege in the proper manner—"

Puella looked up at Sergeant Oakley. "Uh, Sarge, would you mind? I don't like that nickname anymore." Her old nickname reminded her constantly of her days as a drunk, and that was an image Puella really wanted to shed.

Sergeant Oakley was frankly surprised, and then he smiled. "You know what they used to call me? 'Annie,' so I know how you feel." He patted her on the back.

"Sarge, why'd they stop calling you that?" Puella asked.

"Well, one day before your time I busted the jaw of Second Company's first sergeant."

"Are you married?" Puella asked suddenly. The question came out so quickly it surprised and embarrassed her and later she wondered why she had even asked it.

"Not anymore. Old story. Some women aren't cut out to be a soldier's wife." He shrugged. "She accused me of being married to the army. She was probably right." It was obvious the question had bothered Sergeant Oakley. "Now, eyes front! As each target pops up I want you to double-tap it, two rounds, center of mass. When your weapon empties, do a combat reload and continue shooting. When you hear the buzzer, holster your piece. Are you set?"

"Yessir!"

The man-size targets began popping up at intervals out to ten meters and Puella engaged each one as it came into view. By the time the buzzer sounded only fifteen seconds later she had emptied two magazines, twenty rounds.

"Pretty damned good! All right, safety on, weapon holstered," Sergeant Oakley ordered. "Let's go out and inspect the damage." He popped the ten targets back up. Since the fléchette rounds did not disperse very far at only ten meters, he could see all the targets had been hit at least once. Oakley whistled, "Not bad, not bad. But look here, see? Your rounds are hitting just a tad to the right of center as you look at the target. They're certainly disabling hits, but they're grouping a bit off to the left. Remember, even the slightest variation in trigger squeeze or position can have a tremendous effect on the placement of your rounds. Let's try it again, only this time I want you to use only the tip of your right index finger on the trigger. You were crooking your knuckle over the trigger and that made you pull a bit to the right. Your form was excellent, though, and you were holding the weapon steady. So let's see if we can chew out the center of those targets next time." He put up fresh targets and they started again.

At noon they broke for lunch, which they ate sitting on the firing line. In the few hours they'd been together that morning Sergeant Oakley had begun forming a new opinion of Puella. She had impressed him as truly interested in learning how to shoot. She paid attention and asked intelligent questions. And she neither looked nor acted like the stumblebum she had the reputation of being. "I think you are a natural with a hand weapon, Sergeant. The other guys, they come out here and bang away and manage to qualify, but that's about all. You, on the other hand, you pay attention and you really try to do things right. Before we're done I'm going to have you the best shot in this battalion. Say, we're going to be spending some time together, so can I call you Puella? 'Sergeant' all the time sounds so damned awkward and formal and we're both NCOs anyway. What you say?"

"Sure. What can I call you?"

"Bill. I *hate* 'Billy.'"

"I sure ain't gonna call you 'Annie'!" Puella laughed.

"Well, I'll tell you what. You keep up the good work and everyone's gonna be calling you 'Deadshot'! Let me ask you something though: What's it like to work for Colonel Raggel?"

"Well, it's the best job I've ever had, Bill. He works me day and night, but he and Steiner treat me like I'm a valuable member of the battalion."

"I've known Krampus Steiner for years, Puella. He's rough but he's fair. He never beat up anybody in this battalion who didn't deserve it."

"Steiner sez you virtually run the battalion S3 shop, Bill."

"Aw," Oakley said, shaking his head, "the lieutenant's a good officer, just doesn't know the ropes yet. The major who was the S3 before your Colonel Raggel sent him home; he not only didn't know the ropes, he didn't care to learn them. Anyway, I been in the army for over thirty years now and this is not the first S3 shop I've ever worked in. But tell you what, it's turning into the best because your colonel takes a personal interest in everything we do. You know that; we worked together on the goddamned training schedule he wrote for the battalion and he did a better job than I could ever do."

Puella was beginning to like Bill Oakley. He was calm and patient and tolerated her mistakes with good humor, all the attributes of an excellent teacher. In her drinking days she'd never seen much of him. In those days she thought of nondrinkers as pantywaists, not one of the boys, arrogant and judgmental outsiders. But now that she was looking at drunks from the other side of inebriation, she was beginning to realize what a boor she'd been. Oakley's ears stuck out from the side of his head like jug handles, in contrast to Puella's, but he had an infectious smile and his unruly blond hair made him look like a teenager. That he never mentioned a word about Puella's missing ear impressed her. He was looking at her as a person worth his time as a trainer. He was not just hanging around until she got so drunk he could toss her on her back.

"Well, Deadshot," Oakley said, finishing his coffee, "let's get back to work. Projectile rounds this time! Fifty meters! Hubba, hubba!"

By the end of the day Puella was putting most of her shots into the black on the man-size target at fifty meters and was really feeling comfortable with the M26.

Mess Hall, Fort Keystone

The Seventh Independent Military Police mess facility was a battalion mess complete with its own staff of cooks and bakers. Kitchen police was performed by the enlisted men of the battalion assigned to the duty by their first sergeants. Each company had the duty for a period of one week. In the Lannoy army, cooks and bakers were the most dissolute soldiers of all. That was because they lived essentially an independent existence, which was necessary if they were to keep the mess in operation. They served under the supervision of the first cook, a senior sergeant who should have been retired years ago, and the biggest drunk in the battalion. Colonel Raggel went through their ranks with a scythe, reducing them so drastically that the men left were too busy to think about anything but running the mess. The quality of the food served there improved overnight.

It was also good because Raggel and every officer under him ate every meal there. When someone burned the stew, he knew about it. A small part of the mess hall had been set aside for officers and senior noncommissioned officers, but Colonel Raggel often ate with the men from the companies, and he encouraged the other officers to eat with their men also. Officers were allowed to go to the head of the line, but Raggel often stood with the men. "When we go into the field, officers will be the last men to eat in my battalion," he often said.

Sergeant Queege ate (nobody ever "dines" in a military mess hall) with Sergeant Major Steiner at a table set off to one side of the mess. In the early days, they had cut the line and eaten their meals hurriedly so they could get back to work. Nobody ever complained about Steiner, but Puella often got dirty glances when she went to the head of the line by herself. That bothered her because she was not used to cutting lines, but without the privilege she could never have gotten her work done. But, as Colonel Raggel's program began to take effect, work had slackened off at the battalion HQ. That is one reason Puella was able to spend time on the range. But she still ate quickly in the mess because she felt jealous eyes on her as she sat there, and she did not like that.

Sergeant Major Steiner was aware of what had been going on, so he started inviting other senior noncoms to join them, including his old friend Senior Sergeant Oakley. After that first day on the range, Oakley joined them at every meal. The old sergeant major knew Oakley and that the way he looked at Puella and engaged her in conversation meant that he wasn't just sitting there to eat with them. Eventually Steiner would excuse himself, saying something like, "You two talk muzzle velocities and foot-pounds of energy; I'm goin' over to Fourth Company's table there and knock some heads together," and leaving Puella and Oakley to finish their meal together. As long as Steiner was roaming the mess hall nobody had eyes to stare at Puella.

"Puella," Oakley began one day after Steiner had left their table, "I've got to go to Mainside sometime today or tomorrow. If you can get away, come along with me. We'll visit the exchange, maybe have some *real* chow. What do you say?"

Puella grinned. "I thought you'd never ask, Bill."

CHAPTER
TWENTY-SIX

The Rebetadika Homestead, Three Hundred Kilometers Southeast of Sky City, Haulover

Unlike the other destroyed homesteads the Marines had visited, which had all been engaged in farming, mining, lumbering, or light manufacturing, the Rebetadika homestead had been set up as a musicians colony. Haulover's population was large enough for it to have homegrown musicians and other artists, but the tycoons and bureaucrats who ran the planet had little use for creative people and insisted that they engage in "productive" work instead of what they called the "childish" pursuits of music and other arts. The musicians were the first to rebel and move out of the cities, towns, and farms to establish a place of their own, where they wouldn't be badgered by the people they called "Philistines," those who didn't appreciate their art.

The day after Ensign Daly sent his message to Fourth Fleet Marines HQ requesting navy surveillance assistance, Sergeant Williams and fourth squad went to the Rebetadika homestead, which was named after a kind of restaurant with live music in Athens on Earth. This one affected Williams in a way none of the other destroyed homesteads had. As a child, he'd wanted to be a musician and play a pipe organ when he grew up. Either that or drums. Something big and loud, anyway. But he didn't have access to a pipe organ, and his parents wouldn't allow him to bring drums into the house—they thought drums were too big and loud to be entrusted to a child. Especially in their house. So the young D'Wayne Williams had gone in another direction and learned to play chess. He became good enough at chess that by the time he finished secondary school he was a ranked junior player on his home world, Adak Tanaka. He was good, but not good enough to win in professional competitions. But by the time he reached that realization, he'd seen a few Confederation Marines and been mightily impressed by their dress reds. So when he finished his schooling, being qualified for little more than chess instructor, he enlisted.

In the Marines, he'd been surprised to discover that the need to think many moves in advance in chess was of great benefit to an infantryman; it increased his ability to anticipate orders, and to outthink his opponents when he was a fire team leader on independent actions. And the ability to think several moves ahead also helped when he applied for Force Recon.

So that day, away from Ensign Daly, who was at a different homestead with Sergeant Kindy and third squad, Williams put his energies toward trying to think several moves ahead of the raiders while his men searched through the rubble of the destroyed homestead.

He didn't think the raiders had been scared off by the presence of two Force Recon squads; the raiders had an entire continent and a number of populated islands to strike at, they showed no pattern in choosing sites to strike, and the nine Marines couldn't spread far enough to provide any sort of reasonable security for the many homesteads that hadn't been hit. Moreover, the raiders displayed a great deal of sophistication. A Marine blaster squad would have trouble destroying structures as thoroughly as the raiders did; the raiders must have stealth aircraft, since they'd left no radar signatures; and they'd left no trace of the people at the homesteads.

No, nine Marines hadn't scared off the raiders. Ergo, they were lying low.

But why?

What were their plans?

And where was their base? It could be more than a month

before the navy arrived to lay a string-of-pearls to locate it. *If* Fourth Fleet Marines agreed on the need, and *if* the navy agreed with the Marines, and *if* the navy had a starship in position to deploy to Haulover. Which meant that it was incumbent on the two squads of Force Recon Marines already planetside to somehow find the raiders without help, using only their own skills and the resources they'd brought with them.

So, where were the raiders, and what were their plans?

What would Sergeant Williams do if he was leading the raiders?

Several Kilometers Outside the Rebetadika Homestead

Intelligence reaching the Grand Master had told him that the Earthman Marines were being just as unimaginative as he'd expected in examining the destroyed outposts; they visited them in roughly the order in which they'd been destroyed, only occasionally visiting one of the more recent sites. So, while he had sufficient Masters, Leaders, and Fighters to thoroughly surround every one of the outposts, he elected to send only one squad each to three of the sites that hadn't yet been visited by the hated Marines, two of the oldest, and one more recent. One Master, two Leaders, and nine Fighters were more than sufficient to capture one of the Earthmen, and to fight and kill the others if necessary—a task made much easier since the Marines had split their forces.

One of the three sites the Grand Master selected was the Rebetadika homestead. Not that the Grand Master knew, or even cared, what the Earthmen called their outposts.

The transport craft hadn't landed when it had brought the squad to the vicinity of the homestead site at dusk, but rather hovered over a deep pool in an otherwise shallow stream, allowing the squad members to jump into the water. The Master leading the capture squad knew that the original raiding party that had destroyed the outpost had paralleled the stream from

just a few meters away on its way to and from its aircraft. He
also knew that when the Earthman Marines came, they would
follow the tracks of the raiding party. That was why he selected the stream in which to lie in wait. When the Earthmen
came along, he would give the order and his Leaders would
lead the Fighters in springing out of the stream to capture one
of the Marines. And to kill the others.

This plan wasn't in strict accord with the orders the Master
had received from the Over Master who had assigned the mission; he was supposed to position his Leaders and Fighters
in locations where they might capture one of the Earthman
Marines when he was out of sight of his squadmates, and to
avoid other contact if possible. But the Master believed more
glory would accrue to him if he killed other Earthman Marines
in addition to capturing one. He could always say his squad had
had no opportunity to capture one of the enemy in isolation so
he'd had to take more aggressive action. Besides, as long as the
mission was successful in capturing one of the Marines, nobody was going to question the Leaders and Fighters to make
sure the Master had run the mission exactly according to instructions.

So they waited in the water through the night. When the sun
was halfway up the morning sky, they heard the sound of an
approaching landcar and took positions. One Leader, the one
nearer to the outpost site, lay with his upper half on the bank so
he could watch for the approach of the Earthman Marines. The
Master, the other Leader, and the nine Fighters lay submerged,
their lungs collapsed, breathing through their gills. Out of sight
from the path the raiding party had taken.

The Rebetadika Homestead

Fourth squad came up as empty-handed as they had at any of
the other destroyed homesteads. Maybe emptier—they hadn't
even found bone shards. Corporal Belinski, Lance Corporal

Rudd, and Lance Corporal Skripska gathered in front of Sergeant Williams, who was sitting at the base of a tree, lost in thought. They sat, forming an inward-facing circle, with Belinski opposite Williams and the two lance corporals flanking the NCOs. All of them had their helmets and gloves off so they were partly visible to one another.

"We've checked everything except their egress passage," Belinski said when Williams barely seemed to notice their presence.

Williams grunted, an absent acknowledgment that someone had said something.

"You want us to check it on our own, or are you going to join us?"

Just as absent a grunt.

"You feeling okay?" Belinski rolled onto his knees. "I'm going to check your readings." He reached for Williams's chest to feel for the pocket that held the squad leader's medical diagnostic card.

"Hmm? What?" Williams straightened up and brushed Belinski's hand aside. He looked around, blinking at his men. He shook his head sharply and *whooshed,* as though letting out a pent-up breath. "Sorry, I was thinking. Trying to figure things out."

Belinski rocked back onto his heels and wrapped his arms around his knees.

"Did you come to any conclusions?"

"You tell me. Check me on this." Williams looked at his men, waited for them to nod. "I don't believe we scared the raiders off." The other Marines nodded; they didn't think so either. "I think they're waiting, watching to see what we do."

"Do you think we've been under observation?" Skripska asked.

"It's possible. Very possible." Williams looked unfocused into the distance. "I think," he said slowly, "they're planning to take us on, try to kill us, once they have our pattern." He grimaced and shook his head. "We've become very predictable. We're pretty much examining these sites in the order they were attacked."

"Shit," Belinski muttered. "That means they can be any-where we go, and be waiting for us when we get there." Without looking around, he lifted his helmet and put it on.

"Button up," Williams ordered, and they all donned their helmets, slid chameleon screens into place, and pulled on their gloves. As soon as they were effectively invisible, he stood and said, "If they've been watching us, they know exactly where we are. Let's move." He led the way to another tree thirty meters distant; the Marines followed by watching the ultraviolet markers each had on the back of his helmet. They took to the ground in a wagon-wheel formation, facing outward, feet together in the middle.

"If they want to attack," Williams said on the short-range circuit, which couldn't be detected more than ten meters away, "they pretty well have us where they want us. Four of us, and who the hell knows how many of them. Everybody, rotate through your infras and magnifiers. Use your light gatherers to look into shadows. Use your ears."

The four Marines lay quietly for half an hour, cycling through their infrared and magnifier screens, and sometimes the light gatherers, even occasionally using two in conjunction. They turned up the volume on their helmets' external mikes so they could hear farther, and softer, sounds. As far as they could tell, they were the only humans in tens of kilometers of the Rebetadika homestead.

"That doesn't mean nobody's watching," Williams said at the end of the half hour of fruitless searching observation.

"You know what I'd do if I was them and I wanted to wipe us out?" Rudd asked.

"Spit it out," Williams ordered.

"I'd set an ambush along the raiders' back trail."

"So would I," the squad leader agreed. "Here's what we're going to do."

They went several kilometers before they saw anything.

Along the Raiders' Back Trail, at the Streamside

The Marines

Force Recon Marines normally went out very lightly armed, not more than one blaster per squad. Their normal job was intelligence gathering, not fighting, and carrying defensive weapons rather than offensive ones discouraged the more aggressive among them from fighting when they could hide or slip away unnoticed. This time, Sergeant Williams wished all four of the members of his squad were carrying blasters instead of hand blasters; only Lance Corporal Rudd had a blaster. Each of them also carried a knife. Their main advantages were their invisibility; their chameleons were more effective than those worn by Marines in FISTs, and they also damped down their infra signatures—in case the enemy had infra capabilities—making them effectively invisible in that wavelength as well. Still, if a force of unknown size was in fact waiting to ambush them, Williams wished his squad had more firepower.

The Marines were spread on line; Corporal Belinski had the right flank, walking along the far bank of the stream; Lance Corporal Rudd walked to the left of the back trail; and Lance Corporal Skripska had the left flank. Williams himself was between the back trail and the stream.

The Skinks

The Leader watching for the Earthman Marines to come along the back trail waited patiently. He had learned patience the hard way when he'd been a Fighter trainee—by having patience beaten into him by the Leaders who trained him. Some of the other trainees had died from the beatings because they wouldn't, or couldn't, learn patience. If he'd allowed himself to think about it, he would have thought that the squad's taking positions as soon as the Master heard the approaching land vehicle was needless. He would have thought that the hated ones would spend most of the day examining the site of the outpost and not come this way until the sun was well down the afternoon sky. But along with learning patience, the Leader had learned not to think. "If the Emperor wants you to think, we will teach you to think," the training Leaders had said as they beat the trainees who dared to think. And when the Leader had been selected for promotion from Fighter, he had indeed been taught to think—but only to the extent a Leader should think. It was not a Leader's place to think the things that a Master should think. Being trained not to think beyond that which was required of him, he didn't think to wonder about whether there were only four Earthman Marines who would approach the ambush position, or nine of them, or an even greater number.

The Leader did not think at all as he waited patiently for the Earthman Marines to come along the back trail. He knew he might well not be able to see the hated Marines with his eyes; he'd been along on two of the earlier observation missions and knew that the ancient enemy had some means of tricking the eye so they could not be seen visually.

But the People had a means of detecting unseen people: Along their sides they had sensors, surgically embedded during infancy, that picked up the electrical fields given off by living creatures. So he knew that, even though he might not be able to see the Earthman Marines with his eyes, he could still detect their approach when they were about fifty meters away. And fifty meters was well within the effective range of the acid guns the members of the ambush squad carried.

There! The Leader felt the approach of an enemy! To his left front, where he'd been watching. He looked, but saw nobody, which he'd expected. But then he sensed another Earthman, and he was almost directly to his rear! What were the Earthman Marines doing coming from that direction? Were there more of them than he'd expected? He turned around as he slid under the water to notify the Master of the approach of the hated ones.

The Marines

Corporal Belinski paid most of his attention to the line of trees along the edge of the stream bank and the land away from the water, only occasionally glancing across the stream to look for the UV telltales that would let him know where the rest of the squad was. His hand blaster was drawn, held at the ready, its muzzle pointing side to side, up and down, with each movement of his head and eyes. If an enemy suddenly appeared before him, he wouldn't have to waste even a nanosecond in shifting his aim before he could fire. He had set his screens on automatic rotation, switching from visual to infra to magnifier to light gatherer and back again. Most people would find the constant change in vision so disorienting they would soon be unable to walk in a straight line, much less interpret what they were seeing. But Belinski had been in Force Recon for long enough that he could observe his surroundings in so unnatural a manner and hardly even notice the difference; his optic lobe was trained to decipher what he saw in the four different modes and combine them into one visual. He also had one small window open on his heads-up display; it displayed what his motion detector picked up. For more than a kilometer, the HUD showed nothing that his eyes didn't identify as local plant or animal life.

Sudden movement on his HUD made him jerk his head to the left. What he saw was too brief a glance for everything to register immediately, but it was enough to make him take cover. He was able to recall nearly all of what he'd seen in that brief flash as he reported to Sergeant Williams: a smallish, nearly naked man with saffron skin, and a tank arrangement on his back. A hose led from the tanks to a device held in one hand. When the man went underwater, slits seemed to open on his sides, and gouts of air boiled out of them. He had barely shown in infrared.

Belinski looked along the stream, in the direction the man-creature had swum. He saw at least five more of them. All completely submerged. All nearly naked. All wearing tanks with hoses leading to handheld devices. All with slits pulsing on their sides. All nearly invisible in infrared.

CHAPTER
TWENTY-SEVEN

Along the Raiders' Back Trail, at the Streamside near
the Rebetadika Homestead, Three Hundred Kilometers
Southeast of Sky City, Haulover

The Skinks

The Leader swam against the current as rapidly as he could.
As he passed each Fighter, he gripped the Fighter's arm and
twisted him toward where he'd sensed the Earthmen; he turned
half to the near bank, the others toward the far bank. Finally, he
reached the Master and told him what he'd sensed but not seen.

The Master ordered the Leader to continue passing the word
along the line of Fighters then headed downstream and began
organizing the Fighters there to attack, or counterattack, the
Earthman Marines. He wouldn't have had to reorganize his
Fighters had the Marines only come along one side of the stream
as he'd expected them to. Did that mean there were many more
than the four or five Earthmen he'd expected? The Master and
four Fighters were soon joined by three more Fighters and one
Leader. The Master placed them.

The Master lay on the streambed and looked to the banks
on both sides. But the ripples on the water's surface broke up
the refracted image too much and he wasn't able to make out
the Earthman Marines he knew must be there. Not that he had
expected to see them with his eyes.

The Leader who had sensed the approaching Earthman

Marines, and the remaining two Fighters, left the stream on its left bank and crept forward to determine if there was an enemy force on that side, or only one enemy. If there was only one Marine, they were to capture him while the Master and the rest of the squad dealt with the Earthmen along the right bank.

The Marines

"Down!" Sergeant Williams ordered when Corporal Belinski reported the strange people in the stream.

Lance Corporal Skripska faced out from the stream; his area of responsibility was the squad's left flank and rear. Lance Corporal Rudd, with the squad's sole blaster, watched the entire front, though he paid particular attention to the stream. Williams rolled to his right when he went down, almost to the lip of the bank; he wanted to see what Corporal Belinski had spotted but he was at too acute an angle to see through the reflections on the water's surface.

"Tell me again, Harv," Williams said when he was unable to see anything.

Belinski had only gone to a knee when Williams gave the "Down!" order; he knew he wouldn't be able to see into the water if he went prone. His vision was somewhat broken anyway because of the acute angle from which he was now observing.

"They moved," he reported. "I see five, make that six—no, seven—of them. They're lying across the bottom of the stream now, facing in our direction. None are looking directly at any of us." Belinski couldn't see the other members of the squad from where he was, but he had them on his HUD.

"They're completely submerged?" Williams asked.

"That's an affirmative, honcho. I don't see anything that looks like a breathing apparatus. I'd say those are gill slits on their sides, and they're breathing water."

"And they aren't doing anything, just lying there?"

"That and holding those nozzle things like they're weapons."

"Buddha's Blue Balls," Williams swore to himself. These had to be the raiders, but this was *strange,* them being underwater like that. What should he do next? He wasn't bothered by the fact that his Marines were outnumbered—and probably outgunned, if those tank-fed nozzles were weapons. The enemy didn't have infra goggles or screens to see them by, so they wouldn't know exactly where the Marines were to fire at them, while the Marines could see their opponents. No, the problem he faced was, the raiders—and he was sure now that that must be who these people in the water were—hadn't taken any overt action yet. *Damn,* but he needed the string-of-pearls, or some sort of secure satellite comm support. Without it, he couldn't communicate privately with third squad or Ensign Daly—the Haulover commsat only allowed for open communications.

Well, he was a Force Recon squad leader; he was supposed to be able to think on his feet and make decisions that could change the course of a war, or even decide the fate of an entire world.

Now, how could he communicate with someone who was underwater, and was probably armed, and was likely to shoot him if he exposed himself to open communications?

"Harv," he said, "maintain and let me know if anybody moves."

"Aye aye," Belinski answered.

The Skinks

The Leader and the two Fighters assigned to go with him used the cover of a recently broken branch that trailed into the stream to haul themselves out of the water and clear and close their gill slits. A few abdominal pumps, combined with sharp shoulder shrugs, reinflated their lungs, and they resumed breathing air. They set out at a trot.

The Leader was well trained, and skilled at his job. He led his two Fighters two hundred meters into the thin woods before turning in the downstream direction. Along the way, he utilized every bit of cover and concealment available so that any Earthman Marines in his path wouldn't see him before he could sense them. He led the way as a Leader should and frequently looked back at his Fighters to make sure they were also utilizing every bit of cover and concealment available to them. Even doing everything they did to avoid detection, the three made good time. That didn't stop the Leader from wishing they were wearing their uniforms; the dun-colored uniforms blended better with the ground between the trees and bushes than their saffron skin did and would have allowed them greater speed. But he didn't wish it too hard; he had to go with what he had. Besides, naked sides gave his electric field sensors greater sensitivity than they'd have under his uniform shirt.

Two hundred meters from the stream, they'd sensed no Earthmen, nor any animate life larger than a medium-size dog. When they didn't encounter any Earthmen after going downstream a hundred meters, the Leader turned toward the stream where he'd sensed the Earthman Marine on the stream bank.

The Marines

Corporal Belinski was getting very edgy. He knew those people lying on the bottom of the streambed *had* to be breathing somehow. They *couldn't* be breathing water; those opening and closing slits along their sides *had* to be an optical illusion caused by the distortion of refraction and movement in the water. But *how* were they breathing? The tanks on their backs didn't seem to have any connection to the face masks the men weren't wearing to begin with. Nor were there bubbles rising from them; surely rebreathers would be visible. Were they lying on their breathing apparatuses? The first one Belinski had seen, the one lying half above the water on the opposite bank, had rolled over, exposing his front before he completely submerged. Belinski hadn't seen anything on the strange man's chest.

All right, all right, Belinski told himself, *his apparatus was waiting for him in the water. Had they somehow managed to get their hands on Confederation Marine chameleon material?*

he wondered. It wasn't common for unauthorized people to get hold of chameleons. Rare, but not unheard of. Yeah, that must be it, their breathing apparatuses must be chameleoned. Nonetheless, it was unnerving to look at those odd people in the water, completely submerged, without any evident way to breathe.

Belinski was so intent on the strange men in the water that he briefly let his attention stray from his surroundings. A sudden shriek from his motion detector sent him diving forward and to his right—the shriek meant that a largish body was moving within five meters of his position. The only largish bodies in the vicinity of the Rebetadika homestead were people.

Belinski hit the ground, rolled away into a sitting position, and turned to face his rear; the muzzle of his hand blaster tracked with his eyes.

The Skinks

The Leader came up short. He'd detected the electrical emanations little more than twenty meters earlier, but movement, the movement of things growing on the ground, movement that looked like the body of a large man impacting grasses, weeds, twigs, bare ground, hitting and rolling away, and accompanied by the sounds of a man jumping to the ground and rolling away, told him that he'd already reached the Earthman Marine whose position he sought. He didn't waste time wondering how he had had gotten so close to the Earthman before detecting him. He shrilled an order, and his two Fighters sped with him to the place where he thought the Earthman was.

There was a sudden blaze of fire from the Earthman's position, and the Leader joined his ancestors.

The Marines

Corporal Belinski would later be able to reconstruct with a high degree of accuracy what he saw when he turned around, but little of it immediately registered on his conscious mind. What *did* immediately register was three smallish men, clad only in loincloths, carrying nozzles in their hands that were attached by a hose to tanks on their backs. The nozzles were pointed in his direction, but not directly at him—they shouldn't have been pointed directly at him since he was effectively invisible in his chameleons. The one in the middle screamed something, and the three charged. Belinski didn't hesitate, but fired his hand blaster at the one who had shouted the order to charge.

He blinked, momentarily stunned, when the man he'd shot flared up with a *whoosh* of flame.

He shook off the shock at seeing the man flame up quickly, but the other two were so close that they were on him before he could shift his aim to one of them. One landed clumsily across Belinski's legs then clambered up to grope for and find his left arm. The other hit hard on the right side of the Marine's chest, knocking him back. That one's left hand grappled with Belinski's right. He opened his mouth wide, exposing sharply pointed teeth, and bit down hard on Belinski's arm.

Belinski screamed, as much in surprise as from pain. He struggled. He was much bigger than his assailants; if they'd been standing, the two nearly naked men would have barely reached his shoulder. But they were strong for their size. The Marine tried to fling off the one pinning his left arm, but the man had his arm bent at an angle where he had little leverage, and Belinski couldn't shake him. Belinski tried to turn the hand holding his hand blaster to shoot at the one biting him, but that man shook his head violently, tearing the muscles and nerves in Belinski's arm and scraping the bones, forcing his hand to open and drop his weapon. With his free hand the man found Belinski's abdomen and slammed his fist into the Marine's solar plexus.

Reflexively trying to cover his middle, Belinski lifted his shoulders off the ground and raised his arms almost to the vertical before another blow to his solar plexus almost blacked him out. The two attackers let go and, moving with almost incredible speed, flipped him over, bound his hands and feet, and wrenched off his helmet. They looked around for their Leader, and saw the scorch mark on the ground where he had flared up. Uncertain what to do next without someone telling them what to do, they looked at each other. Then one remembered the overriding orders for the raiders and growled them at the other, who nodded.

Crouching low, they picked Belinski up and raced away, carrying him away from the stream.

The Skinks

The Master saw the sudden movement when the Leader and his two Fighters attacked the Earthman Marine above the left bank of the stream. He gargled an order, and the seven Fighters arrayed to his front sprang up from their ready positions on the streambed and brought their weapons to bear on the right bank. They began firing without waiting for further orders, or taking the time to reinflate their lungs. Greenish streamers of a thick fluid arched out of their nozzles, spattering everywhere they struck. At first their shots were random, as they hadn't yet detected the locations of the Marines above the stream. Then they began to sense the electrical emanations, and aimed their shots. But the shots all went long. By then, two of the seven were gone, flared into their constituent molecules and elements when they were hit by plasma bolts.

The Master hadn't risen from the water with his Fighters; he was confident that they would quickly panic the Earthman Marines so he could then lead them to capture more than the one on the left bank. But by the time he saw that the Earthmen weren't where his Fighters were shooting, the enemies' plasma bolts were coming much closer. He darted to the cover of the right bank and rose up as he cleared his gills and inflated his lungs. He barked out orders to the Fighters to adjust their aim. But his orders came only in time to reach his sole remaining Fighter, who didn't live long enough to make the adjustment before a plasma bolt flashed him.

Realizing that he was alone except for the remaining Leader, and confident that the other Leader and the two Fighters with him had captured the Earthman Marine on the left bank, the Master dove back underwater and began swiming upstream as rapidly as he could, trailing the remaining Leader.

But the water was shallow, and an Earthman Marine saw him and sent him to join his dead Fighters.

The Marines

Sergeant Williams saw the flash on the opposite bank, but before he could turn around to see what was happening with Corporal Belinski, he heard the *whoosh-sizzle* of Lance Corporal Rudd's blaster, and another *whoosh* from the stream ahead of him. He looked in time to see a dying flare above the water and six smallish, nearly naked men standing chest deep in the water, pointing nozzles in the direction of the Marines. Williams snapped off a bolt from his hand blaster, and his eyes popped when his target flared up. When the flare died down, he saw no one there, nor in the water below, where the flames had licked. He rolled to dodge a streamer of greenish fluid coming from one of the nozzles, needlessly, as it turned out, since the streamer sailed above him to splatter on the ground about twenty meters to his rear. He didn't know what the fluid was, except that it had to be a weapon. He fired again just after Rudd took a second shot and saw two more brief pillars of fire leap from the surface of the water. Lance Corporal Skripska moved when the firing started, and now flared another of the enemy. A harshly shouted order came from out of sight under the bank an instant before Rudd took out the final standing man.

Williams heard a splash from where the shout had come, then waited a few seconds to see if anybody else jumped out of the water before leaping to his feet and running to where he'd heard the splash. From his feet, he saw into the water better than he had lying down, and spotted another one of the small men swimming rapidly away. He fired at it, but the refraction caused him to miss. Rudd and Skripska also saw the fleeing swimmer, and both fired repeatedly, until one of their bolts connected and fire briefly boiled underwater.

Williams was stunned by the brief firefight, but now wasn't the time to analyze it. "Skripska," he ordered, "secure the left flank and rear. Rudd, watch the front. Keep sharp watch for more of them. Belinski, sound off. . . . Harv, sound off!"

But Corporal Belinski didn't reply.

"Listen up," Williams said to his two remaining Marines, "something happened to Harv. Both of you get to the bank. On my order, we get across as fast as we can. If nobody shoots at us we'll go to Harv. Sound off when you're in position."

In less than half a minute the three Marines were ready to cross the stream. In not much longer they were on its other side, heading toward where Belinski had been. They saw signs of the struggle, including a spray of blood, and a scorch mark on the ground a few meters away. They found Belinski's helmet and hand blaster. But Belinski himself wasn't there. And he was too far away for Williams's site map to pick him up.

Williams swore. That was another reason they needed the string-of-pearls; the string-of-pearls could pick up Belinski's ID bracelet and tell them exactly where the missing Marine was.

But a trail of blood drops pointed the way from the stream. They could follow it and they did, at a fast trot.

The footprints told the Marines they were chasing two small men. And unless those men were very dense, they were carrying a heavy burden. Burdened or not, the footprints of the two small men were set far enough apart to show that they were running.

Fifty meters from the water, the trail turned upstream.

"Step it out," Williams ordered, and picked up the pace. He didn't think the small men could maintain their current speed for long, not carrying ninety-five kilos or more of Marine and gear. But if they were going that fast they must be meeting someone—maybe a whole bunch of someones. Williams wanted to catch them before they did.

The enemy didn't slow down over the next kilometer, or meet anybody else. The Marines pressed, stepping up from a fast trot to a slow run.

Finally, three kilometers beyond where they'd begun following, the Marines drew in sight of the two nearly naked, small men carrying Belinski.

"Tackle," Williams ordered, and broke into a sprint.

Rudd and Skripska went with him. Rudd was faster and got ahead of the others. Skripska managed to catch up to Williams and keep with him. When Rudd was twenty-five meters from the men carrying Belinski, the two suddenly realized someone was after them. They hesitated momentarily, looked uncertain about what to do as the Marines closed on them. Then they barked at each other, dropped their burden, and spun about, grabbing and raising the nozzles of their weapons. They both fired, narrowly missing Rudd, who snapped a shot back at them. One of the two flared up, and Rudd zigged just as the other sent another stream of greenish fluid at him. He screamed when a droplet hit his arm, but still dove into the remaining enemy.

In seconds, Williams and Skripska were with Rudd, helping him to wrestle the small man down and tie his hands and ankles.

"Son of a bitch," Skripska swore when they were finished, "but he's a tough little bastard." It really had taken all three of them to bring the little man under control.

"Check Rudd," Williams snapped at Skripska, then turned to Belinski. The corporal was conscious and breathing; the only thing wrong with him other than the bite on his arm was that his hands were turning blue from his wrists being tied too tightly. Williams quickly released him. He made sure the corporal's uniform had provided him with a broad-spectrum antibiotic, then wrapped his arm with synthskin. Belinski started rubbing his wrists to get circulation going again.

Williams went to where Skripska had cut open Rudd's sleeve. Rudd had his helmet open; sweat was pouring down his face and he was biting his lower lip.

"What in the name of the seventy-three virgins?" Williams exclaimed. A ball of thick greenish fluid, the size of the end of a man's thumb, was bubbling in a hole in Rudd's left biceps.

"I tried to smother it," Skripska said, shaking his head. "Didn't work."

"Damn, only one thing to do." Williams drew his knife then turned to Skripska. "Get a grip on his arm, hold it still for me." Then he said to Rudd, "Sorry, Marine, but I have to cut that out."

"Do it," Rudd said tight-jawed.

Williams started cutting the flesh around the bubbling mass. Red blood flowed into the hollow, then mixed with green when Williams flicked out some of the cut flesh and . . . and . . . green stuff, was all Williams could think to call it. He cut some more and flicked again. Flesh, blood, and the green fluid spattered onto the ground.

"Suction," the squad leader ordered. Rudd used his right hand to thumb his medkit open and pull out the small suction pump. Williams grabbed it from him and began sucking blood out of the cavity in Rudd's arm. A lone bit of greenish fluid remained at the bottom. He gouged it out and peered at it on the tip of his blade, then used the pump to suction it up.

"Secure this for analysis," he said, shoving the pump at Skripska. Then he dug into Rudd's medkit for bandaging materials. He packed the wound and wrapped it with synthskin. "Painkiller, meds?" he asked Rudd.

Rudd nodded; he wasn't sweating as heavily now. "I had my system inject painkillers, a pain blocker, and antibiotics. I'll be ready to move in a minute or two."

"Good." Williams turned to Belinski. "What happened?" he asked. Belinski gave him the short version of his capture while the squad leader bandaged his arm. "All right, let's head back with our prisoner," the squad leader ordered.

They took turns carrying the little man over their shoulders. They quickly learned that they had to gag him, as he kept trying to bite—and his teeth were very sharp.

Headquarters, Emperor's Third Composite Corps

The second Leader, the one who had swum upstream ahead of the Master in command of the failed ambush, was the only one who made it to the pickup point. The Pilot Master flying the transport that came to pick up the raiders and their captive refused to wait for possible survivors once the Leader told him about the Earthman Marines winning the fight in the stream.

Back at the headquarters of the Emperor's Third Composite Corps, the Leader was hauled before the Grand Master to explain what had gone wrong with the mission to capture an Earthman Marine. Once he'd told everything he knew, he was beheaded, because the Master who had failed in his mission wasn't present to be punished for his failure. Then a Senior Master was sent with forty Fighters to find out what had happened to the Leader and two Fighters who had attempted to capture an Earthman Marine. They found where the Leader and one of the Fighters had died. They also found where the other Fighter had been captured.

The Grand Master went into a fury when he found out a Fighter had allowed himself to be captured instead of dying in a cleansing fire. He issued orders to find and immolate that Fighter, no matter where the Earthmen held him.

CHAPTER
TWENTY-EIGHT

En Route to Sky City, Haulover

Lance Corporal Skripska drove the landcar as fast as he could, but it took more than two hours for fourth squad to get back to Sky City. There wasn't a straight road between the Rebetadika homestead and the capital, and most of what there was wasn't paved. The pain in Lance Corporal Rudd's left biceps was so severe that it got past the analgesics and threatened the pain blocker, so Sergeant Williams hit him with a knockout. Full circulation came back to Corporal Belinski's hands early on, though there was enough residual tingling to give Williams concern that he might have suffered nerve damage. Williams and Belinski kept close watch on the prisoner. Early on, Williams questioned the small man, but he tried to bite whenever the gag was removed, so after a while Williams stopped trying. At least the prisoner stopped struggling and trying to break his bonds once they put him in the landcar.

When they were still a hundred kilometers from Sky City, Williams was finally able to establish secure comm with Ensign Daly the old fashioned way, by bouncing radio waves off the ionosphere. Daly and third squad were already nearing the city.

"We ran into them," Williams reported. "I've got two wounded and one prisoner."

"Who's hurt and how badly?" Daly's first concern was for his people.

"Belinski and Rudd. The raiders were using some weapons

I've never even heard of—they shoot some sort of acid. A splash of it got on Rudd's arm. I had to dig it out. He's got a hole in his left biceps that goes all the way to the bone. I've got a sample of the acid—and one of the weapons. The prisoner's a tough little bastard, with pointed teeth. One of them bit Belinski's right forearm, tore it up quite a bit."

"I'll have a doctor on hand to tend to them when you arrive. What about the prisoner?"

"I tried to question him, but every time I took the gag off he tried to bite me. The way he looks at us when we talk, it looks like he doesn't understand Standard English."

Daly grunted. "I've been to worlds where almost nobody spoke English as their primary language, but I've never met anybody who didn't speak it at all. Any idea where he's from?"

"Not a one. I've never seen anybody like him. He's really strange-looking. Has to be some serious inbreeding going on in his near ancestry. And he's strong; it took three of us to subdue and bind him."

"Show him to me."

"Coming up." Williams used his comm to take 2-D pictures of the prisoner and send them to his commander. He did as close as he could to a full-body shot, a close-up of his profile to show the sharp convexity of his face, one of his exceptionally broad feet with the webbing between the toes, and a close-up of his side to show the faint marks on it.

"Does he have any injuries?" Daly asked while waiting for the pictures to be taken and transmitted.

"Only minor scrapes and bruises from the scuffle when we captured him."

When he saw the images, Daly asked, "Who outside of your squad knows about the prisoner?"

"You're the only one I've talked to."

"Good. Don't tell anybody. I'm not handing this prisoner over to the locals. I'll prepare a room in Marine House to keep him in. When the navy finally gets here, I'm turning him over to them. What happened to his clothes?"

"That loincloth is all he was wearing. Same for the others we saw."

"All right, we're at Marine House. I'll start getting the doctor and preparing a strong room. What's your ETA?"

Williams checked the remaining distance. "Twenty minutes, standard."

"See you then. Daly out."

Rudd came to by the time they reached Sky City. He was surprised to see it was dusk.

Marine House, Sky City

A doctor wasn't the only person waiting for them when fourth squad pulled up in front of Marine House. Planetary Administrator Mullilee was there, and Chairman of the Board Miner was on his way. Ensign Daly, Sergeant Kindy, and Corporal Nomonon were outside to meet them. Mullilee joined the Marines in front of the house. Skripska pulled in at an angle that didn't allow Mullilee to see inside the landcar.

"Reporting back, sir," Sergeant Williams said, saluting Daly. "Where's the doctor?" He gestured at Belinski and Rudd. The two injured Marines, like their squad leader, had their helmets and gloves off so they could be seen. The synthskin and bloody skin around it on their arms showed clearly through cut-open sleeves.

"He's getting set up in the kitchen," Daly said. "Let's get you two to him." He waved the Marines ahead and took Mullilee by the arm to take him back inside so he wouldn't notice Kindy and Nomonon getting into the back of the landcar.

As soon as the front door closed behind Daly and Mullilee, Skripska started the landcar and drove around to the rear of the house.

"Careful around him," Skripska said. "He likes to fight, and he's stronger than he looks."

He pulled in close to the back door of the house and got out to help the others pull the prisoner out of the backseat. At first, the small man went passively, but he began struggling as soon as he saw he was being taken inside.

"Grab his feet!" Kindy shouted; he was holding the prisoner's right arm. He looped his right arm through the prisoner's, then grabbed his left arm. "Help Skripska with his feet," he ordered Nomonon, who'd had the prisoner's left arm.

Even with Kindy holding the prisoner's arms firmly, and another Marine on each of his legs, carrying the man was difficult, and they almost dropped him twice before they got him into the small room that had been prepared for him. The room held a chair, a small table, and a narrow bed—all of which were bolted to the floor. The windows were securely covered so nobody could look from the outside and see who was in it. They forced the prisoner onto the chair.

"Sorry about this, sport," Kindy said as he wrapped packaging tape around the prisoner and the back of the chair, "but we've got to keep you still and quiet for a while." He knelt to secure one of the prisoner's legs to a chair leg, and fell back with a thump when the small man kicked him.

"What was that?" a suspicious voice called from the front of the house.

"Nothing," Kindy called back. "I tripped on something, that's all."

Quickly, and more carefully because of the kick, the Marines got the prisoner's legs secured. When they went to the front of the house, Kindy left a minnie on a windowsill to keep an eye on the prisoner.

Inside, Daly got Williams, Mullilee, and the two wounded Marines into the kitchen before Mullilee had a chance to notice that three of the Marines weren't present. He had Belinski and Rudd strip off their shirts as they went. Williams rolled up his sleeves for greater visibility.

"Dr. Tabib," Daly said to the white-haired, white-coated man who stood next to a table with medical accoutrements laid out on it. The doctor was washing his hands with something from a spray can. "Here are your patients. Corporal Belinski suffered a human bite on his lower arm. Lance Corporal Rudd was hit by some kind of acid that ate a hole in his upper arm."

If the doctor was at all discomforted by seeing half-men approaching him with no visible means of support, he gave no sign of it. "Human bite? That can be very—" Tabib began, then the rest of what Daly said registered. "Acid? Come here, young man." He waved at Belinski, blinked when Rudd stepped forward. "Ah, *you* have the acid burn? Let me see." Rudd held his arm out to the doctor, who prodded the synthskin covering his wound. "Very interesting dressing." He looked up at Daly with a question in his eyes.

"It's called synthskin, sir," Daly explained. "Standard field dressing in the Confederation military. If it's left on long enough, it bonds with the surrounding skin."

"Ah, I see. Then we should not leave it on long enough, neh?"

"No, sir, we should not." Daly reached in to show Tabib how to remove the synthskin dressing.

"Ingenious." Tabib examined the dressing, then glanced up at Mullilee. "We should get this *synthskin*. It could save lives when people in the homesteads are injured and have to wait for good medical assistance." He returned his attention to Rudd's arm without waiting to see how Mullilee responded. "Very professional packing. Who did it?"

"I did, sir," Sergeant Williams said.

"You are a surgical assistant?"

Williams let out a surprised laugh. "Not hardly, sir. That's just the field expedient first aid that Force Recon Marines are taught."

"Impressive." Tabib continued removing the packing and began examining the deep hole in Rudd's arm. He used an absorbent ball to blot the blood that was seeping into the hollow. "All the way to the humerus. And how did this happen?" He looked into Rudd's eyes.

"We were ambushed by raiders, sir," Williams said. "They had guns that shoot streams of acid."

"Acid guns?" Tabib looked back and forth between Daly and Mullilee. "I've never heard of such things."

Mullilee looked shocked. Daly didn't, but said, "I've never heard of them either, sir."

Tabib looked back at Williams. "How did you clear the wound? Its walls are abraded."

Williams drew his knife. "With this, sir. Then I suctioned it out—along with a drop of the acid that was still in the bottom of the wound."

"Yes, I see the scoring on the humerus from your knife," Tabib said. "Where is the sample?"

"Lance Corporal Skripska has it, sir. I believe he's still parking the landcar."

They heard the front door open and the sound of voices.

"See who's there," Daly told Williams.

The squad leader moved to where he could see into the main room. "It's Chairman Miner. He's talking at Jaschke and Ellis." Daly gave him a look. "*At* them, sir. It's *not* a conversation."

The doctor manipulated Rudd's arm during the byplay involving the front door. "I believe the tissue can be regenerated, even with the primitive equipment we Hauloverans have. If not, your arm may be crippled for life."

They heard a *thud* from the back of the house, and Miner called out, "What was that?"

Daly and Williams didn't know exactly what the thud was, but they knew it must have to do with the prisoner. They both headed for the front room to forestall Miner from going to investigate. Before they got there they heard Kindy call out, "Nothing. I tripped on something, that's all."

"We'll see what's 'nothing,' " Miner snarled, and started through the room to the hallway leading to the back of the house.

"Chairman Miner," Daly said loudly, interrupting the chairman of the board. "How good of you to come, sir."

"What's this about you killing the raiders?" Miner demanded.

"One of my squads found some of them, sir. Sergeant Williams was just about to tell us what happened." Daly stepped aside and gestured for Miner to precede him into the kitchen.

With a brief glance toward the rear of the house, Miner went where Daly directed. Dr. Tabib had just finished redressing Rudd's wound and was starting to examine Belinski's bite wound.

"Your work again, Sergeant?" Tabib asked. When Williams said Skripska had dressed Belinski's wound, the doctor shook his head. "If either of you decide to leave the Marines, I won't hesitate to hire you as my assistant." He half listened as Williams described the action outside the Rebetadika home-stead to the others.

Williams gave a fairly accurate description of the firefight; the only significant details he left out were the raiders vapor-izing in flame when they were shot, the fact that they seemed to breathe underwater, the capture of Corporal Belinski—and the prisoner. He also exaggerated the number of raiders and said the Marines had been driven off by superior firepower.

"But you said their guns had a range of only about fifty me-ters," Miner objected. "Your blasters fire farther. Couldn't you have pulled back and shot them all?"

"Possibly," Williams said levelly. "But if we stood off, we wouldn't have been able to see all of them; for that matter, maybe we *didn't* see all of them anyway. So while we were standing off, picking off the ones we *could* see, some of them could have been maneuvering around behind us." He shrugged. "With-drawal in this case was the better part of valor."

Miner grunted. He wasn't satisfied with the answer—and his suspicion that the Marines didn't deserve their reputation was strengthened.

When Williams was through with his report, Dr. Tabib broke in. "Take it easy with that arm," he told Belinski, "and come to my office tomorrow so I can check it again. In the meantime, take these—the dosage is marked on the label." He reached into his medkit and handed Belinski a small bottle from it. "You," he said turning to Rudd, "I want you to come with me to the hospital so we can begin the tissue-regeneration process."

Rudd looked at Daly, not sure he should go with the doctor.

Daly hardly had to give it any thought. "We don't know how long it'll be before you have access to navy medical facilities. So go with him." Then to Tabib: "Doctor, how long will you have to keep him?"

"The regeneration should only take a week or two. Why?"

"Sir, he won't be in therapy constantly, will he? Could he be treated as an outpatient?"

Tabib considered the question for a moment, then nodded. "As long as he's on time for all of his treatments and doesn't do anything to aggravate the injury, I guess so. But if he does anything to retard the treatment, or misses a treatment, then I'll have no choice but to hospitalize him."

"Thank you, Doctor, I'll see to it that he makes all of his treatment sessions—and that he's on time for them."

"All right, then. Mr. Rudd, if you will come with me?" Tabib said as he repacked his implements. "Mr. Mullilee, could you do me the favor of providing us with transportation to the hospital?"

"Y-Yes, I can do that," Mullilee answered, speaking for the first time since fourth squad returned to Marine House. He hastened to lead the way out to his landcar. Miner glared at the Marines, but left with the others.

Moments later, third squad and Skripska joined the rest of the Marines. Skripska had taken time to change out of his chameleons into garrison utilities. Kindy went directly to the kitchen.

"What were Mullilee and Miner doing here?" Williams wanted to know.

Daly made a face. "We don't know any doctors here, so I called the constabulary and asked who they used. It turned out their doctor had strict orders to notify Miner and Mullilee if we ever requested his assistance. So he called them, even after I asked him not to tell anybody."

Kindy came back with bottles of beer for everybody and began passing them out.

Williams shook his head. "I guess it makes sense," he said. "Especially if Miner's involved with the raids."

"Yes, the raids. Now what the hell *really* happened out there," Daly demanded as soon as everybody had a beer and was settled.

"I'll let Belinski tell you what happened to him," Williams said. "Otherwise, everything happened just about exactly the way I told it in front of the locals." He grinned grimly. "I only left out a couple of details."

Daly didn't interrupt, or allow anybody from third squad to interrupt, while Belinski told his story, and then Williams filled in most of the details he'd left out of his earlier account. There was another thing he mentioned at the end.

"When we caught up with the two carrying Belinski, it was, well, it was odd. They hesitated before they dropped him and turned to fight us. It was like they were waiting for orders from somebody."

The room was silent for a few moments when Williams finished. Daly finally broke the silence.

"A couple of things. First, I'm glad Dr. Tabib didn't ask to take the acid sample with him. Even if we have to wait a month for the navy to show up, I want our own people to analyze that acid. Second, are you crazy, or do you think we are? People don't vaporize when they're shot by a blaster! They just don't do that. And they don't breathe underwater, either."

Williams nodded. "I've always believed the same thing. But as sure as"—he was about to say "as sure as Muhammad has pointy teeth," but remembered the prisoner's pointed teeth, and changed it to—"as sure as Buddha has hairy blue balls, that's exactly what they did today. At least ten of them vaporized in huge gouts of flame when they were shot. And two of them left scorch marks on the ground."

"Why only two if you flamed ten of them?" Ellis asked.

Williams snorted. "Because eight of them were in the water when we shot them, that's why," he said.

Ellis had the grace to look embarrassed.

"Speaking of people doing strange things, what's the prisoner doing?" Daly asked.

Kindy glanced at his minnie feed, as he'd done occasionally since leaving the secure room. "Struggling against his bonds. The same as he's been doing ever since we left him alone. Doesn't look like he's managed to loosen anything, though."

"Let's go take a look at him," Daly said.

The prisoner stopped struggling when the Marines crowded into the small room; he twisted his head around and glared at them. Kindy went directly to him to check the bindings. The prisoner hadn't managed to budge any of them.

"Remove his gag," Daly said. "I want to talk to him."

"Careful, he bites," Williams added.

Kindy looked curiously at Williams; he hadn't seen the deep gouges on Belinski's arm. Still, he stood behind the prisoner to remove the gag, and stepped back as soon as he had. Even at that, the prisoner didn't miss by much when he twisted his head around to bite.

"Damn!" Jaschke exclaimed. "Did you catch the teeth on him?"

"Yeah, I did," Belinski said drily.

"Oh, right."

"On premodern Earth, some warlike, primitive peoples filed their teeth," Daly explained. "Maybe he's from a world where people wanted to revert to that kind of culture."

When he heard that, Kindy got busy with his comp. After a moment he said, "Sorry, boss. According to my database, none of the couple hundred human worlds were settled by people who wanted to file their teeth."

"Where are you from?" Daly asked the prisoner, moving to where the small man wouldn't have to twist around to see him.

The prisoner growled something unintelligible and punctuated whatever it was he said by spitting at the Marine officer. Daly calmly looked at the spittle that marked the chest of his shirt, then quickly stepped forward and slapped the prisoner across the face. He pulled back just in time to keep from getting bitten.

Daly shook his head. "That's a no-no, mister. Don't bite the hand that decides when you get fed. I'm Ensign Jak Daly, Fourth Force Recon Company, Confederation Marine Corps. What's your name?"

The prisoner growled again but didn't spit this time; maybe he *had* learned not to bite the hand that . . .

"This interrogation will go a lot easier if you speak Standard English," Daly continued. "I certainly don't understand the language you're using." He looked at the other Marines. "Do any of you recognize his language?" They all shook their heads. "Interesting. In this group, I imagine we'd recognize almost every language in common use in the Confederation." He gave the prisoner a hard look. "And I believe everybody in the Confederation speaks at least *some* Standard English. So stop playing language games and switch to a language we can all understand."

The prisoner looked at him blankly for a moment, then growled a few syllables that none of the Marines could recognize.

Skripska felt a rumbling in his midsection. "I'm beginning to feel a bit hungry," he said. "Do you think he is too?"

Daly stared at the prisoner for a moment. "Could be," he said. "Did you secure him so he can have a hand free to feed himself without being able to undo his bonds?"

"Affirmative," Kindy said.

"Well, it's about that time. Whose turn is it in the kitchen?" Daly didn't need to ask, he knew the rotation; he was looking for a reaction from the prisoner, but didn't get one.

"Let's go," Jaschke said to Ellis. Then to Williams: "What do you think he likes to eat?"

Williams shrugged. "Those guys spent a lot of time in the water. Maybe he likes fish."

"Fish it is, then," Daly ordered. "Make everything something that can be eaten with fingers; I don't want to give him a knife or a fork." When Jaschke and Ellis left to prepare their dinner, he said, "I want to take a look at that weapon."

"I'll get it," Skripska said, and left the room. He poked his head back in a moment later. "You don't want to look at it in front of him, do you?"

"No. Take it to the front room. I'll join you in a minute."

"Sure thing, boss."

Daly stood looking at the loinclothed man for a moment then tapped his own chest and said, "Daly." He tapped a finger on Kindy's chest and said, "Kindy." Pointed at Williams and said, "Williams." And so on with the other Marines still in the room, then finished by pointing at the prisoner.

The small man had followed the introductions with slowly growing understanding. When Daly pointed at him, he growled two syllables.

"Say it again? Daly," he said, pointing at himself, then at the prisoner.

The same two syllables, but slower this time. They sounded like "Buben."

"Buben? Your name is Buben?"

The prisoner nodded. "Buben, Buben," he growled.

"Now we're getting somewhere," Daly said, but he wondered just how far they could get if the prisoner really didn't understand Standard English.

CHAPTER
TWENTY-NINE

Pistol Range, Fort Keystone, Arsenault

The day of the match between the teams of the Seventh Independent Military Police Battalion and First Battalion, Third Regiment, dawned bright and hot. At zero-seven hours it was already 33.8 degrees Celsius in the shade. Most of the personnel of both battalions were present, as well as guests from other units in Task Force Aguinaldo. All in all, it was a huge crowd.

"Let's get this over before noon or we'll all be down with heatstroke," General Aguinaldo quipped as he took a seat in the stands erected for the occasion. Sitting immediately to his right was Major General Chester Miles, the commanding general of the infantry division from Hancock's World, and on General Miles's right was Lieutenant Colonel Pommie Myers, the challenger; on Aguinaldo's left sat Colonel Raggel, the challenged. From the beginning Myers found it difficult to keep his mouth shut, so anxious was he to impress the two general officers. At one point he leaned forward and shouted across the two generals, "Hey, Raggel! I like my steaks medium rare, hahaha."

Looking over the broad expanse of the thousand-meter range visible from the bleachers, General Aguinaldo shook his head; the heat waves were shimmering in the near distance, presaging a grueling, hot day. He could look down on the fifty-meter course where sidearm training took place. The range control and safety officers were in place; the two teams were set up on the firing line; the judges under General Cumberland had checked and rechecked the scoring system; range personnel had checked and double-checked the operation of the target system. All the ammunition the shooters planned to use had been carefully inspected to make sure it was regulation and serviceable. Inspectors had also verified by the batch numbers that each round contained a standard military load and there were no "hot" rounds on the range. The trigger pull on each weapon had been carefully tested to ensure it fell within the standard deviation for military sidearms, between 1.7 and 2 kilos.

The preparations had been under way since six hours. All was in readiness.

Colonel Myers babbled on about how good his team was. But it was obvious from the sweat rings under his armpits that he was beginning to wilt in the heat. "Pommie," Aguinaldo said, "better save your breath and drink some water or we'll be carrying you off this range before the match is over."

Mid-Morning, Several Days Earlier, Commander's Office, Seventh Independent Military Police Battalion

Both teams had had ten days to prepare for the match. The MPs, as the challenged unit, had the right to establish the rules. "Let's keep it simple," Colonel Raggel had told his team, "standard fifteen-hundred-point course of fire, a hundred and fifty rounds per shooter, solid shot only, barricades, weak hand, strong hand, standing, kneeling, prone positions, all that. You set it up, Sergeant Oakley."

"Very good, sir. Sir, we need to know more about our opponents, find out who we're up against. Can we get MPI to do some snooping?" The battalion's Military Police Investigation Unit had been rather idle since the battalion had deployed to Arsenault because there was not much police investigation involved in preparing for battle with the Skinks.

Raggel turned to Sergeant Major Steiner. "Who's the best guy down there?"

"Warrant Officer Jimmy Santos, sir."

"I'll have him released to do some snooping. It'd be illegal for us to use MPI agent funds so I'll furnish him the money out of my own pocket to lay bets on the outcome of the match. You know the betting'll be heavy. If we win, give me back what I put in, and I'll give the winners what's left over as a special commendation. If we lose . . ." He shrugged. "Anyway, he can use the money to get the ground pounders to talk about their shooters. You tell him what you need to know. All right, guys, get to it. Give me periodic progress reports."

WO Santos was a short, compact young man exuding an air of quiet competence. "The lieutenant said the colonel said you needed help, Billy. The old man gave me all this cash," he said, waving a wad of credits, "so I figured you need a fourth hand for poker." Santos was known as an inveterate gambler. "Hi, Puella," Santos greeted Sergeant Queege as he took a seat with the three marksmen. "Haven't seen you around recently. Where'd you get that tan?"

"On the range." Puella grinned, nodding at Sergeant Oakley.

Oakley returned her grin, then said to Santos, "Jimmy, we need to know who we're up against. Can you drift over to Mainside, hang out at the beer garden, find out what the infantry has to say about the guys on their team? The money is to lay bets. Colonel Raggel figures that way you can get the gravel pushers to brag about their guys."

"Right. If we know who they are we can find out a lot about them," Santos answered. "I'll be the battalion's bookie and tell 'em I'm layin' the bets for all the guys back here. It'll be a snap. You let ol' Jimmy the Sherlock loose and I'll get what you need."

Three days later Santos made his report. "Good news and bad news, guys. The bad news is you're dead. The good news is it'll be fast."

"Aw, what the *fuck*?" Sergeant Maricle blurted out, exchanging a nervous glance with Puella.

"I mean it. Their top guy is a Sergeant Darryl Kries. I met him the other night. Tall, slim, mean-looking rascal, walks like a gunfighter, silent as a statue and serious as death. And I found out he's a protégé of a guy called Tam Le."

"Oh, holy shit!" Oakley exclaimed, burying his face in his hands. "You guys know who Tam Le was?"

"Never heard of him." Maricle shrugged.

"Tam Le was only the finest pistoleer in the history of firearms. He won six times straight in the Interplanetary Matches on N'ra. He won all six with possibles. That's six *perfect* scores, all hits in the X-ring. Nobody's ever done it before or after."

"Is he still around?" Puella asked.

"No. The story I heard is he was killed hang gliding off Honolatu Mountain on Carhart's World."

"That's a pretty damned stupid way to go," Maricle commented.

"Especially if you do it at the age of 116. And this guy, Darryl Whatshisname, trained under Tam Le?" Oakley turned back to Santos.

"That's the word. The others are Corporal Rick Totaro, another silent type, but he and Kries train together all the time, and Sergeant Andrew Grills. Now, Grills is the comedian, always joking around but said to be another crack shot. Boys, I think you ought to call this whole thing off before you get yourselves massacred." Santos grinned. "Naw, just joking."

"Very funny, Jimmy." Oakley gathered his thoughts. "Okay, Darryl trained under Tam Le—but that doesn't mean he *is* Tam Le. The other two might be good but we're better. We have to go into this match convinced we're going to win. You both know that even the best shooters have bad days. Well, these guys are going to have a bad day, and we're going to give it to them. If you *think* you're going to lose when you step out on the firing line, you *will* lose. It's that simple. Jimmy, can you go back up to Mainside, lay some more bets? This time you let it be known that their Darryl Whatshisname—"

"Kries.—"

"—Kries, is a nobody, a poor student, a *lucky* shot, overrated. You tell those guys we've got *Annie Oakley* on our side," he said, grinning at Puella, "and she's gonna wax their M26s for 'em. But Jimmy, just who are these guys, infantrymen who're so damned good with sidearms? That's unheard of."

"Medics. Their principal weapon is the M26, and I guess they figured if that was the only thing between them and the enemy they'd better be pretty good with it. Can't say they're stupid in that regard, can we? And old Kries? Word is he's just a gun nut from long before he joined his army. Word is he paid out of his own pocket for instruction from Tam Le, and Tam Le, he didn't come cheap."

"We've got to respect this guy, but we can beat him. Jimmy, go back to Mainside and lay some more bets."

"You got it. Say," he said, "if we win all the bets I've been making we'll not only eat like kings, we'll come out ten thousand credits to the good!"

Pistol Range, Fort Keystone

"Shooters, move to the firing line!" the range control officer ordered. Both teams moved to the firing points. "Lock and load and holster your weapons!" On this order they would fire two magazines containing six rounds each. The range safety officer walked down the line, checking each weapon. The M26 was a hammerless, double-action-only pistol. Its firing pin was spring-loaded, and when the weapon was in battery, a stud on the rear of the slide protruded. The safety officer touched each weapon to be sure it was loaded.

Puella stood at the firing line, her arms by her sides waiting for the order to commence firing. It would come when the targets popped up. Her stomach churned. She glanced over at Maricle just to her right. He smiled and winked at her. She wondered how he could be so calm. She just knew that she was so nervous that she'd screw this order up and embarrass everyone. She glanced to her left. The three challengers stood loose and easy. The short one called Andy looked at Puella, smiled, and said, "Oh, sugar snaps!" She couldn't help smiling back, and that one simple act caused the tension to drain out of her.

The target was the standard silhouette, 60.96 cm by 114.30 cm. At a mere seven meters she knew she couldn't fail to get each round into the X-ring. At fifty meters, that might be more difficult.

"Ready on the firing line!" A few seconds of silence and then the targets popped up. "Commence firing!"

Puella got all twelve rounds, including a reload, in 8.5 seconds. She could see her hits clearly, all dead center. The weapon's slide locked open on the last round. She dropped the magazine and held it up for the safety officer to see. He checked each shooter's weapon before allowing them to be holstered. "Alibis?" the range control officer asked. There had been no malfunctions. "Step back from the firing line. Do not handle your weapons! Reload your magazines while the targets are scored," the RCO announced.

After each order the targets were changed for fresh ones. The old targets were scored electronically and then double-checked visually by the judges, who only then entered the official scores on each shooter's scorecard. The shooters were allowed to see their targets and the scoring, and if they did not protest, the scores became official. Each shooter had scored 120 points on the seven-meter course, perfect scores. Puella glanced at Kries's target and almost let out a gasp. His hits had cut a hole in the target precisely 2.5 by 2.5 centimeters! Truly remarkable. Puella's hits had all counted for ten points each, but her spread was much larger than Kries's.

"That boy is good," Bill whispered from behind Puella, "but his groupings will spread out as the ranges increase. Remember, it isn't the size of your group that counts, it's the point spread. This stuff is showmanship, nothing more. And remember, it's the team's score, not the individual's that counts. Grills's and Totaro's groups are no better than yours. And watch your trigger squeeze. At two kilos it can really screw you up if you jerk that trigger." Puella smiled to herself. This made her feel a little better. She wasn't the only nervous one; she could see that Bill was nervous, otherwise why repeat what every shooter knew by heart? Bill's own group measured 3 by 3 centimeters. He looked out over the range toward the fifty-meter target line, wavering in the heat. "Now the going gets rough," he said.

By the time the first match was over the aggregate team scores stood at 1447-90X points for the challengers and 1481-80X for the Seventh Independent MPs. While the infantry scored higher in the X-ring than the MPs, the challengees made up for that with more hits and no misses in the other rings; the infantrymen counted three misses on their targets, that is, rounds that had hit outside the seven ring. Corporal Totaro called out good-naturedly to his teammate Grills, "Those twenty misses were all yours, Andy!" Grills only grinned and hollered back, "Oh, sugar snaps!"

Puella had the highest individual score of her team, as did Kries for his. Kries caught her eye and saluted in her direction. Puella had never felt prouder of herself in that moment. She grinned and waved back at him. The infantrymen were taking their loss very well, she thought, but their commander wasn't.

The MPs were ecstatic when the judges announced the aggregate scores. "You lucky bastards!" Myers screamed, standing and shaking a fist.

"Sit down, Colonel!" General Aguinaldo ordered, then he whispered something into General Miles's ear and then leaned over and said something to Colonel Raggel, who descended from the stands to congratulate his team. "One more performance like that and we eat like kings," Raggel said with a grin.

They took a break between orders to hydrate and rest. "You did really well," Oakley told his teammates, "but next time, who knows? The heat's getting to us all. We can't afford to screw up on this next match. How do you feel, the two of you?"

"Never better!" Puella answered immediately, her eyes flashing.

"Just getting started, Coach," Maricle answered. "Nobody puts the 'nix' on Nix." He exchanged high fives with Puella. In the exhilaration of the contest both of them had forgotten the animosity that had developed between them earlier. They were partners now, doing the best they could and doing it well.

General Aguinaldo came down to congratulate both teams. "I've never seen better shooting, Senior Sergeant," he told Oakley. "Are you sure none of you are really Marines?"

By the time the second and final match began the temperature had risen to a sizzling 36.6 degrees Celsius. All the shooters except Puella began to feel the heat and the strain as the match progressed. She had perspired heavily during the first match, but now the sweating had stopped and she did not even feel thirsty. She was thriving, and before long was actually beginning to enter that rare state of physical and mental ecstasy known as "gunner's high," where she no longer felt her body but seemed to float on the firing point, her M26 a mere extension of her mind, as in a trid game where all she had to do was *think* and the weapon pointed and discharged itself.

By the time she finished the last order at the fifty-meter range, cleared her weapon, and held it up for the range safety officer's inspection, she knew she'd fired the impossible "possible," and that is all she remembered until she returned to consciousness lying on the ground, with Sergeant Darryl Kries kneeling beside her.

"Looks like the heat got to you there, young lady." Kries smiled. "I gotta tell ya, though, I've never seen such shooting. You finished before anybody else, but when you collapsed on us, General Cumberland halted the match."

"Y-You mean—" Puella croaked as she tried to rise.

"Yeah. We couldn't continue with you lying out there. He called off the match for now. I mean, we were almost done when we had to stop to haul you off the line and get your body temperature down. That gave everybody an unexpected rest and a chance to hydrate, which nobody would've gotten if we'd finished the match. So he said that wasn't fair. We'd have to fire the whole order over again when you were back on your feet, which you ain't gonna be for a while. My legs were wobbly too. I'm glad he called it off."

Someone squatted next to Puella. It was General Aguinaldo. "I have something to show you, Sergeant." He nodded at one of the judges who presented Puella's target. The entire X-ring had been shot out. "You scored fifteen hundred points on that match, Sergeant, a perfect score. Nobody'll ever take that away from you. When you're feeling better, come and see me. We could use a marksman like you in the Corps." He got to his feet. "This match is over," he announced. "The judges have canceled it on a technicality. And I declare that we all get under some shade, barbecue some steaks and drink some beer, because you've all earned it." He put his arm around Darryl Kries's and Bill Oakley's shoulders and guided them toward a grove of trees where the barbecue had been set up. "We might could use you two in the Corps, gentlemen, even if you were outshot by a woman."

"Oh, sugar snaps!" Andy Grills muttered, trudging behind them to the BBQ.

"I want a rematch!" Lieutenant Colonel Myers screamed at Aguinaldo's back.

"Anytime, Pommie," Raggel said, helping Puella to her feet. "I don't think Pommie's going to be around for the next one," he whispered. "And don't let anyone tell you otherwise, Sergeant Queege. We won, based on your score alone."

Puella turned to Sergeant Major Steiner. "Top, you remember that time on Ravenette, when I ate those slimies in a bet with my first sergeant? I thought that would make me famous." She shook her head.

"Well, you're famous now. We used to call you 'Queege old Squeege,' but now the boys are calling you 'Annie Oakley.'"

Orderly Room, Headquarters, Seventh Independent Military Police Battalion

"I have something to tell you," Colonel Raggel said. He, Sergeant Major Steiner, and Puella were sitting in the battalion orderly room. It was several days since the match. "I'm leaving."

"What!" Steiner exclaimed.

"No!" Puella protested.

"Yes. I'm due to be promoted to brigadier general very soon and General Aguinaldo wants me to take over General Miles's division." He smiled. "Old Pommie Myers has been sent home too."

"When do you leave, sir?" Steiner asked.

"Soon as a replacement can be found for me here. But there's something I want to show you two right now." He reached behind him and produced two handsomely embossed folders. One contained Puella's promotion warrant to the grade of senior sergeant. The other made her eyes pop.

Across the top of the vellum certificate was embossed a handsome, full-color reproduction of the Lannoy Army Silver Medal of Valor. She read the certificate: "'CORPORAL PUELLA QUEEGE, 21993000, SEVENTH INDEPENDENT MILITARY POLICE BATTALION, DID, ON OR ABOUT . . .'

"This was on Ravenette!" she gasped.

"Read on," Colonel Raggel said.

"'. . . IN THE TOWN OF PHELPS ON THE WORLD KNOWN AS RAVENETTE, WHILE TEMPORARILY AS- SIGNED AS A PATROL OFFICER TO THIRD COMPANY, SEVENTY-EIGHTH MILITARY POLICE BATTALION, TWO HUNDRED AND TWENTY-SECOND INFANTRY DIVISION, DISTINGUISHED HERSELF BY CONSPICU- OUS GALLANTRY AND INTREPIDITY . . .'

"I can't believe it." Puella sighed and laid the certificate down. "How did—"

"Easy. I contacted General Barksdale Sneed, the former CG of the Fourth Composite Infantry Division, to which the Seventh Independent and the 78th MPs were assigned when you were on Ravenette. He prepared the recommendation. Your army chief of staff approved it. I'm going to announce your promo- tion and present you with the medal tomorrow morning. I have a bunch of other commendations to pass out. And I'll announce the imminent change of command. But I wanted you to know first. Sorry you have to wait until tomorrow to put on your new chevrons." He held out his hand. "One more thing. I'll be needing a good sergeant major and a good senior sergeant up at division. Either of you interested?"

At first both were silent. Steiner was the first to speak. "Who's gonna help the new CO run this battalion if you're gone? Thanks, Colonel, but I think I'll just stay here. Aw, shit, boss, I'm too old for the infantry." He laughed. "But your askin' me to go with you is the finest compliment I've ever received. Better than any medal."

"Oh, I agree with that, sir!" Puella blurted out.

"Well, what about you, then, Puella?"

"Well, sir." Her face turned red and she looked at her feet, then she shifted her weight nervously. "Uh, it's like this, sir. I had an announcement to make too, sir, but you beat me to it and now I feel like I'm deserting you."

"What in the hell do you mean by that?" Raggel asked.

"Well, I'd be proud to go with you, sir! You've done more for me than anybody! I mean, I'd love to go with you, sir, but, and I would've told you, but I was just waitin' for the proper time to . . ."

"Now's as good a time as any. Spit it out."

"Well, sir, I took General Aguinaldo up on his offer. I'm transferring to the Confederation Marine Corps."

CHAPTER
THIRTY

Marine House, Sky City, Haulover

Lance Corporal Skripska had laid the weapon out on a table in the front room. Daly pulled up a chair to examine it. Two tanks, one larger than the other, were attached to a packboard similar to a type the Marines had seen in military museums. The board had four straps: two shoulder straps, one chest strap, and one in the right place to go around the waist of a small man. The tanks were connected at their bottoms via a boxlike structure. A flexible hose led from the bottom of the box to a nozzle and grip that closely enough resembled the trigger-receiver group of a blaster to make it clear what it was. There were gauges on the tanks and the suspended box. The markings on the gauges looked like slightly curved lines placed almost randomly across each other. While Daly touched the weapon here and there, he was careful not to touch anything that looked like a control, and kept clear of the obvious trigger.

When he was finished going over everything else, Daly looked again at the gauges and said, "Either it's almost full or it's almost empty. Tomorrow we'll go someplace and test it." He peered at it some more before saying, "You know what this reminds me of? Back in the twentieth century, some armies—including the U.S. Marines—had a weapon called a 'flame thrower.' It had some sort of flammable liquid in two tanks, and compressed air in a third." He looked at the other Marines.

"The liquid was sticky, so when it hit someone it stayed right there and kept burning. Hit someone with a big enough splash and he turned into a living torch."

Corporal Nomonon grimaced. "Ooh, nasty."

"I had to dig that acid out of Rudd's arm," Sergeant Williams said. "It was still eating its way through. That flame thrower sounds just as bad."

"I'm going to secure this in my room for now," Daly said. "I'll put it in the landcar before dawn—I don't want the locals to have any idea we have it." He rose and picked up the weapon just as Corporal Jaschke came from the kitchen.

"Soup's on," Jaschke announced.

"Can half of everything fit into one serving bowl?" Daly asked.

"Ah, yeah. It won't be all that appetizing like that, but I can do it."

"Do it. Kindy, Williams, Belinski, put four chairs and a table in the prisoner's room. The four of us will eat with him—all of us serving from the same bowl to show him it's not poisoned. Everybody else eat in here. Oh, and provide a pitcher of water and five glasses."

Secure Room, Marine House

Buben, the prisoner, was still secured to the chair, which was bolted to the floor and facing the small table, which was also bolted down. He watched suspiciously as Sergeant Williams and Corporal Belinski put the bowl with the food and the water pitcher on the table that Sergeant Kindy had placed in the center of the room. He seemed to count the glasses and small bowls that Ensign Daly had brought in. Despite the suspicion in his expression, his nose quivered at the smell of food, and a bubble of drool appeared on the middle of his lower lip.

"Are you hungry, Buben?" Daly asked. "Would you like to eat?" He tilted the serving bowl so the prisoner could see into it and scooped a healthy serving into one of the smaller bowls, which he handed to Belinski.

Using his fingers, Belinski popped a piece of fish into his mouth and made a production of chewing and swallowing before taking another mouthful. Daly repeated the process with Williams and Kindy, then served himself and ate a bite. Buben's eyes followed each movement and more drool started dripping down his chin, but he didn't say anything.

"All right, Kindy, work your magic with his bonds so he can eat."

"Aye aye," Kindy said. He put his bowl on the table and wiped his fingers on a napkin before he stood and stepped to the prisoner's side. He moved at a leisurely pace until he reached for the binding that restrained the small man's right forearm. Then he went fast, loosening the bond and stepping out of the way.

Buben made no aggressive movements when his right hand came free; instead he opened his mouth and used his free hand to point at it.

"Sure, Buben, I'll be happy to feed you," Daly said, putting his own bowl down and filling the last one. He stood, and staying on the prisoner's left side, reached around to put the bowl on the small table in front of his chair.

Buben didn't try to bite Daly when Daly's arm was within reach. Instead, he leaned forward as far as the tape holding him to the chair back allowed and began plucking fish, vegetables, and potatoes out of the bowl and stuffing them into his mouth. When he finished eating, Daly put a napkin in reach, but the prisoner looked at it uncomprehendingly.

"How about some water, Buben," Daly asked. "Are you thirsty?" Again, he served the other Marines and himself, and they all drank before he poured a glassful for the prisoner.

The small man gulped the water down and reached his glass over as far as his bindings allowed.

"More, Buben? Certainly." Daly held the pitcher over the

offered glass and refilled it. The prisoner didn't gulp the second glass quite as fast as he had the first. "Would you like more food? Or are you full now?" Daly indicated the serving bowl.

The prisoner placed his glass on the table in front of him and held out his bowl. This time, he took time to examine the potatoes and some of the vegetables before eating them.

"Looks like he's never seen a spud before," Kindy remarked.

"Or green beans," Belinski added.

"Different folks, different strokes—or, in this case, cuisines," Williams said.

Daly looked at the prisoner's belly, which was now slightly distended, and said, "Pretty soon we're going to have another problem—he's going to need to make a head call."

"You can handle it, boss," Kindy said. "I've got full confidence in you."

"Thanks, Him," Daly said drily. "I love you too."

The others chuckled.

Daly used a napkin to wipe his fingers and mouth then pointed at the napkin he'd placed in front of the little man. "Don't you want to clean up a bit?" he asked.

The prisoner blinked at Daly then looked at the napkin in the ensign's hand.

"Like this," Williams said, and demonstrated.

Hesitantly, the prisoner picked up the napkin and dabbed it at his lips, then scrunched it up and worked his fingers through it, an expression of wonder on his face.

"Never seen a napkin before either," Belinski observed.

"Either that or his world has a caste system," Daly said, "and he's in a low caste that isn't allowed napkins. You notice he didn't look for eating implements either, but went right to it with his fingers. And he didn't show any surprise when we ate with our fingers."

Williams shook his head. "He's an uneducated peasant, a serf. Probably illiterate as well."

Belinski sighed. "You'd think we'd have done away with that by now and made everybody full citizens."

Kindy snorted. "You'd be surprised how many people left Earth to settle new worlds because they wanted to return to 'the good old days.' Sure, 'good old days,' with lords and ladies, peasants, indentured servants, women as chattel. Give me modern civilization any day."

"So it's possible that Buben really doesn't speak any Standard English," Daly said, and cocked his head at the prisoner. "An illiterate, uneducated peasant. He isn't much use to us, is he? Pity we wasted that food on him."

"Yeah, it is," Williams said, catching on to what Daly was doing. "No point in keeping him around."

Daly seemed to give the question some consideration, then said, "We're going to test that weapon of his tomorrow. We can take him along and test it on him, see exactly what the acid does to human flesh, how long it takes to kill someone."

"And then," Belinski said, also understanding what Daly was doing, leaning forward with a vicious grin, "we can give him a bolt from a blaster, and you can see for yourself how they flare up."

"That'll sure get rid of the evidence," Kindy added. "I sure wouldn't want to be accused of abusing a prisoner."

"Excellent thinking, Sergeant! We'll do exactly that. I'm certainly interested in seeing it for myself. Not that I believe it's literally true, you understand." Daly turned to look speculatively at the prisoner.

Buben had craned his head around to look at them with interest while they were talking, but his face gave no sign that he understood a single word they said. Now he focused on Daly and bowed his head. He used his free hand to indicate that he needed to relieve himself.

"Either he really didn't understand us or he's got exceptional control over his face," Daly said. "So everybody be alert for him to try to break away while we take him for a head call."

The prisoner was docile when they took him to the nearest bathroom. They had to show him how to use the facilities but had no other problem, not even when they took him back to the secure room and bound him to the bed.

Ensign Daly prepared another message to send via drone to Fourth Fleet Marine Headquarters on Halfway. The message began with a detailed account of the firefight at the Rebetadika homestead, though Daly hesitated over including some of the details—people simply *didn't* flare up into vapor when shot with a blaster, and they couldn't breathe underwater either. People at Fourth Fleet Marine HQ were liable to think he'd suffered a brain injury or chemical imbalance when they read that. But he was also feeling a real sense of urgency. And if people at 4FMHQ thought he'd gone around the bend, they might speed up getting the navy to send a starship to Haulover, a navy warship and some more Marines. After the events of the day, Daly suspected that whoever the raiders were, they needed to be dealt with forcefully, and with more power than two Force Recon squads could bring to bear. He ended his report with detailed descriptions of the captured weapon and the prisoner. Included with the written descriptions were images, 2-D and trid of both, along with an account of the prisoner's behavior. Almost as an afterthought, he appended a recording of the prisoner's speech. He was positive that 4FMHQ would be able to identify the language. They'd just as positively be able to identify where the raiders had come from. After some internal deliberation, he added a strongly worded plea to get the navy to Haulover fast; he knew he could keep the acid-shooting weapon secure until the navy showed up, but he also wanted to keep the prisoner out of local hands and wasn't sure how long he could keep the small man under wraps.

As trepidatious as Daly felt about the reception some of the details in his report would receive at 4FMHQ, he had no such misgivings about the reaction to them at Fourth Force Recon headquarters. Force Recon Marines saw—and did—things that were stranger than could be conceived of by the headquarters pogues.

The Wee Hours, Approaching Sky City

A Senior Master led a Master, two Leaders, and six Fighters on the road to the capital of Haulover. The Master drove the landcar they'd captured from an Earthman outpost. The Leaders had grumbled between themselves about stealing a landcar without killing the Earthmen in the outpost, or destroying the buildings, but not loudly enough for the Master or the Senior Master to overhear. Had they been overheard, they would have been disciplined, and discipline in the Emperor's army was severe; and if they survived the discipline they would be reduced to mere Fighters with no chance of being returned to the position of Leader. The two Leaders didn't know, but they suspected the Master was likewise displeased. If he was, he didn't complain within their earshot. Both Leaders had served under the Senior Master leading them that night, and knew him to be an exceptionally harsh disciplinarian. They suspected that if the Master complained about doing nothing more than stealing the landcar, the Senior Master might well have executed him on the spot for protesting the Grand Master's orders.

The six Fighters had no opinion on the matter.

The Master drove the Earthman landcar. It was a very quiet vehicle. Which was fortunate, since the Master had little experience of Earthman landcars and had difficulty starting it and then confining it solely to the road. Had the vehicle not been so quiet, the theft would have awakened the Earthmen at the outpost, and the real People would have had to kill them—as the Leaders, and probably the Master as well, desired to do. As it was, the Master *did* drive the landcar off the road a few times, and even collided with a tree once. But by the time they reached the plateau on which Sky City perched, the Master was driving the landcar as though he'd been doing it since his youth.

The ten were garbed in Earthman clothes, since they were going into the Earthman city and might be seen by someone who questioned their presence. They could kill such a person, of course, but would do so only if letting the person live jeopardized their mission. They were *required* to kill any of the Earthman Marines who might be in their house—and the captured Fighter if he was there. But killing a questioner might draw unwanted attention to the group and thereby alert the Earthman Marines so that the mission to kill them and the captured Fighter could fail. That was why the Over Master who planned the mission assigned a Senior Master who spoke the Earthmen's primary language to command it. The Senior Master should be able to deflect any potential challenges simply by talking.

Once they killed the Earthman Marines and their prisoner, they could kill as many of the Earthmen of Sky City as they desired. But most important was killing the Earthman Marines and the captured Fighter. The killing of their enemies would surely bring out any other Earthman Marines who might be hiding on the planet to where they could be killed by the Emperor's Third Composite Corps. Or bring large numbers of Earthman Marines there if none were present.

It did not matter if the ten members of the raiding party lived to return to headquarters. If the mission was not successful, they *would* not return.

The landcar strained climbing the road to the top of the plateau; it wasn't meant to carry as many passengers as it held. Still, it reached the top of the plateau three hours before dawn. The map drawn by the Masters and Leaders who had earlier scouted the location of the Earthman Marines' quarters was true and easy to follow. The raiders saw few other people or vehicles along the way. When they reached their objective, the driving Master drove a hundred meters farther before stopping. The ten got out and hid their weapons, projectile throwers taken on raids against the outposts—weapons better suited for fighting inside the house than the acid shooters they normally used—under their Earthman garments then headed for their strike positions along the sides and rear of the building. The Master and two Fighters took position along one side, next to windows; the two Leaders and two Fighters by windows on the other side; the Senior Master and the remaining two Fighters went to the rear entrance to the building.

While the strike team arrayed itself around its objective, a pair of observer Masters took positions more than half a kilometer away. Regardless of developments, they were not to engage in the fighting at the Earthman headquarters. If none from the strike team survived their mission, the mission of these two was to report what had happened.

Marine House

Corporal Nomonon yawned and checked the time for what felt like the two hundredth time, but it was only a couple of minutes after his last time check. Normally he'd be much less restive during guard duty. But his normal watches were in the field, and there he could patiently maintain watch for twenty-four hours without moving. Twice that long if necessary. But one lousy hour inside Marine House, *that* was driving him nuts. It was the first time they'd had an overnight watch since they arrived on Haulover; it was also the first time they'd had a prisoner to watch over.

Nomonon's eyelids drooped and his head lowered. His chin fell to his chest and bounced right back up. "Damn!" he swore softly. "Can't fall asleep." He wasn't thinking of being disciplined for falling asleep on guard duty, he was more concerned with the ragging he'd get from the other Marines if he fell asleep during a lousy one-hour fire watch. He decided to stand and take a look through the house. Not that there was anything to look at or for, but walking around would keep him awake.

He was in the kitchen getting a drink of water when he heard a whistle from behind the house, followed immediately by the tinkling of glass from the back door.

CHAPTER
THIRTY-ONE

Marine House, Sky City, Haulover

<u>The Skinks</u>

The raiding party didn't have any communications devices; they didn't want to risk alerting the Earthman Marines by having their transmissions intercepted. The Senior Master commanding the mission looked along both sides of the building to verify that his raiders were in position and had withdrawn their weapons from under their clothing, then took his own place next to the door on the back of the building and blew a short blast on his whistle. On that signal, one of the Fighters with him poked the muzzle of his weapon through a pane of glass in the door and reached in to fumble for the securing mechanism and fling the door open.

The scouts who drew the map that led the raiders to the quarters of the Earthman Marines had not been able to enter the building, so the raiders didn't have an accurate layout, but the scouts had been able to see enough from the outside to know that a hallway led from the back door to a large front room, and that several smaller rooms opened off the hallway.

The Senior Master ushered the two Fighters through the door ahead of him. They raced to a door on the left and opened it, filling the hallway with thunder by firing their weapons into the room beyond. The Senior Master himself threw open the first door on the right and dashed inside without firing. No light came into the room from outside, but he turned on the light globe hanging around his neck. He had to blink against the sudden brilliance, but then he lowered nictitating membranes over his eyes and was immediately able to see reasonably clearly. The room was unoccupied—except for the captured Fighter.

With a cry of triumph, the Senior Master ran to the narrow bed where the Fighter was secured. As he pulled a bottle from one pocket in his pants, and a spark maker from another, he ignored the Fighter's shouted words: "The Earthman Marines, they treated me well! They are not evil!" The Senior Master opened the bottle and doused the Fighter with the accelerant it contained, then lit the spark maker and jumped back far enough that the resulting flames wouldn't ignite him. It was necessary to vaporize the Fighter in cleansing fire; if he was merely killed, his body would remain behind to possibly tell the Earthmen who they were, and where Home was.

Only after the body of the captured Fighter was returned to its component elements did the Senior Master become aware that he had heard a *sizzle-whoosh* from the hallway, and saw the bright light that flashed there.

The Marines

At the sound of the whistle and breaking glass at the rear of the house, Corporal Nomonon roared out, "INTRUDERS!" and spun to race from the kitchen to the front end of the hall; in one movement, he dropped the glass from which he'd been drinking and went for his sidearm. He was so intent on what was happening at the rear of the house that he almost missed the sound of breaking glass behind him. Reflexively, he dove to his left and rolled to face the kitchen windows, completing his draw and pointing his hand blaster toward where he'd heard the noise. His reflex movement was fast enough; two projectiles, accompanied by *BOOMS!* magnified by the confines of the room, slammed through the space he'd just occupied.

Two smallish men holding projectile rifles were clambering

through the windows. He squeezed the trigger of his hand blaster and blinked in shock when one of the small men immediately flared into flame. The other twisted and flowed, moving as fast as Nomonon had moved diving from the initial projectile fire, to escape the fireball. He moved far enough, fast enough that Nomonon's first shot at him missed. But the invader flashed into vapor at the Marine's second shot.

Nomonon hadn't seen the third intruder, who had been behind the others. But in his last seconds of consciousness he felt the impacts as the man fired his rifle through the window and put three rapid projectiles into the Marine's chest.

The Skinks

With the first part of his mission accomplished, the Senior Master turned his attention to the sounds and lights from the hallway, the *sizzle-whoosh* and flashes of brilliant light. He also heard the guttural shouts of his own troops mingled with the harsh, confused cries of the Earthman Marines. In the hall, he saw the scorch marks where one of the Fighters had been immolated by the terror weapons wielded by the Earthmen—weapons terrible because they didn't merely kill but ignited the oil-permeated cells of the bodies of the People and vaporized them. He also saw the scars burned into the walls and floor of the hall by plasma bolts that had failed to strike the other Fighter who had entered the room across the way. That Fighter stood just inside the opposite door, patiently, even placidly, awaiting orders.

A plasma bolt struck the doorjamb near the Senior Master's head. He flinched and belatedly realized that his light globe was still on, that its glow must have drawn the fire. He flicked the light off and waited for more fire to come his way. When none did, he signaled the Fighter across the way to get ready to poke his Earthman projectile thrower around the corner of the door and blaze away down the length of the hall. The Fighter mimed what he would do when he received the order, and the Senior Master was satisfied.

The Senior Master wished he'd thought to bring a periscope, or, failing that, that he had a mirror that he could use to look down the hallway without exposing himself. But he had neither. Not that it would necessarily matter, not if the Earthman Marines were wearing their invisibility uniforms. The Senior Master stripped off his shirt and turned to face the front of the house, to better sense the locations of the Earthmen. He signaled the Fighter to do the same.

What he felt made him jump to the side and draw his projectile sidearm, then empty the weapon through the corner of the walls toward the front of the house.

The electric emanations he felt along his sides didn't change, and he nodded to himself. He hadn't been present during the debriefing of the Leader who was the sole survivor of the previous day's encounter with the Earthman Marines, but he'd listened to the recordings, so he knew the Earthman Marines could be much closer than their electrical emanations would indicate. That was why he was surprised and had emptied his sidearm through the wall. But since his projectiles had no discernible effect on the enemy, he deduced that there was something in the invisibility uniforms that damped the electric signals, making the Earthmen seem farther away than they actually were.

He inserted another magazine into his sidearm while he analyzed anew the signals he was receiving. He didn't know the layout of the house, or how the electric conduits snaking through it or other sources of electric signals might be masking the locations and numbers of the Marines. But he had not risen to Senior Master and would not have been in line for promotion to Over Master had he not been able to locate the electric field of a life-form in a jumble of other signals.

Closer to the front of the house, inside rooms near the far end of the hallway, were three or four Earthmen; two on this side of the hall, one or two on the other. Two or three more were beyond that, to the left side, a single one and either one or two more, he couldn't tell for sure. Of his own troops, he sensed one on the right side of the front part of the house and two on the left. With the one across the hallway, that meant he had four remaining, to face at least five and possibly seven of the enemy. Against those odds, it was likely that he and his troops would die. But they had accomplished their primary mission, and would take at least half of the Earthman Marines with them when they died.

That would be a satisfactory conclusion to the mission.

The Marines

Corporal Jaschke was a sound sleeper, but not so sound a sleeper that certain noises couldn't penetrate his consciousness and bring him to instant wakefulness. High among the short list of *Get-Up-Right-Now!* sounds was an alarm cry from another Marine. So when Corporal Nomonon shouted, "INTRUDERS!", Jaschke was rolling out of bed and reaching for his weapons before his eyes were even open. In that second, he had achieved enough situational awareness to recognize the *thump* and gasp from the other side of the room as Lance Corporal Ellis doing the same things he'd just done.

Confused sounds came from other parts of the house. A hand blaster went off in the kitchen, along with the sharp *crack* of projectile-throwing rifles. There was the tinkling of breaking glass from the side wall of the living room. And gunfire at the end of the hallway near the back door—along with a *whoosh,* as though something had gone up in sudden flame.

As he grabbed his helmet and pulled it on, Jaschke scrabbled to the door and eased it open. He slid his light-gatherer screen into place and eased his head into the hall at floor level, his sidearm in his hand poking in front of his face. He was in time to see a smallish man, who looked very much like the prisoner except that he was dressed and armed, step out of the room opposite the secure room. Without hesitation, Jaschke snapped a plasma bolt at the intruder.

The man blazed into all-consuming flame—just like Williams

and his men had said. Thinking it wasn't likely that the intruder was alone, Jaschke fired several more bolts down the hall, skittering them along the walls and floor, hoping bits of plasma would break off and splash into the room the intruder had come out of. He felt Ellis moving into the doorway, facing toward the front of the house.

The Skinks

On the left, two Leaders and two Fighters waited at two windows for the signal. One window led into a large open space, the other into a room that looked like sleeping quarters. When they heard the Senior Master's whistle from behind the house, they burst through the windows, one Leader and one Fighter through each.

The Fighter who was first through the sleeping room's window landed in a shower of glass on a sleeping body. He rolled over the bed to the floor and sprang onto the next bed, knife in hand. But the Earthman Marine he expected to land on and quickly dispatch had been jarred to instant movement by the shattering of the window glass, and was already rising—the Fighter's knife stroke scored the Earthman's side instead of being the death blow it should have been. Somehow, the Earthman simultaneously grabbed and twisted the Fighter, and turned his twist into a full half-circle swing, slamming the Fighter headfirst into the wall, momentarily stunning him.

The Earthman Marine who had been landed on by the Fighter followed him off the bed; he wasn't on the bed when the Leader leaned through the window and fired several shots from his projectile thrower into it—the Leader didn't realize his target had moved. He raised his eyes to look across the dark room and saw a darker shadow that was upright and larger than the Fighter who had gone through the window. He shifted his aim to pump several projectiles into the dark shadow that had to be one of the enemy and pulled the trigger. But before the Leader could get off more than one shot, the Earthman who hadn't been in the bed where he had fired rolled to his knees and fired a bolt of plasma into the Leader. The two Earthmen were momentarily shocked by the fire that bloomed from the Leader, and recoiled from the flames . . .

. . . just as the stunned Fighter regained awareness, and realization that his initial attack on the Earthman he was supposed to kill had failed. He located the Earthman Marine and screamed as he lunged off balance to stab him. But the lone projectile that the Leader had gotten off before he flashed into fire struck the Earthman and knocked him back, making the knife thrust miss and the Fighter tumbled to the floor. The first Earthman saw him in the brief light from the Leader's blaze and snapped a shot at him, vaporizing him instantly.

The Marines

Sounds of gunfire from multiple directions snapped Ensign Daly from his sleep. Like the other Marines, before he went to sleep he placed his weapon where his hand would automatically fall on it if he woke suddenly. He grabbed his hand blaster as he rolled out of bed and faced the door of his room. He squatted in the darkness, listening to the sounds of blasters and rifles. He heard firefights in the sergeants' room, either the living room or the kitchen, and in the back hall. It wasn't Marines in one place fighting off aggressors in one place; both kinds of fire sounded from all three locations. Whoever was attacking must have used multiple points of entry and engaged the Marines in every place that they were in Marine House—except for Daly's room, the only one that wasn't immediately accessible through doors or windows.

Daly reached for his helmet and slipped it on with the light-gatherer screen in place, then duck-walked to the door and listened for sounds in the hallway outside it. When he didn't hear any noises right outside, he slid the door open and eased his head out. He didn't see anyone, not even when he turned on the infra screen. The sounds of combat had stopped.

"Count off. Sitrep," he said softly into the all-hands circuit, not knowing whether anybody else had donned their helmets yet, but suspecting they had. He was right.

"Kindy. We got two of them. Williams is down." Sergeant Kindy sounded more shaken than Daly had ever heard him.

"Jaschke. Ellis and I are all right. We've got at least two bad guys pinned in the rooms near the back door. I'm afraid they got to the prisoner."

"Belinski. Skripska and I are okay. We're across the hall from Jaschke and Ellis, same sit."

"Nomonon, sound off," Daly ordered when Corporal Nomonon didn't speak. That didn't necessarily mean anything because the fire watch probably didn't have his helmet with him. "Has anybody seen Nomonon?" Nobody had.

"Kindy, how bad is Williams?" Daly asked, rising to a crouch and creeping into the hallway. He checked the bathroom while listening to the situation reports.

"He's got a puncture wound from a projectile rifle and a shallow cut on his side. Also some burns from when one of those things flashed up too close to him. I've got him patched up. He's conscious."

"All right. Kindy, I'll let you know when I reach your room. Come out then. We'll check the living room and kitchen. Use your infra; I've got my light gatherer. We'll clear the living room. Everybody else, hold your positions. Sidearms are the preferred weapons for fighting in the house. Questions?" He didn't expect any, and none came. "Him, stand by, I'm on my way."

Seconds later, he signaled Kindy that he'd reached the door to the sergeants' room. Kindy slid the door open and joined him in the hall. Using hand signals because he didn't want his own voice or Kindy's covering any sounds made by anybody who might be in the living room or kitchen, he told Kindy what they were going to do. Kindy gave him a thumbs-up.

Daly duck-walked along the right side of the hall while Kindy crawled on elbows and knees. They stopped when they

reached the end of the hall. Without sticking his head out of
the hall Daly scanned the room from as far as he could see to
the right all the way to the left. He didn't see anybody through
his light gatherer, but he did see the window was broken out.
He switched to his infra and scanned back the other way.
Again, he didn't see anybody—which didn't mean nobody was
hiding behind furniture.

Kindy, meanwhile, scanned the room left to right with his infra, and back with his light gatherer. Using hand signals, Kindy
indicated that he'd spotted a glow behind a chair near the front
door.

The Skinks

Neither the Leader who had come through the window into
the large open space nor the Fighter with him had fired his projectile thrower—they didn't have targets. They heard the
sounds of fighting in the hallway to the rear of the building and
in the sleeping room next to them. The Leader led the way to
the far side of the large room, toward where he sensed one of
the three soldiers who had come into the food room. There, he
made contact with the Master, who was the only survivor of
the trio who had entered the house from that direction. He
sensed faint radiation from a body he could barely see lying in
the doorway to the food room. The faintness of the emanations
implied that that Earthman Marine was dying, and he rejoiced.

Elsewhere in the house, he sensed two pairs of Earthmen in
rooms astraddle the hallway, and three more in the direction
of the sleeping room the other Leader had entered, but he
couldn't tell if they were in the sleeping room or in the hall
he'd glimpsed as he went through the large room. Aside from
his Fighter and the Master the two of them had joined, he only
detected two of his own, at the far end of the long hallway.

He awaited orders. He did not have to wait long. He and his
Fighter turned and aimed their stolen Earthman projectile
throwers toward the end of the hall, where the projectiles could

go through the opening of the hall and continue into the sleeping room.

But before they could fire, an Earthman Marine burst from the mouth of the hall to the front wall of the room, and one of the enemies' weapons fired, sending its ball of plasma into the Fighter, whose dying flame lit up his end of the room, exposing both himself and the Master to anyone looking in their direction. The Leader hesitated a beat, but then obeyed the Master's orders and began firing his projectile thrower in the direction of the hall opening. His finger managed to pull on the trigger three times before a plasma bolt joined him to his ancestors.

The Marines

Ensign Daly saw three rapid muzzle flashes and fired two plasma bolts their way, staggering them right and left. He would have fired more but the first bolt lit up that end of the room when the enemy blazed up.

"Kindy, report," Daly snapped into his helmet comm.

"Shit, I'm hit," Kindy gasped.

"How bad?" Daly didn't like the sound of Kindy's voice.

"In my right shoulder. Hurts like hell."

"Can you get back to your room? Get into your chameleons?"

"I . . . I'll try."

That was bad; Force Recon Marines never said they'd *try*, they always said they'd *do*.

"Hang in there, I'm on my way." Daly stood high enough to look over the furniture and used both his infra and light gatherer. He didn't see anyone, but crossed the room to Kindy's side as quickly as he could anyway. It was a good thing he went fast; several rapid-fire bullets sped just behind him. He dove over Kindy and hit the deck. He grabbed the squad leader and dragged him to the sergeants' bedroom. His light gatherer showed him where a medkit was, and he quickly got bandages, a painkiller, and a pain blocker out of it and applied them. He spared Williams a glance; the other squad leader was unconscious, but his regular breathing showed no signs of distress. Daly got back on the all-hands circuit.

"Listen up. Both squad leaders are down. I'm going outside and around to the kitchen; there's somebody in there. After I take him out, I'll help with the bad guys you've got pinned in the back. Just hold them in place.

"Hang in there, people," Daly whispered to the squad leaders.

He went out the window the intruders had come in through. A moment later, he was crouched below the shattered kitchen window. He'd used his infra screen on the way around the front of Marine House, looking for sentries or reinforcements for the invaders, but didn't see anyone, not even signs of anybody watching from nearby houses. He switched to his light gatherer and popped up to give the kitchen a quick sweep, then ducked back down. He'd seen only one person in the kitchen, kneeling behind the wall next to the door to the living room, holding a civilian handgun. He raised back up and took careful aim before firing a plasma bolt at the figure's back. Even though he'd seen the light cast by flashing bodies twice before in the past few minutes, he blinked at the direct sight of one flaring up before him. Using both his infra and light gatherer, he scanned the kitchen again, and as much of the living room as he could see. He didn't see anybody else. He turned his ears up and listened for sounds from within, but all he heard was the first calls of "What's going on?" raised from nearby houses.

"I got the one in the kitchen; the front of the house seems to be clear. I'm coming around to the rear now. Somebody keep an eye on the front, just in case I missed anyone."

He dashed to the rear of the house.

The back door stood open, and Daly raced past it to the window of the unused bedroom on its left. The window wasn't broken. He looked in and saw one soldier leaning back against the far wall with his head turned toward the open door to the hallway. Without hesitation, he bashed the glass in with the butt of his hand blaster and torched the soldier. Even before the light of the dead man's fire began to fade, he smashed out more of the glass, then dove through the window, cutting himself in several places on the broken glass. He hit the floor and rolled, looking into the corners he hadn't been able to see from outside. Nobody was in them. He scrabbled to the doorway and poked his weapon through it to fire into the doorway opposite.

A brilliant flash replied to his shot, and he bolted across the hall, diving into the secure room and looking for more enemy. But the room was empty.

He lay panting for a moment before saying into his all-hands circuit, "I got them. The rear of the house is clear. Are any of you in your chameleons?"

"We all are," Corporal Belinski answered. "How about you?"

"Only my helmet." Daly looked down at himself and gave a rueful laugh. "Other than that, I'm naked. So, since you guys are invisible and I'm entirely *too* visible, how about if you make sure the house is secure. And check Nomonon." He looked at himself again and noticed blood flowing from multiple cuts. "Oh, yeah, and I need a medkit."

"On it, boss." Jaschke rattled out orders to the other three Marines.

Lance Corporal Ellis brought Daly a medkit before the Marines conducted their search of the entire house. Daly patched his wounds as best he could, then went to his room to get dressed when the search revealed no more enemy. Belinski, as the next most senior uninjured Marine, called for medical assistance and notified the constabulary. He decided to let Daly wake Planetary Administrator Spilk Mullilee to give him the news. All they found of the intruders were scorch marks.

CHAPTER
THIRTY-TWO

Marine House, Sky City, Haulover

Ensign Daly was just waking Planetary Administrator Mullilee when he heard the sirens of approaching emergency vehicles. *That's fast response,* he thought. Belinski had just placed the call for medical assistance a moment earlier.

"Mullilee," the planetary administrator said groggily.

"Sir," Daly said to Mullilee, "Marine House was just attacked. We succeeded in defeating the attackers but I have several wounded. We've already called the hospital for emergency care and transport. We also notified the constabulary."

"Buddha's Blue Balls," Mullilee swore, abruptly sounding wide awake. "D-Don't do anything until I get there. I-I'll get there as fast as I can."

"Right. Daly out." He cut off comm. Daly had no intention of not doing anything—he had injured Marines to attend to, and he was going to do everything necessary to care for them without waiting for anybody. He was already heading to the sergeants' bedroom while he spoke to Mullilee.

"How are they?" he asked Corporal Belinski as he entered the room. Belinski and Lance Corporal Skripska were closing a stasis bag on Sergeant Kindy.

"Not good," Belinski said. He glanced at Corporal Jaschke, who was kneeling over Sergeant Williams.

"I've got him stabilized," Jaschke said. "Good thing emergency medical is responding so fast."

"What about Nomonon."

"He's in the other stasis bag. Ellis is watching him. In the kitchen."

Belinski and Skripska rose from installing their squad leader in the medical bag that would maintain him in an effective state of suspended animation until he could get proper medical attention.

"Nomonon is real iffy," Belinski said. "If the navy doesn't get here in a hurry . . ." He shook his head.

Daly nodded, and swallowed a lump that formed in his throat. Nomonon had been one of his men when he'd been a squad leader, before he went to Arsenault to attend Officer Training College. He looked at Kindy; Kindy had been one of his men as well. Williams had joined the company after Daly had left for Arsenault. Without another word, Daly turned on his heels and headed toward the kitchen. Before he got there, the sirens stopped in front of the house and Lance Corporal Ellis opened the front door.

But it wasn't the emergency medical vehicles that Daly had assumed, it was the constabulary.

"What's going on here?" demanded a man with sergeant's pips on his collar. "We got reports of gunfire from this location."

Daly turned from the kitchen to the constable. "We were attacked," he said. "I've got casualties. Where are the ambulances we called for?"

The constable sergeant shook his head. "I don't know anything about any ambulances. All I know is we got calls about gunfire from around here." He turned around and spat out a series of orders to the men who accompanied him. They went off, weapons in hand, to search the grounds of Marine House and the surrounding area. Then he turned back to Daly and said, "You say you've got casualties?"

"Three men, seriously wounded."

The constable got on his comm to call for ambulances. "They're already on their way," he said when he signed off. He cocked his head at the sound of approaching sirens. "That must be them now. I'm Sergeant Watchman, who the hell are you?"

"Ensign Jak Daly, Fourth Force—"

"Yeah, you're the Marine in charge here. Heard about you. My people are checking around outside. Now how about you tell me what happened in here?"

Before Daly could relate what had happened, two ambulances shuddered to a stop in front of the house and four medics piled out of them, carrying what Daly assumed were civilian medkits.

"Where are they?" the first medic through the door asked.

"One in a stasis bag in the kitchen. Two more in that room." Daly pointed. "One in a stasis bag, one badly injured but not bagged."

"Stasis bag?" the first medic asked, but didn't wait for an answer. He led one medic to the sergeants' bedroom and sent the other pair to the kitchen.

"I've heard of these," one of the medics murmured as soon as he reached the kitchen. "Wish we had them. Maybe someday." He knelt to examine the med readings on the stasis bag's front. "Is he dead?" he asked. "I don't see any vital signs."

"The stasis bags slow things down far enough that signs don't always show," Ellis explained, a touch of hopefulness in his voice, like he didn't believe what he said himself. "It holds someone in a sort of suspended animation."

"What should we do with him?" the medic asked uncertainly.

"Just get him to the hospital. Don't try to give him any treatment yet."

"All right, if you say so," the medic said doubtfully. "Give me some data on him." He got out his comp and asked a series of questions—name, age, home, nature of injuries, and more—and entered the answers into his comp. While he did that, the other medic went back to the ambulance for a gurney.

In the sergeants' bedroom, the chief medic checked over

Sergeant Kindy while the other medic took down the answers to the routine questions.

Finally, satisfied that Kindy was properly stabilized, the chief medic said, "Whoever patched him up did good work." He looked at Williams in the stasis bag and murmured something envious about offworld technology. He and his assistant went to the ambulances for gurneys.

Before the constables allowed the ambulances to leave, the sergeant asked the medics a few questions. He wasn't fully satisfied with their answers; the stasis bags prevented them from giving firsthand descriptions of the injuries of the bagged Marines.

After he let the ambulances leave, Watchman turned to Daly. "You were going to show me what happened here."

"Detachment up!" Daly called, and began talking while his few remaining men assembled. "It began with Corporal Nomonon, who was on fire watch."

Watchman raised an eyebrow when Daly said he had a man on fire watch; he wondered why the Marines kept an overnight watch, but didn't comment on it. Not yet, anyway. Instead, he observed and listened quietly while the Marines walked him through what had happened. He took in the secure room, the manacles, the furniture bolted to the floor, and the charred mattress and bedding, but still didn't say anything about the state of things. He barely blinked when Daly and the other Marines told him about the attackers' vaporizing when hit by the plasma bolts shot from blasters—that was merely another anomaly in their account that would need further checking. Just then, all he wanted to do was gather data without putting anybody's guard up.

They had completed the tour of Marine House and the recounting of what had happened when Planetary Administrator Spilk Mullilee showed up. But he wasn't alone; he came in the retinue of Chairman of the Board Smelt Miner. They didn't arrive to the tune of sirens, or even the screech of tires breaking to a stop outside. The first the people inside knew of the arrival of Mullilee and Miner was the chairman's raised voice.

"Constable, disperse those people! Send them home. I don't care *who* they are, get them away from here!" Then he swept through the entrance of Marine House.

"What in the name of the Goddess of Monumental Screwups did you do here?" Miner demanded, taking in the scorch marks on the living room floor and a half-burned easy chair. "Were you trying to burn the house down? Did you want to get rid of any evidence of your incompetence?"

Ensign Daly pointed to the broken windows and the blood pooled on the floor where Corporal Nomonon had been shot. "There was a fight," he said tightly. "I've got three men seriously wounded and in your hospital. Two of them might not survive."

"Four casualties," Corporal Belinski said softly. "You forgot yourself."

Daly ignored him. "As for the burned places, I don't know how or why, but when we shot the people who attacked us they went up in flames."

The remaining Marines nodded their agreement.

"I've never seen anything like it," Corporal Jaschke said.

"People don't do that when they get shot by blasters," Lance Corporal Ellis added. "They just don't flare up." He looked haunted.

Mullilee looked sick, listening to the Marines. "How badly did they—whoever they were—hurt you?" he asked.

"Sergeant Kindy and Corporal Nomonon are injured so badly we had to put them in stasis bags to keep them alive until they could get proper medical attention. Sergeant Williams should be in one as well, but we only brought two. And if a Confederation Navy starship doesn't arrive on station soon enough, the two bags might not keep them alive until one does. And I have no idea how long that may be."

"Wh-What about you?" Mullilee asked. "Someone said you're hurt."

Daly grimaced. "Just a few cuts, nothing serious."

Miner looked at the collection of civilian rifles and handguns piled in the middle of the room. "I only see one knife there. What happened, did you have a knife fight with one of them?"

Daly shook his head. "I came in the back window to flank the last of them." He didn't explain further when Miner looked at him questioningly.

"These are all civilian weapons," the chairman of the board said. "Are you sure you didn't kill some locals and then try to get rid of the evidence by burning them?"

"Do you know any way to make a human body burn to vapor and do nothing more to its surroundings than leave a scorch mark on the floor?" Daly asked. "I certainly don't. These people . . ." He shook his head. "These *creatures* simply *whooshed* up in flame when we shot them with our blasters."

"People just *don't* do that," Ellis said again. His eyes were wide enough to show whites all around.

"Snap out of it, Marine," Jaschke said, giving Ellis's shoulder a shake. With Kindy out of action and Nomonon maybe dead, he was acting squad leader and had to take charge of the situation.

Ellis shook the hand off and turned his back to the civilian authorities, looking away from the signs of battle. He took a deep, shuddering breath to calm himself. And then another.

Jaschke stepped around to look at Ellis. He put a hand on Ellis's shoulder and leaned his forehead on Ellis's. "You're Force Recon now, Ellis," he murmured. "Sometimes we see things that other Marines only see in their worst nightmares. You were with us on Ravenette. That was a straightforward operation, just going in and snooping and pooping behind enemy lines, getting intel, and hitting them where they thought they were safe. Sometimes we don't have any idea what we're up against. When that happens, we show the enemy that whatever they can do to us, we can do worse to them."

Ellis was breathing more calmly and his eyes no longer looked haunted. "What worse can we do to these . . . these *creatures*?" he said. "We don't know how many of them there are. They might have already killed one of us, and they've wounded half of the rest."

Jaschke chuckled. "You know what they say about Marines: 'The difficult we do immediately. The impossible might take a little longer.' So we're up against the impossible. Or at least the improbable. We'll figure it out, don't worry. And we've got a navy starship coming to give assistance. They'll string their pearls around this planet, and then we'll have the bad guys right where we want them."

"When's the navy going to get here?"

"When they do, that's all."

A corner of Ellis's mouth twitched up in a wry half-smile. "And as every Marine knows, the navy's always late."

Jaschke grinned back. "Except when they're dropping Marines into harm's way." He gave the junior man's shoulder a comradely shake.

While Jaschke was steadying Ellis, Daly continued talking to Chairman Miner, though he mostly directed what he said to the planetary administrator. Miner still seemed suspicious of the Marines, but had stopped asking if they'd actually killed innocent citizens of Haulover and tried to disguise the fact. Mullilee continued to look sick. Sergeant Watchman listened carefully for any discrepancies between what Daly told Mullilee and Miner and what the Marines had said before. There weren't any—and the Marine officer left out the same details he'd left out when showing Watchman around.

"Now, if you gentlemen will excuse me," Daly finally said, "I have some people in the hospital who I need to check on."

"A-And get yourself tended to," Mullilee said.

"I'm all right."

"You're bleeding." Mulilee pointed at Daly's shirt. A red stain was spreading over his ribs.

Daly nodded. "And get myself tended to." He didn't ask but he wondered where General Vojak was. Surely, the Haulover minister of war had more business here than the civilian chairman of the board did.

Headquarters, Emperor's Third Composite Corps, Haulover

The Grand Master sat cross-legged high on his dais, with four sword-armed Large Ones arrayed to his rear and sides, and was attended by a diminutive female who poured and tested his steaming beverage before he drank.

The two Masters who had served as scouts, observing the action at the base of the Earthman Marines in the capital city of this Earthman world, prostrated themselves before the Grand Master and related what they had seen. They spoke in turn, loudly, so that their voices were not fully absorbed by the reed matting mere centimeters from their downcast faces. The Great Master who served as the chief of staff stood to one side of the Masters, sword in hand. An Over Master, also with sword in hand, stood to the scouts' other side.

The Grand Master listened with little indication that he was paying attention. The two Masters stopped talking when the Grand Master clapped his hands, signaling another diminutive female to make an appearance. The Grand Master rasped a few words at her, and she disappeared, only to reappear a moment later, bearing a small tray with a covered dish and a single flower in a fluted vase. This second female approached the Grand Master and bowed deeply, setting her small tray on a low table near the Grand Master's side. At a growled, raspy command, she knelt and sat on her heels to uncover the dish on her tray. Using food sticks, she stirred the contents of the dish and delicately picked up a morsel, which she put into her own mouth. She masticated slowly and then swallowed. She opened her mouth wide, exposing tiny, pointed teeth to the Grand Master. He probed her mouth with a finger to ascertain that she had indeed swallowed the morsel. Turning his attention from her as though she were no longer there, he growled, and the Masters resumed their discourse of the night's events.

The Grand Master gave no indication of his reaction to the discussion, but he approved of the locations from which the Masters had observed—just beyond the search area—which came into play once the local authorities arrived and searched the area for other raiders. The Masters told the Grand Master of the gunfire they'd heard coming from inside the Earthman Marines' base, and of the flashes of light they'd seen. He particularly appreciated hearing about the bodies that were carried out of the building after the fight was over. The bodies told him the Earthman Marines had suffered casualties, that the fighting wasn't at all one-sided. Although the fact that there was no more fighting once the local authorities arrived indicated that none of the strike team had survived the battle.

When all the others had gone, the Masters had crept close to the building and listened at the broken windows. Both of them spoke the Earthman language, which was part of why they were chosen for the scouting mission. They heard enough to know that the raid's primary objective had been achieved; the captured Fighter was dead and properly immolated. Beyond that, the Grand Master learned from the story told that the hated enemy had suffered severe casualties, and that gladdened the Grand Master's heart.

The Grand Master may have seemed to have totally dismissed the second female from his awareness, but he continued to pay attention to her aspect. When, after some minutes had passed, she showed no sign of distress from the morsel she had eaten, he waved a hand in a manner that instructed her to lift the dish in front of his face so he wouldn't have to look for it to spear morsels with his food sticks while he nibbled at the small food offerings inside it. He was finished eating and had dismissed the second female by the time the Masters finished their tale.

Well satisfied by the report of the raid, the Grand Master rasped a series of curt orders, and a short parade of females filed into the hall, bearing two low tables for the two Masters to sit behind and two pots of steaming beverage, along with two covered dishes. The two Masters took their places and partook of the Grand Master's food and beverage. They basked in the distinction of the Grand Master's favor, a favor

almost as great as being promoted to Senior Master—
promotions they now expected to receive in the near future.

Marine House, Sky City, Haulover

The constabulary had a light cordon of officers around Marine House, two on each side, providing security, when a
Haulover army vehicle dropped Ensign Daly off on his return
from the hospital. Daly didn't say so, not to them, but he was
glad they hadn't been there a few hours earlier when Marine
House was attacked. If the constabulary had been there, he was
sure he'd have fewer wounded Marines. But he was equally
certain that there would have been several dead constables.
Maybe all of them. Whoever the attackers were, they were
fighters. The constables were watchmen; they wouldn't have
stood a chance against fighters.

And why were police constables guarding Marine House?
Surely that was a job for the army. Daly made a mental note to
contact General Vojak when he got the chance and ask him.

"Detachment, on me!" Daly called out when he closed the
door to Marine House behind him. He appeared solemn as
the remaining four Marines assembled in the living room. He
looked each of them in the eye.

"Nomonon didn't make it," Daly finally said. "There was
too much trauma, too much bleeding, before we could get him
into the stasis bag. I had them clean the bag out and put Kindy
into it." He looked at them again. "Both squad leaders are out of
action, so we have to do some reorganizing. Belinski, you're
senior, which makes you the acting squad leader. Jaschke,
you're assistant squad leader. When you have to operate in
two-man teams, go with the lance corporal from your original
squad. We'll take another look when Rudd comes back, which
should be in a couple of days." He paused to swallow. "Sooner
if we need him."

"Questions?"

"What do we do next?" Belinski asked.

"We're Force Recon. Barring other orders, we gather intelligence. Anything else?" Daly looked at his four men; there weren't any more questions. "I'm going to file another report with Fourth Fleet." He headed for his room.

Daly had spent the time in transit from the hospital back to Marine House thinking of what he was going to say in this report. All he had to do now was put it into order, code it in, and upload the report to the Mark IX Echo along with a launch order. But all he could think about for some time was the things that had happened every time he found himself in command of more than one squad.

He'd taken over command of second platoon on Atlas after everyone senior to him in the platoon had been killed or wounded. And they suffered more casualties. He'd taken charge when the tsunami hit the town of Oceanside on Arsenault when he was on liberty there during Officer Training College. People under him died. Now he was in command on a mission that didn't require an officer, and one Marine was dead and two more were in stasis bags. He beat himself up over the losses, trying to figure out if people under him had died because of some deficiency in his leadership. But it was a question he couldn't answer easily so he forced himself to put it aside and get about the business at hand.

TO: Commander, Fourth Force Reconnaissance
       Company Camp Howard, MCB Camp Basilone,
       Halfway
FROM: Commander, Force Recon Detachment,
       Haulover
RE: Mission Update
1) In the early hours this date, Marine House was
attacked by an enemy force of approximately ten
persons. One Marine KIA. Three Marines WIA, two of
them currently in stasis bags awaiting arrival of Conf.
Navy warship. All aggressors KIA. Prisoner detailed in
previous message KIA.

2) All: NOTE: ALL aggressor KIA vaporized upon
being struck by plasma bolts fired from hand blasters.
All surviving Marines involved in action witnessed
vaporization. I have never heard of such a thing, and
need whatever data is available on such incidents.
3) I strongly suspect that there is more than a small
raiding force from another human world present on
Haulover. Possible alien sentience?
4) Request a full Fleet Initial Strike Team be
dispatched to Haulover as soon as possible.
5) Need Navy string-of-pearls right now.

Daly stopped and read over the message. Yes, it said everything it needed to. Even though the people at Camp Howard
were going to wonder if he was ill with that "Possible alien sentience?" sentence. But how else to explain the vaporization?

Daly and his men were Force Recon; he added one more line
to his message before sending it off:

6) Continuing mission.

CHAPTER
THIRTY-THREE

A Confederation Navy Essay in Orbit Around Haulover

Bosun's Mate First Tigure Sean was in charge of the Essays laying the string-of-pearls when the CNSS *Broward County* went into orbit around Haulover. It wasn't as good as being on the bridge, where he could hear all the comm between the captain and the Marines planetside, but Lieutenant Commander Bhimbetka would likely wear a headset, at least for his initial contacts, and only the duty comm officer and chief radioman would be able to hear any of the comm anyway. Here on the Essay, though, Sean could tap into any of the string-of-pearls' channels and pick up anything he wanted to hear. Provided what he wanted to hear wasn't scrambled or on a visual-only channel.

The first thing he found that was very interesting was that the Force Recon Marines planetside had sent a message drone to their headquarters on Halfway just a few hours earlier. The second was that Captain Bhimbetka was very interested in that message, and had ordered the Marine commander up to the ship.

That second item didn't come through the data he was scanning from the string-of-pearls, it came in a direct message from the *Broward County*—Sean was to take his Essay planetside as soon as he finished laying the string-of-pearls and pick up the jarhead ensign and carry him to orbit.

Captain's Quarters, CNSS <u>Broward County</u>

Lieutenant Commander Aladdin Bhimbetka made sure the door to his cabin was secured before he opened his wall safe and removed the sealed orders he'd received along with the "any Confederation Navy starship" drone message. He took the vacuum-wrapped orders to his desk and sat before breaking the seal. He found it interesting that inside the first vacuum wrap was another along with the expected crystal. He inserted the first crystal into his console and began reading. The beginning of the message was background about a hostile alien sentience, much of which he had already learned, followed by a supposition that said aliens were now on Haulover—which he had suspected as soon as the *Broward County* had found the "any Confederation Navy starship" change of orders. The sealed orders went on to say that he was to deploy his string-of-pearls upon arrival at Haulover—which he had already done before he opened his safe to retrieve the orders. He was to meet immediately upon arrival with the commander of the Marine Force Recon detachment planetside. If the Marine commander had intelligence that met any one of a string of criteria listed in the orders, Bhimbetka—or whichever starship's commander received the sealed orders—was to open the second set of sealed orders and follow them. If none of the criteria were met, the second set of sealed orders was to be locked away until his starship was relieved or ordered off station around Haulover.

After reading the first set of sealed orders, Bhimbetka picked up his comm and called the bridge.

"Ensign Tallulah, sir."

"Ensign, has the SOP Essay returned yet?"

"No, sir."

"Contact, who's got it, Chief Sean?"

"Yes, sir, Bosun Sean."

"Tell Chief Sean to head planetside ASAP and bring the Marine Force Recon commander to orbit. Also send my compliments to the Marine CO and my wish to meet with him at his earliest convenience. Tell him Sean's on his way to get him."

"Aye aye, sir."

Bhimbetka put his comm aside and considered the implications of the doubly sealed orders. Then he went to his Combat Information Center to see what the string-of-pearls was finding out about Haulover.

Marine House, Sky City, Haulover

Ensign Daly was in his room trying to decide on his next step when a long-anticipated but not-yet-expected tone sounded on his satellite comm. He moved in front of it and opened the connection. "Ensign Jak Daly," he said to the young face that appeared before him. "How can I help you?"

"Ensign Hedly Tallulah, CNSS *Broward County*. We just arrived on station in orbit around Haulover. I have a message for your commanding officer."

"That's me." Daly hoped the navy ensign, who probably had time-in-grade on him, wasn't going to give him a hard time about being so low-ranking at his age. The navy officer didn't.

"Sir, Captain Bhimbetka's compliments. He would appreciate your meeting with him aboard the *Broward County* at your earliest convenience. An Essay is currently en route to Beach Spaceport to bring you up."

"What's its ETA?"

Tallulah glanced to the side, checking the Essay's progress. "About two hours, sir."

"Tell your driver I'll meet him. And I've got four wounded, two in stasis bags, who I want to bring up."

Tallulah blanched at "four wounded"—evidently he knew that Force Recon operated in very small units, and realized that the detachment's casualties were very heavy.

Two hours? Daly thought. *Plenty of time. And the Essay's coxswain obviously never drove Essays for Marines; Essays carrying Marines to planetfall came straight down and never*

took as long as half an hour from orbit to surface. Two hours?
The squid had to be coming down in multiple orbits instead of
subjecting himself and his shuttle to the stresses of a combat
assault landing.

Beach Spaceport

Ensign Daly stood just inside the passenger terminal, watching from the observation windows. Lance Corporal Rudd, who
had driven him to the spaceport, stood near his left shoulder.
Sergeants Kindy and Williams, in their stasis bags, were on
gurneys attended by a pair of medics from the hospital. Corporal Belinski stood between the gurneys. Everything Daly figured he'd need for show and tell with the *Broward County*'s
captain was on crystals in his shirt pocket.

"There it is," Rudd said, pointing.

Daly looked where Rudd pointed and saw the brilliance of
an Essay's breaking jets headed toward the landing strip. He
heaved a deep breath. It was a damn shame the navy couldn't
have arrived earlier; he might well have had one more live Marine, and fewer wounded. He looked around for spaceport personnel, someone to direct him and his people to the correct
gate to meet the Essay, and saw a woman in what looked like a
pilot's uniform coming toward him.

"Ensign Daly?" the uniformed woman said when she got
close.

"Yes, ma'am," Daly said, stepping forward.

"Your shuttle is about to land. If you and your men will
come with me, I'll take you to the gate." She looked at Daly
and Rudd, but avoided glancing at the gurneys and the stasis-
bagged Marines on them. Daly also noticed that she didn't give
her own name.

"Thank you," Daly said, and gestured for her to lead the
way. He looked back to make sure the medics attending the
gurneys were following before stepping out himself.

Haulover was a new world; most of the spacecraft that visited it were cargo ships bringing supplies needed to establish and maintain the colony, and their orbit-to-surface landers came into the cargo terminal, not the passenger terminal where the Marines were to meet the Essay. So the walk to the gate was short, not much more than fifty meters. The nameless woman could have simply told Daly where to go. But she guided them, then quickly departed after turning them over to the gate attendant. This uniformed functionary not only looked at the standing Marines, he looked sadly at the stasis bags. He didn't introduce himself either, but merely asked Daly and the others to seat themselves until the Essay arrived at the gate. The medics rolled the gurneys to the nearest chairs and sat, but Daly, Belinski, and Rudd remained standing.

They didn't have to wait long, they'd heard the screaming of the Essay's touchdown while they were walking to the gate. Shortly, they heard the Essay's engines wind down outside, and were ready to go out as soon as the attendant opened the gate.

A bosuns first and a seaman who stood at the foot of the Essay's ramp saluted when Daly approached. The Marine was reassured when he saw they were both dressed in blue work uniforms; they were working squids, not ceremonial sailors.

"I'm Ensign Daly. You're my taxi?"

The bosun grinned. "Yes, sir. Sean's taxi service, at your service." Then he saw the gurneys and his expression turned solemn. "Sean's ambulance, maybe. Don't worry, sir, I'll drive like I've got an admiral with hemorrhoids on board; I'll get your people into orbit without aggravating their injuries."

"I appreciate that."

With a few businesslike words, Sean and the seaman took the gurneys from the civilian medics and wheeled them aboard the Essay, where they secured them. Daly and his other two men followed and strapped themselves into the webbed seating Sean directed them to.

Marine Essays launched almost vertically after a short forward roll. Sean took off more sedately, and the trip to rendezvous with the *Broward County* in orbit took three hours. Daly relaxed in his seat and tried to sleep, but was unable to. Neither Belinski nor Rudd seemed to sleep either, though both of them kept their eyes closed for most of the ride and neither attempted conversation.

Once aboard the *Broward County,* they were met by an ensign and two corpsmen. The ensign led Daly to the captain's cabin while the corpsmen took the others to the starship's sick bay.

Captain's Quarters, CNSS <u>Broward County,</u> in Orbit Around Haulover

"Welcome aboard, Ensign," Lieutenant Commander Bhimbetka said, rising from his desk to shake Daly's hand. "I'm always happy to have a Marine come to visit." He waved Daly to a small chair positioned between the side of his desk and his narrow bed. "I trust my medical department has taken your casualties in hand?"

"Yes, sir, they met us as soon as we came aboard."

"Fine. Now, what can you tell me about what's happened planetside?" Bhimbetka turned his comp monitor so Daly couldn't see it. "Start at the beginning."

Daly briefly recounted the state of the homesteads he and his Marines had investigated, then spoke at greater length about the encounter between Sergeant Williams's squad and the Skinks at the Rebetadika homestead, and the prisoner and weapon they brought back. Bhimbetka occasionally nodded and made a note. He looked reflective while Daly told about the predawn attack on Marine House, and took more notes.

When Daly finished his account, the *Broward County*'s skipper turned his monitor to show it to Daly. "This is a checklist. If you reported any *one* of the items on it, I have been instructed to open a second set of sealed orders." He got out the second set of orders, broke its seal, and read. His face registered surprise as he did. He shook his head. "You don't know about the Skinks, do you?" he asked when he was through reading.

When Daly admitted he didn't, Bhimbetka gave him a quick briefing on the Skinks. "As you can see," Bhimbetka said, gesturing at the checklist, "your report meets nearly every item. You seem to be lacking only uniforms, swords, and giants."

This was the first Daly, or anybody else on Haulover, had heard of the hostile aliens, and he was startled by the news. But he understood the urgency of the situation. He forced himself to recover quickly, told himself that he and his Marines had twice met the Skinks in combat, and twice defeated them, and that they weren't to be feared as supernatural beings out of a childhood nightmare. Later, he could scream at the unknown.

Bhimbetka asked, "Do you have a copy of your latest message to Fourth Fleet Marines with you?"

"Yes, sir."

"These orders," he said, indicating the second set, "instruct me to forward your mission reports to Task Force Aguinaldo on Arsenault." He saw the question on Daly's face and said, "It appears that your Commandant has been tasked with assembling and commanding a special task force to deal with the alien threat." He held up a hand to forestall questions. "That's all I know about TF Aguinaldo. So give me a copy of your message." Bhimbetka quickly put together the message he was required to send, telling the appropriate people that the Skinks were present on Haulover.

When that was done, Bhimbetka stood. "Come with me; we need to find out how many of these Skinks are on Haulover." Daly got to his feet and followed as Bhimbetka briskly led the way through the ship's narrow passageways.

Along the way Daly asked, "Sir, you saw no sign of a possible starship in the vicinity?"

"That was the first thing we looked for when we returned to Space 3." Bhimbetka didn't seem offended by the question. He cocked his head momentarily, then added, "Maybe I should check for traces of starship passage that don't match the commercial vessels that have come here."

Then they reached the radar shack.

Radar Shack, CNSS <u>Broward County</u>

"Do you have anything yet?" Lieutenant Commander Bhimbetka asked an ensign as soon as he entered radar.

"No, sir, we're still doing our preliminary mapping," the ensign replied.

"Ensign Herovasti, this is Ensign Daly," Bhimbetka introduced them. "Herovasti is my radar officer." He looked Daly in the eye. "The *Broward County* is a small starship; we don't have a ground-surveillance section."

"Yes, sir, I understand," Daly said. "I've been on destroyer escorts before. I've always been impressed with just how much can be done with such a small crew."

A smile briefly quirked Bhimbetka's mouth. "And you know how to shovel it at a dumb squid too."

"No, sir, I mean that sincerely," Daly said with a straight face. "DEs have been my transportation on several deployments."

Bhimbetka looked him in the eye, then nodded. "All right, tell Mr. Herovasti where you believe the section should start searching." He added to the radar officer, "Get Tutka in on this."

"Aye aye, sir." Before Herovasti could turn to call him, a second class petty officer stepped to his side.

"A large starship will have a chief running its radar and surveillance section," Bhimbetka explained to Daly. "Here, we've got a second class doing the job." He glanced at Tutka. "And a fine job he does.

"Now, I'll leave the three of you to it. I'll be on the bridge." The captain was gone before anybody could call for attention.

"How do you want to work this?" Herovasti asked Daly.

"I was about to ask you the same." Daly looked around the radar shack. It was a small, cramped space with barely enough room for the officer, three crewmen, and their equipment. "How complete a map do you have so far of the main continent?"

Herovasti looked at Tutka.

"Just about complete," the second class answered.

"Then we'll look over your shoulder," Herovasti said. Tutka

took his station and the two officers crowded in behind him, necessarily pressed side to side in the small space.

Daly leaned forward to examine the map that came up on Tutka's display. "Let me point out the locations of the raids," he said, and took the stylus that Tutka offered him. He got out his personal comp and, working from its data, plotted the destroyed homesteads on the map. "This one is where one of my squads encountered the Skinks," he said as he marked the last one.

"We know from evidence we found at the homesteads we investigated that the Skinks travel by aircraft, but we don't know what kind, or the direction they come from. The aircraft have skids rather than wheels or air cushions. But that doesn't necessarily mean anything; we don't have a lot of knowledge of their technology. Judging from the length of the skids and their spread, I estimate the aircraft are capable of carrying up to two squads—that's twenty men," he added in case the sailors didn't know how many men were in a squad.

"So their base could be anywhere within hundreds of kilometers of that area," Tutka said.

"That's right."

The radar chief grunted. "Can I get everybody on it?" he asked.

"I think you better," Herovasti said. He stepped back and touched Daly on the arm, signaling him to step back as well, as Tutka snapped orders to the other two radarmen.

In the passageway outside, Herovasti said softly, "Tutka's good. He'll find whatever's there. And when this cruise is over, I'm sure he'll get transferred to a larger starship and be promoted." He shook his head. "Damn shame DEs aren't authorized first class radar petty officers. I'm going to hate losing him."

Sick Bay

"These two will be ready to return to duty in a week or so," Lieutenant Lekeis, the ship's surgeon, said about Corporal

Belinski and Lance Corporal Rudd. "The other two," he said, shaking his head, "I'm afraid their injuries are beyond the capabilities of my sick bay to deal with. They'll have to stay in stasis until we reach a port with a navy hospital."

Ensign Daly briefly closed his eyes. "But they'll be all right until then?"

"Oh, absolutely. I was able to open their bags and make temporary repairs on their grossest traumas. They're quite stable now."

"Thank you, Doctor. Can I see my other men now?"

"Sure. I can even release them to you if you want. They don't need to stay in sick bay."

"You heard the doctor," Daly said to Belinski and Rudd. "Come along and let's find quarters for you."

"Aye aye, sir," Belinski said. "I don't like hospitals." Then he said to the ship's surgeon, "Not that there's anything wrong with your sick bay, sir. It's just that hospitals are usually full of sick people."

Lekeis laughed. "Sometimes I feel the same way, Corporal."

There was nothing more to do aboard until the radar section came up with something, so Daly, Belinski, and Rudd returned planetside. Daly had the Essay take Corporal Nomonon's body to the *Broward County* on its return trip.

CHAPTER
THIRTY-FOUR

Marine House, Sky City, Haulover

Planetside, the Marines spent a great deal of time discussing the Skinks and coming to grips with the idea that the raiders were aliens seemingly bent on the destruction of humanity. To Corporals Belinski, Jaschke, and Lance Corporals Rudd, Skripska, and Ellis, the alien nature of the enemy presented an intellectual challenge rather than a cause for fear.

"After all," Belinski explained, "they caught us by surprise twice, and we beat them twice."

On the third day, Daly got a call from the *Broward County*. The radar section spotted an aircraft landing at a homestead. Beach Spaceport reported that there was no scheduled or otherwise authorized flight destined for that homestead.

Wonder of wonders, Chairman of the Board Smelt Miner had come through with the small aircraft Daly had requested. Daly notified Planetary Administrator Spilk Mullilee and the minister of war, General Pokoj Vojak, while he and his remaining Marines headed for the spaceport. They all carried blasters.

The Marines arrived before the local authorities at the Ikar homestead. They were too late; the Skinks had already done their worst and left. But the *Broward County* had tracked the Skink aircraft on its return flight, and had a fix on where it had landed. Daly headed back to orbit.

Ward Room, CNSS <u>Broward County</u>, in Orbit Around Haulover

The *Broward County*'s ward room was an even smaller space than the radar shack, but it wasn't crowded with equipment so Lieutenant Commander Bhimbetka had a temporary station set up there. He, Ensign Herovasti, and Ensign Daly were able to look over Radarman Second Class Tutka's shoulders as he manipulated the data on his display.

"Show us," Bhimbetka said as soon as the petty officer took position and lit his station. "Start with an overview of the raid locations."

Tutka's fingers danced over the controls and an image of a large swath of ground speckled with several dozen dots. The dots formed a rough oval, some four hundred kilometers on its long axis, with Sky City near one focus.

"That's all the homesteads I know of that have been hit," Tutka explained. "The blinking one is the place that was just hit." His fingers danced again, briefly, and a dotted line appeared on the screen, curving into and then away from the blinking light. "That's the track of the aircraft the raiders flew in on."

"Pull back, show us where it went," the *Broward County*'s captain ordered.

Another brief finger dance caused the oval to shrink and shift far to one side of the screen. The line that curved into the blinking light extended and eventually straightened out. It terminated at a clearing in a forest that blanketed the side of a mountain range a thousand kilometers from the center of the dotted oval.

Daly let out a low whistle; he hadn't expected the Skink base to be so far away from the homesteads. "Can you give us a close-up?" he asked.

"Sure can." Tutka's fingers danced once more and the clearing swelled until it filled the screen. The clearing wasn't large, less than two acres, but there was no sign of the aircraft that had landed there earlier that day. What was in evidence, though,

was a large number of small figures. Daly did a quick calculation and came up with five hundred figures in the clearing.
Some of them were standing in small groups, some strolling
about. But most lay on the ground, obviously relaxing.

Tutka snorted. "They look like they're basking. Makes
sense; they're cold-blooded, aren't they?"

"I don't think so," Daly said, shaking his head. "At least the
one we had as a prisoner seemed as warm-blooded as you or
me." He peered at the screen. "Can you get finer resolution
there?" He pointed at the side of the clearing where it came up
against a cliff.

"Easy." Tutka brought the area Daly indicated into sharp focus. It looked like the mouth of a cave. That was confirmed a
few minutes later when some of the figures outside went into
the cave mouth and others exited into the open.

"We need to find out how many are there," Bhimbetka said
softly. "But it'll take days. And then only if we have sufficient
facial-identification capabilities—and we can get sharp enough
resolution from the string-of-pearls."

"No can do, sir," Tutka said. "I can work wonders with what
we've got, but that's asking too much of the equipment a DE
carries."

Bhimbetka looked at Daly. The Marine looked back at him.

"Sir, I have an aircraft planetside. I'll need your people to run
cover for me, keep me from running into any Skink aircraft,
while I get a team close enough to run a recon on that clearing."

"My ship will give you everything you need, Marine,"
Bhimbetka said firmly.

Twenty Kilometers from the Skink Clearing, One Thousand Kilometers Northeast of Sky City, Haulover

The small civilian aircraft that Chairman of the Board Miner
had loaned the Marines made a safe landing on a remote, unim-
proved road. They'd gotten there without having to deviate
from their planned route. It was a matter of a few minutes'

work for the six Marines to move the aircraft under trees and camouflage it. Ensign Daly knew that because Radarman Second Class Tutka could barely find it, and he knew where it was.

"All right, Marines," Daly said once he was assured that the camo job was sufficient, "this is where we earn our keep. Let's do it."

Lance Corporal Skripska crossed the road, following an azimuth toward the distant clearing. Daly followed him, trailed by Corporal Jaschke and Lance Corporal Ellis. Corporal Belinski and Lance Corporal Rudd stayed behind to guard the aircraft. Belinski and Rudd had objected, but Daly insisted that their wounds needed more healing time. He said that the *Broward County*'s surgeon hadn't yet cleared them for full duty so he was keeping them on light duty.

Skripska set a brisk pace for the first twelve kilometers, but slowed down as the four Marines neared the clearing. Skripska used his "eyeballs, Mark I" to watch where he was going; Daly rotated through bare eye, infra, and magnifier; Jaschke used mostly infra, but mixed in bare eye; Ellis, walking backward for the most part to watch their rear, also used infra and plain view. In addition to the visual searches, they all had their ears turned up, and Daly and Jaschke also had motion and scent detectors running in the corners of their HUDs. Daly was also using an electronic emissions detector. The forest they traversed was densely packed with thick-boled trees that sprouted sturdy-looking branches a few meters above the ground. The main branches were often close enough that they nearly touched the branches of other trees, forming a tight latticework above.

They were less than a kilometer from the clearing before they found sign of the enemy.

The Skink Clearing, One Thousand Kilometers Northeast of Sky City

"Freeze," Daly ordered on the short-range circuit. His electronic emissions detector had picked up something. He tweaked it to get a finer reading and used his magnifier and light-gatherer screens to examine the tree the detector said was the source of electronic emissions. *There,* about three meters up the trunk of a tree, he could make out a reflection from a skillfully hidden vid lens.

That's odd, he thought, *vid cameras don't emit, they absorb.* The lens didn't seem to be pointed at the Force Recon squad so Daly ordered his men to stay in place. He stepped to the side, farther out of the camera's probable cone of vision, and approached the tree. When he was closer, he discovered the source of the emissions—on the side of the trunk away from the lens was a microwave transmitter. Evidently it was feeding what the lens saw back to the Skink base. He soft-footed back to the squad and led them around the security device. They evaded several more passive detectors before they encountered a live sentry, and Daly had to wonder if he'd been right when he said the Skinks were warm-blooded—the sentry showed less in infra than a human of the same mass would.

When they reached the point where they could see the edge of the clearing through the trees and undergrowth, they climbed. The main branches, some four meters up the trunk, were as sturdy as they'd looked from the ground, and the Marines were able to easily move along them and go from tree to tree until they were able to see into the clearing with little to obstruct their view. By then each Marine was in a different tree. They settled in for a long watch.

Over the next six hours, Daly determined that the Skinks rotated in and out at half-hour intervals, about two hundred and fifty at a time, maintaining approximately five hundred outside, looking for all the world like they were basking in the sun. Basking would be necessary if they were cold-blooded. On the other hand, if they lived in caves they might need the exposure to sunlight for the same reasons humans did—to prevent depression and absorb vitamin D. Whatever the reason they were outside, they all went inside at dusk.

When Fourth Force Reconnaissance Company was tasked

with the mission, it hadn't occurred to anybody that the recon squads might have to come up with an estimate of the number of bad guys if only a few of them were in sight at one time—as had been the case when second platoon made its raid on the heavily guarded installation in the Union of Margelan on Atlas—so they weren't carrying face-recognition equipment. The *Broward County* had limited face-recognition capabilities, but its equipment wasn't man-portable. So Daly had to make an estimate filled with uncertainties. How often did the Skinks come out into the sunlight? Once a day? Every other day? Weekly? Several times a day? He had no way of knowing. He also didn't know whether it was the only Skink installation on the planet. All he could do was get whatever information he could about the size of the outfit at the cave he'd spent hours watching.

He prepared a minnie disguised as a Norway brown rat. Ancestral rats had stowed away on the first colony ships to arrive at Haulover, and many escaped into the wild before the first colonists were even aware of their presence. The rats had no natural enemies on Haulover and few local predators found them appetizing so they spread quickly throughout the main continent, where they became pests except in homesteads and other populated areas that took strong measures to keep them in check. Indeed, during the hours he watched, Daly thought he saw a few rats slipping in and out of the cave mouth. He didn't expect the minnie to be able to transmit from inside the cave to the receiver he carried, so he didn't attach a vidcam to its shoulders. Instead he set it to record through its eye lenses.

When the minnie was ready, he let it scrabble down the trunk of the tree he was in and scamper to the cave mouth. Then he put his men on three-quarters watch and settled back to wait again.

Over the next several hours, the Marines flashed brief messages to one another over tight beams. The messages were just enough to ascertain that they were keeping a three-quarters watch—one man sleeping while the others maintained watch.

Twice during that time, groups of Skinks came out of the cave and walked into the forest, while other Skinks returned to the cave. Daly assumed that it was a change of the guard in the forest, though he recognized the possibility that they were security patrols.

Three hours before dawn, the minnie came out and scratched at the base of Daly's tree. He tight-beamed his squad, and the Marines moved back into the forest before descending to the ground. They returned to their hidden aircraft more quickly than they'd approached the clearing.

Marine House, Sky City

Ensign Daly downloaded the minnie's data and the Marines settled in front of the vid to see what the remote device had found.

Inside the mountain was an extensive complex of low-ceilinged, interlinked chambers on several levels. Many of the chambers held war machines: smallish armored vehicles, artillery, aircraft of types the Marines didn't recognize, stacks of munitions, fuel depots, crates with markings that looked too deliberate to be the chicken scratchings they resembled. Huge chambers were filled with what appeared to be foodstuffs, located near what were probably kitchens or other food-service facilities. There was a complete hospital, and more. In short, everything needed to field and sustain at least two full five-thousand-man brigades in the field.

Moreover, there were barracks chambers, each holding what Daly estimated was five hundred men; there were enough such chambers that they might well have held the five thousand men the equipment suggested. Most of the questions Daly had were now answered.

But another was raised.

One of the instructions Daly had given the minnie before he sent it into the cave was a return-by time. The minnie had recorded the entrances to many tunnels it hadn't had time to explore. Daly had no way of knowing where or what those tunnels led to, but it was reasonable to assume they led to more of the same that the minnie had found.

There must be the equivalent of at least a division, probably reinforced, under the mountain.

The Force Recon Marines were going to have to work closely with the *Broward County* to determine whether there were more cave complexes, and go out on their own to explore whatever caves they discovered.

Daly took everything his patrol had learned about the Skink base to the *Broward County* and handed it over to Lieutenant Commander Bhimbetka, who put together a message packet for Task Force Aguinaldo, the minister of war in Fargo, and the Commanding General, Fourth Fleet Marines—the parent unit of the Force Recon Marines on Haulover.

In minutes, three drones were on their way, and Bhimbetka and Daly began planning how they were going to continue their surveillance and reconnaissance of the situation planetside on Haulover.

CHAPTER
THIRTY-FIVE

The Giddings Place, near Wellfordsville, Earth

Treemonisha Giddings lived alone on her small farm a few kilometers outside the village of Wellfordsville. Alone, that is, with six cats, three dogs, two cows, five pigs, a gaggle of chickens and her vegetable patch. She had lived all her life within fifty kilometers of Wellfordsville, alone since her husband of forty-two years had died and her nine children had grown up, married, and moved away.

Treemonisha lived off her husband's life insurance and money her children sent her. That and the things she grew and raised on her farm. She seldom went into town. She wasn't welcome there. "Too damned ornery, that old gal," Tanner Hastings of Hastings's Hardware and General Store would remark, shaking his head sadly, if anyone mentioned Treemonisha. And most of the 653 (plus or minus) residents of Wellfordsville agreed with that assessment. But when Treemonisha made her infrequent visits to Hastings's store to buy supplies, old Tanner treated her with respect and the hangers-on who could always be found sitting about the trid player he kept going gave her plenty of room. "Don't do to mess with ol' Treemonisha," they'd say, shaking their heads. "She's got a tongue on her like a rattlesnake's bite!" So people left the old widow woman alone, and that was the way she preferred it.

She was left alone, that is, until one morning in late March when a very strange creature showed up in her chicken coop.

Dr. Gobels's Laboratory, Wellfordsville

"We've about exhausted all the physical tests we can run on it," Dr. Gobels remarked to Pensy Fogel one afternoon some days after they'd smuggled Moses into his Wellfordsville laboratory. "Now we'll see how intelligent it is."

Fogel snorted. "Not very. All it's ever done is squeal since we brought it here." He nodded at Moses, who was lying inside his cage. "Moses, how old are you?" He winked at Gobels. "God, I have to laugh, calling that thing *Moses*. Moses, how old are you?" Moses only groaned in response. "See? No need to test it, Dr. G., we already know it's an idiot." Fogel laughed harshly. He'd enjoyed probing and sticking Moses and was a little disappointed the physical testing was over.

"Well, it's illiterate, so we can't conduct written tests on it," Gobels said, chuckling. "How old would you say it is? Age six on the human scale? We'll administer the Stanford-Binet X and see where it stands on the Wechsler Preschool and Primary Scale of Intelligence. Take it out of the cage, would you, Pensy?"

As Fogel opened the door to Moses's cage, the little Skink scuttled into the far corner and moaned. "Come on, come on, you little shit, time for another anal probe." Fogel chuckled. He grabbed Moses's leg. The Skink began to shriek. "Maybe its verbal comprehension is higher than we thought." Fogel laughed. "Up your ass, you little bastard!" Fogel chortled, dragging Moses out of his cage. Moses clutched at the bars. Exasperated, Fogel stabbed him with a small electric prod that caused him to squeal and lose his grip.

"Go easy, Pensy! We've got to relax it as much as possible. Give it some of that sweet drink it likes. Strap it into the captain's chair." The device was a couchlike instrument into which Moses normally was strapped for physical examinations. He began to shriek as Fogel placed him into the thing. "Easy, easy," Gobels said. "Easy, Moses. No hurty-hurty. Here, drinky-drinky?" He shoved a straw into Moses's mouth and squeezed a small plastic bottle containing a carbonated beverage. Much of the liquid dribbled down Moses's chin but he calmed down almost instantly. He'd been conditioned to associate the sweet drink with being left alone for a while since they always gave it to him after the experiments were over for the day. "See, Fogel? Baby wants its bottle!" The beverage was nothing more than a cheap sweetened drink they bought in Wellfordsville, but it contained carbohydrates and nutrients and Moses evidently liked it.

The testing required a degree of patience that Pensy Fogel lacked, so Gobels administered it himself. When at last the testing was done, Moses was given a light sedative and returned to his cage.

"Well, boss?" Fogel asked after Gobels had scored the tests. "Where does it stand?"

"Seventy-five."

"I thought so! A few points above a moron!"

"Umm. Look at these results. On the verbal comprehension it scored very low but on the perceptional reasoning it scored within the normal limits of its estimated age." In the perceptional reasoning test Moses had been asked, among other things, to put together red and white blocks in a pattern according to a displayed model, find a common bond between pictures displayed in a row, and other tasks of similar complexity. He'd done very well on such tests. In the verbal comprehension tests Moses had been asked the meanings of words, how two concepts are alike, and questions about social situations, general knowledge, and so on. In those tests he had scored very low. "That is to be expected since it was not born into human society, and has been raised by religious fanatics." Gobels rubbed his chin thoughtfully. "Maybe we should discount the VCI, or weight it differently."

"Ah, a moron is a moron," Fogel replied, looking at his watch. "What do you say we lock up here and go into town for some of that couscous at Mamma Leone's place?" Mamma Leone's was the only ethnic restaurant in Wellfordsville and the pair ate there whenever they were in town.

"All right. Give it another bottle of juice. Add a mild sedative and return it to the cage."

"Aw, boss, it'll only piss it out in there and make a mess!"
Fogel said.

"Let it. It's its own bed. It can clean it up in the morning.
Come on. If we're going, let's get going."

Moses slept, and when he awakened he found the bright
lights had been turned off and the lab illuminated by tiny night-
lights placed at intervals along the wall where his cage sat. For
once he awoke without noticeable pain anywhere in his body.
He listened intently. No one was in the lab and, evidently, the
living quarters attached to the laboratory were also empty because he could not hear the low voices or the music that usually emanated from there when Gobels and Fogel had retired
for the night. He reached up and gripped one of the metal bars
that formed his cage. It was loose. He had been working on it
for several nights but that night, feeling much better, he was
able to work it completely free. Once that bar was out, others
followed until he'd made an opening big enough to crawl
through. He found a window he could reach by standing on a
bench. It was latched from the inside. He had no trouble figur-
ing out how to release the latch. Then he squeezed himself
through.

It was cold outside and Moses was naked, but that made no
difference to him—*he was free!* He stood shivering in the pale
moonlight. A dirt road twisted off among the trees. He rea-
soned that Gobels and Fogel were away. Fine. He'd follow the
road, and if the headlights of a vehicle approached, he'd find
cover in the woods.

Moses's verbal comprehension might have tested low, but the
Brattles had taught him Standard English and he knew what
the word *moron* meant, and he resented Fogel's use of that
word to describe him. He also knew other words the Brattle
boys had taught him, naughty words, and now he said them
aloud in the quiet darkness. "Fuck you!" he said, shaking a tiny
fist at the laboratory. "Fuck you! Fuck you!"

The Giddings Place, near Wellfordsville

The moon was down when Treemonisha found herself startled awake by the most awful squalling coming from her
chicken coop. "Damned foxes!" she snarled, leaping out of bed
and thrusting her feet into the boots she always kept sitting
ready on the floor. She grabbed the shotgun propped against the
nightstand and shuffled to the front door. Standing on the porch,
she broke open the breach and felt with her fingers that the gun
was loaded. "I got a surprise for you," she whispered, tiptoeing
across the yard to the chicken coop. Holding a flashlight in her
mouth, the shotgun under her right armpit, a finger on the trigger guard, she ripped open the henhouse gate, snatched the light
out of her mouth, and shined it inside. At first she saw nothing
but flapping wings and feathers. And then she saw it: a small
child crouched shivering in a corner, its back up against the
wall, its feet encased in droppings.

Treemonisha blinked and shined the light full on the tiny figure. His eyes were closed tight in his strange little face; his
arms were tightly wrapped around his knees. He was shivering
uncontrollably. "Good God, child, what you doin' in my henhouse?" was all Treemonisha could say at first. Then she said,
"Come on out of there now! Come on! Let me get you inside
the house, boy, and out of this cold. Come on." She transferred
the shotgun to under her left arm and extended her hand
toward the boy. There was something in Treemonisha's voice
that told him he could trust this mountain of a woman. "Don't
send me back!" he pleaded as she dragged him into the yard.

"Back where?"

Moses shrugged. "Back there!" He gestured toward the
woods across the road from her house.

Treemonisha shined the light over the boy. "Damned if you
ain't the strangest-lookin' child I ever did see," she exclaimed.
"What the hell they been doin' to you, boy?" She examined the
bruises and scabbed-over puncture wounds on the boy's arms
and legs. "Good Lord!" she gasped. "Boy, what is your name?"

"Moses. Exodus 2:10, 'And she called his name Moses: and she said, Because I drew him out of the water.' "

"Good God, what have I found here?" Treemonisha sighed, looking down hard on the little boy. In the east the sky was beginning to turn a bright red. She glanced at the sunrise and smiled. It'd be a nice day and now she had someone to talk to. "Moses? Moses, eh? Well, Mr. Moses, I ain't Pharaoh's daughter and I didn't find you in the bulrushes. I found you in the chickenshit!" And she laughed, and there was something in that laugh, so different from Pensy Fogel's, that made Moses laugh along with her.

Treemonisha smiled down on her sleeping Moses—that was how she'd begun to think of him, as *her* Moses. She'd washed him, treated his wounds, and fed him a Wellfordsville breakfast—eggs, fried potatoes mixed with fresh onions, crisp bacon, toast, rich coffee—and he'd eaten as if he were starving. Now he slept in her deep feather bed. She knew he was not totally normal and suspected he had come from somewhere up north where disfigured babies were still being born. It was up there most of the bombs had been dropped during the conflict they called the Second American Civil War. No doubt that's where the boy had come from, probably abandoned by his parents who had just given up trying to raise him as a normal child. She knew from the bruises and scars on his little body that someone had abused Moses terribly, and that made her very angry.

Treemonisha started at the loud, insistent knocking on her front door. "What the—" But instantly she *knew* that whoever it was, they were after her Moses. She sprang to her feet—no trace of the stiffness that belabored her ninety-odd-year-old bones—and went to the door. Cautiously, she opened it a crack. Outside stood two men.

"Good afternoon, madam," one said. He held up an official-looking identity disk. "I am Dr. Joseph Gobels and this is my escort, Mr. Fogel. We are from the Fargo Child Protective Services Bureau. We are looking for a missing child. Have you seen this one?" He nodded at Fogel, who stepped forward and thrust a trid image of Moses at Treemonisha.

Now, Treemonisha Giddings was a good poker player. She shook her head, and her facial expression did not belie the instinctive terror that raced through her body alerting long-dormant defensive systems. "Never seen him. Good day to you, gentlemen." She made to close the door.

"Ah, one moment, please!" Gobels stuck his foot in the door. "We know he's here, Miz, ah, I didn't catch your name?" When Treemonisha refused to answer, he rushed on, "You must give him to us or there will be very unpleasant consequences, madam! There will be legal action and law enforcement involvement—"

Despite her advanced age, Treemonisha was a big, strong woman, as people are who live their entire lives on farms. She shoved the door hard and was rewarded by the pleasant sound of something breaking in Gobels's foot. He screeched in pain and terror and stumbled backward into Fogel.

"How do you like it, you perverted bastard?" she shouted, and with her right arm she grasped the pump shotgun sitting just inside the door, worked a round into the chamber, and leveled it at the pair. This time her finger was inside the trigger guard. "Now git the hell off my property, you two, or I swear by God I'll put a hole through you so big you can drive that landcar through it!"

The door slammed solidly shut behind the two as Fogel helped Gobels stumble back to their landcar. Once inside the vehicle, Fogel said, "Good thing we planted that tracer on the little shit, otherwise we'd never have found him."

"We've got to get him back, Pensy!" Gobels raged, pounding the dashboard in frustration. "We've *got to*!"

"Well, goddamn, boss, how we going to do that? That old bitch'll blast us for sure with that antique of hers! Besides, we can't go to the authorities. Shit, we'd be in it up to our necks if they ever found out what we did with our specimen, didn't turn him over like we were supposed to. Best we just wait. One of these days he'll come out and we can snatch him, no problem."

"We've got to get him, Pensy. Oh, goddamn, she broke my fucking foot!" Dr. Gobels groaned. "We've *got* to get him and right now! We are on the verge of the greatest scientific breakthrough since—"

"I don't follow, boss."

Gobels shook his head. "Remember those DNA samples we sent off to be run?"

"You got them back? You didn't tell me?" Fogel looked hard at Gobels, a small flame of anger beginning to burn way down inside him.

"Well, I was going to. I *am* telling you! We've got to get him back and we've got to do it right soon!"

Fogel held up his hand. "Damn me if I'm going back to that place. No! Your specimen is not worth getting shot over!"

"It is if you'll just listen to me for a second!" Gobels protested.

"Why, then?"

"The Skinks! *I know what they are!*"

EPILOGUE

General Anders Aguinaldo stood at the window looking out into the rain. It would be light soon. Why, he wondered, did military crises *always* seem to occur during the hours of darkness?

He had just been awakened by the shift officer in the communications room. The flimsy he held loosely in one hand bore stupendous news.

Aguinaldo breathed deeply the fresh aroma of wet, growing things. A cool, damp breeze swept through the open window just as one of the ubiquitous flying insectlike creatures disintegrated in the electrical field that served as a window. *That's what* they *do,* he mused silently. *Skinks flared up when hit by a blaster,* he reflected. "The more the merrier," he whispered.

Someone entered the room behind him. Aguinaldo did not need to turn around to see who it was. He held up the flimsy of the message that communications had delivered to him only a few minutes ago. "Read this, General," he said without turning around.

Lieutenant General Pradesh Cumberland, Deputy Task Force Commander, took the message and read it.

The rain drummed even harder on the roof. A flash of lightning stabbed through the air just over the trees. Aguinaldo counted silently, *One thousand one, one thousand two, one thou*—a clap of thunder rolled over the building.

"Buddha's Blue Balls!" General Pradesh whispered behind Aguinaldo's back. He meant the contents of the message in his hand, not the thunder. "That thing this ensign's men captured was a Skink, no question about it. According to the string-of-pearls surveillance, there are plenty more where that one came from."

Aguinaldo turned away from the window and grinned. "Our marching orders, General."

"It's dry on this Haulover place, I assume?" Pradesh grinned as he handed the flimsy back to his commander.

Aguinaldo laughed outright. "I don't know, and I don't give a kwangduk's scraggly ass! Get the staff and my commanders up here right now. We've got a long day ahead of us. Meanwhile, I'm going over to communications. I have a message of my own to send out." He punched Pradesh lightly on the chest as he passed by. The mission Task Force Aguinaldo had been preparing for so hard and for so long was on.

Comm Shack, Task Force Aguinaldo

"Goldie," Aguinaldo shouted as he stepped into the task force communications center, "put your dirty pictures away, tell yer ne'er-do-well communicators to get their fingers out of each other's asses, and get cracking!" "Goldie" was Lieutenant Nate Goldfarb, one of the three shift officers assigned to the communications center.

"Maybe I should have held that message up until after breakfast, General," Goldfarb quipped. He had been the first to read the message so he knew what was coming.

"You knew precisely that this was going to happen," Aguinaldo replied. "I know because all you guys were pretending to be very busy when I came through the door just now. Not your usual posture, I regret to say." He grinned at the enlisted communicators. "You warned them I was coming." He chuckled as he sat at an empty console. The enlisted clerks grinned. Aguinaldo always poked lighthearted fun at them when he came in, a habit he'd developed since taking command of the task force. Another habit of his is that he did his own writing. Other officers would *dictate* their communications, then change them several times before sending them and raise hell if a clerk made a mistake trying to translate the verbal garbage that most of them passed off as military writing. Not Aguinaldo, he wrote his own message texts.

"Look over my shoulder as I write this, Goldie. You figure out the exact quadrant where this Haulover place is and address this directly to President Chang-Sturdevant, Ultra Secret, Eyes Only, NODIS. I don't want *any* further distribution beyond the people it's addressed to—and address them *by name*. Info addressees: The Honorable Marcus Berentus, Minister of War; General Alistair Cazombi, Chairman, Combined Chiefs. That's it."

"You don't want to info anybody else, sir? Chief of Naval Operations? Chief of Army Staff? Commandant of the Marine Corps? Our staff, originating command who sent the alert message?"

"I trust the president and her highest military advisers to decide who among that Heptagon bunch needs to know what's in here. They're all a bunch of chairborne warriors back there; this needs to go to the fighting commands. But first the Old Lady. My staff and commanders are already coming up here. I'll tell them personally. We'll take care of the other commands with a separate message. I want you to attach this through a back channel to our fleet commander with my personal instructions to get it into a drone and on its way immediately. Naval liaison will know all about this when I get with the staff in a little while. All right, open your dictionary, I'm only a former enlisted Marine they kicked upstairs so he wouldn't wreck the Corps. Here goes.

" '1) MADAM PRESIDENT, I HAVE THE HONOR TO INFORM YOU THAT THE ENEMY HAS BEEN SIGHTED,' insert the place and planetary particulars here, Goldie, 'THERE HAVE BEEN SIGNIFICANT CIVILIAN AND SOME MILITARY CASUALTIES,' add in what that ensign reported about casualties on Haulover, 'ENEMY STRENGTH

ESTIMATED BY NAVAL FORCES IN ORBIT AROUND HAULOVER MINI-
MUM 10,000 PERSONNEL; ENEMY INTENTIONS REMAIN UNKNOWN
AT THIS TIME, BUT GIVEN HIS WELL-KNOWN PRACTICE OF HIDING
AND FORTIFYING TROOPS AND POSITIONS, I FEEL THIS ESTIMATE
(10,000) IS TOO LOW. THEREFORE, I AM DISPATCHING A RELIEF
FORCE STRONG ENOUGH TO DEAL WITH A FULL-SCALE INVASION
AND ATTEMPT TO OCCUPY THE PLANET HAULOVER AS A STEPPING-
STONE TO MORE IMPORTANT AND LUCRATIVE TARGETS IN HUMAN
SPACE. ADEQUATE FORCES WILL BE HELD IN RESERVE TO DEAL
WITH CONTINGENCIES. ENTIRE TASK FORCE IS ON ALERT FOR IM-
MEDIATE DEPLOYMENT. YOU SHALL RECEIVE PERIODIC UPDATES.

" '2) I AM INFORMING CONFEDERATION MILITARY COMMANDS
AND POLITICAL ENTITIES OF HAULOVER INCURSION BY SEPARATE
MESSAGE.

" '3) RESPECTFULLY REQUEST ALL SCIENTIFIC AND EXPLORATORY
ASSETS NOW BE CONCENTRATED ON DETERMINING POINT OF ORI-
GIN OF ENEMY FORCES.

" 'AGUINALDO.'

"What do you think, Goldie?" Aguinaldo looked up at the
lieutenant.

"Deathless prose, sir."

"Okay, next message." His fingers flew over the keys. "I
want this to go to the commanders of all the Confederation
forces with info to the chiefs of all the armed forces of all the
Confederation member worlds. Info the president, Berentus,
Cazombi, the service chiefs:

" '1) THIS MESSAGE IS A WAR WARNING.

" '2) RETRANSMISSION IS AUTHORIZED TO COMBATANT COM-
MANDERS ONLY.

" '3) AN ENEMY ALIEN FORCE HAS LANDED ON,' give the particulars here, 'ESTIMATED STRENGTH OF INVADING FORCE ESTIMATED
TO BE AT LEAST CORPS SIZED, AS MANY AS 100,000 PERSONNEL.

" '4) YOU ARE HEREBY ORDERED TO DEPLOY, TWENTY-FOUR-
SEVEN, ALL RECONNAISSANCE AND SURVEILLANCE ASSETS IN
YOUR RESPECTIVE AREAS OF OPERATIONS. REPORT TO THIS HQ
IMMEDIATELY, REPEAT, *IMMEDIATELY* ANY SUSPICIOUS ACTIVITY.

NO INCIDENT IS TOO INSIGNIFICANT TO REPORT. LOCAL COM-
MANDERS HAVE FULL DISCRETION TO USE DEADLY FORCE AGAINST
ANY THREATENING ENTITIES DETECTED IN THEIR AREAS OF RE-
SPONSIBILITY. PLACE ALL COMBAT, COMBAT-SUPPORT TROOPS,
AND NAVAL FORCES UNDER YOUR COMMAND ON ONE-HUNDRED-
PERCENT ALERT.

" '5) ALL MESSAGES GENERATED IN RESPONSE TO THIS ORDER
WILL BE CODE NAMED "*HAULOVER*," GIVEN *FLASH* PRECEDENCE,
AND ADDRESSED TO ME PERSONALLY.

" '6) STAND BY FOR CLARIFICATION AND FURTHER ORDERS AS
THIS SITUATION DEVELOPS.' "

Lieutenant Goldfarb's eyebrows arched. *Flash* in communications code meant imminent enemy contact, and never having
been on the cutting edge of a war, he'd never seen such a message. "That'll get their attention," Goldie whispered. "It might
also get some innocent folks fried."

"I'll take that chance. Goldie, after this goes out you'll be
getting a flood of incoming messages. Give joint action to G2
and G3, info everybody else in staff and command. Now, I
want this next one sent *directly* to that ensign on Haulover,
Daly, with info to his chain." The message read:

HOLD THE LINE. HELP IS ON THE WAY. AGUINALDO.

Headquarters, Task Force Aguinaldo

"Bitch of a morning, eh?" General Pradesh Cumberland
chuckled as he sipped his coffee. The task force staff and commanders had just departed the headquarters briefing to begin
their troop deployment missions.

Aguinaldo stretched and yawned. "Why does all this always
seem to happen between taps and reveille? Why can't wars
start at noon?"

"That was the quickest staff meeting we've ever had. I think
it only took fifteen minutes to write the operation order for
those troops."

"I think this is it," Aguinaldo said. "Haulover is an ideal

place to start a world-hopping campaign. Fine. We'll draw them in and then kill them once and for all. And sooner or later, we'll find out where they come from and shake their nest to pieces." He grimaced, smacking a fist into a palm with a dull *whack* to emphasize destruction of the Skink "nest." "But they aren't stupid," he mused. "They know as much about us, more in fact, than we know about them. Our weapons and tactics, how we think, how we operate. We bloodied their noses on Kingdom. They'll have learned from that. You bet they'll have some surprises for us this time."

General Anders Aguinaldo was right about that.

Read on for a glimpse of

WINGS OF HELL

the next Starfist novel
by David Sherman & Dan Cragg

The Grand Master sat at state on a raised dais in his hall. Idly, he watched as a diminutive female knelt before the low lacquered table sitting at his side in convenient reach of his hand. The female poured hot liquid from a delicate pot into a small cup on the table next to a slender vase that held a lone long-stemmed flower—the only ornament on the table. He continued to watch as she placed the pot on the table on the other side of the vase; then she picked up the small cup and delicately drank it down. Drinking complete, the diminutive female replaced the cup, sat back on her heels, folded her hands on her thighs, and waited as impassively as the four Large Ones stood to the rear of the Grand Master, swords ready in their hands to protect their lord from attack. Only then did the Grand Master look away from her and raise a languid hand in signal.

In response, a column of diminutive females appeared from a side entrance to the hall, each bearing a pot of steaming liquid, and went in precise order around the hall, kneeling next to small lacquered tables that sat between the pairs of Great Masters and Over Masters who knelt in ranks before the Grand Master. Each table held two small cups flanking a slender vase with a single long-stemmed flower. The females poured steaming liquid into the cups, then placed the pots on iron trivets that lay behind the tables on the reed mats that covered the floor. The Great Masters and Over Masters were the senior staff of the Grand Master's corps, and the commanders of his major combat elements and their seconds.

Once all the Great Masters and Over Masters had been served, the Grand Master returned his attention to the female who had served him. When he detected no sign of distress in her countenance or posture, he nodded. She poured a fresh cup of liquid for the Grand Master. The Grand Master took the cup from her hands when she offered it to him, faced the assembled Great Masters and Over Masters, and raised the cup in salute.

He waited a beat or two for the assembled upper-rank Masters to raise their cups in return, then spoke: "To our coming great victory!" He quaffed the steaming beverage, then held out the cup for the female to take and refill. The Grand Master's voice was rugged and raspy; as with nearly all Masters of the Emperor's army who attained such high rank, he had not exercised his gills in so long that they had atrophied, allowing air from under his arms, as well as from his lungs, to exit through his larynx, and affect his voice.

When the Grand Master offered his toast, the assembled staff and major combat unit commanders replied in kind and quaffed.

"The Master, Leaders, and Fighters who attacked the Earthman Marines in their own lair did not survive their mission," the Grand Master rasped. "But they killed or wounded many of the enemy. The survivors will have already sent a report on the encounter to their headquarters. The report will surely tell the Marine commanders that we are here, on this Earthman mud ball, and they will send more Marines for us to fight and kill." He grinned, exposing pointed incisors. "We shall soon complete plans for the coming fight, and we will rehearse them until both our staffs and our fighting forces execute them flawlessly.

"This time, as never before, we *shall* defeat the Earthman Marines!"

Finished speaking, the Grand Master extended his hand for the female kneeling near his side to hand him his refilled cup. He raised the cup in another salute and roared, "Victory!"

The hall reverberated with cries of "Victory!" from his staff and senior commanders.

Lieutenant General Pradesh Cumberland, Confederation Army, Deputy Commander of Task Force Aguinaldo, less formally known as "the Skink Force," stood in the doorway of General Anders Aguinaldo, late Commandant of the Confederation Marine Corps, and cleared his throat.

Without looking up from his console, Aguinaldo said, "Come on in, Pradesh."

Cumberland did so, shaking his head, wondering not for the first time how the Marine knew he was at the door. *Or am I the only one who clears his throat instead of knocking?* He closed the door behind himself.

"I've been going over the most recent personnel reports," Aguinaldo said as he finally looked up and waved his deputy to take a seat. He smiled wryly. "Ever since I sent that war warning to the commanders of Confederation forces, I've been inundated with requests—make that demands—from planetary presidents, prime ministers, dictators, and oligarchs that I immediately return to their control the forces they committed to the Skink Force, to defend their home worlds." He snorted. "I even have demands from the senators from each of those worlds insisting that the units be returned."

"But we—you—can't do that!" Cumberland said.

"And I won't," Aguinaldo agreed. "We'll need every one of those units by the time this is over. Besides, several of them are already in transit to Haulover." He shook his head. "So much for the distribution limits I put on that message."

"You knew the limits would be ignored."

"I did, indeed." He leveled a look at his deputy. "I think my war warning woke them up as much as the president's public announcement of the Skinks' existence."

"A wake-up call they likely needed."

"So long as it doesn't cause a panic. I'm letting the president deal with that." Aguinaldo turned his console around so

Cumberland could see it. "A fresh communication from what I've dubbed 'Confederation Forces Haulover (Provisional).'"

Cumberland quickly read the message:

TO: CG, TF Aguinaldo, Arsenault

FROM: Bhimbetka, Aladdin, LtCmdr, Cpt. CNSS
           Broward County

RE: Update of enemy order of battle, Haulover

Sir:

Following detailed analysis of string-of-pearls mapping of Human world Haulover, determination has been made that enemy force is probable 50,000. Perhaps not all are combatant. Map with locations of sightings of enemy, including estimated types of units and numbers, is attached.

> Respectfully submitted,
> Bhimbetka, *Broward County*

"A probable force of fifty thousand," Cumberland murmured.

"Which number probably doesn't include support troops. So I'm staying with my earlier estimate of one hundred thousand enemy."

"It could be more."

"Indeed it could. That's why I'm standing up the XXX Corps in addition to the XVIII Corps. If we need them, they'll be ready to go on a few days' notice."

Cumberland tipped his head back for a moment, thinking. He nodded sharply. "Andy, there was an American general in the late twentieth century, name of Powell. He established what came to be called 'the Powell Doctrine.' It essentially said that you should never enter a war unless you have overwhelming force on your side."

Aguinaldo mentally rifled through his memories and quickly found the Powell Doctrine. "And it only held for a few years before someone with more faith in machines than in men scrap-heaped it." He thought for another moment, then added, "As I recall it, Powell won his war against a huge army in a matter of days."

"And the man who didn't want to use enough soldiers made a war that threw his country and a large part of the rest of the world into a turmoil that lasted far too many years."

"Your point is taken, Pradesh. You're a good thinker; that's why you're my deputy. I will issue orders for XXX Corps to deploy to Haulover as soon as shipping is available for it."

"Overwhelming force, sir?"

"Overwhelming force."